STEPHANIE FAZIO

BISECTER

Syafant Press

*To Andrew, without whom this book would never have
been written*

PROLOGUE

BEFORE

Hurry up," I call over my shoulder, laughing.

"Can't…too fast…." Henri, the second-fastest child in the Subterrane, flops onto the cave's floor.

Barely winded, I double back. I lean over him, grinning. "Does this mean you give up?"

Henri groans.

"He gives up," Destinel, my best friend, announces. She waves a small flag over Henri's head to mark his loss. "I pronounce Hemera the fastest runner in—" she looks at me while she thinks, "—in the entire world!"

"Ha!" Henri gets to his feet. "She's only fast because she's weird."

"I am not." I cross my arms. "You think just because I'm a girl you should be faster and stronger than me?"

Henri's lower lips juts out. "I *would* be faster and stronger than you…if you were human."

"I'm human," I retort.

"Are not!"

"Don't be rotten, Henri," Destinel says. To me, she adds, "Don't pay any attention to him. He's just bitter."

"I'm not the only one who says it, and you know it," Henri persists. "All the Dwellers say there's something wrong with you. They say…."

I don't wait to hear the rest of what they say about me. I don't wait to hear Destinel's rebuke, or for my gathering tears to spill. I run as fast as my legs will take me back to the Subterrane. I almost knock over a guard and several chattering old women on my way through the tunnels, but I don't stop until I reach the cave I share with my mother.

My foot catches on the hem of my cloak, and I almost fall headlong into my mother. She catches me just before I barrel into her.

"Darling, Mer." She laughs, shaking her head. "You're so fast, even your legs can't keep up with you."

Her smile fades when she sees the look on my face.

"What's wrong?"

"Henri says I'm not human," I confess, burying my face in her cloak.

"Oh, Mer." My mother strokes my hair.

"But is he right?" I look up at her, my black eyes blurring until her face swims in and out of focus. "Am I so different from you and the others?"

"Of course, you are," she says, smiling down at me.

Before my tears have a chance to spill from my eyes, my mother wraps her arms around me. "You're so much better, so much more."

"I am?" I ask, my voice wobbling.

"I'll tell you a secret," my mother offers. She waits until she has my full attention. Lowering her voice to a whisper, she says, "They say those things because they're jealous of you."

I wrinkle my nose. "They won't even look me in the eyes."

My mother sighs. "The Dwellers have their reasons for being afraid. But if you are brave enough to hold your head up high, it will always be enough to carry you through."

I sniffle, and give my mother a wobbly smile.

"I have something to give you," she says.

I watch her, my mouth slack, as she unfastens the delicate silver chain around her neck. The small key dangles from the chain as she hands me the necklace I've never seen her take off.

"You're giving me your necklace?" I ask, hardly daring to hope.

"Indeed, I am." My mother strokes my hair.

I let my fingers brush over the silver, exploring the key's ridges.

"This is the key to my heart, darling Mer. And it belongs to you."

"It's perfect," I say, still fascinated by the way the silver reflects the lantern light.

"I have something else for you." My mother reaches under her bed and pulls out a parcel wrapped in rough cloth.

"What's all this for?" I ask, jumping up and down, unable to control my glee.

My mother gives me a knowing look. "Have you forgotten what today is?"

I think for a moment. "My birthday!"

"Your *twelfth* birthday," she says, handing me the parcel.

I tear it open, revealing a newly-made sling.

The weapon isn't much to look at—just a small leather pouch that rests between two ropes. But by swinging the ropes with the right amount of speed and releasing one end at the precise moment, the rock nestled in its pouch will fly through the air with deadly force. My father taught me how to use it, along with the rest of the weapons in the smithy. Even though Henri and Destinel have gone on to practice with wooden swords in hopes of getting a real one, I've always preferred the sling.

"I love it!" I cry.

"It's the Captain's gift to you," she says.

I look up at her in surprise. "Father made this for me?"

"Captain Harkibel," she corrects gently.

"Why did he have to be gone for my birthday?" I pout.

"Captain Harkibel is very busy. He's arranging a trade deal with Subterrane Jevin."

When I don't say anything, my mother takes the sling from my hands. "Come, we'll go out to the forest to practice."

"And can we pick—"

"Rupyberries?" my mother finishes, giving me a knowing smile. "Yes, and maybe I can even talk Cook into making a pie with them." She winks and offers me her hand.

As we walk up the tunnels, my mother gives my hand reassuring squeezes. We pass guards along the way, who bow their heads in respect to her.

"Go in darkness, Lady Harkibel, Hemera," they say in greeting.

They always keep their eyes fixed on my mother, and even turn their heads to avoid looking at me. I know their greeting is only for my mother's sake.

"Go in darkness," my mother replies, wrapping one protective arm over my shoulders.

"Lady Harkibel," Henri's mother runs down the tunnel after us. "Please," her breath catches. "My newborn is showing signs of sweating sickness."

My mother takes her outstretched hand. "Give her two teaspoons of boiled giphee root and bathe her with ice water four times a day." She gives Henri's mother a reassuring smile. "Young Sirrel will be just fine."

"Thank you, my Lady." The woman squeezes her hand. Her gaze slides to me, her mouth thinning into a disapproving line.

My mother extricates her hand from the woman's. "I've used the same treatment on my own daughter," she says, giving Henri's mother a cool look. "And look at how perfect she's turned out."

The woman swallows, her gaze flicking to the challenge in my mother's eyes before turning to the ground in front of her.

"And did I hear Marca say something about the children gathering in your cave later today?" my mother asks.

The woman's mouth opens and closes like she's a fish.

"I'm so clumsy and forgetful," my mother continues before the other woman can speak. "I misplaced the scroll telling us the time I should bring Hemera over. Do remind me of the time. Lowest day, was it?"

My mother is neither clumsy nor forgetful, and we all know it. The other woman nods, looking a bit ill.

"Fabulous." My mother wraps both her arms around me. "Hemera will see you then."

"Yes, my Lady. Thank you, my Lady."

She hurries away without another glance in my direction.

"Never you mind her, Mer," my mother says. "Let's go get some rupyberries."

My mother bends to adjust the hood of my cloak, making sure I'm completely covered in the protective material, before leading me onto the Outside.

Once we're in the forest, I run ahead of her along the path I know by heart. I gather handfuls of the fat, sweet rupyberries. Only a few of the berries manage to find their way into my basket rather than my mouth. My mother's laugh rings out when I race back to her, startling the kynthia birds perched on her shoulder. I go to her, a handful of yellow flowers in my hand and my mouth stained purple from the sticky rupyberry syrup.

"You really are a wonder, darling Mer," my mother says.

Shaded by a large script tree, she takes the blossoms and braids them into my hair with deft, sure movements. "You are strong, and not just in the ways everyone can see." She ties off the braid and spins me around to look at her.

"Beautiful," she murmurs.

"Even with my eyes?" I ask.

"*Especially* with your eyes."

A crash through the brush silences us both.

"Hemera," my mother says, her gaze intent on something I can't see. "Climb as fast and as high as you can up that script tree. Whatever happens, don't come down, and don't make a sound."

"But—"

"Go now!"

My mother never raises her voice, so when she does now, I know better than to question her. I begin to climb, even as a cold fear settles in my bones in spite of the day's blistering heat.

I do as I'm told and don't stop until I've reached the topmost branches. When I don't dare climb any higher for fear the branches will break beneath my weight, I peer down at the ground through the leaves.

At first, I don't understand what I'm seeing. My mother, as small as a doll from this height, is holding a long branch out in front of her. I'm about to call down to her, when I see movement in the trees.

A scream catches in my throat.

It's the closest I've ever been to one before, but there's no mistaking the hulking beast striding straight for my mother. No other creature has such scaly, sun-roughened skin…no other creature walks on two legs like a human, but has a crooked, bowed back that makes it appear almost animal.

The creature lets out a deafening roar. My mother raises her branch.

CHAPTER 1

3 WEEKS LATER

I try to pull on the adult's cloak that is far too big for me. My feet get tangled up in the heavy material pooling at my feet, and I fall face-first onto the floor of the cave.

"You're so klutzy," Destinel chuckles. She tries to help me up, but she only manages to get herself tangled up in the mess of fabric and falls to the ground beside me.

We roll around on the ground, laughing until Destinel snorts, which only makes us laugh harder.

My stomach cramps; it's the first time I've laughed since the funeral, which was weeks ago. It's good, at least for a little while, to be able to think about something else.

"You both act like you're five years old." Henri stands, hands on hips, leering down at us.

"Says the boy who cried like a baby when he was the first one out of the races this year," Destinel gloats.

Henri's eyes narrow. Even though the Dark God festival was months ago, Henri still hasn't gotten over the humiliation of entering the race and losing on the first lap.

"You shut your mouth," Henri begins, but I interrupt him.

"Maybe if you'd shut *your* mouth during the race, you wouldn't have thrown up all over yourself," I say.

Destinel snorts. Henri rolls his eyes.

"If you both had a brain between you," he says, "you'd be playing Dwellers versus Halves instead of dress-up."

"The Captain said killing Halves isn't a game," I say, repeating the words my father said the last time he caught Destinel and I playing that very game.

"That's true," Henri says, and I can tell from the look on his face he's about to say something cruel. "Maybe if Hemera had taken it seriously, her mama would still be alive."

His words are like a slap to my face, made all the worse because they echo what I've been telling myself ever since it happened. If I had done something, anything, my mother might still be alive.

"Why you little," Destinel starts forward, her murderous gaze fixed on Henri.

I want to tell her to stop, that he's right, but my throat won't work.

Henri takes a step back from Destinel, but he's not finished yet. He keeps his beady eyes focused on me. "Mama says now that Lady Harkibel's dead, we don't have to pretend to be nice to you anymore." Henri gives me a knowing smirk. "Now I don't have to pretend you aren't a freak."

"You shut your stupid mouth, Henri," Destinel shouts.

"And you," Henri sneers, "You're just a sad little orphan living off the charity of the rest of the Dwellers in Subterrane Harkibel."

Destinel's mouth shuts with an audible click of her jaw.

Henri's taunts are always worse because they're true. Both of Destinel's parents died from the Burn after getting lost on the Outside and being unable to find their way back to the Subterrane before high day.

The look on my best friend's face makes my mouth remember how to form words. I try to think of the meanest thing I can say to Henri that will shut him up.

"Just because your papa trades his dinner ration for drink," I say, "doesn't mean you can't afford some manners."

At the expression that crosses Henri's face, I feel a little sorry. But then I remember what he said about Destinel and my mother. I don't feel bad anymore.

"Why I oughta…." Henri lifts his hands and curls them into fists.

Even though Destinel is taller than me, I step in front of her, protecting her in case Henri decides to strike.

"No, you really ought not to," a different, deeper voice replies. Brice, the head scout's son, takes Henri's fist and forces it back down.

Brice is two years older than us and a scout in training. His parents were my mother's closest friends in the Subterrane, and she used to bring me with her to his family's cave. Brice was always nice to me, even when our mothers weren't watching, although I always felt a little shy around him. We haven't talked much since my mother died.

Brice releases Henri's arm, giving him a look that dares him to raise it again.

"I'm sorry about your mom, Hemera," Brice says.

Unlike some of the other children, whose parents shooed them over to talk to me when they thought my father was watching, I believe he means what he says.

Even though it has been weeks since my father and I buried her, the mention of my mother still makes my vision blur.

"Thank you," I stammer.

Brice's mother ducks into the cave. When she spots Brice and me, her gaze softens.

"Hemera, how are you holding up?"

She takes one look at me, and shakes her head. "Never mind, I'm a fool to ask you that." She dabs at her eyes with the sleeve of her cloak. Her kind, familiar face invites me to speak the words I've kept locked away since her funeral.

"I miss her," I whisper.

Destinel puts her arm around me, and I lean against her.

"We've lost the best of us," Brice's mom says, still wiping at her eyes. "She's the only reason Subterrane Harkibel still exists."

She's referring to the time my mother single-handedly defended the Subterrane's women and children from an attack. It was before I was born, but I've heard the story so many times I feel like I was there.

When the dreaded Halve creatures attacked the Dwellers and almost wiped Subterrane Harkibel off the map, my mother stood in front of the cave where all the women and children hid. With just her sword and a ferocity not even the Halves would test, she drove them away.

Those same monsters are the ones who took her from me.

"Sometimes it helps to talk about those who are no longer with us," Brice's mother says. "I know it's been difficult for you, with the Captain gone so much. If you'd like, you could talk to me."

What could I say?

I could say I'll never forgive myself for letting this happen to her…that I should have done something…something more than cower and hide. I should have been brave like her.

I could say I don't know how to do any of this without her.

"Hemera?"

I start at the sound of my name.

Brice's mother is looking at me, her forehead creased in concern. "Is there anything you'd like to get off your chest?"

I try to swallow, but my throat is too dry. I reach for the waterskin hanging over my shoulder, but my hands are trembling too much for me to take hold of it.

I stare down at the ground. "No," I say. "There's nothing."

I couldn't stop the tears that were leaking from my eyes as I ran out of the cave. Destinel had wanted to come with me, but I told her I just needed some time alone.

Destinel understands what it's like to lose parents, but her parents died from illness. My best friend can't possibly imagine what it's like to watch your own mother be murdered before your eyes, when you did nothing to stop it….

I might have gone to the Captain's cave in search of the one person who could understand what I'm feeling, but my father is already gone again—off to some Subterrane somewhere to trade something.

I can't bear to go back to the sleeping cave I shared with my mother and see her empty bed. So instead, I go down to the lowest level of the

Subterrane and close myself inside the small cave that holds the Subterrane's Dark God shrine.

I kneel at the foot of the biggest statue, lace my fingers together, and ask the Dark God to protect my mother as she takes her first steps into the darkness.

I don't know how long I stay there, minutes or hours.

A faint rumbling makes me open my eyes. At first, I think it might be the drums beating out a message for the whole Subterrane to hear. But the vibrations aren't those of the drumbeats.

It isn't until the support pillars lining the cave begin to tremble that I understand what is happening. The cave, with seven layers' worth of pressure sitting on top of it, is collapsing.

I fly to my feet as the walls of the cave begin to shudder.

Crack.

Dirt rains down on my head and into my eyes. Panic squeezes against my throat, choking me as the dust finds its way into my lungs. The pillars that support the tunnel shake again. One by one, their solid foundations begin to crumble.

Run, Hemera. Run now.

I'm fast, but my legs are weighed down by grief and fear. There's already rubble blocking the tunnel out of the cave, and I have to claw my way through the dirt and stones to make a path. In a few more seconds, I'll be trapped down here, buried underneath seven levels of caves and tunnels.

My screams are drowned out by the sound of debris filling the path. My vision is blurred from the sting of bits of stone.

"Help! Someone help me!"

But there's no one to hear me. I'm alone.

My lungs scream as I choke on the stale air. Sweat streams down my back, pressing my thick cloak even more tightly to my body. A buzzing sound fills my head. I can't breathe.

There are too many rocks. The tunnel is impassable, and I'm trapped.

My shaking limbs betray me and I fall to the ground. Two slabs of fallen rock balanced against each other are all that shield me from being completely buried.

The rocks stop falling…for the moment. It won't be long before they start again. My body is wracked with shivers in spite of the suffocating heat. How much longer until my air runs out?

My heart stops at the sound of muffled voices above me. A giddiness takes hold of me as hope surges in my chest.

"Help! I'm down…."

Rock dust catches in my throat. I double over as far as the cramped space will allow, coughing.

"Please," I try to yell, but the coughing has stolen my voice.

"Pillar must have broken and caused a chain reaction," a voice says from above. "The whole tunnel's caved in. Do you think anyone's down there?"

No matter how hard I try to scream, I can't manage anything above a whisper.

"Hemera Harkibel was down there."

Yes, I'm down here! Please.

The same voice continues, "The *Bisecter.*" The hatred in this word is like a punch to my already aching gut. "Leave her."

Acid surges up through my throat. *Leave me? They couldn't….*

"She's my best friend. You help her right this instant or I'll go down there and get her myself!"

Destinel. Even with all the dirt and stone between us, I know her voice.

"Get the kid out of here," a voice says.

I hear screaming as Destinel is dragged away.

"Destinel's right. We can't let her die regardless of what she is," someone else argues.

"We might be caught in another cave-in ourselves if we try to save her," a high-pitched female voice cuts through the others.

"If we save her, we'll put the entire Subterrane in danger. Let nature take its course."

No! They can't just leave me down here to die.

My father would make them rescue me if he was here. If my mother was alive….

Dirt slides down the wall and into my precarious shelter. I cover my face with shaking hands. There is nowhere else for me to go. I'm being buried alive.

"High day's coming," someone says. "We'll send messengers to the Captain and figure out how to clean up this mess later. In the meantime, section off the tunnel so the rest of the Subterrane doesn't get taken down, too."

Hysteria edges in all around me. I squeeze my eyes shut, but the darkness behind my eyelids makes me feel like I'm falling.

I will die here.

My eyes snap open at the sound of moving rocks. My cheeks burn as the salt from my tears mixes with the cuts on my face. I wrap my hands around my knees and brace myself for the crush of stones. But the ceiling doesn't collapse.

"Hang on, Hemera," a voice calls.

There is scuffling above me, as though stones are being moved one by one.

"One more big one," the voice calls down, less muffled than it had been before.

There is more movement above me, and then the ceiling begins to collapse.

"Hurry!" Brice yells as he scales down the tumbling rocks and grasps my outstretched hand.

CHAPTER 2

NOW

I light a candle with one hand and slip my other into the belled sleeve of my cloak. Ignoring the material's clumsy weight as it drapes over me from head to toe, I duck under the low opening of the cave and into the tunnel.

I slink along the path, keeping close to the wall, willing myself to blend in with my surroundings.

If my mother were here, she'd tell me to hold my head up high. But she isn't. So I keep my gaze down as though there's something fascinating on the ground in front of me.

My hand reaches unconsciously for the silver key hanging around my neck, *the key to my mother's heart.* My fist swallows up the delicate piece of metal, feeling the borrowed strength burrow into my bones.

Two guards pass me on their way to the Outside. Like me, the men's cloaks are pulled tight about them so every inch of skin will be hidden when we step into the deadly sun. One of them becomes very busy adjusting his gloves the moment he sees me. The other looks at the stone ceiling, the covered oil lanterns spaced along the wall…anything to avoid looking at me.

It's my pitch-black eyes that remind the other Dwellers I don't belong.

Such a shame, I've heard the older women whisper. *She'd be a real beauty if it weren't for those* eyes.

I press one hand against the damp earth wall as I walk and clutch my necklace with the other. Something about the closeness of it all makes my chest tight and my breathing sharp. Since the cave-in five years ago that nearly claimed my life, I keep waiting for the ceiling to fall again and bury me alive. Just the memory of the falling earth makes me stumble.

Pick up your feet before you fall and embarrass yourself, Hemera.

The main tunnel of Subterrane Harkibel winds its way up to the surface through seven levels of packed earth passages. I skirt around the edge of the underground lake to avoid the parts slippery with mud. A Dark God statue, the replacement for the one that was swallowed up in the cave-in, stands sentry beside the lake. In a ritual almost as familiar to me as breathing, I kneel in front of the statue.

"We will meet when the darkness comes," I murmur, repeating the phrase we're taught before learning even our own names.

Other hooded and cloaked figures do the same, leaving more space around me than necessary as they kneel to pay their respects to the Dark God.

Two drumbeats reverberate through the hard-packed wall. *Low day; time for work.* Everyone is hurrying now, and I'm crushed against the wall as guards, scouts, and miners crowd into the tunnel. My chest tightens in that familiar, suffocating way. Ever since the cave-in, crowded and dark places make me want to either scream or pass out.

Breathe, Hemera, I command myself.

My hand fumbles for the silver key. I close my eyes for a moment, trying to remember the glint of metal on the cream skin of my mother's neck. The image is clear enough, but when I try to imagine the sound of her voice when she said, "It's the key to my heart, darling Mer. And it belongs to you," the memory is just out of reach.

"Hemera."

I'm jolted out of the memory at the sound of my name. I realize I've been standing in the middle of the tunnel, clutching my necklace, and earning more than a few disapproving stares as the other Dwellers step around me.

Idiot, I tell myself. The last thing I need is to give them any more reasons to shun and avoid me.

"Captain doesn't want any more emeralds. You're cutting rubies today." The head miner shoves a pickax into my hand without looking at me before disappearing back into the crowd.

The gems that grow in the Subterrane's mines as naturally as weeds in the crop field give us an endless bounty to trade with the other five Subterranes—and endless work. *Survival is not for the faint of heart,* my father likes to say. My father, Captain Harkibel, is the leader of our Subterrane. Those of us who live in the Subterrane territory, the network of six Subterranes connected by trade routes and shared information, are the Dwellers.

"What a grumpy old toad." Destinel makes a rude gesture at the head miner's back. She yawns, slinging an arm over my shoulders. "Want to skip work and rub itching cabbage on Henri's pillow?"

"Love to." I grin at the thought. "But if a Dweller shirks her work assignment—"

"Then the delicate balance of the Subterrane's existence will be threatened," Destinel finishes. She even links her hands behind her back and paces back and forth in a perfect imitation of the Captain.

I shoulder my pickax. "Those rubies aren't going to cut themselves, and the healers will probably poison you if you're late."

Destinel scowls. "Like those cranky old women need me to mix one more pot of Burn salve," she mutters.

The scent of yeast and spices wafts through the tunnel leading to the dining cave. My mouth waters, but I won't be able to collect my ration until after my work assignment. I inhale again, but the scent of bread is gone. There is only the lingering stink of dank earth and worms.

"Say hello to the Outside for me." Destinel gives me a wave before ducking into one of the smaller tunnels.

The main tunnel is filled with Dwellers now. We look like sand-colored ants, wrapped in our identical cloaks and hurrying uphill to the Outside. The cloaks are heavy and stifling, but they are all that protect us against the Burn. Even during low day, the only time it is safe to leave the Subterrane, a person's skin will sizzle and blister the moment it meets with direct sunlight.

Although the sun never sets below the horizon, we still use it to keep time. Our working and sleeping hours are marked by the oval path of the sun as it travels overhead from north to south during high day, and then back to north along the horizon during low day. We sleep in the Subterrane, under layers and layers of dirt and rock, when the burning rays of the high day sun make it impossible to venture beyond the walls of the cave.

Dwellers exchange greetings as we wait for the guards to crank open the two sets of stone coverings that keep sunlight from filtering into the Subterrane's entrance. Some of the children push through narrow gaps to get nearer to the ladders propped against the tunnel's last, steep incline. There are twelve hours of low day. They cannot be wasted.

I pull on my gloves and tuck them into the belled sleeve of my cloak. A gentle tug on my cloak draws my attention downward. Sirrel, Henri's younger sister, stares up at me.

"Mama says anyone who looks you straight in the eye will be cursed for six generations."

"Six generations is very specific." I squat down until I'm eye level with the little Dweller girl. "If I'm so dangerous, then why are you talking to me?"

Sirrel grins. "*I* know you're not evil. Your hair's too pretty." She reaches out a finger to stroke the loose curls dangling at my face.

I smile at her. I've always gotten along better with the youngest Dwellers than the ones my own age—with the exception of Destinel and Brice, of course. Maybe it's because they haven't learned they're supposed to be afraid of me yet.

"Sirrel!" The girl's mother shoves her way through the throng of Dwellers, almost knocking a man over in her haste. "What did I tell you about talking to *her*?" the woman scolds.

If Destinel were here, she'd have something witty and biting to say that would make the woman's ruddy face turn even redder. If Brice were here, he'd stare her down until she lowered her head in shame.

"Rarr," I mutter under my breath. For Sirrel's sake, I bare my teeth like I'm some kind of rabid animal.

Sirrel giggles. Her mother gives me a withering look. She wipes the sleeve of her own cloak over the girl's hand where it touched my hair.

I try to ignore the familiar hurt that squeezes my heart. *Does she think her daughter will catch what I have, like some disease?*

"Make way, scouts coming through."

My breath catches. Even the sound of his voice sends a warm tingle through me.

Brice brushes a hand against me as he passes, reminding me of the first time he touched me. He was grabbing my hand, pulling me out of the landslide of stone and dirt that was trying to swallow me. And then, afterward, he brushed the dirt from my cloak and pulled bits of debris from my hair.

"Stop ogling him." A girl standing near me rolls her perfect, normal brown eyes at me before turning to her friend. "Like *she'd* ever have a chance with *him*."

They both laugh.

I can feel my pale skin turn scarlet. I swat at an insect buzzing around my face, but I miss and end up slapping my own cheek instead. I duck my head as the two girls laugh harder.

Brice's beautiful green eyes slide from me to the girls. His jaw tightens. I wait until his attention is on me again and give him a slight shake of my head.

It's not worth it, I tell him with my eyes. If the Captain found out about us....

"Isn't he gorgeous?" the girl, still chortling at my expense, asks.

"Brice." Her friend sighs out his name. "What I wouldn't give to have those arms wrapped around me."

It's the best feeling in the world, I imagine telling her. *I would know.*

"He's *so* brave. He's definitely going to be Captain someday. I wish—"

All conversations stop at the sound of the stone covering to the Outside grating against its hinges.

"Hoods up," a guard calls.

As if we're one body instead of many, we draw up the hoods of our cloaks so the stiff brims keep our faces shadowed from any sunlight overhead. Gloves are pulled onto hands, shielding the last bit of skin as sunlight spills onto the path. We surge forward.

"Go in darkness," I tell the guard. He grunts without meeting my eyes.

It's these small slights, the ones that add up over the course of hours and days, that remind me I don't belong…that I'm something different…something wrong.

I climb the ladder and step through the hole in the ground separating Subterrane Harkibel from the Outside. Sweat begins to stream down my back, making me curse the cloak that is both a nuisance and my lifeline.

The crowd of Dwellers thins as some veer off toward the crop fields. Others head down to the river to draw endless buckets of water for the thirsty crops. Under my father's direction, the growers are constantly experimenting with new varieties of plants that can withstand the sun's intensity. The blacksmiths are working on special plates of metal, which my father is trying to make into armor. Thus far, no one has been able to develop armor that will protect us from the Halves but won't make its wearers melt in the sun. *Climb aboard the wheel of change, or be crushed beneath its weight*, my father always says.

The scouts are already making their way through the narrow, guarded opening in the stone wall separating the Subterrane from the forest that lies beyond. The rest of us traipse along the weathered path, pickaxes in hand, to the mine.

Rickety ladders lead down into the jewel pit, where buckets attached to ropes wait to be loaded with treasure. The bulk of what we harvest goes to Subterranes Jevin and Aria, which pay in much-needed lamp oil and the special material from which our cloaks are made. The rest are given to the Duskers. *Sacrifices to the Dark God*, they tell us. But every time they come, more of the jewels are pinned to their gray cloaks, rather than left to rest on their Dark God shrines. If anyone else notices, they don't say so.

I almost groan out loud as the head miner dumps five empty buckets at my feet. Mining is hard, monotonous work. And because I'm stuck next to the same two trash-talking, pickax-wielding men all day, the company falls just shy of intolerable.

I take up my place along a portion of wall gleaming red from the sparkle of rubies and drive my pickax into the gray wall. A spray of rock sends up a puff of dust. Even though I turn my head to the side, my face is covered in the fine powder.

The dust is the worst part. It leaves white streaks in my dark hair, the only part of my mother's beauty I inherited. The dust makes my tongue feel thick and chalky, and is permanently embedded in the creases of my gloves.

"Someone help me with this." The man beside me strains against a boulder blocking his access.

"Not you," he growls as I move to help. I shrug my shoulders and grit my teeth, telling myself I don't care. *You are more than what they see.* My mother's words, which always sounded wise and true when they came from her lips, ring hollow in my head.

A scream of agony cuts through the usual sounds of the day. I drop the fist-sized ruby in my hand and run in the direction of the cry.

CHAPTER 3

A small crowd has formed around a man whose leg is caught beneath a boulder. The stone is so large it dwarfs the four Dwellers who heave and groan against its weight. The stone doesn't budge.

"Dark God save me!" The man writhes on the ground, the droplets of his blood like small rubies scattered across the stones. He twists his body as though trying to rip his leg off. I shudder and resist the urge to look away.

Try as they might, the others aren't making any progress with the stone.

I could help, I think as I watch the men struggle. I *should* help. But my father's words echo in my head, a constant warning. Don't do anything to draw attention to yourself. Don't let them see what you can really do.

The man's screams are so loud I can't hear myself think. Before I consider what I'm doing, before I can think about what it will mean, I push my way to the front of the crowd.

I only meant to lift the stone enough for the Dweller to drag out his leg, but the entire boulder comes off the ground. One of the miners trying to help is drawn more than a foot off the ground when he doesn't let go.

There's a collective gasp from the onlookers. They all turn to stare at me. For several moments, no one speaks. No one moves. I focus my attention on keeping the rock I'm still holding up from falling back on the Dweller's leg.

"You can gawk after you get him free," the head miner barks.

The others pull the man—unconscious now—from beneath the stone before I let it fall back to the ground. It settles with a thud that makes the ground shudder.

A short laugh escapes from me as I look down at my dust-covered gloves. I always knew I was strong, but it's been years since I've done anything even close to testing my limits. I forgot how good it feels to use, rather than resist, my strength. I should feel tired, exhausted even, from the strain of lifting something so enormous. Instead, I just want to do it again. I give the boulder a satisfied look.

"Papa!"

I recognize little Sirrel's voice even though I can't see her face as the tiny cloaked figure runs straight toward us.

To my surprise, the girl doesn't run to her father, who is being carried back to the Subterrane so the healers can tend to him. Instead, she collides with my legs, wrapping both arms around my knees and kissing my cloak.

"You saved Papa! You saved Papa!" she cries over and over again.

A rush of emotions hits me—gratitude for Sirrel's affection, satisfaction to have been able to help…regret I hadn't been brave enough to act when my own mother needed me….

"It's alright." I pat her small back. "Your papa is going to be fine."

She blinks away tears as she squints up at me. "I was coming back from the river and I saw—I saw—" She swallows another sob. "But you saved him! You're the strongest Dweller in the whole entire Subterrane!"

I don't try to hide the smile spreading across my face. No one ever talks about my differences like they're something to marvel at. Maybe I should stop hiding all the time. Maybe I should let them see me for what I am every once in a while….

"Here now." One of the miners lifts Sirrel off her feet and places her on the ground behind him. "You best not be speaking with the Bisecter."

The sting of his words leaves me speechless. The stupid smile plastered on my face dissolves.

"She saved Papa," Sirrel argues, pointing a small, gloved finger at me.

I try to tell her it's okay, that she shouldn't worry about me. But the words stick in my throat.

Two of the miners exchange a look, and then one of them lifts the squirming, screaming child and carries her back toward the Subterrane.

Her shouts of protest are soon lost. When I turn back, the others are staring at me.

"You really are one of them, aren't you?" a miner who has never before spoken to me asks. He makes no effort to hide his disgust.

"Did *they* teach you that trick? Or were you just born like them?" another sneers.

"I—"

"The only thing human about you is your pretty looks," chimes in a third, "and even those are ruined by your eyes."

They laugh.

"Filthy Bisecter. If Captain Harkibel wasn't your father, you would've been dragged off to Malarusk years ago."

The blood drains from my face. It's true; my father has always protected me, even gone so far as to hide me so the Duskers wouldn't find out about me.

You are more than what they see. You are more than what they see. I chant my mother's words over and over again as I wait for the tightness in my throat to ease.

A few of the miners throw suspicious, hateful glances in my direction. I try to make my way back to the ladders, but I stumble on something unseen in my path. My feet get twisted up in each other.

Not now, Hemera!

I try to regain my balance, but it's too late.

I hit the ground hard, gravel biting into my palms through my gloves, as I roll into an undignified position. The men laugh as they stalk past me.

"Clumsy and a freak," one of them says. "What are the odds?"

I wait until they're gone before I pick myself up. I look down at the ground through blurred vision.

I just saved a Dweller's life, but it doesn't matter. To them, all I'll ever be are the black eyes I share with the Halves.

CHAPTER 4

I blink away the tears threatening to spill over.

My gaze moves past the protective wall to the forest, where the beasts we all fear are lying in wait. With every rustle of leaves, I can imagine seeing the monstrous Halve creatures waiting for some unsuspecting Dweller to cross their path.

The first time I heard about the Halves, it was from the Duskers. They told the story that I have since heard word-for-word at the closing of every Dark God festival.

"No one knows from whence they came or for how long they've existed," the Dusker boomed across the crowd of Dwellers. "But we all know the horror they've brought upon us."

He went on to talk about how the Duskers would protect us so long as we continued to pray for darkness and make sacrifices to the Dark God.

It's the same promise they've been making for generations, and still, there is no darkness, and the Halves are still murderers.

The Halves, so-called for their vague resemblance to humans, are hunched over, grotesque beasts. They only go out in the low day like the rest of us, but they don't need cloaks; their rough, scaly hides protect them from the sun. The Halves are bigger, stronger, and faster than any human, but they are witless; they know only how to murder and destroy. Some Dwellers believe the first Halves were once humans who got the Burn but somehow survived, but no one knows if that's true.

When I was a small child, I overheard a Dweller woman telling her granddaughter about me. Before then, I hadn't understood why the Halves and my name were often whispered in the same breath.

"A few months before the Captain's daughter was born," the woman explained to her granddaughter, "a group of Halves attacked Subterrane Harkibel. During the battle, a Halve made it past the guards and began to attack the women and children hiding in the Subterrane. Hemera's mother was very brave, and tried to protect the children. She put herself in harm's way to defend them.

"When Lady Harkibel's dagger sliced through the Halve's body, its poisonous blood landed on her. Welts rose on her arms and spread across her body. She should have died when the poison got into her blood. Instead, her welts healed and she became the only person ever to survive contact with Halve blood."

My mother lived, but the healers told her there was no hope for her unborn child.

My survival was called a miracle…until I opened my eyes, and the healers looked into the wide, black stare of the Halves.

The healers decided the unborn baby had absorbed the poison that should have killed my mother. By taking the Halve's blood into my own, I became something different—neither human nor Halve. My father came up with the word *Bisecter* to describe the anomaly, but it soon became a title the Dwellers used to isolate and humiliate me.

It was only because my father was the Captain that I was not thrown out of the Subterrane to die.

✳ ✳ ✳

I can't hide my black eyes, but until today, my father was the only one who knew I inherited the Halves' strength.

I wipe my dirty cloak sleeve across my face. There's no sense in standing around and waiting to see what will happen once news of my inhuman strength spreads through the Subterrane.

I measure the long shadow my body casts across the ground. *Lowest day,* which means there are six more hours before the sun reaches deadly heights again. The miners' pickaxes clink against the stone walls of the pits. As their insults churn in my head, an aching loneliness creeps over me.

Propping my pickaxe against one of the ladders, I begin to walk in the opposite direction.

Clumsy and a freak.

A desperate need to see Brice pulses in my chest. The thought of his arms wrapped tight around me sends prickles of anticipation down my spine and makes my feet move almost of their own accord.

I don't stop until I reach the protective stone wall enclosing the land above Subterrane Harkibel. Brice is the best scout in the Subterrane, which means he'll be stationed in the large clearing where Halves are known to pass through in greater numbers.

My heart beats faster. If anyone sees me sneaking away from my work assignment, I could be locked in the prison caves. Worse, I might come across a Halve before I find Brice.

Freak. Unnatural. Bisecter.

I feel an irresistible urge to see one of the only people who doesn't flinch at the sight of my black eyes. I pick my way over the crumbled part of the stone wall until I'm on the other side. There, I pause.

When the two guards pacing alongside the wall turn their backs, I take my chances, and run.

I reach the base of an enormous script tree and duck under its thick, green branches. The air smells like river and new leaves. It's the forest's scent. It smells like Brice.

Taking what feels like my first deep breath in days, I scan the ground for the unworn path I know by heart. I follow the narrow trail that winds around thick tree trunks. I move slowly, listening for the telltale trample of Halve feet, ducking behind tree trunks whenever an animal scurries through the brush. After the better part of an hour, the clearing appears.

The first time I came to this clearing, it was by accident. It wasn't long after Brice rescued me from the cave collapse. I felt lost and alone in a way I never had before. I hadn't realized how much my mother protected me from the other Dwellers' hatred and fear until she was gone. After Henri and two other kids shouted insults until my ears rang, I ran out of the Subterrane without any plan or care for where I was going.

I was running from the Subterrane, but also from the dreams that haunted me each high day.

I discovered the cave behind the waterfall just as low day turned. No sooner had I closed myself into the darkness, the stone door was pushed aside to reveal a boy with brilliant green eyes framed in the swirling waterfall mist.

When the echoes of my startled scream stopped ricocheting off the cave walls, Brice, the only Dweller who refused to leave me for dead, smiled as if we were two normal humans exchanging greetings by the Dark God shrine.

Brice wasn't just admired by every beautiful girl his age, he was also the youngest and best scout in the Subterrane. Even my father spoke highly of Brice, and he usually keeps his praise to himself.

I smile to myself at the memory of Brice, leaning against the wall of the cave, looking as comfortable as I was awkward.

Unlike me, who could find a way to trip over air, Brice's every move was fluid. There was no hint of the stoop so many Dwellers have from a lifetime of ducking through tunnels.

It was the first time I saw—really saw—the golden hair and green eyes every other girl in the Subterrane swooned over.

"Nice to see you, Hemera," he said.

Brice looked right into my eyes, then. No one besides my parents and Destinel had ever had the courage to meet my gaze.

As it did then, the gentle rush of the waterfall fills me with a sense of calm. It's almost impossible to imagine how something as evil as a Halve could exist in a place as beautiful as this. I let out a slow breath as a quiet relief spreads through my tense limbs.

I kneel down beside the stream to splash water onto my face. I reach under my hood and try to comb my fingers through the tangles in my thick hair, but it's too matted with sweat and my gloves are too bulky for me to make much progress.

A dark shadow flits behind a tree. The bush to my left rustles. My shoulders tense.

Brice leaps out from behind the tree, dagger in hand.

"Hemera!" His dagger drops to the ground. "I could have killed you."

I laugh, my adrenaline turning to relief. "I missed you."

"And I you." Brice pulls me against his chest. "But you can't just wander into the forest any time you please. Especially since it's your father who makes the rules."

"Is it?" I feign surprise. "I had no idea."

Brice tries to hide the smile tugging at the corner of his lips.

This conversation is familiar. It's the same one we always have whenever I sneak away from my work assignment to be with him. I smile up at Brice, into eyes the color of new leaves.

"You don't always have to do everything he says, you know," I tell him.

"I most certainly do." He picks up his dagger and sheaths it at his belt. "And so do you. He's our Captain." There's pride in his voice.

I raise my eyebrows in challenge. "So, if my father told you to kill me, would you?"

At the look that crosses Brice's face I can't help but laugh.

"That's not funny, Hemera." He glares at me, but the tension in his shoulders is already melting away.

"It's not just about the Captain," he continues. "What if you came across a Halve?"

"Then you and your dagger would save me."

I meant it as a joke, but Brice's chin lifts and he stands a little straighter. "You're right about that."

We look at each other for a moment, just basking in our togetherness.

"Admit it," I say. "Breaking the rules feels good, doesn't it?"

Brice sighs, relenting.

"I'm glad you came." His handsome face, usually so stern, rewards me with his perfect smile. "Even though it's much too dangerous to make a habit."

As he leans down to kiss my forehead, his hair falls over his eyes. It's soft and warm as it brushes against my face.

Brice straightens up and looks into the trees. "Think you can handle things on your own for a few hours?"

The other scout, who had melted against the trees so completely I hadn't even seen him, steps out from behind a trunk. He gives Brice a disapproving look and nods. Brice is the lead scout on his watch, and so none of the others would dare to say what they're really thinking…that Brice shouldn't be abandoning his post when there are Halves about…that he shouldn't be abandoning his post for the likes of me.

Brice doesn't seem to notice the other scout's disapproval. Smiling at me, he takes my hand and leads me toward the rock ledge over which a narrow waterfall flows. When I step onto the slippery rocks, my feet betray me. I wobble, my arms flying like a spastic bird, as I pitch forward.

All that saves me from plunging head-first into the pool is Brice's steadying hand.

If it was anyone except for Brice or Destinel, I would have been embarrassed, but the two of them know me well enough to expect my feet to betray me.

"I swear those rocks were out to get me," I say.

Brice chuckles. "Always too busy looking ahead to pay attention to what your own feet are doing."

"It's not funny," I say.

The Captain stopped teaching me how to duel because he was convinced I was always falling over on purpose. *Learn how to use your feet*, he said, *or for sun's sake grow some new ones.*

I've done neither, as my body likes to remind me.

"I think it's cute," Brice says, leaning under the brim of my hood to kiss me. "I wouldn't want to change a single thing about you."

My heart does a little flip in my chest. I've already forgotten the Dwellers' angry words and their ugly stares. When I'm with Brice, everything they hate about me only seems to make Brice love me more.

When I turn back to him, the look in Brice's eyes sends a fiery heat coursing through me.

The natural cave set back into the depths of rock behind the waterfall has been our secret place ever since he rescued me from the cave collapse.

At first, it was just the act of going somewhere where no one else could find us that held allure. Brice showed me his sketchbook, and I showed him how to use my sling. We talked about everything and nothing, stealing long hours where Brice didn't need to be the perfect, obedient scout, and I didn't have to be the Bisecter.

It was more than two years until we became something different to each other…something so much more.

Brice bends down to light the torch while I pull off my cloak, enjoying the feel of air passing through my loose-fitting cotton shirt and pants. As Brice pulls his own cloak over his head, the outline of taut muscles shows through his thin shirt.

Brice frowns. "I don't like you putting yourself at risk just to see me."

"Choosing me might be the most dangerous thing you've ever done," I retort.

His frown fades, replaced with a thoughtful look. He takes a lock of my hair and twirls it around his finger. "Someday I'll be Captain of this Subterrane," he murmurs, "and then we'll get to make the rules."

My insides warm. Brice and I have talked about it before—the time when my father will choose his successor. It has to be Brice. There is no one better suited to the role of keeping our Subterrane safe.

Brice has been protecting the Subterrane for years as a scout, but when he's the one making the laws, I'll be able to help. We won't just defend the Subterrane from the Halves, we'll hunt them.

It's when we talk about this future that I feel closest to Brice. Of all the Dwellers, he understands my hatred for the Halves better than anyone.

I lock my hands behind Brice's neck to pull his face down to mine. His lips are soft, warm, inviting. Brice wraps his arms around me, drawing me closer. I breathe in his scent as his heart beats against my chest.

He's so alive.

When I step back, Brice's green eyes are alight. They say more to me than any spoken promise. I am his, and he is mine.

"Don't go anywhere," Brice murmurs as he moves to pull the makeshift stone door into place.

Even though the cave is empty save for a couple of blankets and two candles fixed to the wall, it's more home to me than the Subterrane. This cave is the only place I'm free, where I can breathe.

Brice lets out a grunt as he tries to pull the stone door across the cave's entrance. A pang of guilt seizes me. I could lift the door in place with barely a thought, but even with all the other secrets we've shared over the years, Brice doesn't know about my strength. He hasn't been back to the Subterrane since his shift started, and so he doesn't know what I did for Sirrel's father. With any luck, my father will silence the miners before anyone else finds out.

Gossip spreads through the Subterrane faster than a brush fire, but I've learned never to underestimate my father's authority as Captain of Subterrane Harkibel.

When I was ten years old, my father saw me lift five stone blocks out of the jewel pit at once. Together, the blocks were taller than me. I had thought my father would be pleased to see what I could accomplish. I was wrong. My father had dragged me back to his caves.

"The Duskers will take you, Hemera," he said, his face as pale as if he were one of them. "They'll throw you in the Malarusk dungeons. They'll torture you. And then they'll kill you."

Until then, I hadn't known how different I was.

After my mother died, it became more important than ever to hide what I could do.

I stopped testing my strength. I walked everywhere, taking care never to run. I kept my eyes down whenever I passed another Dweller. I thought if I could blend in, the part of me that was less than human might cease to exist.

Guilt eats at me every time I see Brice struggle with the heavy stone door. I know I should tell him everything about me—there have been several times when I almost have. When we're together, though, I can almost forget about what I am.

Brice finally manages to wrestle the door in place. He feels his way to me in the darkness and folds me into his arms.

"Hemera Harkibel." He whispers my name as he traces the outline of my face with his finger.

There is a warm tingling behind my rib cage. His perfect green eyes glimmer even in the dark as I nestle into the crook of his arm. The rise and fall of his chest is so steady, so comforting. He wraps a protective arm around my waist.

"I love you."

Warm in his embrace, I fall into the kind of deep sleep I never reach underground.

* * *

A noise outside the cave jolts us awake. We disentangle ourselves and Brice pushes back the stone door. There is a muffled groan, the rustle of leaves, and then silence.

After another few minutes pass without a sound, Brice whispers, "I'm going to go take a look. You stay here."

Ignoring him, I pull on my cloak. Brice looks like he wants to argue, but instead, unsheathes his dagger and says, "Stay behind me."

Brice leads the way as we track through the brush and around the curved path behind the waterfall. We inch forward into the sunlight, waiting for someone to leap out of the thick shrubs.

We work our way deeper into the brush. I'm beginning to think we imagined the sound, when I see someone lying just off the path.

"It's Taniel," I say in disbelief as I rush over to him.

Taniel was one of the Captain's guards. He was clever, daring, and ruthless. He also disappeared from the Subterrane more than a year ago without even the slightest hint of what had happened.

"Is he alive?" I ask as Brice kneels over him.

Brice turns the man's head so I can see the deep, symmetrical gashes on either side of his neck.

I inhale sharply. "Do you think an animal got him?"

Brice shakes his head. "They're too even for it to have been an animal."

"What are you doing—" I begin, as Brice pulls up the sleeve of the man's cloak.

I gasp.

Bloody gashes cover the inside of Taniel's left forearm.

Brice holds the limp arm for us both to see. "It's a message."

"How did you know—"

But as I squint at the shredded flesh, I realize Brice is right. What had looked like a random pattern carved into Taniel's skin are letters.

"Who could have done this to him?" I ask.

"He did it to himself." Brice nods at Taniel's right hand, which is still gripping a jagged stone.

We squint at the arm together.

"TNGR. Help," Brice reads.

The dead man's bloated flesh is already beginning to blister from exposure to the sunlight, making the letters almost illegible.

"What do you think it means?" I ask.

Brice looks from me to the words carved into Taniel's skin. He seems to be debating something internally. Finally, he says, "TNGR must be short for Tanguro."

"Tanguro?" I ask in surprise.

Tanguro is an abandoned fortress in the Wild Lands far to the North.

According to the stories, Tanguro was built long before the Duskers came to power. It was a great walled territory with a network of caves bigger than any of the Subterranes. When the Duskers resettled everyone into the Subterranes, Tanguro was abandoned. Traders from distant territories who sometimes stopped at Subterrane Harkibel would tell stories about strange and terrible creatures that prowled the lands on the Tanguro side of the mountains. There have also been stories…whispered rumors…that the Halves are capturing humans and keeping them in Tanguro as prisoners. Until today, I didn't believe them.

Taniel wasn't a trader or a scout. What would he have been doing there?

As if echoing my thoughts, Brice says, "The Halves must have brought him there. I've heard they made themselves a lair in the ruins of the old settlement."

"And you think he escaped and came back to warn us?"

Brice nods.

"How far is that?" I ask, when Brice continues to stare at the dead man's arm.

"Taniel must have walked for weeks to get back here." His voice is flat, almost monotone, like seeing a dead man with a warning carved into his skin is ordinary. For all I know, it could be. Brice never talks about scouting with me, just like I never talk about mining.

"Hemera!" Brice's voice is sharp. He's looking at my shadow.

As we puzzled over Taniel's message, the sun crept back up. High day is coming.

If we don't hurry back, we'll be stuck on the Outside during high day. Not even our cloaks would save us then.

"Let's go." Brice stands up.

"It's nearly curfew," I say, beginning to panic. "The Captain will notice if we get back at the same time."

"I won't leave you alone," Brice argues. "There could be Halves."

"You take the river trail," I say, ignoring him. "I'll go back through the woods."

"Hemera," Brice protests.

But I'm already running.

CHAPTER 5

With every step, I imagine the blisters that will soon form on my skin as the Burn cooks my flesh from the outside in. I run faster.

I once saw a Dweller after he got stuck on the Outside during high day. The guards brought his body back to the Subterrane, and when they took off his cloak, there were holes burned straight through his body.

I'm nearly through the open stretch between the woods and the Subterrane when my foot catches on something in my path. My feet give way and I hit the ground face-first. I gasp as my cheek scrapes against bare rock. Before I can even think about moving, a heavy netting closes in around me and sweeps me off the ground.

The net rises until I'm at least ten paces above the earth.

The trap holding me is secured to the branch of a dead tree by a single rope. It creaks as I swing back and forth high above the ground. My body is folded up so tightly in the cramped netting I can barely breathe, let alone move. My cloak does little to stop the rope from chafing as it cuts into me. My screaming and flailing make it worse.

I must be in one of the hunters' traps.

Knowing this snare was set by my own people does nothing to ease my panic. No one will come looking for me before low day. By that time, there will be nothing left except for whatever scraps the Burn vultures leave behind.

As the net squeezes tighter around me, a pinch near my ankle reminds me about the small knife Brice gave me months ago and insisted I keep in my boot. With a tremendous amount of squirming, during which the branch bows and groans, I manage to loosen the knife and begin sawing through the woven ropes. Each strand is wider than the blade of my knife.

Sweat drips off my forehead and stings my eyes. I don't pause to wipe my face. Every passing minute brings me closer to the Burn and to death. Panic and the sun's heat press against me until I can hardly breathe.

With a satisfying snap, a rope breaks and I fall through the netting.

I hit the ground hard. Gasping, I clutch my stomach as I fight for breath. Dark spots flash at the corner of my vision.

I manage to sit up. Someone is running through the near-blinding sunlight toward me.

"Captain?"

"Hemera! What are you doing out here?" When he reaches my side, he's breathing hard. "Do you care so little for both our lives?"

Without waiting for a reply, he yanks me to my feet.

Even though the brim of his hood is drawn forward, blisters bubble up on my father's cheeks and neck as we stagger back toward the Subterrane. My nostrils sting with the stench of burning flesh.

The guards help us down the tunnels of the Subterrane to the healing cave, where the healers flock around my father.

"My daughter!" he rasps. "Help her first."

The healers ignore his orders. It takes three of them to hold him down. The sound of his sizzling flesh mixes with the smell of burning.

I'm too guilt-ridden to do anything besides huddle in a corner as the healers slather Burn salve on my father's blisters. Guards flood the healing cave at the sound of his screams. I should be wailing and clawing at my skin, but I'm not.

Why don't I feel any pain?

When I run my hands over my face and neck, there are no blisters. How could I have escaped the Burn? My father and I were on the Outside for the same amount of time, and he's writhing on the narrow cot as he tries to claw off his own skin.

Oh no.

A low groan escapes me. *The Halves don't get the Burn.*

I rub my hands up and down my arms. My skin looks and feels human, but some of whatever protects them from the sun must be in me, too.

No, no, no. I didn't ask for any of this. I just want to be like the other Dwellers.

I want to scream and tear my hair out along with my father. Instead, I hug my arms tight to my body and try to disappear into the shadows.

From the youngest age, all Dwellers are taught to fear the high day. Wearing my cloak any time I leave the Subterrane is as natural to me as breathing, and so it never occurred to me that I might *not* need it.

Does this mean I would have been safe from the Burn even without my cloak?

My father's eyes roll back in his head and his body goes slack.

"He's dead!" a guard yells, and they all surge forward.

No! Please, not him, I beg the Dark God as I rush to his side. The Captain is the only family I have left.

"Just knocked out," a healer corrects briskly.

Relief floods my limbs. I try to get closer to my father, but the guards make a barrier around him and push me away.

"Haven't you caused enough trouble?" one of them hisses.

The healers bandage my father and then transfer him to a bed in an adjoining cave. Then, they turn to me.

"You were out in the sun? During *high day?*" A healer with a round stomach and fleshy chin wipes the dirt from my face with a rough cloth.

She purses her lips. "And not even a blister on you."

Another healer clears her throat and raises her eyebrows. The other says, "Oh. It must be because...."

"I'm a Bisecter." I keep my chin high even as my heart sinks.

The healer applies a thin sheen of the Burn salve, even though there are no blisters on my skin.

"You aren't worth wasting the salve on," she says as she cleans her hands in a stone basin, "but the Captain would have my head if I didn't do *something.*"

She avoids meeting my eyes.

"Where is she?"

I hear Destinel's panicked voice from the adjoining cave. My friend races into the cave, her arms full of clean cloths and jars of Burn salve. She drops everything at the sight of me.

"Hemera!"

I get a brief glimpse of one of the other healers chasing the unraveling bandages and spilled jars left in Destinel's wake.

"Are you okay? The guards said you were on the Outside after curfew, and then they said you were brought here, and I—"

Before I can even speak, two guards step into the healing cave and grasp each of my elbows.

"What in the sun?" Destinel demands, trying to wrap me in a protective hug.

The guards separate us.

"Hemera Harkibel, you are under arrest for violating curfew."

"But my father," I croak. "I can't leave him."

"Come with us, please."

My eyes begin to water. I force back the tears, not wanting to give the guards, or the healers exchanging victorious glances, the satisfaction of seeing me fall apart.

"This is insane!" Destinel explodes.

The healers have to practically wrestle her to keep her from chasing after us. I don't hear what else she's shouting as I'm led out of the cave.

I'm trembling so much my legs don't remember how to work. If it wasn't for the guards gripping me, I would have fallen all over myself.

Still gasping and trying to regain my composure, I let the guards escort me down the tunnel that snakes around the underground lake. The Dark God statue's knowing glare seems to follow me down the path. The guards drag me on, deep into the bowels of the Subterrane.

I have been to the prison caves on the seventh level with my father before, but never as a prisoner. If the walls caved in down here, there would be nowhere for me to run, nowhere to escape. The guards don't seem to notice my ragged breathing as they yank me forward.

They push me through a narrow, iron-barred door. The small cell is bare except for a single candle. The door creaks shut. The key turns in the lock, and then the boots tramp back up the tunnel.

Stupid. I pace around the small cell. *How could I have been so stupid?*

My teeth are chattering even though it's hot as an oven down here. All I can think about is my father covered in blisters, screaming as the healers held him down. He could have died.

Aside from Brice and Destinel, my father is the only person who cares what happens to me.

✳ ✳ ✳

How long have I been in this cell? Hours at least, maybe even days. The candle has long since burned out. The darkness smothers me.

If you are brave enough to hold your head up high, Mer, my mother used to tell me, *it will always be enough to carry you through.*

Still, it's all I can do to keep from whimpering as heavy footsteps stomp down the tunnel. I move to the door and cling to the bars as the light from the guard's lantern bounces around my tiny cell.

"Is my father alright?" I call out.

"The Captain's fine," the guard replies.

My relief is short-lived.

"You are found guilty of breaking curfew." The lanky guard's voice is flat. "You are hereby sentenced to twenty lashes. Your punishment will commence immediately."

Gulping, I squeeze my fists until I feel my nails cut into my palms. *Be brave,* I command myself.

The guard unlocks my door. I allow myself to be steered up the maze of tunnels. *Twenty lashes.*

Another guard falls into step behind me. We pass the dining cave, where a group of Dwellers waiting for their dinner rations point at me. Without looking back, I know they will follow behind the last guard. They won't miss the chance to see the punishment of Captain Harkibel's daughter, the Bisecter.

There is a crowd already waiting in the meeting cave, which is the only place large enough to hold all of the Dwellers at once. My father, his face covered in bandages, stands on the wooden dais in the center of the circular cave. The sight of him standing fills me with an overwhelming sense of awe. He doesn't look like someone who nearly died from the Burn.

The guards lead me to the dais as the other Dwellers file in, whispering excitedly. Everyone falls silent as my father begins to speak. His voice carries clear and strong despite his bandages.

"The high day curfew, put into law by the Duskers, is necessary for the protection of us all."

Shame prickles along my spine; not for breaking curfew, but for being the cause of the blisters under my father's bandages.

"Ten lashes will be given for putting the Subterrane at risk."

A murmur of disapproval runs through the crowd. Twenty lashes had been promised.

He looks at me. "With the recent disappearances, there is added responsibility on us all."

A guard hands my father the leather whip. Another guard binds my hands to the wooden stake in the center of the dais. I grit my teeth, staring straight ahead.

I catch Destinel's gaze in the crowd. Her face is Dusker pale, and there are two guards gripping her shoulders to keep her from running straight to me. Her mouth is moving in what I'd guess is a prayer. I try to give her a smile to let her know I'll be alright, but I only manage a wobbly grimace.

My father leans over me as though checking to make sure the knot around my wrists is secure. The bristles of his close-cropped, graying beard tickle my ear. He whispers, "You are strong, daughter. The strongest of us all."

His hand hovers over my mother's key necklace, and his message is clear: be brave. Like her. When he straightens back up, my father's lips are pressed in a tight line.

I clench my jaw. *Hold your head up high.*

But even as I think the words, my mind fills with the image of my mother's bloodied face and unseeing blue eyes.

The first crack of the whip reverberates through the cave. A strangled cry escapes me, even though I swore to myself I wouldn't make a sound.

Pain rips up and down my spine even after the sound of the whip has died. Waiting for the next stroke is as unbearable as the lash itself. My screams are drowned out by the jeers of the crowd.

Four, five...my body will be torn apart by the time he reaches the tenth stroke.

My fists are clenched so tightly my nails bite into my palms. When the count reaches seven, the beating stops.

I cringe at the sound of the whip hitting the packed dirt floor of the cave.

The crowd's disapproving boos sound far away. My father says something, but I don't hear what. I sink to the ground, unable to support my own weight. A guard steps forward to untie my hands.

My back feels like it has split open from the base of my neck to just above my waist. Drops of blood dot the dusty ground as I rise to my feet, blinking to keep my vision from going dark.

"Serves you right, Bisecter!" a woman snarls as the guards help me walk through the crowd. "You should be thrown out like the beast you are!"

The sting of her words, ones I've heard all my life, cut deeper than the wounds across my back.

The guards bring me back to my sleeping cave, where I collapse onto the bed. My fiery back throbs as I lie motionless on my stomach. Eventually, I give in to the desire to close my leaden eyes.

✳ ✳ ✳

When I wake, the guards are gone, but I'm not alone. My father, his face a mess of purplish, partly-healed blisters, is looking down at me.

"How are you feeling?" he asks.

"Better," I say, surprised to find it's the truth.

I run my fingers along the rough bandages a healer must have wrapped around my back as I slept. I find the knot in the cloth at the base of my spine and loosen the bandage. It's crusted with dried blood. With the tips of my fingers, I explore the depths of my wounds.

A muffled sound of surprise escapes my parched lips.

What I was certain were bone-deep cuts have turned into little more than scratches. It doesn't even hurt when I press on the flesh where I was lashed.

Did I imagine the beating?

But no—dried blood covers the bandages and my sheets.

"Nothing?" my father asks, studying the look on my face.

I shake my head in confusion. My throat has gone dry.

"It's your blood," he says. "I wasn't sure it would affect you the same way as them." His voice takes on the hint of excitement it gets when he has made some great new discovery. "In all my years as a healer, I never saw anything like it."

In spite of the oppressive heat in my cave, a shudder wracks my body. "The Halves?" I manage.

My father nods. "They possess extraordinary healing powers." His thin lips curve up in a rare smile. "And so, it appears, do you."

For a moment, we just stare at each other. I have so many questions I don't know where to start. I don't even know if my father will be able to answer them. So little is known about those monsters.

We're both jolted out of our thoughts as four drumbeats in quick succession echo through the tunnel.

"Dusker inspection!" a guard outside my sleeping cave shouts, even though we all know what the drumbeats mean.

I yank on my cloak. By the time I turn around, my father is gone. I push away my disappointment, telling myself I'll be able to talk to him later. I slip into the tunnel along with the other Dwellers. Each level gets more crowded as we move in a body up to the meeting cave. Everyone is talking at once.

"Did the Captain know they were coming?"

"I wonder what news they bring."

The Duskers are always discussed with some combination of fear and reverence.

Everyone rubs a hand over the stone Dark God statue on our way into the meeting cave. Some even kneel down before it to pray as if it will somehow curry them extra favor.

I stay at the back of the crowd with the hood of my cloak drawn up. If they ever discovered me, the Duskers would kill me on the spot for being like the Halves. It's only because my father is Captain Harkibel that none of the other Dwellers have turned me in.

The Duskers became powerful right around the time people started being slaughtered by the Halves in droves. According to the stories, the enormous underground citadel, Malarusk, was presented to one of the original Duskers by the Dark God himself. The Dark God tasked the Duskers with protecting the six Subterranes, which offered a safe haven from the harsh sunlight and wild beasts. Anyone who challenged the Duskers was exiled to the Banished Lands.

Snatches of the Dwellers' whispered conversations reach me as I stand against the wall of the cave. Nervous glances are thrown at my father. Everyone wants to know if he will give any lawbreakers up to the Duskers.

The law is all that separates us from chaos, the Duskers always say. *Without it, we are no better than the Halves.*

The four men in gray cloaks are escorted onto the dais. One of them, the one wearing the black armband of the Captains, towers over the rest. I recognize the cut and shape of an enormous emerald I mined myself gleaming at the collar of his cloak.

A break in the gray material is just wide enough to expose the man's eyes and a strip of pale, chalky skin. It is a source of pride among the Duskers; the whiter the skin, the purer the bloodline. Supposedly, Arlow Harkibel, one of the original Duskers and my great-great-great grandfather, had skin so pale it was possible to see through to his bones.

"Hemera!" Destinel fights her way through the crowd to me, her face awash with relief. She throws her arms around me.

"Sorry," she gasps, dropping her hands to her sides like my back was made of fire. It takes me a moment to realize she thought she was hurting my lash wounds.

"Shh," a Dweller standing nearby gives us a stern look.

"I'm okay," I tell Destinel in a whisper.

"I tried to come see you, but the guards wouldn't let me." Destinel's eyes start to water.

I reach down and give her hand a squeeze.

My father stands to the side of the dais, scanning the crowd. His hard gaze lands on me for a moment before it moves on again. For some reason, it makes me long for my mother. When she was alive, she was always beside me in the meeting cave, a protective hand resting on my back. I swipe a hand across my eyes and force my attention back to the dais.

After greeting the Captain and sharing news (Subterrane Leonold is quarantined for sweating sickness, and grain production is improving at Subterrane Jevin), the Duskers begin their speech with the same story they always tell. All of the Dwellers know it by heart, but we are expected to listen with rapt attention as though we've never heard it before.

"There will come a time when this endless day ceases and the darkness comes," the Dusker Captain begins.

His words are muffled by the gray material covering the lower part of his face, which is part of the Dusker uniform.

"The Dark God sent a vision, a world where Dwellers live without fear of the sun, where there is only darkness. It may be years or generations from now, but the sun will set, and darkness will come.

"Go in darkness."

"Go in darkness," we echo.

The Duskers kneel on the floor of the dais as they hold up the charcoal statues of the Dark God. I mutter the prayers along with them, but my attention is drawn away from the statues to a group of scared-looking Dwellers huddled together and whispering.

I edge closer to a woman in the group who stands nearest to me.

"What's going on?" I ask.

The woman looks at me with disgust, avoiding my eyes.

"What's going on?" Destinel echoes.

The woman gives me another distrustful look, but the thrill of whatever news she has is irresistible. She leans closer.

"Haven't you heard?" she whispers. "One of the Dwellers was captured by those dreadful mutant Halve creatures."

She glares at me as she utters the word "Halve."

"Who?" I ignore her glare.

Our Subterrane is lucky; only a few Dwellers have been captured by the Halves so far, but none of them have returned.

Except Taniel.

The woman leans closer to Destinel and me. She whispers conspiratorially, "It's that handsome scout, Brice."

CHAPTER 6

All of the air rushes out of my lungs. It's like I have been thrown into the river and can't reach the surface. It feels like being buried alive.

Brice has been captured by the Halves.

The Duskers finish their prayer and begin their inspection of the Subterrane for any violations. My father is nowhere in sight. He must have returned to his cave.

I stumble away from the crowd of Dwellers. My father will be furious his best scout has been captured and will send out a rescue party. *Brice will be back before high day,* I tell myself.

I run down five levels to the Captain's cave. Without pausing to catch my breath, I burst through the door, pushing past a guard who tries to stop me.

"Captain!" My voice is hoarse with fear. "You have to help—send out a search party." I gulp a quick swallow of air. "Brice has been captured!"

My father sits behind a large oak desk littered with rolls of script tree bark. He steeples his fingers on the desk in front of him. He is wearing his black armband, the emblem of the Captains, and a gray sash in honor of the Duskers' visit slung across his shoulder. He is the image of everything I am not: calm, collected, and unconcerned.

"I know Brice has been captured." His tone is calm, his expression unreadable.

My father holds up his hand to stop the flood of anger about to burst from me.

Unhurried, he faces me across the desk. "When your arrest was announced, Brice came to me. He tried to stop your lashing by telling me about where you were. About how you found Taniel."

For a moment, I'm speechless. *Why would Brice do that? If the Captain finds out about us….*

My father continues, "When he told me about Taniel's…note…." A strange look passes across his face before he continues, "I assigned Brice to lead a small band of scouts to Tanguro to investigate."

My lips move, but no words come out.

My father makes a small gesture with his hand, as though inviting me to sit in the single chair across from his desk. I don't move.

My father shrugs. "No more than eight hours after they set out, the guard I assigned to Brice's company made his way back to the Subterrane. He was injured, and the Halves left him for dead. He lived just long enough to report that Brice and the others were taken captive."

A scream is lodged in my throat.

My father pushes back his chair and stands. "There has been talk of the Halves making a lair of sorts at Tanguro." He taps a map lying open on his desk. "Apparently, they are bringing their prisoners there."

I already know all of this, I want to yell. The words carved into Taniel's arm are burned into my memory. *TNGR. Help.*

"You have to send out a rescue party," I choke out. "You have to do something!"

I force myself to release my mother's key before I rip it off its chain.

"Hemera," my father says in his Captain voice, "it is my duty to protect the Subterrane and its Dwellers. It has become clear the mission to Tanguro is too dangerous. I cannot sacrifice any more lives for the sake of one scout."

This can't be happening. I want to scream, rip the calm from my father's face, *do something.*

"If the Halves took Brice back to Tanguro, then he is lost to us," the Captain continues. He stares at me while I struggle for breath. "I've done this to protect you, daughter."

Protect me? A sick feeling of realization washes over me.

"What have you done, Zeidan?" I demand, stepping forward until we're nose to nose.

All of the air leaves the cave at once. *No one* calls the Captain by his first name.

The guards step forward, their hands on the hilts of their swords, but my father puts up a hand to stop them.

"I will not tolerate disrespect from any of my Dwellers." His eyes narrow until they are little more than slits. "Not even from my own flesh and blood."

"I don't need your protection," I retort. "I need your help. Send out a rescue party."

My father shakes his head, like he's pitying me. It makes me want to punch something.

"You are young and know little about the world," he says. "I chose Brice for the mission to give you time to understand—"

"I understand," I interrupt, "that Brice loves me. And I love him." The words are out of my mouth before I can stop them.

His lip twitches in a humorless smile. "You think so, do you?"

I raise my chin. "Yes."

"If the scout knew what you can do…if he knew your differences were more than just your eyes…?"

His question hangs in the air as we glare at each other.

"So, that's it then?" I ask. "You're just going to sit here and do nothing?"

My father's silence is answer enough. Swallowing the scream threatening to rip free from my throat, I push past the guards and out of the cave.

Brice saved me during the cave collapse when everyone else would have left me for dead. He never would have abandoned me to the Halves. And I won't abandon him. If no one will help me, then I'll go after Brice myself.

Hot, furious tears threaten to spill over as I push past another set of guards.

My mind is spinning by the time I reach the main tunnel. My father said the Halves were bringing prisoners to Tanguro. That's where they'll take

Brice if they don't kill him first. *No,* I correct myself. *Brice is alive. And he needs me.*

I've never traveled beyond the borders of our land and have only a vague idea that Tanguro is somewhere far to the North. That doesn't matter, though. Already, visions of rescuing him swim through my head.

But it's not just the thought of Brice making me bolder than I have ever felt before. If I can reach Tanguro, I can make the Halves pay for what they did to my mother. I put my hand over the silver key, where it rests above my heart.

"Apologies," says a deep voice behind me, "but it is the Captain's orders that we confine you for your own protection."

Two guards step in front of me. I turn from one to the other, staring at them open-mouthed for several seconds. When they don't move, I try to brush past them. In a swift motion, they draw their swords and cross them in front of my path.

My head begins to throb.

One of the guards, whose pointy chin is made longer by a curling goatee, says, "We will escort you back to your sleeping cave."

I don't have time for this, I want to scream.

But both guards are gripping their sword hilts. Their grim expressions make it clear they will throw me back in the prison caves if I try to resist. With no other choice, I allow myself to be led back down to my cave.

I slam the door in the guards' faces and begin to rummage through the pile of belongings beneath my bed. The only thought in my mind is Brice and how I'm going to rescue him. My hand searches until I find the only weapon besides my dagger I'm allowed to keep outside of the smithy. My sling.

It's the same one my mother gifted me on my twelfth birthday, right before she was killed. I know it was really from my father, but I remember how the wrapped parcel looked in her hands. When I hold the sling, I can almost remember the soft touch of her fingers on mine as she handed it to me.

I shove the weapon into one of the deep pockets in my cloak, along with my dagger.

They won't take him away from me, I promise myself. *Not him, too.* The thought both reassures me and makes my blood boil.

I lie down on my bed, forcing my breathing to slow. I won't be able to go anywhere until the guards leave. Until then, I know I should rest. But all I can think about is Brice. To keep myself from imagining him at the Halves' mercy, I force myself to think about him in the way I know him best.

I think about droplets of water on the bare skin of his arms as we swim in the shaded pool behind the waterfall. The spray of water that arcs over me as he flicks his hair. The way his laugh rumbles deep inside his chest as he holds me in his arms. The way he tells me I'm beautiful, black eyes and all, and I believe him.

As helplessness settles into my bones, my mind turns to darker memories. I remember when, three years after my mother died, Brice's parents were killed by Halves during their patrol. Rumors surrounded the specifics of their deaths, but both Brice and the Captain were quiet on the matter. Brice told me the whole story one day when we skipped out on our work assignments to go to our cave.

Brice told me he had been out with his parents, who were both seasoned scouts. They were tracking a few of the Captain's guards who had gone missing a few days earlier. When the Halves appeared out of nowhere, his family was overpowered and his parents were killed. Brice managed to get away only because the Halves were distracted by a herd of stags they decided to hunt instead.

My hand found Brice's as he talked about his hatred for them, his need to repay them for what they took from him.

I understood those feelings well.

All the Dwellers hated and feared the Halves, but I had never before met someone else whose every high day was haunted with dreams of them. Our shared hatred for the beasts brought me close to Brice in a way I had never felt with any of the other Dwellers. It made me realize I could trust him.

Brice made me a promise that day: that when we were older, we'd leave the Subterrane and hunt the Halves together. He told me I wouldn't have to face them alone.

It was after that time that things began to change between Brice and me.

Without discussing it, Brice and I started meeting in the cave behind the waterfall more often. Sometimes we would talk. Other times, we would sit shoulder to shoulder, and I would silently watch Brice sketch beautiful images onto pieces of script tree bark.

When Brice told me I was the only person he'd ever shared his drawings with, it made something crack open inside my chest. A flood of feelings I had kept buried since my mother died flowed out.

And then he kissed me. Even knowing what I was. Before that moment, I hadn't known what it felt like to truly be alive.

It was that feeling…the one that stayed with me for days…that made me realize I was falling in love with Brice.

Two short booms and one long jolt me out of my thoughts. My heart lurches. The drums' reverberations send the trinkets on a wooden shelf by my bed rattling to the floor. I run to the door before my brain registers what is happening. The door is unlocked and the two guards meant to be watching me are gone.

The drumbeats come again. *Two short, one long.* The Subterrane is under attack.

CHAPTER 7

y the time I reach the main tunnel, the archers have amassed in the entrance of the Subterrane. Their bows sing as their arrows leave them. I peer between bodies to see what they're shooting at. Then I see them.

Halves. The beasts are barreling through the unfinished section of stone wall, straight toward the Subterrane.

Even from this distance, their bodies are monstrous, hulking. Their rough, weather-stained hides are covered in black scabs. They carry wooden clubs in their scaly fists.

It's the closest I have been to a Halve in seven years. Hatred burns in my chest.

The first Halve to reach the Subterrane seems not to notice it is pierced with six arrows. Thick, brown blood streams down its flesh. The beast bares its rotting teeth as the archers fire arrow after arrow. It doesn't falter. The Halve swipes its club across the line of men, splintering their bows in a single motion.

Battle cries erupt as the Halves break through the line of archers and charge the guards.

In front of me, a Halve pummels a man with its fists. The Dweller pulls a dagger from his belt and plunges it into the Halve's flesh. I watch in horror as blood from the Halve spatters the man's bare hand.

The Dweller tears back the sleeve of his cloak, not caring that he's dangerously close to stepping into the sunlight. His skin is smoking where the Halve's blood landed, and there are already red welts that are oozing a foul-smelling fluid. The man shrieks as he claws at his arms, like he's trying to rip his skin from his body.

A strangled scream erupts from my own throat. Grabbing the man's fallen dagger from the ground, I throw it at the beast. The blade misses the center of the Halve's neck and cuts deep into its scaly shoulder. It lets out a tremendous roar before shoving its way through the panicked Dwellers and back toward the forest. I want to scream, cry, turn around and run back into the safety of the Subterrane. But there's a wall of panicking Dwellers behind me and Halves pressing us in on all sides.

Be brave, Hemera.

My mother would never have run away; she would have tried to help. I fight my way through the crowd to the man whose shrieks have reached a deafening pitch. His forearm is bloody and raw.

Swallowing the bile in my throat, I tear a strip of my shirt beneath my cloak and try to press it over the welts to keep the poison from spreading, careful not to touch the infected skin myself. The man's screams grow louder.

"Come on!" A firm grip tugs me away.

It's one of my guards. He drags me to my feet and pushes me back toward the Subterrane.

"What about him?" I try to shout, but my voice is carried away with the rest.

Arrows fly from every direction. Through the screams, the boom of the drums carries from the Subterrane.

A giant shove sends me sprawling on the ground. A man groans and crumples where I had been standing moments before.

The pointy-chinned guard who had been herding me toward the Subterrane lies motionless on the ground. An arrow from one of our own archers sticks out of his chest. In the commotion, I must have stepped in the path of one of our archer's arrows. The guard pushed me out of the way to be killed instead.

My knees tremble as I sink down beside the man. I can't just leave him lying here where he'll be trampled. I grab his cloak to drag him out of the path of the stampeding Dwellers, but I'm knocked to the side by a group of the Captain's personal guards who are fleeing.

"Hemera, run!"

My other guard is fighting his way toward me.

A sickening thought fills my mind. *Where's Destinel?*

I shove my way back through the crowd with renewed vigor. I have to find my friend.

I see Henri, battling a Halve three times his size. His sword matches the Halve's club blow for blow, but the Halve is too strong. Henri is weakening. I manage to grasp my sling with trembling hands, but when I try to open my leather pouch full of stones, it overturns and all of my ammunition spills to the ground.

"If you want to help," Henri grinds out between sword strokes, "save the elders and children." Henri goes down on his knees. I move forward to help him, but he shouts, "Save Sirrel!"

I turn and don't look back, not even when I hear the sickening thud of a wooden club meeting flesh.

"Where's Destinel?" I grab a passing healer, gripping her cloak to keep her from running away.

The healer has a glazed-over expression, and just stares at me like she has no idea who I am.

"Where's Destinel?" This time, I shout it in the woman's face.

The healer still doesn't say anything, but her eyes flick to a pile of bodies stretched out in front of the Subterrane's entrance. They're all wearing the green armband of the healers. My heart beats out a fearsome rhythm.

I don't remember reaching the pile of corpses. I don't remember pushing aside their broken bodies as I searched for my friend. I only remember finding her, with her blood-streaked cloak and petrified expression. I sink to the ground, cradling my friend in my arms.

It's the first time Destinel hasn't returned my embrace. My chest heaves as sobs tear free from my throat.

The battle rages around me, but I can't move, can't even think. Fear hangs over everything like a dense haze. The coppery smell of blood hangs in the air.

I can't stay here.

As gently as I can, I lower Destinel's body to the ground. I kiss her temple, and then force myself to my feet.

Another man's scream is cut off by a Halve's club a few paces from me. I stare at the carnage surrounding me. What should I do? Where should I run? Everyone is sprinting in different directions, shouting the names of their family as they trample the ones on the ground crying out for help.

In the midst of the fallen bodies is a dense cluster of Halves. They surround a man who wields a sword, but every moment the circle of Halves closes more tightly around him.

Even at this distance, I recognize my father in the center of the Halves. *No! Not him, too.*

There are too many of them for my father to fight alone. I mutter a prayer to the Dark God as I draw my sling from beneath my cloak. I push my way against the tide of the crowd. Pausing just long enough to choose a jagged stone from the ground, I wind my sling and take aim. Someone grabs my arm just before I release the ropes.

"Let go of me!"

"Come with me," the guard pants, his face shining with sweat.

"No, the Captain—"

"His orders were to keep you safe," he yells.

The guard drags me away from the Subterrane, where the Dwellers battle Halves near the entrance, toward the stone wall.

"No!" I turn back to the Captain.

No matter what my feelings are for him right now, I can't just abandon him. He's my father.

"The Captain's order was to keep you safe," the guard says again, pulling on my arm.

My breathing is fast and shallow. Even when I cover my ears with my hands, I still hear the screams. The ground is stained red from Dwellers' blood.

"I'm not leaving him." But even as I say the words, more Halves fill the space between us. I would have to fight my way through all of them. I can't even see my father anymore.

"We have to go," the guard pants. "Now."

A sob rips free from my throat as he pulls me out of the path of flying arrows, past the broken stone wall, and into the barren land between the Subterrane and the forest.

As soon as we pass into the undergrowth, a wooden club swings at me. I barely have time to duck before the club crashes into the tree behind me. There are six, seven, eight of them, maybe more. I scream.

A Halve grabs my cloak. Its rotten teeth are bared as it wraps a hand around my neck.

Dark spots explode at the corner of my vision. Desperate to lessen the pressure against my throat, I push against the Halve's thick forearm.

Crack.

The Halve lets out a deafening screech as its tree trunk-thick arm goes limp.

I gasp. The Halves are stronger than any creature alive, and I just broke its bone with my bare hands.

"Run!"

I turn back to the sound of the guard's sword crashing against a wooden club.

He is far behind me, trading blows with a Halve. The Halve swings its club again, and then the guard is on his knees. His sword gives a violent jerk as he blocks another swing.

"Watch out!" I yell as the Halve draws back its bare, misshapen foot.

There is a sickening crunch of bone.

The guard's screams fill the forest. Before I can take another step, the Halve brings its club down over the guard. His cries are cut off.

"No!"

The guard is dead, killed by the beasts whose poisonous blood pumps through my veins.

The Halve's black eyes lock on me.

CHAPTER 8

The Halve's heavy footsteps are right behind me.

Keep running. Don't look back.

Branches slice across my cheeks as I tear through the forest. I run until I'm surrounded by dense trees and the only sound is the pounding of my heart.

I have only been running for a few minutes, but I'm deep into the forest. The Halves are nowhere in sight. The realization stops me cold.

No Dweller could outrun a Halve. I really am like one of *them*.

Sinking to the base of a tall script tree, I bury my face in my hands. But I don't have the luxury of feeling sorry for myself now. I listen for the sound of heavy feet trampling the brush, for the sight of their hideous bodies, for their snarls.

Everything is quiet. I'm alone.

I should have stayed to make those monsters pay for what they did to Destinel and Henri and all the other Dwellers. Did Sirrel survive, or was her small body added to the pile with the others? I hadn't even seen her in the chaos.

I should have stayed to defend the only home I've ever known. The image of my father surrounded by Halves is burned into the backs of my eyelids. I want to go back, but reason tells me it's too late. There were too many of them, and they were too strong.

Self-loathing curls around my heart and squeezes.

How could I have left my father so easily? He has protected me for my entire life. And I just abandoned him to the Halves. Shame heats my face. If my mother were alive….

Anger begins to gather inside me. It's an easier emotion than grief, and I cling to it with all I'm worth. Destinel was my best friend, and my father was the only family I had left. And now, because of the Halves, they're both gone.

Clenching my hand into a fist, I drive it into the first thing it meets. My fist plows straight through the trunk of an old script tree, the wood splintering as it breaks apart. The tree shudders, its leaves raining down from the canopy above. The wood groans as it begins to topple over.

I have to leap to the side to avoid being crushed underneath the fallen tree.

I stand, dumbfounded, as the forest settles back into silence. Knowing I just took down an enormous tree should scare me. I should look down at my gloved hands and curse their strength. I wait for the familiar self-disgust, but it doesn't come.

I curl my hands into fists. *Revenge.* My heart beats in time with the word as it passes through my lips.

I will kill every last Halve at Tanguro. I won't stop until they're all dead, or I am. A shiver of anticipation passes through me. My mind starts to clear, and my thinking sharpens.

I take stock of the few possessions I have on me. There's my sling, two full waterskins, a roll of script tree bark, a stub of a blackwood pencil, and the two Sustum bricks we are given for the high day meal. Seeing the Sustum brick rations makes a pang go through my chest.

My father concocted the recipe for Sustum bricks back when he was a healer, before he became Captain Harkibel, to keep the scouts alive during long missions. The bricks are held together with a strange-smelling, sticky substance. They have an unpleasant gritty feel on the tongue and are nearly tasteless, but they serve their purpose. *Learn to see the world upside down, inside out, and backwards,* my father always used to say. *Only then can the true discoveries be made.*

With an effort, I push my father's voice and the guilt tearing at my insides from my mind as I repack my meager supplies in my cloak's deep pockets. *He's gone,* I tell myself. Destinel and all the other Dwellers of Subterrane Harkibel are gone. All I have left is revenge. *And Brice.*

I need a plan.

Looking around, nothing seems familiar, and I have the sinking feeling I'm already lost. But then I see the two lines of crooked trees I've seen a thousand times. I let out a deep breath. I'm a short way from the cave behind the waterfall. I must have run in this direction out of habit.

* * *

It seems impossible that the gentle rush of water and smell of wild flowers could still exist after everything that has happened. Even as I make my way through the clearing, I keep waiting for Brice to jump out from behind a bush, to tell me with laughing green eyes that it was all just a joke, to wrap me in his arms and kiss me.

He doesn't appear.

I slump to my knees in the clearing, unable to support the weight of my body. *He's gone. Brice is gone.* The words crush me from the inside out until I can't breathe.

A howl in the distance jolts me out of my stupor. High day is coming.

I pull myself up from the ground and follow the path around the side of the waterfall. I duck through the opening of the cave—our cave—and close myself into darkness.

I'm alone.

As I settle into the folds of the blanket, the last conversation I had with my father comes back to me. *If he knew your differences were more than just your eyes....*

"You're wrong," I say into the darkness.

Brice would still love me even if he knew I'm as strong and fast as the Halves. He would understand.

I clench my fists at my sides. Why didn't I tell Brice everything when I had the chance? I knew him too well, trusted him too much, to keep something so enormous from him.

As I stare into the darkness, my wandering gaze finds the black circle on the far side of the cave. I leap to my feet. How could I forget the section of wall Brice hollowed out to store his weapons?

Standing on my toes, I reach into the hole. My searching hand grasps a cloth-wrapped bundle and a thick roll of script tree bark that is almost too far back to reach. My pulse pounds in my ears.

It's too dark in the cave to read the scrawls on the bark, so I put it in the pocket of my cloak while I concentrate on the bundle. Inside the cloth are two sharp daggers, an extra waterskin, and three Sustum bricks.

"Thank you, Brice," I say into the too-quiet cave.

As soon as it's low day, I'll head north. I'll find the North Road. It used to be the major thoroughfare between the territories before the Duskers banned unapproved travel outside of the Subterranes. I know from my father's maps of the territories that the road starts at the narrow point of the river and runs all the way from the Subterrane territory through the Banished Lands and to the mountains. If I can find it, the North Road will be the straightest path to the Wild Lands and Tanguro.

Sleep is the last thing on my mind, but there's nothing else I can do until low day. I won't be any good to Brice if I die from exhaustion before I reach him. I think of the words carved into Taniel's arm.

TNGR. Help.

I grit my teeth against the bitterness that fills me—bitterness at what the Halves have taken from me and what I am because of them. If they've hurt Brice….

As I lie in the dark cave, every part of me aches for him. I trace my fingers over my lips the way Brice sometimes did before he leaned in to kiss me. Being here in our place, alone, makes me remember the first time Brice told me he was falling in love with me. Even now, recalling the way those words fell from his lips, a jolt of feeling races down my spine.

"You do know what the other Dwellers say about me, don't you?" I had asked him once.

"I do." Brice leaned down to kiss my brow, tightening his arms around me like he could protect me from their insults.

"Aren't you afraid I'll bludgeon you to death or zap you with my eyes?"

My question was serious, but Brice laughed.

"I've killed enough Halves to know you're not one of them. Even your eyes are different. Yours are deep and endless, not murky like theirs. I could get lost in your eyes."

My heart pounded a frantic rhythm as he closed the distance between us.

"I love you, Hemera Harkibel," he whispered, right before his lips met mine.

* * *

Brice. He's gone.

"I'll make them pay," I promise the darkness.

I will spend the rest of my life hunting the monsters that have stolen everything from me. It's what I should have done years ago, but I was too much of a coward.

I have to get to Tanguro. Only then will I be able to kill the ones responsible for taking Brice and murdering both of my parents.

CHAPTER 9

I wake with one hand curled around my mother's necklace, and the other clutching the hilt of one of Brice's daggers.

I leave the cave as soon as it's low day. I put on my cloak, tie the bundle with Brice's daggers and food to my back, and crawl out of the cave and into the sunlight.

As soon as my eyes have adjusted to the brightness, I dig into the deep pocket of my cloak and pull out the piece of script tree bark Brice left with the knives. My trembling fingers are clumsy as I unroll the rough bark we peel from the trees and use to write messages.

A small laugh escapes me. It's a map. Hardly daring to believe my luck, I squint at the pictures and labels covering the scroll.

I twist the map around in my hands, mesmerized by the amount of detail. Brice is good at drawing; he could make images come to life on a piece of script tree bark with nothing more than a blackwood pencil. But that doesn't explain why or how he made this map.

The drawing shows lands far beyond the Subterrane territory, where no scout would ever travel. Two parallel, curved lines on the far-left side of the bark show the bends in the river that snakes around Subterrane Harkibel and the other Subterranes to our south. To the East of center, Brice has drawn Malarusk, the Dusker citadel. There is a blank space due north, with *Banished Lands* scrawled at the top. Ridges and peaks on the topmost edge of the bark must be the mountains that mark the beginnings of the Wild Lands, which hold the abandoned fortress of Tanguro.

A thick, straight line that begins above Subterrane Harkibel and travels up the map must be the North Road. There are even small dots marking the location of travel caves.

The travel caves were dug before the Duskers' time, when people lived all throughout the land and were constantly moving in search of new food sources. Since the Dusker travel ban, though, only Captains and traders are allowed to travel outside their own Subterrane.

I can use the travel caves to escape from the sun and any other deadly creatures that might be stalking the lands between here and Tanguro. As long as I'm not seen by any Duskers along the way....

Closing my eyes, I mutter a quick prayer to the Dark God. Whatever the reason Brice had for keeping this map, it is going to lead me to him. It's like he somehow knew I would need it.

Giddiness sweeps through me. *I'm coming, Brice.*

I take one more look at the map, plotting my route, and then roll it up and tuck it into the bundle slung across my back.

As I walk, the small stones I have been collecting in the leather pouch on my belt click together in time with my steps. My sling is tied to the outside of my cloak where I can grasp it if I need to ward off any animals. *Or Halves.* The thought sends a shudder through me, and I pick up my pace.

Even though the sun is low, sweat streams down my body beneath the cloak. Every itch is unreachable through the thick material. My hair, which has come loose from its knot beneath my hood, is a sodden, tangled mess.

Take off your cloak, says a small voice in my head. *The Burn can't hurt you.*

Tempting as it is to strip off the cumbersome material, the thought of the Halves' leathery, hideous skin stops me. *What if exposing my skin to the sun makes it look like theirs?* I draw my cloak tighter around me.

The trees begin to thin. Energy surges through me at the sight of the wide dirt path of the North Road. It's right where Brice's map said it would be.

I pause behind a tall bush and peek around the side. If I'm seen by any travelers, my journey will be over before it begins. But everything is quiet. The North Road is empty as far as the eye can see.

Stars begin to dance across my vision, and I realize I've been holding my breath. I let it out, listening to the gentle whoosh of air. I move out from behind the bush and stride up the steep bank to the road.

The crackle of parched leaves makes me snap my head around.

I don't have time to draw my sling before an arrow whizzes past my right ear. It lodges in the tree trunk behind where my head had been a moment earlier.

"Halt!"

The command is unnecessary as I'm already standing as still as a Dark God statue. Instinctively, I raise my hands to show I'm unarmed.

"If you so much as think to move, you'll be dead before you can even whimper," a low voice snarls.

The man, who is standing behind me where I can't get a glimpse of him, undoubtedly has another arrow fitted to his bow. There is no question I would be dead before I could even reach for my sling, let alone turn around and take aim. My knees start to wobble.

"Please," I say, not needing to fake the quiver in my voice. "I mean no one any harm." I turn my head to the side, but then snap it back at the sound of a bow string being pulled taut.

"What are you doing here, and where have you come from?" His voice has lost none of its gruffness.

Is he a Subterrane Captain? One of the criminals from the Banished Lands? His voice isn't muffled like he's wearing one of the Dusker hoods. The thought brings some small relief.

"I'm lost." I'm unable to form my story in my head before the words are out of my mouth. "My Subterrane was overtaken by Halves, and I ran into the woods. I've been searching for other survivors, but you are the first living person I've met."

"Turn around so I can see your face. Slowly!"

I obey and get my first glimpse of my attacker. The first thing I notice is the arrow nocked in his bow and pointed at my chest. The second is the broad, double-bladed axe hanging from a leather strap across his body. There's also a lute hanging from a cord around his neck. It looks ridiculous next to the axe.

"Don't move a muscle," the man growls, even though I'm barely breathing.

His voice sounded like it would belong to a large, bearded man who dresses in animal hides and wears a tattered, filthy cloak. I expected his skin to be marked with years of dirt, and to be spotted with dark blisters indicating onset of the Burn.

It takes me several moments, therefore, to register that the harsh voice belongs to a slender, almost fragile-looking man. He's no more than an inch or two taller than me. He's older than I would have guessed, too. Not as old as my father, but his honey-colored hair is tinged with gray and there are fine lines spidering out from the corners of his eyes. The man's cloak is a drab brown, without any markings that might give a clue about which Subterrane he belongs to. His shoulder-length hair is in a simple plait, and he wears no jewelry. He regards me through bright blue eyes that, for some reason I can't name, seem sad.

I take in all of this in an instant. There is something not quite, but almost familiar about this man.

He shifts his arrow. For a moment, the material of his glove lifts and I can see the strange black ink designs covering his right hand.

Dwellers from Subterrane Leonold brand their hands with the image of Darkness Peak, the mountain where Duskers commune with the Dark God, but the pattern on this man's hand is different. It looks like a sun with flames swirling out from its center.

"What's your name?" The man's voice snaps my gaze away from his hand.

"Hemera Harkibel," I answer automatically.

Stupid.

Now he knows which Subterrane I'm from and that I'm the Captain's daughter. He'll kidnap me for ransom, or worse, turn me over to the Duskers for breaking the travel ban. If the Duskers find me—if they discover what I am—I'll be worse than dead.

Something flashes in the man's eyes before his face becomes impassive again. He doesn't say anything about my father or Subterrane, though. He could be one of the barbarians who live in the Banished Lands, but he doesn't look like a criminal.

"I haven't seen eyes like yours in any human I've met before," he says, stepping forward to study me.

I lower my gaze to my dusty boots. My pulse throbs.

When I don't say anything, he asks, "Where do you plan to go now that your Subterrane is destroyed?" The arrow is still fitted to the bow, but his arms have slackened.

"I know some people, distant relatives, who were expelled from the Subterrane territory and live in the northern part of the Banished Lands." I babble, relieved for the change in subject. "I'm going to find them."

After staring at me for several moments, the man says, "Better steer clear of the North Road. The Halves use it on their way to and from Tanguro."

A jolt of fear shimmies down my spine before I steel my nerves. "Halves or not, I'm going north."

I back away from the man. My eyes are fixed on his arrow, but he's made no move to aim at me again.

"Don't be foolish enough to think you can make the journey alone," he says. "They'll kill you before you reach your family's cave. If the Halves don't get you, the Burn will."

"Thanks for the warning," I reply, "but I'll take my chances."

"It's your funeral, then."

He speaks the words like he doesn't care, but I see real concern deepening the lines of his face. I get moving before he gets any grand notions of trying to rescue me and bring me back to wherever he came from.

I can feel the man's eyes on my back as I walk toward the North Road, but he doesn't try to stop me. Resisting the urge to look back, I trip and stumble my way up the embankment on jellied legs.

It was right to get away quickly, I tell myself. Who knows what he would have done when he figured out who—and what—I am. Still, though, I would have liked to know who this man is and what he was doing here. I can't shake the feeling I've seen him before.

I stay on the side of the road bordered by stones. At least if I see someone coming, the rocks will offer some cover.

I keep up my pace for hours without further incident. I'm fit from my work in the mines, but my energy won't hold forever. I nibble on a Sustum brick and take small sips from my waterskin without stopping. My eyes scan the horizon in search of any sign of movement.

I stop to check my progress against the map. By the looks of it, I should reach the mountains bordering Tanguro in three weeks' time. Even knowing it will exhaust me faster, I begin to jog.

A muffled sound makes me come to a skidding stop.

The hairs on the back of my neck prickle. Crouching behind one of the larger stones, I unhook my sling from my belt and place a stone in its leather pouch. I flick my wrist to set the ropes whirring by my side.

I wait for several minutes. When I hear nothing, I peer around the side of the stone.

I barely have the wits to stifle my scream.

CHAPTER 10

At least twenty Halves are on the road.

They are still too far to see clearly, but they're headed this way. And they are approaching fast. Their swollen, bare feet send up clouds of dust.

I stay crouched behind the stone, trying to decide what to do. There is nothing but bare desert on either side of the road. It is miles back to the trees, and if I try to run, they'll see me. *Maybe if I stay very still….*

The ground trembles from the pounding of their feet as they begin to pass my hiding place.

I crouch lower to the ground as their muffled grunts and wheezing breaths grow louder. The stink from their sweat makes my eyes water.

When the ground stops shaking and the sounds grow fainter, I rise to my feet and step out from behind the rock. The Halves' dust cloud is already far down the road. Most of them are running on all fours, making them look like a herd of wild beasts.

Savages.

Before I can release the pent-up air in my lungs, one of the Halves at the back of the group stops running. It rises up from all fours to its full height and sniffs the air. Its monstrous head scans the road from side to side, and I know the moment its hideous black eyes lock on my own.

It lets out a low, rumbling growl. The others stop running and stare as it gestures toward me with its gnarled hands.

My stomach lurches. I don't wait to see what they will do. Swinging the ropes of my sling, I release one end and watch the stone sail through the air.

My stone hits the Halve between its eyes. It drops to the ground with an audible thud. Furious cries erupt from the others as they race back toward me. I swing again, but my arm is trembling and my stone flies wide. Before I can try again, they're upon me. One of them grabs my right arm and wrenches it behind my back. Another barrels into me with so much force all of the air is pushed out of my lungs. A third wraps its scaly hand all the way around my throat and squeezes.

Panic takes over as my vision begins to darken. Without thinking, I use my free hand to grasp the Halve's arm. I pull down with all my strength, trying to free my airway from the crushing force.

A choked yelp of surprise bursts from me as the Halve's body flips over mine. I duck to avoid its flailing limbs.

The Halve lands on its side at least a pace away. The others let go of me, grunting their own shock at what I've just done. Adrenaline coursing through me, I turn to the nearest Halve and reach up to punch its chest.

It flies into the air. There must be two feet of space between its body and the ground as it sails in an arc away from me. Its lifeless body makes a shallow crater when it lands on the hard ground.

But there's no time to celebrate or marvel at my strength. More Halves are already on the move.

Many of them hold wooden clubs in their massive, scarred hands as they close the space between us. Their unblinking black eyes, the ones I share, bore into me from their distorted faces. They surround me.

My brief snatch of confidence erodes as I stare at their hideous faces. My sling hangs by my side as I wait for the same death that took first my mother, and then my father.

I've failed.

The Halves move closer. The ones in front brandish their clubs as cruel, guttural sounds burble up from their throats. Tears spring to my eyes even as a stooped Halve rushes toward me on all fours, its club gripped between its jagged, yellow teeth.

If I die, there will be no one to rescue Brice.

The thought makes something inside me snap. I fumble with the knife in my belt. Lunging at the beast, I drive the blade through its flabby midsection. Thick, brown blood oozes from the wound.

"For my parents!" I scream.

Its blood has seeped through my gloves, but none of the poisonous welts appear on my hands. Their blood—the same blood that runs through my veins—doesn't harm me. I wrench my knife out of the Halve, watching as the life drains from it. Illness sweeps through me, but I thrust my dagger into the Halve again.

These creatures are monsters.

"Come on!" I wave my blood-slicked fist in the air.

The other Halves advance. They step over the one that has collapsed in an oily puddle of its own blood.

My mother's voice echoes from somewhere deep inside me. *Be brave, Mer.*

I slash at an arm that grabs for me. The Halve shrieks as blood oozes from the deep gash along its scaly forearm. It darts forward and knocks the knife from my hand. The beast's reeking breath blows hot on my face. I stare into its black eyes.

The Halve emits a muffled *oof!* when I elbow its sunken chest. It falls to the ground, but three others take its place. A Halve raises a club above its head. The image of my mother, in the same position I'm in now, flashes through my mind.

The club flies toward my upturned face. The hood of my cloak falls back and the sun's brightness blinds me. I make a weak effort to pull the hood back over my head with my free hand.

The club's shadow crosses over my face. *This is how it ends.*

The Halve seems suspended with its club poised for the strike. And then it topples forward. A feathered arrow pierces its neck.

I look up to see the man I thought I left behind hours ago. He stands at the road's edge, felling one Halve after another with his arrows.

The Halves that are still alive are maddened with terror, trampling the dead to get away. Some of them are running on all fours. I use my sling to kill two more Halves as they race back the way they came.

It's not long before the man and I are alone amid the bodies strewn across the ground. I'm breathing hard, sick from the smell of blood.

The man walks over to the first Halve he killed and yanks his arrow from its body. He doesn't even flinch at the squelching sound.

I walk between the lifeless bodies, stepping over blood streaked across the road, to the first Halve I killed. Wrapping my hands around the hilt, I tug Brice's dagger out of its stomach. The feel of the blade rising from the Halve's innards makes bile rise in my throat.

"Don't!" The man lunges toward me just as brown blood lurches up from the wound, covering my gloves and dripping into my sleeves.

He looks at my hands, first with wild panic, and then tilts his head as I stand before him with my dripping knife.

"The blood, it doesn't poison you." It's more of a statement than a question. His expression is a mixture of bewilderment and relief.

Fear twists my gut. There is no lie that can explain why the Halve blood doesn't hurt me. But even as I watch the man's bushy eyebrows furrow in growing impatience, something about him makes me want to tell him the truth. Maybe it's the hint of darkness that seems to lurk behind his gaze that makes me think this man has encountered creatures far more evil than me. Besides, if he was going to tell the Duskers about me, he would have done so rather than risking his own neck to rescue me. Before I can think better of it, I tell the man about what I am.

There is a long pause when I've finished speaking. His eyes meet mine, and I almost keel over from pure shock when I don't see any hint of hatred or disgust. He doesn't fear me.

"We need to get off the road," is all he says. His expression is unreadable.

A Halve that lies belly-down in the dirt at the edge of the road is not yet dead. It twitches as blood leaks from a wound in its neck. Its body convulses for a few more seconds before it goes still. I turn away in disgust, but as I turn, something wedged beneath its body catches my eye. It looks like a scroll of script tree bark.

The man has noticed it, too. He tries to roll the body of the Halve over. Sweat trickles down his forehead as he grunts from the effort, but the corpse is at least twice his size and too heavy for him to budge.

"Let me." I bend down, digging my fingers underneath the Halve's tough flesh.

I anchor my foot against a stone and then pull up. The body lifts straight up into the air and then lands with a dull thud several paces away.

A choked sound of surprise escapes my lips. This time, I was ready for my strength to be enough to move the body. But I wasn't prepared to lift it ten feet in the air....

I'm not even breathing hard.

The man and I look at each other. His mouth hangs open.

"I didn't mean...." I look down at my hands as though they're something separate from the rest of my body.

"Incredible," the man whispers.

I give him a sharp look, but his awe seems genuine.

"Aren't you afraid of me?" I ask.

The man stares up, as if measuring the distance the Halve's body reached at its highest point.

"No," he says. "I'm not afraid of you."

There is a sick feeling in my stomach as I walk over to where the Halve's body has come to rest. The scroll of script tree bark is still clutched in the beast's fist. I use my knife to pry its hand loose and slide the bark out. A sense of foreboding makes my hands tremble as I unfurl the scroll.

"What in the—?" The man looks over my shoulder at the drawing.

In the center of the scroll is a drawing done in perfect likeness...of me.

An unpleasant chill travels up my spine.

"It's you!" the man exclaims as I stare at the image.

"I know," I force my mouth to form the words. "It's mine."

Brice gave me the drawing months ago. He made it for me when he was away on a long scouting trip. I kept it in my sleeping cave, on the shelf beside my bed. I hadn't moved it since Brice gave it to me.

The man pulls the lute from around his neck and plucks out a tuneless song. "Where did it come from?"

"My sleeping cave in the Subterrane," I shake my head, trying to make sense of it all. "But why would a Halve take it?"

"Maybe when they plundered the caves, they took whatever they found there. I guess this one just took a liking to your picture. It could have been the eyes." The man shrugs, but as he goes to put the lute away, his hand wavers.

"They didn't come from the direction of the Subterrane territory, though." The man gestures in the direction the Halves approached from.

He's right, I realize with a jolt. The Halves were coming from the north, which means they can't be the same ones that attacked the Subterrane. Unless they went around the Subterrane territory and then circled back….

The wide, black eyes mirror my stare as I hold the drawing at arm's length.

"Let's get out of here," the man says.

Burn vultures have smelled the blood and are circling above us.

I clutch the drawing in my hand as I follow him off the road. We move deeper into the trees until we're out of the Burn vultures' sight. The man sits down on a boulder and lays his double-bladed axe on the ground beside him. He grips the neck of his lute as he studies some moss on a rock. Finally, he says, "You are well-prepared for a scared young Dweller who was not expecting to flee her Subterrane."

The moment he finishes speaking, his eyes flick upward to judge my reaction.

My cheeks grow hot. I stutter over an explanation, but nothing coherent emerges.

"You're a pretty decent shot with that sling of yours," he continues. There's a gleam in his eyes, like he's enjoying my discomfort. "I've never seen anyone move that fast before. Knife work needs some improvement, though."

I'm at a complete loss for words.

I surprise us both when I ask, "What's your name?"

The faintest hint of emotion flashes across his face before it's gone, which makes me wonder if I just imagined it. After a long pause, he says, "Dayne."

Dayne. I had hoped his name would reveal something of where he came from, but it doesn't.

After another brief pause, he continues, "And you, Hemera, have not been honest with me."

My stomach turns at the way his eyes bore right through me. I twist and untwist the ropes of my sling.

Dayne stares at me with raised eyebrows. "Let's have the truth this time."

Taking a deep breath, I decide to venture close enough to the truth that Dayne will believe me.

I begin pacing, unable to stay still. "What I told you before was mostly true. My Subterrane was destroyed by the Halves, and I survived by running into the forest. I'm traveling to Tanguro because if anyone from my Subterrane is still alive, the Halves will bring them there."

I try to keep my face blank even though my heart is racing. It seems best not to mention Brice's name, or say anything else that's too specific until I know more about this stranger.

At the very least I expect Dayne to ask me more questions, or demand that we go back to the ruins of Subterrane Harkibel to prove my story. I fidget while I wait for him to say something. If he tells the Duskers about me....

Dayne surprises me when all he says is, "You'll never reach Tanguro without help. There are all sorts of dangers on the road your sling will not protect against."

I stop pacing.

Dayne continues, "Even if you somehow make it, how do you plan to rescue prisoners who are guarded by dozens, more likely hundreds, of Halves?"

I sink down onto the ground. It's true, I hadn't considered how I would rescue Brice. I sort of just assumed it would all work itself out if I managed to reach Tanguro. Now, that plan seems foolish.

"What you say may be true," I say, "but there's nothing left for me where I came from. I'll do everything I can to get north or die in the attempt."

My brave words are weakened by the slight quaver in my voice.

"So, you're going to take down a hundred Halves with two bits of rope and some pebbles?" Dayne's lips are pursed.

I scowl.

"Excuse me, but I need to be on my way," I tell him. "Thank you for your help back there."

I walk away from Dayne. My foot catches on a root in the path, and I stumble. I grab at a bush's thorny branch to steady myself, but its shallow roots tear free. I tumble to the ground with the bush clutched in my arms like a prickly baby.

I grit my teeth together. *Well done, Hemera.*

I can hear Dayne chuckling as I right myself, which makes the blood in my temples pulsate.

"Wait!" he calls as I stalk away with the last shreds of my dignity.

He's beside me in a moment. "I will accompany you on this crazy journey of yours."

"Why?" My eyes narrow in suspicion. "If the journey is as dangerous as you say, then why not travel as far away as you can get?"

"Who knows? Maybe I'll find someone worth saving at Tanguro, too." His face grows serious again. "Besides, you need someone to teach you how to use those daggers of yours."

I huff, still irritated that he doesn't think I'm capable of reaching Tanguro alone. On the other hand, though, it's obvious he knows how to survive in the wilderness and fight the Halves. Such skills could prove useful in helping me to rescue Brice….

"Alright," I say, after a short deliberation. "But we better get moving."

CHAPTER 11

Dayne falls into step beside me. "We need to get farther away from the North Road and find shelter before the sun turns."

I glance at my new companion out of the corner of my eye. Where is he from? Where was he headed? What's his business in these parts? He's not from Subterrane Harkibel, and he's not wearing the Duskers' armband that grants permission to travel....

Dayne outpaces me, leaving me alone with my thoughts. I touch the corner of Brice's drawing as we walk.

I remember when Brice gave it to me. It was after he returned from his longest scouting mission yet. I could barely eat or sleep for the entire month he was gone. I had no idea when he would return. Worse, we had argued before he left the Subterrane.

He wouldn't tell me where he was going, saying only it was on the Captain's orders. From the way he was talking, I knew he expected to encounter Halves. I begged him to take me with him. I didn't want him to face that danger alone, but more than that, I was desperate to begin what we both had fantasized about for years—taking our revenge on the monsters who had stolen my mother and his parents.

Brice said he loved me too much to let me put myself in that kind of danger, and that he wouldn't jeopardize the Captain's trust by letting me come with him. When I told Brice I would come, with or without his permission, he threatened to tell my father. We yelled at each other and said things we didn't mean. The next low day, Brice left.

When he returned, our reunion had been full of tears and apologies. He gave me the drawing he made of me, telling me that not a moment had gone by during his absence when he hadn't thought about me.

After that, we spent hours just wrapped in each other's arms, relishing in our togetherness. It was like the hurtful words we exchanged before he left had never happened.

"Hemera." Dayne's voice snaps me back to the present. I startle at the way he's studying me with his intensely blue eyes.

He's about to say something else, but then turns his ear toward the trees. Dayne puts a finger to his lips. Something about the look on his face makes me go still.

"Hemera," Dayne's voice is so low I have to lean forward to hear him, "can you climb that touch-me-not without setting it off?"

I follow his gaze. The tall branches sprout clusters of small, round pods, each filled with hundreds of the knife-sharp spikes that give the tree its name. Any pressure against the pod will burst its soft outer shell and send all of the spikes flying outward. The spikes pierce the first object they meet and are impossible to dig out.

"I can climb it."

"Then do so. Quickly."

I follow Dayne's order, resisting the urge to ask what's going on. I climb up the trunk as quickly as I can manage in my heavy cloak. When I reach the branches covered with touch-me-not pods, I slow my pace, careful to avoid brushing against them.

There's a fork in the branches that will not put me in danger of touching the pods. Just as I pull myself into the fork, I hear voices below.

I look down to see how far Dayne has climbed, but I'm alone. Peering through the leaves, I see Dayne on the ground far below, one hand resting on the handle of his axe.

The voices grow louder as three large, bearded men come crashing through the trees. They're so engrossed in an argument with each other they nearly walk right past Dayne.

One of the men sees him, though, and shouts, "Here, here! I tol' you we were on the righ' path!"

The men circle Dayne like Burn vultures. A shudder passes through me, which jostles the branches nearest me. I hold my breath, but none of the pods move enough to touch each other.

"He's just a lil' ole guy," says one of the other men. "Prolly not carryin' too much, but maybe he has information."

Even though my view is partially blocked by the thick leaves, I can see the men's rotting teeth. There is no doubt these men are criminals from the Banished Lands. They look like they haven't bathed in weeks, maybe months.

"I would be happy to provide you with any information I can," Dayne says. His voice is musical compared to the sounds of these barbarians as they tramp through the brush.

"See this ole' hand?" one of the men growls, holding up a gloved fist that looks to be covered in dry blood. "I kill'd the last guy with this. He was polite and frien'ly-like, just like you. It wasn' enough, though," he shakes his head in mock disappointment.

"We need supplies," the second man adds. "And the direction of caves that migh' be in need of…our assistance…."

The man strokes his fist and grins as his sentence trails off. Dayne steps back, and I imagine it's to remove himself from the range of the man's stench.

The third bandit growls, "You are goin' to lead us to the nex' Subterrane. Can' waste all day walkin' aroun' with no idea of where we're headed. You have one hour to lead us straigh', or we kill you."

I still don't know whether to trust Dayne, but if I do nothing to help him, he'll soon be dead. These thieves have no reason to spare Dayne's life even if he does tell them where to find whatever is left of Subterrane Harkibel.

My hand runs along the handle of the knife in my belt. I could never get down from the tree without the men hearing me. My sling would have been an option, but I have no stones left. Looking around, I see bunches of the spiked touch-me-not pods dangling within reach.

I wrap the belled sleeve of my cloak around my glove for added protection and reach up toward one of the branches. I pluck the stem that hangs above one of the pods and cradle it in the folds of my cloak, holding my breath the whole time.

The men's voices are getting louder and angrier. I place the pod in the leather pouch of my sling, and push back the heavy, clumsy sleeves of my cloak. I take aim, careful that my winding arm doesn't jostle any of the surrounding branches and send the spikes flying toward me.

At the precise moment, I sling the pod about twenty paces away from my tree. There's a whoosh as the pod's spikes pierce through leaves and wedge themselves into tree trunks. Without waiting for the thieves' reaction, I let another pod fly ten paces to my left. The third one goes about as far as the first, but in the opposite direction.

I peer through the dense leaves to the ground below. The bandits stand back-to-back and are arguing with each other about the source of the noise.

"I tell you, they're closin' in on us!" one of the thieves growls. "They mus' 'ave followed us from the las' cave. I tole' you tha' we shoulda kilt those dirty kids! Now they 'ave us surroun'ed."

"Those chil'ren weren't fit to walk to the edge of their crop fields, let alone follow us. You moron, it's the 'alves. They've sniffed us out!"

I wind my arm once, releasing a touch-me-not pod as close to the men as I dare. There is growing panic in their voices as they back away from Dayne. One of the men moves to a space beneath my tree where my visibility isn't blocked by the leaves. I re-load my sling and aim a pod at the bandit's face.

My ammunition hits its mark. The man stumbles backward, dazed. He lets out a bloodcurdling scream as the spikes fly into his face and neck. That's enough for the other two bandits. They run.

Dayne moves into my line of focus, picks up the fallen bandit's knife, and slides it into his chest. The man's screams are cut off.

I shudder at the ease with which he ends the man's life. Killing Halves is one thing, but—

"Alright, Hemera," Dayne calls up to me. "You can come on down."

When I reach the ground, the suspicious glare Dayne wore when we first met has disappeared.

"That was some quick thinking you did up there," he says. "I thank you."

The hard lines that streak the corners of Dayne's mouth soften into something that almost—but not quite—resembles a smile.

"Well, I owed you from before, anyway." I look away, embarrassed.

Dayne clears his throat. "Shall we continue on?"

When I hoist my bundle onto my back, the map slips out and lands near Dayne's feet. Before I can snatch it back, Dayne stoops to pick it up. He unrolls the script tree bark and studies it.

"Er, someone, a friend in my Subterrane...it belonged to him." I twist a frayed thread of my cloak around my finger. I never mentioned anything about this map in my earlier story.

Dayne looks up from the map and studies me.

I should stop talking. But instead, I say, "He was sent on a scouting mission the day before we were attacked. He gave me the map to hold onto for him. He said prisoners were being taken to Tanguro, and he planned to go there when he returned. It was pure chance I still had the map when the Subterrane was attacked."

"This friend of yours knows his way to Tanguro." Dayne squints at the map. "He even marked the travel caves along the North Road."

I squeeze my gloves into fists to keep from fidgeting.

Without taking his eyes off the map, Dayne says almost to himself, "What I wouldn't have given to know about these…." He rubs at the place on his right glove where I know the blazing sun tattoo marks his hand.

When he sees me watching him, he rolls up the map and taps it against his hand.

"Do you have any idea how valuable this is?"

I don't know what answer he expects me to give, so I don't say anything.

"If this is accurate, we might be able to reach Tanguro without having to worry about certain death from the Burn, at least."

If Dayne noticed that my story doesn't line up, he doesn't say anything.

Dayne looks at our shadows. "Sun's getting high, and I don't like to hang around this close to the road. There's an open stretch we'll need to cover before high day."

After plotting our route, Dayne gives me back the map, which I roll up and tuck into my bundle. I follow Dayne as he leads us toward a steep hill that, once we've passed over it, will make us invisible to anyone on the road.

The scorched land crumbles beneath our feet, and Dayne offers his hand to help me over the rocks at the base of a hill. Instead of taking it, I ask, "Who uses the North Road these days?"

"Halves, mostly. Occasionally Duskers. Although with the threat of Halves, the Duskers don't often venture far from Malarusk." A grim smile tugs at his lips. "They're good at hiding in their citadel and letting the Dwellers do their dying for them."

I look at Dayne in surprise. The Duskers protect the Dwellers, not the other way around.

I open my mouth to speak, but Dayne raises his fist without even looking at me. A shiver runs up my spine.

The ground beneath us begins to shake.

CHAPTER 12

Stones hurtle down the hill toward us.

My first thought is it's a Dusker trap. I've heard of them lying in wait to catch violators of the travel ban.

Or maybe they were just waiting for me.

Dayne grabs my arm and pulls me out of the rocks' path. We narrowly avoid an uprooted tree that's hurtling down the hill in the flow of earth. The entire hill is crumbling before us.

When the rocks stop falling, I look around with wild eyes for the Duskers' gray cloaks. I expect the black arrows from their dreaded crossbows to come whizzing at us.

With trembling fingers, I take out my sling. My fingers fumble in the dirt for a sharp stone fragment to place in the leather pouch. It will be a pathetic defense against even a single Dusker, but my daggers would be even less useful. Getting close enough to a Dusker to use it would mean certain death at best. Capture and torture in the Malarusk dungeons would be worse. I shudder at the thought and grip my sling.

Dayne stands beside me with his axe in one hand and a spear I didn't even know he had in the other. I squint through the eddies of swirling dust to the crumbled hilltop, ready for an army of Duskers to descend on us.

No one appears.

I release the pent-up air in my lungs, but Dayne keeps his weapons drawn.

"It was no force of nature that caused those rocks to fall," Dayne says, breaking the eerie silence. "You stay here and keep that sling of yours ready. I'm going to go have a look up there."

Nodding, I tighten my grip on my sling.

It's so quiet. *Too quiet.* Maybe Dayne is with the Duskers after all and has gone to warn them about me. But where could I hide? The trees are too far away; the Dusker arrows would find me long before I reached them. My limited options swirl in a disorganized haze as fear settles in my stomach. Finally, when I can't bear waiting any longer, I edge closer to the bottom of the hill where the stones have piled up in a great heap.

A muffled squeak from the mound of rocks makes me leap backward.

"Dayne?" The air is still too dusty for me to make out anything farther than a few paces from where I'm standing. *Did I imagine the noise?*

"Help!"

This time, there is no mistaking the cry. The voice is coming from partway up the broken hill. I pick my way through the toppled stones, careful not to fall and break my legs.

"Help me! I'm buried!"

The voice is too high-pitched to be Dayne's. I keep my sling and dagger ready in case I'm walking straight into the Duskers' waiting arms. *Not that either weapon would do me any good if they're waiting to ambush me.*

"Where are you?"

The cry grows closer and more desperate. "Please! My leg is caught!"

I throw my pack and sling on the ground to use both of my arms to shift the stones away from the voice, which is coming from below ground.

As I pull away a slab of stone that is three paces long, a gloved hand reaches up to grab mine. Holding the stone aloft with one hand and scooping aside rubble with the other, I stare at the person emerging from beneath the fallen rocks.

Dayne appears beside me as the small person scrambles out from beneath the rubble. A boy, covered from head to foot in dust the color of filthy brick, scrambles onto the ground in front of us.

Before the boy can utter a word, Dayne points the blade of his axe at his thin neck.

"Dayne!" I gasp. "What are you doing?"

He ignores me, addressing the boy in the same harsh voice he used when I first met him. "Who are you, and what are you doing here?"

Even beneath the layers of grime that cover the boy's bone-thin face and tattered cloak, I can see he's trembling. He can't be older than eight or nine. His hair is matted with sweat and sticks up in every direction. His head seems too big for his twig-like body. The boy doesn't look strong enough to stand, let alone attack the two of us.

"I was stuck under the rocks," the boy stammers after a tense silence.

"You with the bandits? Where's your cave? Are there more of you?"

The boy's eyes dart from me to Dayne.

"Dayne, put your axe down!"

Surprised by my tone, Dayne lowers his axe without argument.

"Are you alright?" I ask, trying to keep my voice even to show we mean the boy no harm. His brown eyes are wide and seem to pop right out of his scrawny face.

Without looking away from me, the boy points to his leg. Blood trickles across the rock by his feet.

"He's hurt!"

Dayne, still holding his axe in one hand, kneels on the ground to tie a strip of his shirt around the boy's knee.

"We've got to get this cleaned up. Infection will kill him soon enough if the sun doesn't get to him first." Dayne makes no attempt to spare the boy from this diagnosis.

"Do you have any family? Any friends?"

The boy doesn't answer. He stands in his too-big cloak, shivering in the baking sun.

"Are you alone?" Dayne persists.

When the boy manages a slight nod of his head, Dayne hoists him over his shoulder and picks his way through the rubble down the hillside. I gather my fallen pack and sling and trip over the rocks behind them.

"Where are you taking him?"

"Back to the river. We have to wash this knee and see what the damage is. Then, I'd like us to get back under cover of the trees before we attract every Halve and bandit this side of the mountains."

Dayne handles the boy as gently as he would a sack of grain.

Where is the boy from? How long has he been out here? He looks frail enough for a breeze to knock him over. A trail of blood speckles the ground in his wake.

Dayne drops the boy onto the riverbank to inspect the wound. In the shade of an overgrown bush, he pushes the boy's cloak aside.

His knee is swollen to at least twice its normal size. The wound leaks blood, which leaves muddy streaks down the boy's leg.

I draw in my breath as I see the sliver of stone wedged in his flesh. The boy's screams turn more to howls as Dayne works his fingers around the tender area.

Dayne is going to pull the stone out of the boy's knee. My stomach curdles. I clutch the boy's hand, both to offer him comfort and to steady myself.

"On three," Dayne grunts. "One, two, three!"

An agonizing wail from the boy subsides into pitiful whimpers as Dayne extracts the stone, holding it between his forefingers. I can't take my eyes off the oozing hole in the boy's knee and the tattered skin.

Dayne's gaze softens just a little as he lifts the boy to his feet. He is gentler this time, and even mutters some encouraging words as he helps the boy limp to the water's edge.

I cover my mouth to keep from echoing the boy's screams as his knee is submerged in the water. The boy utters several curses when Dayne begins to scrub the boy with a rag and a bar of soap he produced from somewhere in the depths of his cloak. The boy's shrieks become more vicious as Dayne nears the injured knee, and after a short battle, Dayne throws the soap at the boy and growls, "Here, do it yourself. But for sun's sake be quiet about it, or you're going to attract every Dusker and Halve this side of Malarusk."

When he rejoins us on the bank, the boy is dripping and almost clean. Without the layers of grime, he somehow looks even frailer.

Tossing me a fresh piece of cloth, Dayne says, "Bandage his knee. Tight enough to keep the blood locked in, but don't cut off his circulation."

We sit in a sliver of shade so the boy can roll up his cloak. Blood still leaks from the wound, but it looks less hideous now that it's clean.

Dayne watches me work with a critical eye. "We'll need to mend those tears in his cloak before he gets the Burn."

"Thanks," the boy mumbles when I've finished.

"You have anything you want to tell us?" Dayne demands.

After a brief pause, the boy asks, "You don't have anything to eat, do you?"

His voice is pitiful. I dig a Sustum brick out from my pack and hand it to him, along with my waterskin.

The boy gobbles up the entire brick and downs the contents of my waterskin in two gulps.

"Thanks! I haven't eaten in days!"

The boy dabs the remaining crumbs from his palm and licks them off his fingers. I watch him with a horrified fascination. The children in Subterrane Harkibel were thin, but this boy, with his hollow cheeks and bulging eyes....

"Hemera, pull out that map of yours and find us the nearest cave to spend the high day," Dayne says. "And then I'm going to rustle us up a proper dinner."

We find the cave on Brice's map easily. It's obvious the cave has been long-abandoned before we set foot inside; it's overgrown with plants and tree roots. It would be impossible to find unless someone already knew it existed.

Thank you, Brice.

There is still an hour before high day. While Dayne is out hunting, I make camp.

"I'm Hemera," I say, trying to distract myself from the boy's sickly features. "My Subterrane was attacked by Halves, and now I'm traveling north in search of any captives."

The boy's eyes fill with tears. He wipes the dirty sleeve of his cloak across his nose.

It's alright," I say, putting my hand on his shoulder. "You don't have to tell me who you are if you don't want."

The boy sniffs and then says, "My name's Wokee. My settlement was destroyed by Halves."

A short bout of hiccups stops Wokee from saying anything else. I pat his back and offer him a clean cloth to wipe his face.

"Settlement?" I ask tentatively.

Wokee nods, blowing his nose on the cloth and then balling it up into his small fist. "Our home."

At the empty look I give him, he adds, "In the Banished Lands."

My brow furrows in confusion. Only criminals and barbarians live there. I even heard some of them had lost the ability to speak and communicated in grunts like the Halves.

"We're not all bad like the Duskers say," Wokee says, sensing my thoughts.

"Then why do you live in the Banished Lands?" I blurt out before I can stop myself.

"We've lived in the Banished Lands ever since Grandpapa was expelled from Subterrane Jevin." Wokee shrugs. "And now it's home." His thin face twists into a sad smile. "Or at least, it was."

Wokee doesn't say why his family was forced out, and I don't pry.

As I try to disguise our footsteps leading from the road to our camp, Wokee tells me about the caves where he lived with a dozen other families until the settlement was attacked. I listen in fascination as he talks about his mama, a cloaker who could stitch a cloak twice as fast as even the most skilled in Subterrane Harkibel, and his papa, a trader. They sound ...*normal*...nothing like the exiled criminals the Duskers always described.

It's not long before the boy is smiling, revealing a dimple in his right cheek.

"I haven't talked to anyone in days. Except for the birds, but they don't talk back." He grins. "I didn't think anyone would ever find me. I got so hungry I even ate *worms*."

He crinkles his nose in disgust, which makes his numerous freckles bunch together on his cheeks.

Wokee's mouth falls open as he watches me lift an enormous stone above my head to hide the entrance to the cave from any prying eyes.

"How can you lift that?" His wide eyes seem like they will pop right out of his face.

I shrug. "Tell me more about your parents," I say, trying to change the subject. Instead of answering me, Wokee comes closer to inspect my work.

"The men in my cave were strong. You're...you're like nothing I've ever seen," Wokee flails his hands as he grasps for the words. "How much can you lift at once?"

My father's warnings echo in my head.

"I'm not stronger than anyone else," I snap.

Wokee's lower lip trembles.

"Well let's see," I say, awash with guilt. What threat could this little boy be to the likes of me?

I pile the largest stones I can find on top of each other until the pile sways and threatens to topple. I bend over, keeping the stack steady by bracing my body against it, and lift up.

Wokee claps his hands and laughs with glee as I launch the pile of rocks up and over the makeshift wall.

"Whoa!"

I can't help but smile; Wokee's reactions are so opposite from what I'm used to.

"How far can you throw that one?" He points to a boulder that is as wide and tall as I am.

Wokee's dimpled smile makes me pick up the rock. I pull my arm back, but it catches on the branch of a dead tree I hadn't seen. As I try to free myself, the unstable rocks beneath my feet shift. I land on my backside, the huge rock still held above my head. A puff of rock dust rises from the impact.

I wince.

When Wokee starts to giggle, I crack a smile. It's not long before he's laughing so hard he snorts, which reminds me of Destinel. Instead of making me sad, though, it warms me to this boy. I can't help but join in with his uncontrollable laughter.

It takes minutes for us to compose ourselves. When we have, I make a show of checking to make sure there's nothing blocking my arm, and then let the boulder fly. It sails more than three paces in the air before it lands on another rock and fractures. My veins swell with the strength of the Halves' blood.

"That's *amazing*!" Wokee squeals.

His enthusiasm is contagious, and I find myself grinning along with him.

"Have you ever seen someone use one of these before?" I take the sling out from my belt and place a stone in the leather pouch. Wokee watches as I wind the sling by my side, faster and faster until the ropes are a blur.

I release the stone. It moves too fast to pick out against the bright sky, but three loud pops come from the direction in which I aimed the stone.

Wokee limps over to a line of trees to investigate.

"Hemera," he shouts. "Your stone went straight through three trees!" He jumps up and down on his good leg. "*Through* the trees! Three of them!"

Wokee is dancing around the trees. "What else can you do?"

"Well," I bite my lip. "I'm a fast runner."

"Show me," the boy commands.

When I hesitate, Wokee folds his arms over his chest.

Shaking my head and stifling a laugh, I draw a line in the dirt with my toe. I position myself at the imaginary start line.

"Say go," I tell Wokee.

At his signal, I take off.

The wind is cool as it passes through the thick material of my cloak. My long hair fans out behind me as I dart around obstacles in my path.

I stop after less than a minute. When I turn around, I utter a yelp of alarm. Wokee and the rock wall are no longer visible.

My stomach twists in knots. *What have I done?*

I retrace my steps, more slowly this time. I follow the marks of footprints in the dirt and places where the grass is still pressed down from my weight.

I haven't tested my speed since I ran in the race during the Dark God festival, and I was just a child then.

The race held on the last day of the Dark God festival is a grueling ten laps around the outside of the Subterrane, in our cloaks. Everyone who saw me at the starting line laughed at the little Bisecter child who thought she could compete with the Subterrane's fastest runners.

I won the race, beating the fastest Dweller in the Subterrane by four laps. I always knew I was faster than the other kids, but before this race, I had never tested myself against the adults in the Subterrane. It was the first time I knew beyond any doubt that I was as different as the other Dwellers said.

My father told everyone I had cheated, that I ran two of the laps instead of all ten. I left the winner's circle red-faced with shame. The Dwellers' boos followed me all the way back to the Subterrane. After that, I swore I wouldn't stand out from the others. If I forgot I was different—if I never tested myself again—they might, too.

I believed what my father said, that I had somehow miscounted the laps. It was the only explanation for why I was so much faster than the other Dwellers, wasn't it?

It wasn't until the other day, when I outran the Halves in the woods, that there was no mistaking my speed.

Bisecter. One of them. *Freak.* The Dwellers' insults echo as if they're surrounding me. I clamp my hands over my ears, but the motion does nothing to shut out the sound of their voices.

The campsite comes into focus after more than a quarter of an hour of steady walking. A small figure bounds toward me.

"You ran faster than anyone I've ever seen!" Wokee yells. "I wouldn't have believed it if I hadn't seen it myself!"

My smile falters at the sight of Dayne, who leans against the stone wall with his arms crossed over his chest. His mouth is ajar.

"I saw you run."

"I...."

"That was an incredibly stupid thing to do." His voice is cold.

"I know," I whisper, staring at the ground.

"Do you have any idea what the Duskers would do to you if they knew?" His glance flicks to Wokee, who is watching our exchange with interest. "They have spies, you know."

"I'm sorry." My cheeks are hot with shame.

Dayne steps in front of me, waiting until I meet his gaze.

"They're terrified of the Halves as it is," he says. "What do you think they'd do if they found out how powerful you are?"

"But I'm not," I protest.

Dayne slits his eyes. "Let's just make certain that no one else has any reason to wonder." Dayne glares from me to Wokee. "Got it?"

Wokee and I exchange a guilty look as we follow Dayne like scolded children back inside the wall of our camp.

CHAPTER 13

A swollen boar's carcass lies on the ground outside the cave. Dayne barks out orders to us as he prepares the meat. Grateful for something to do besides wilt under Dayne's scowl, I make trips back and forth to the river to fill our waterskins and gather firewood.

The travel cave is small, but free of the slimy worms that make their home underground. Dayne finishes smoking the meat while Wokee runs back and forth between us, asking how much longer until it's ready.

The meal tastes better than anything I ever ate in the Subterrane. We recline against the cave wall, sucking on the bones. When I pull the stone covering over the mouth of cave, Dayne takes out his lute. The soft melody in the darkness makes my eyelids heavy.

After Wokee has licked his fingers clean, he curls up in a corner of the cave and begins to snore. If it weren't high day, I would be concerned the noise would attract every Halve and Dusker from here to Tanguro.

"We'll never get any sleep with that racket," Dayne complains as I ball my cloak into a makeshift pillow and shift it under Wokee's head.

When Dayne stops playing, I say, "What you did back there, killing those Halves," I pause. "Where did you learn how to fight like that?"

I'm still curious about Dayne. It doesn't escape me that aside from his name, he hasn't told me anything about himself.

Dayne regards me, his eyes pinpricks in the darkness. "It's not important," is all he says.

He goes back to plucking at the strings of his lute, humming softly. My eyes are beginning to close when his voice jars me awake.

"So, who'd the Halves take from you?"

His question throws me off guard, and I can't stop the word before it's out of my mouth. "Everyone." The bitterness in my voice is unmistakable.

"Your parents?"

I nod before realizing he can't see the movement. "Yes."

"Both of them?"

I think about my father, surrounded by the Halves, with no one coming to help.

"Yes."

"What happened?" Dayne's voice is soft enough that I can tell he's lost his family to the Halves, too.

I surprise myself by telling him about the attack on the Subterrane. Tears roll down my cheeks as I remember clutching Destinel's lifeless body, and my unfulfilled promise to Henri that I would protect Sirrel. Shame heats my cheeks, but the words pour out as I tell Dayne how I abandoned my father. How I ran.

Dayne strikes a match and lights a stub of candle. He holds it up until the cave is illuminated in soft light. I hear Dayne's sharp intake of breath.

Following the direction of his unblinking stare, I see it's directed at my necklace, which has come loose from the collar of my shirt. The intensity of his gaze is unsettling.

"My mother gave it to me," I say, like I need to defend myself for wearing it.

My words seem to jolt Dayne out of his thoughts, and he nods slowly. "Your mother..." he swallows. "You said the Halves killed her...?"

I try to read the expression on Dayne's face, but he's busy fiddling with his lute.

I haven't told the story to anyone except for Destinel and Brice. They had known me, and so they understood the grief and guilt I carried with me like a second skin. I've just met Dayne, but something about the sadness I've seen pooled in his eyes makes me think he'll understand.

"My father was gone trading jewels to other Subterranes," I begin. "I was angry because he hadn't come back in time for my birthday. My mother took me into the woods to pick rupyberries to distract me."

I remember the little black kynthia birds perched on her shoulder. The kynthia fly higher than any other bird and are not harmed by the sunlight. She always said they reminded her of me.

I still remember the way my mother's blue eyes, the ones I wished I had inherited rather than my monstrous black ones, sparkled in the sunlight.

I remember the crash in the underbrush…my mother's command for me to climb the tree.

Stupid. If I had just stayed by her side….

Dayne lights another candle, and the glow lights up his face. There is raw emotion in his eyes, and I think again that he must also have lost family to the Halves.

The terror that gripped me on that day comes back to me in a rush. *Breathe, Hemera.*

"What happened?" Dayne asks quietly.

I can remember watching the beast raise its wooden club over its head like it was yesterday.

"She tried to fight it." My voice cracks. "But she never stood a chance."

In the silence that follows, I feel the familiar presence of the questions that have clung to me since that day.

What would have happened if I had made a noise, distracted the Halve, jumped down from the tree? What if we fought it together?

"That must have been very difficult for you," Dayne says.

"Difficult," I repeat, but my mind is far away, back in the woods with my mother.

Her silky dark hair, always brushed to gleaming perfection, was strewn across her face. A trickle of blood traced a line to her jaw. The light in my mother's eyes faded until they were an unfamiliar, milky gray.

I held her as her skin cooled and stiffened like hot wax in the mold.

Even then, I knew nothing would ever be the same. Never again would she lull me to sleep with stories about strange and colorful creatures that lived beyond the mountains. Never again would I have her comfort and company when the other Dwellers ignored me. Never again….

She was gone.

I had no tools to dig a grave, but I spent hours clawing a shallow hole into the ground. My hands were raw and blistered, but I didn't care. I rolled my mother into the hole, arranging her arms so she would rest more comfortably. But as I knelt beside the grave, fat tears blurring my vision, I couldn't bring myself to push the piles of dirt over her beautiful body.

"My father found me next to her grave, just before high day."

Wokee has stopped snoring, and my voice is loud in the cave.

My father's face went Dusker pale as he took me in, with my dirt- and tear-streaked face, kneeling by the grave. He stood motionless for several seconds before falling onto his knees beside me. He gathered me into his arms as I sobbed. When I looked up at him, his eyes were red and brimming with his own unshed tears.

He didn't say a word to me; there was nothing to say. He just held me until my sobs turned to exhausted, heaving breaths. And then my father lifted me up and carried me away from my mother.

We never spoke about that day again. But the memory of my father's arms wrapped around me, holding me while I cried beside my mother's grave, gave me comfort during the loneliest high days.

"You must have been very young," Dayne says, his voice full of sympathy.

"I was twelve years old."

The familiar suffocating feeling is back. I press my head against the wall and grip my mother's key, forcing myself to breathe.

When Dayne speaks, the softness in his voice twists my heart.

"Get some rest now, Hemera."

Wokee's snores have resumed, but rather than irritating me, the sound drives out the screams echoing in my thoughts. I lean against the wall of the cave. With the sound of Dayne's lute and Wokee's snores in my ears, my eyes start to close.

For the first time since Brice was taken, I feel less alone.

CHAPTER 14

As soon as it's low day and we've hidden the evidence of our stay, we begin to walk. I pull out Brice's map, tracing our progress with my finger.

"That's where we're headed." Dayne taps the upper right-hand corner of the map.

I measure the distance from our current location to the spot where Dayne is pointing, and groan. It looks like we've hardly covered any distance at all. At this rate, we'll be lucky if we ever make it to Tanguro. But one look at Wokee, who is limping along several paces behind, forces down my impatience.

As I squeeze the map back into my pack, my fingers brush against the drawing I took from the dead Halve. A chill grips me when I think about the Halve in my cave, rifling through my belongings.

What was it about the drawing that made the Halve clutch it even as it drew its last breath?

"What I propose is that we travel through the forest," Dayne says as I shove the drawing deeper into my pack. "It will take longer than if we stayed near the road, but it's our best chance of passing undetected."

I shake my head. "It will take too long." Taniel's words, *TNGR, Help,* are never far from my mind.

"We're better equipped to take on a few thieves than an army of Halves or Duskers," Dayne says.

He's right, of course, but I can't ignore the fluttering panic that has been growing in me ever since I heard Brice was captured.

"Now get that sling of yours out and keep it at the ready, just in case," Dayne says. "Wokee, what can you offer besides a supreme knowledge of bad words?"

Wokee gives Dayne a sheepish look. Ducking his head, Wokee produces a small, curved dagger from his belt.

"I'm pretty good with this." He twirls the knife between his gloved fingers in a practiced motion. "And no one ever notices me because I'm small and quick." To demonstrate, he darts around a dead tree, wincing at the added pressure on his knee.

Dayne watches Wokee's performance. His mouth twitches into a grin, which he masks when Wokee looks back at him for approval.

"Alright then," Dayne grumbles. "Both of you stay alert."

We trek uphill until lowest day before we break. I didn't think Wokee would have the strength to keep up with his wounded knee, but his energy seems to be as boundless as his chatter. He grasps fistfuls of rupyberries and throws them up in the air, trying to catch them in his mouth as we walk.

Wokee distracts us from the heat with stories his mother used to tell him. He's overcome with a fit of giggles at the end of a tale about a wild pig who turns into a human, only to realize he's naked. His laughter is infectious. Dayne throws his head back, and for a moment, I catch a glimpse of his face without the deep creases. It makes him look years younger.

As the sun climbs back up toward high day, we make our way to the nearest travel cave marked on Brice's map. This one is larger than the last, with tunnels and chambers that go deep underground. It must have once been an outpost for trading between the Subterranes and those in the Banished Lands before the Duskers outlawed travel.

"Smells like no one's been here in years," Wokee wrinkles his nose as I roll up my cloak to make a pillow for him, a practice that is becoming routine.

Dayne lights a single candle from his pack before settling himself against the wall of the cave. "Lucky we have that map of yours," he yawns.

His eyes narrow to slits when he notices me staring at the sun tattoo on his right hand.

"So, what's your story?" I ask, forcing my gaze away from the swirling black lines. "Where are you from?"

And why are you helping me, I want to add.

"None of your damn business, that's where."

The sting of his words shocks me into silence.

I move to the other end of the cave, preferring Wokee's earth-shattering snores to Dayne's sullenness. I kneel on the ground and mutter my Dark God prayers, which I've been neglecting. When I open my eyes, Dayne is watching me.

"You know the Dark God isn't real, don't you?"

I gape at Dayne. Dwellers are dragged off to Malarusk for crimes much smaller than questioning the Dark God's existence. "The darkness is coming," I sputter, repeating the Duskers' mantra.

"Don't quote their rot to me," Dayne snaps. And then, more softly, "Can you imagine a world in which the sun disappeared for even part of the day?"

He pauses while I try to picture it. I can't.

"The darkness is just another one of the Duskers' false promises they use to keep the Dwellers complacent."

I have no idea what Dayne is talking about. The Duskers are ruthless in their justice, but if they weren't, the Subterrane territory would turn into another Banished Lands. There would be murder, disease, starvation….

"Dayne," I begin. "What have the Duskers done to make you hate them so much?"

Before he can respond, a rush of fetid air passes through the cave. Dayne's candle flickers, and then goes out. There is a scuffling noise from somewhere in one of the adjoining tunnels.

"What was that?"

In answer, a deep, menacing roar fills the cave.

Something hot and coarse tears against my face as I'm knocked to the ground. I land on a rock, biting down hard on the side of my cheek.

I hear a scream, a snarl, and taste blood.

CHAPTER 15

With trembling fingers, I fumble around in my pack until I find the matches. It takes several tries for me to strike one. In the few moments before the match flickers out, the cave is illuminated.

An animal, so big it stretches the entire length of the cave, is sprawled on the ground. The wooden handle of Dayne's axe sticks out of its muscled back.

I spit out a mouthful of blood as I explore the raw inside of my cheek with my tongue. As my racing pulse settles, I clutch the wall to support my wobbling legs. My foot catches on something—someone—on the ground. Looking down, I suck in my breath at the sight of Dayne's body beneath the dead beast.

"Dayne?"

My whisper is met with silence.

Grabbing one of the beast's forelegs, which is as large as me, I yank the animal off Dayne.

Please, please, please don't be dead.

Dayne gasps, coughs, and mumbles a few curses.

"You're alive!" I throw my arms around him.

"Easy does it," he says hoarsely. "Where's the boy?"

Wokee's dark outline moves from where it's pressed against the wall of the cave farthest from the beast.

"Come on, you big scaredy," I try to joke, but my words hang hollow in the air.

Dayne tries to sit up, mumbles something about his head, and falls back to the ground. His head hits the earth with a dull smack before I can break his fall.

"Dayne?" Wokee whimpers. "Is he—"

I squat down next to Dayne and press my fingers to his pulse. "Just knocked out." The words give me more relief than I should feel for someone I hardly know.

"What is that thing?" I motion toward the body beside us as I try to arrange Dayne in a more comfortable position.

The beast has two fangs, each the length of my arms, hanging down from its muzzle. It must weigh more than a dozen of the burliest Dwellers together. Its yellow eyes, glazed over in death, stare unseeing through tufts of matted black fur. In spite of its size, the animal has feathered wings folded over its broad back. A giant purple tongue lolls between its jagged fangs.

"Oh, a hyenair!" I answer my own question as I finish my inspection of the beast. "I thought they were just a legend."

"Not a legend." Wokee's voice is barely more than a squeak. "They come down from the mountains to hunt humans when they can't catch anything else."

He's shaking.

I go to him and put a hand on his bony shoulder. He huddles against me.

"One of them ate Wodell." Something between a hiccup and sob escapes from Wokee.

"Wodell?" I ask.

"My twin brother." Wokee's body begins to quake anew, and I wrap both my arms around him.

"It just grabbed him with its mouth and flew away."

The despair in Wokee's voice sends an ache through my heart.

"We tried to throw rocks and chase after it, but...." Wokee pulls away from my embrace and stares up at me. "I should have tried harder to save him."

I know that look in Wokee's eyes all too well. I was around his age when I saw my mother murdered.

"If you had been there, you could have stopped it," Wokee looks up at me. "You're so fast and strong." His eyes gleam with unshed tears.

I give his thin hand a squeeze and swallow my own bitterness and regret.

"Hemera," Wokee is wide-eyed with panic. "There's something else in here."

"Where?" I squint, willing my eyes to see through the darkness.

Wokee's small finger points to a black tunnel at the other end of the cave.

A growl, so faint I can barely make it out, reverberates along the tunnel. The hyenair's mate? My palms begin to sweat.

"Get out your knife and stay with Dayne."

I take my dagger out of my belt with my right hand and wind my sling in my left.

I pass through two open chambers before the noise comes again. This time, it's closer. Too close.

I look down. Two wide, yellow eyes stare up at me from a tiny body that is a sliver of a shadow in the darkness.

I bend down to get a closer look, holding my dagger out in front of me. The animal lets out a squeaky howl. It's no bigger than the palm of my hand, with ears far too big for its scrawny body. One of its ears stands straight up while the other flops across a yellow eye. Its fangs hang down from its upper lip in a miniature replica of the giant Dayne killed. But even its teeth are too small to seem threatening. On its back are two nubby wings.

The creature licks my hand with its sandpapery tongue. When I tickle its neck with a finger, the cub nuzzles against my hand. Its fur is long and soft, and sticks up in every direction. It fits in both of my palms when I scoop it off the ground and carry it back to the cave.

Wokee has managed to light a candle, which he holds in trembling hands. The shadows stretching across the ground make the dead hyenair look even more fearsome.

The tiny cub squirms out of my arms and bounds over to the body of the dead hyenair. It sits with its hind legs splayed, looking from me to the dead beast. It curls itself into a tight ball and whimpers. My chest aches with sympathy.

"What's that?" Wokee asks fearfully.

"It's the hyenair's baby."

The cub wedges itself between its mother's enormous, lifeless paws.

I know how you feel, I want to tell it. I bend down and wrap the cub in my cloak.

"W-what are you doing?" Wokee hugs the wall as he edges closer.

"It'll die if we just leave it here."

The cub wriggles free from the folds of my cloak and rolls onto the ground. Wokee leaps to his feet, grabs the cub by the scruff of its neck, and draws his knife. The creature's tiny wings beat the air ineffectually.

"Wokee, no!" I gasp.

"It's a hyenair," his voice is edged with hysteria. "It killed my brother!"

"But we just killed its mother."

Dayne awakens, muttering to himself as he explores the knot at the base of his skull. He reaches into his pocket and pulls out a flask filled with something that makes him shudder and cough. He drains the flask and lets it fall to the ground.

"Quit your arguing," he growls. "Do you want every Halve in a hundred miles to hear you?"

I'm so relieved Dayne is awake I want to hug him again. It's only the scowl on his face that makes me think better of it.

"It'll grow up and kill us in our sleep," Wokee persists.

"I'll train it," I promise, cradling the cub in the safety of my arms.

I offer the cub a handful of water from my waterskin, which it laps. It relaxes against my hand as I stroke the soft feathers of its tiny wings.

Wokee, who is still glaring at the cub, moves around to the other side of the cave and sits on the ground with a huff.

"Any chance you can get this carcass out of here?" Dayne turns on me. "I'd turn it into a stew, but I'm not quite up to it."

Draping my cloak over the cub so it won't be able to see, I grab the dead animal's paws and drag it down the tunnel.

When I come back carrying Dayne's axe, Wokee is glaring at the quivering lump under my cloak.

"Better rest now," Dayne says as he slumps against the wall. "We'll need to be off as soon as it's low day."

CHAPTER 16

I wake to the sight of the cub, still curled nose-to-tail beside me, with one ear flopped over his face. The cub blinks his round, yellow eyes and flutters his tiny wings. He stands on wobbling legs, takes a step forward, and then falls back on his rear end. He opens his mouth, exposing his miniature fangs, and lets out a high-pitched squeak. I give him a strip of dried boar's meat, which he remains occupied gnawing until we break camp.

"He needs a name," Wokee announces as he helps shove the last of our belongings into my pack.

"I thought you didn't want to keep him," I tease.

"He's too small to hurt anyone," he replies, like it should be obvious to me. "Maybe if he stays with us, he won't want to kill anyone when he grows up."

"Why don't you come up with something to call him?" I suggest.

Wokee squats down to look at the cub. "Wodell and I used to pretend to be monsters. Grandmama made us a costume to go with our favorite monster, and we'd hide under it to scare the bandits that came sometimes. We called it Vlaz." He gives the cub an appraising stare. "I think that'd be a good name for him."

The cub flutters his wings as if in agreement.

"Vlaz it is, then," I smile.

When we step out into the sunlight, I pull out the map. We bend over it, and my eyes flick to the X marking Tanguro.

Dayne echoes my own thoughts when he says, "Lot of ground to cover."

Vlaz stays close beside me as we walk, following the strip of dried meat tied to the corner of my belt.

"We're going to have to go back onto the Road to cross the river." Dayne unstraps his axe. "You both wait here while I scout ahead."

"I'll go—"

"Stay with the boy." Dayne's voice is commanding. "And keep the fur ball quiet."

Reluctantly, I let Wokee pull me behind a boulder. When I look forward, Dayne has already disappeared into the hazy sunlight.

Neither Wokee nor I speak. I squint straight ahead, waiting to see the outline of Dayne returning to us.

The first sound to interrupt the silence is a squeaky growl from Vlaz. The fur on the top of his back stands on end. Both of his long ears are pricked forward, and his small wings flutter. I turn back to follow the direction of Vlaz's gaze.

I hear them before I see them. And then I see the smoke from their fire, no more than fifty paces away.

"Duskers," Wokee breathes.

"Can't be. We're nowhere near Malarusk."

"New recruits making their pilgrimage to Darkness Peak," Wokee whispers. "At least, that's what Grandpapa always said." He flicks his glance at the imposing mountain in the distance. Darkness Peak rises straight ahead, formidable as the Duskers themselves. The ash gray peak stands alone amid the endless red-brown scraggy mountains cutting across the landscape. It's the place where the Dusker Supreme is said to be able to commune with the Dark God.

A nervous tingle raises the hair on the back of my neck.

If they discover us here, will they kill us on the spot, or drag us back to the Malarusk dungeons? I wrap my cloak tighter around me as a chill spreads through my body.

My pack squirms. Before I can react, Vlaz sails through the air. His tiny fangs are bared. His nubbed wings beat furiously, but don't keep him airborne after his initial leap. He disappears beyond the boulder.

"Vlaz," I hiss. But the cub is long gone.

There is shouting and the unmistakable click of crossbows being loaded. I peek around the boulder and stifle a scream. Two pairs of gray boots are headed straight toward us.

I draw my dagger. "Wait here," I tell Wokee.

"But Hemera—"

"Wait here!"

I know the exact moment the Dusker sees me. His eyes are shadowed by his hood, but he stops and draws his crossbow. The black-tipped arrow is pointed straight at me. I can't move. I can't breathe.

"What the? Argh!" The Dusker's crossbow drops to the ground as he twists around in circles, trying to kick Vlaz off of his leg. When that doesn't work, the man pulls a long, curved dagger from his belt. Without thinking, I run forward. The man doesn't know whether to stab me or Vlaz, and I take advantage of his indecision.

I thrust my knife into the Dusker to the hilt. I gag as my blade cuts through living flesh.

Before the Dusker even hits the ground, and before I come to my senses, I load my sling and release a glass-sharp piece of rock. The second Dusker falls.

I twist around, dagger and sling ready for the next attacker, but no one comes. It's quiet.

My legs tremble as the Duskers' warm, sticky blood congeals on my gloves. I turn and vomit into a bush.

These are not Halves, but men. And I killed them. With barely a thought or any effort. Everything the Dwellers ever said or thought about me, about how dangerous I am, has just become true.

The last things the dead men ever saw were my black eyes.

"You okay?"

Hearing someone else speak makes me jump out of my own skin.

"I'm sorry, I didn't mean to. They were just there, and then, and then—" I'm babbling.

"Don't say sorry," Wokee commands. "Those Duskers deserve all you gave them and more."

The cold hatred in Wokee's words should shock me, but I feel numb.

I want to look away but can't. Seeing these leaders of all Dwellers dead by my hands makes me think of my father. If he knew what I've done, he would—

"What happened?" Dayne, axe in hand, strides up to us. His eyes shift from me, to Wokee, to the bodies splayed out at my feet.

My stomach lurches into my throat. I trip over myself trying to grasp my fallen knife and land in a trembling heap on the ground.

Wokee tells Dayne what happened, while I stay where I've fallen, just staring at the Duskers. One man's hood has come loose, revealing a mangled face. It looks like every bone was shattered on multiple occasions, leaving his face scar-ridden and contorted. Even in death, blisters from the Burn are surfacing on his exposed skin.

Wokee interrupts his own story to ask, "Why does his face look like that?"

There is a long pause. Finally, Dayne says, "Sometimes, the Duskers make deals with their prisoners; if they agree to join the Duskers and spread their laws, their crimes will be forgiven. They do this," Dayne nods at the man's distorted face, "to the prisoners who accept the deal…to test whether they're strong enough to deserve what comes with being a Dusker."

I reach out to a tree to steady myself. "How do you know that?"

"They tried to recruit me once," Dayne replies.

His mouth is set in a straight line and I know better than to ask any more questions.

"Well anyway, you made short work of these ones, Hemera. Well done." Dayne bends down to regard Vlaz, who is busy shredding my bootlace with a single claw. "And you just earned yourself a permanent spot in our company, as far as I'm concerned."

Vlaz lets out a self-important roar, which is more of a squeak.

"Yeah, good job," Wokee adds. It's unclear whether he is talking to me or Vlaz.

I just stare at my companions. It's unheard of to kill a Dusker, let alone two of them. I've never even heard of someone trying to attack the Duskers. At least not since the rebels disbanded generations ago. And here these two are, praising me for something that would earn us all a short, miserable life in the Malarusk dungeons. The Duskers protect the Dwellers, and it's our duty to honor them. And yet….

I think of my father, surrounded by Halves with no one to help him. Where were the Duskers when he needed them?

Dayne looks down at his shadow. "Come on. Let's get out of here before any more come."

* * *

"My father will never let us be together."

The smile fades from Brice's face. When he lowers his head to brush his lips against my neck, I forget whatever I was planning to say.

I smooth a strand of hair off his face. His green eyes take my breath away.

"We need to stop seeing each other," I say in a rush before I lose my nerve. "If he finds out about us…."

Instead of pulling away from me like I expect, Brice smiles and leans closer. "Hemera."

My name rumbles through his chest and sends a small shiver through me.

"Nothing could make me stay away from you." He wraps his arms around me.

Brice…the loyal scout…defying his Captain. For me. Breaking all of the rules for me. It makes me feel wanted, loved, in a way I haven't felt since my mother died.

I nestle against his shoulder, listening to the rhythmic beating of his heart. "I just wish we could stay like this forever."

Brice cups my cheek in his hand, leaning over me until our eyes are level. "Whatever else happens, know this." The raw emotion in his eyes ignites a fire inside me. "I love you, Hemera Harkibel."

When his lips touch mine, I am no longer the Captain's daughter. I am not the Bisecter. It's just us, tangled up in each other until I can't tell where one ends and the other begins. His kiss holds the promise of forever.

✷ ✷ ✷

I grasp for the feeling of Brice's steady arms around me as the memory fades. My mind is so filled with thoughts of Brice that when Dayne stops walking, I almost knock into him.

We've been wading through tall reeds for hours, so it's impossible to see what's ahead. Dayne must have heard something because he's clutching the handle of his axe until his knuckles turn white. I loosen my sling and grasp a small stone from my pouch, even though I see no sign of movement. Wokee wraps Vlaz closer in his cloak in case the cub decides to let out one of his high-pitched growls.

When two birds soar out of a nearby tree and shatter the silence with their cries, we all jump. Dayne relaxes his grip on the axe. "Must have been it," he mutters.

We take one short stop before lowest day. All of us are eager to put the Duskers far behind us. All that keeps me from dwelling on their scarred faces and bloodied cloaks is the thought of reaching Tanguro.

Dayne adjusts the sleeve of his cloak, and for a moment, I can see his tattoo. The black curls of the sun's rays dance along the back of his hand as he extends his fingers.

Something I heard once, a whispered conversation about Soldiers of the Light, comes back to me now. The tattoo…Dayne's hatred for the Duskers….

"Are you one of the rebels?" The question is out of my mouth before I can think better of it.

I know the question is ridiculous; the rebels are nothing more than a memory of something that died years ago. No one challenges the Duskers anymore.

But Dayne doesn't laugh or scoff as I would have expected. His eyes flash before his face becomes a mask again. He closes his right hand into a fist and thrusts it back into the belled sleeve of his cloak, hiding the sun symbol. "It's from a long time ago. Means nothing now."

"Ouch!"

Vlaz's tiny fangs have sunk into Wokee's forearm. Before he can grasp him, the cub is out of his arms and running.

"I'll get him," I call, already sprinting after the cub.

I push through the tall reeds, calling for Vlaz. The unpleasant sensation I'm being watched takes hold of me. It has gone very quiet. I stop to listen.

Something cold and metal presses against the back of my neck.

"Don't move an inch, or I'll slice your head off," a deep, male voice commands.

CHAPTER 17

My stomach lurches, but I stay still. *Duskers.* They must have followed us. *They know what I did.* My blood runs cold.

"Step forward!" the voice commands.

At the same time, the man's hand shoves me from behind. The blade is heating up against my neck.

"There's others!" a different, female voice calls.

My heart drops. The voice came from the direction I left Dayne and Wokee.

"How many?" my captor growls.

I swallow, feeling the blade press against my neck.

"We got one," the distant voice calls.

I turn at the sound of movement through the reeds. Wokee appears first. His knees are shaking so much he can barely stand. There are two large men who hold their swords against either side of Wokee's neck. A woman with the reddest hair I have ever seen sticking out from her hood follows Wokee's movements with an arrow nocked in her bow.

These people can't be Dwellers, nor do they look like the filthy bandits who tried to attack Dayne and me. At least they aren't wearing the gray cloaks of the Duskers.

"Hurt her and you're dead!"

The blade twitches against my neck. I turn to see Dayne holding his axe to the man's throat. Wokee whimpers as the two men beside him dig their swords into the soft areas beneath either side of his jaw.

"Step away from her, and tell those men to lower their swords," Dayne commands in a clear, threatening voice.

I hold my breath.

Dayne pushes the edge of his axe forward, forcing the man to take a step. "Do it now!"

There is a brief hesitation, and then the man says, "Do what he says."

As soon as the other men step back, Dayne drops his axe and raises his hands.

Before I can ask what he's doing, Dayne says, "We surrender."

Just like that, without even a scuffle.

"No, we don't—" I begin, but Dayne cuts me off.

"Ignore the girl. We'll come without a fight."

It is only the look on Dayne's face that keeps me from saying anything else.

The man giving the orders peers at each of us in turn. "If anyone so much as *thinks* about trying to escape, you all die."

The other men have Wokee's arms locked behind his back as they push him forward. My captor keeps his sword in one hand and his knife in the other. The archer with red hair moves ahead, scouting the reeds on silent feet. I grit my teeth to keep from screaming at Dayne…from demanding to know why he gave up so easily. We could have fought them, run away, done *something….*

But when more men appear from wherever they were hiding and surround us, I understand. Two of them grip my shoulders, one on each side, while more follow in front and behind.

"What are you going to do with us?" I surprise myself by speaking.

The man behind me replies, "We're taking you to our leader."

My stomach drops. They must be Dusker spies. Criminals who buy their way out of the Banished Lands by capturing Dwellers who grow illegal herbs or break the travel ban.

Dayne and Wokee are both silent, so I don't say anything more.

I expect the men to take us southeast, back toward the Dusker territory. Instead, we march without break in a northward direction. This at least gives me some encouragement. If we can get away, we won't have lost too much time. As the sun climbs higher, though, our path shifts westward, away from Tanguro.

My legs ache and my stomach rumbles. Every time I try to turn around to see how Dayne and Wokee are faring, I get prodded in the back by the man's sword.

A cry—Wokee's—makes both my captors and I stop. Wokee is on the ground with one of the men kneeling over him.

"Leave him alone!"

My captor's sword against my neck is all that keeps me from running back to Wokee.

When the man stands, he's holding Vlaz by the scruff of his neck. The cub wriggles and beats his small wings as he tries to sink his teeth into the man's hand.

"Found a stowaway in the kid's cloak," the man calls out.

I catch Dayne's eye for a moment, and he winks at me.

"What should I do with it?" the man asks.

Vlaz hisses and snarls as he dangles from the folds of his neck.

To my relief, the red-haired woman still pointing an arrow at us says, "Hell, he's just a cub. Let him go."

Vlaz plants his bottom on the ground, his luminous yellow eyes fixed on our company. The men push us forward again and I lose sight of him until, a few minutes later, the cub comes trotting up beside us.

When we reach a dense cluster of trees, we stop. The leader reaches into his cloak and produces an armful of cloth scarves. He distributes them among our captors, and without a word, they bind the scarves around our eyes.

"Attempt to remove your blindfold or run away, and you will be dead."

I force myself to hold still as the scratchy material folds my eyes into darkness.

At first, I take small, scuffling steps, convinced my already-clumsy feet will trip over a stone or root. Our captors lead us over flat ground, though, so it doesn't take long before I fall into the rhythm of our marching.

After what feels like hours of walking, we come to a stop. Our captors whisper together. It sounds like there are more of them than there were before, but I can't be sure. We stand for an eternity, the sun baking us through our cloaks, before we're pulled forward again.

The change is instantaneous. The insufferable heat is replaced by a slight breeze, cooling the sweat streaming from my brow. I open my mouth, inviting in the cool air the way a man dying from thirst will swallow water from a stream.

We are no longer on flat ground but walking downhill. When I lose my footing for a moment, I put my hands forward to steady myself. My fingers touch packed dirt. It's like I'm back in the Subterrane.

We must be underground.

A low groan escapes my lips.

My breathing comes fast and sharp. *Should I take off my blindfold? Try to steal one of the men's swords and kill them?*

Too risky. They'll kill Dayne and Wokee.

My captor places an arm on my shoulder, steering me around corners until I can no longer even guess at our direction. I jump backward when a cool mist sprays me from either side, but then open my mouth to let the water slide down my parched throat. The red-haired woman says something I can't make out, and then the scarf covering my eyes is untied.

CHAPTER 18

Wokee and Dayne are beside me, blinking as their blindfolds are removed. The red-haired woman still guards us, an arrow nocked in her bow, but she seems relaxed. The rest of our captors have disappeared. I give Dayne a look, willing him to understand that now is our chance to escape. He won't meet my eyes, though.

Vlaz is huddled against Wokee's leg. His long ears are pinned back and his fur is plastered to his skinny body as the water trickles from the ceiling and splashes onto him. His eyes are fixed with more than curious interest on a silver fish darting to and fro in a tiny pool.

We're standing on smooth, wet stone. The packed dirt walls I felt earlier have been replaced by slick gray rock, which surrounds us on three sides. A flowing sheet of water covers the cave's cavernous opening.

Sunlight streams through small, angled holes in the rocks far above our heads, which allows the beams to reach the highest part of the wall without coming close to touching us. Red, orange, and pink flowers spring out of the wall's crevices. The air is perfumed with the flowers' scent, and cool from the mist. It's the most beautiful place I've ever seen.

Little black birds flit into the cave and then dart back out through the falling water. Kynthia birds, my mother's favorite. It's the first time I've seen one since she died.

Look at the way they fly, Mer, so high and fearless. Just like you....

I close my eyes and wait for the tightness in my throat to ease.

Men and women stride through the cave, barely sparing us a glace, before disappearing around large rocks. They all wear different cloaks and are a mix of skin colors, piercings, and other markings of the Subterranes.

Some are unmarked by any Subterrane. None of them, at least, wear the gray cloaks of the Duskers.

This place must be one of the settlements in the Banished Lands, although it looks nothing like the barren, dangerous caves described in the Duskers' stories.

Why have we been brought here? What do they want with us?

I tug the hood of my cloak forward so my face is covered in shadow. Whoever they are, I don't want them to notice my eyes.

A young man passes through the cave. He glances at us, and then slides to a stop. His eyes widen.

He's tall and clean-shaven, unlike the shaggy-bearded men who captured us. His skin is unlike either the pasty Duskers or the reddened, spotted variety of most Dwellers. It is a coppery bronze, matched with eyes the color of honey. His sharp jaw and straight nose make him look both handsome and arrogant.

"Incredible. You're Dayne Clarion. I'm just…honored…." He walks up to us and shakes Dayne's hand reverently.

His right hand is covered by the same sun design inked into Dayne's skin.

"Dayne Clarion?!" The red-haired archer drops her bow. She looks from the young man, still gripping Dayne's hand, to Dayne. Her jaw goes slack.

"Don't tell me you didn't recognize him," the man says.

At the red-haired woman's expression, the man grins. "The guys are going to give you hell about this later."

"I'm so sorry," Red Hair says to Dayne, her curls bouncing with every word. "Truly, I didn't know…should have looked at your face…." Her cheeks have turned as red as her hair.

In spite of my confusion, I can't help but feel satisfied at her discomfort. *Serves her right.*

The mere mention of Dayne's name draws a dozen people through the sheet of falling water. They all talk at once, elbowing each other to get closer to Dayne.

"Dayne Clarion!" someone calls. "It's him!"

More of them pack into the crowded cave. Now that I'm looking, most of these people have the sun tattoo on their right hand. I want to ask Dayne about it, but a crush of people separates us.

An older, stooped man clasps Dayne's hand in both of his. "I never expected to see you here again. Welcome home!" His grin reveals a missing front tooth.

I watch, open-mouthed, as an endless stream of men and women file into the cave. They talk excitedly as they wait on line to shake Dayne's hand. Every one of them is marked with the sun tattoo.

Choruses of "thank you for coming back" and "what are you doing in these parts?" and "are you organizing an attack?" echo from all sides. Wokee and I manage to exchange a puzzled look through the crowd.

Dayne stands in the midst of the chaos, uttering a terse word here and there in response to the eager questions. He seems neither surprised by, nor to welcome, all of the attention.

The man with the golden eyes who first recognized Dayne squeezes closer to him.

"I'm Wade," I hear him say.

Dayne barely glances at him, but he persists. "How did you do it, Dayne? Jadem would never tell us."

"I heard he was brought here as a prisoner before he was recognized," a woman near me says to someone else. "How could you *not* notice you were blindfolding Dayne Clarion?!"

Dayne's expression is growing surlier by the minute, although the people who surround him don't seem to notice. They continue to pepper him with questions and praise. Finally, Dayne breaks his silence and says, "Get Jadem."

"She's been summoned," the archer with red hair replies breathlessly. "And sorry for you know—" She flaps a hand at our discarded blindfolds.

Dayne gives her a curt nod, "The rest of you clear out of here."

At that, everyone files back out through the tunnel behind the waterfall, still chattering.

"What was all that about?" I demand as soon as we're alone.

Before Dayne can say anything, a massive figure steps through the waterfall.

I can't help but gasp at the sight of the woman towering before us. She's taller and wider than any woman I've ever met, her bulk taking up most of the cave's opening, but that is nothing compared to the rest of her.

Her face is distorted, with long scars stretched across her eyes and cheeks. It reminds me of the Dusker I killed, except it looks like her wounds were from many years ago. A displaced bone in her jaw makes her entire face lopsided. Her left eye is missing, replaced by a jagged scar that runs the length of her face. When she reaches up to push aside a wisp of gray hair, I see the sun tattoo on the back of her hand.

Wokee whimpers and moves behind Dayne as the woman's voice fills the cave.

"It's good to see you, Dayne. I never expected you to come back, especially blindfolded and at the sword-point of a few of my soldiers. You must be getting careless."

Her mouth twitches into a sagging, crooked grin.

I look to Dayne for some kind of explanation, but his gaze is fixed on the woman.

"Jadem," Dayne says curtly. "If you think your men could capture me against my will, then you are older and more senile than you look. We were passing this way, and your guards made for a convenient escort. Anyhow, we're short on supplies."

Jadem's one eye focuses on Dayne. "My resources are always at your disposal. But I imagine that is not the reason for your visit." She seems unperturbed by Dayne's scowls.

"My young friends and I are headed north…."

Jadem isn't paying attention to Dayne anymore. She has noticed me with my sling dangled by my side, a stone already in the leather pouch. Her scarred mouth drops open.

"It can't be," she whispers.

Her one pale blue eye is trained on me. A shiver runs down my spine.

"What's going on?" I hate the way my voice wavers. Every nerve in my body is poised to run.

"Is it?" she asks Dayne, who gives a slight nod in response.

"Hemera." She says my name with a softness I wouldn't have guessed such a woman could produce. "Is it really you?"

"How do you know my name? How does she know my name, Dayne?"

My words are laced with panic. I wind the sling at my side, making no effort to hide my intentions.

"It's alright, Hemera, she won't harm you," Dayne says.

His sour expression doesn't reassure me.

"I haven't seen you since you were a baby," Jadem says. "You look just like your mother did at your age, except for your eyes, of course."

My breath catches. I tug at my hood to draw it farther over my face. But her words make my sling go limp in my hand.

"You knew my mother?"

Nodding, she gestures toward me. "Please, we have much to talk about."

"Jadem," Dayne starts.

"I take it she doesn't know?" Her voice is so quiet I barely hear.

Dayne shakes his head.

"What don't I know?" I look from one to the other, but neither responds.

Jadem holds out her hand and motions for me to walk through the waterfall.

Still clutching my sling, I turn around to watch as Jadem follows me. I pass through the waterfall and step into a stone room with lush, green vines climbing up the walls.

"Hemera, beautiful Hemera," Jadem shakes her head as she stares at me. "I thought I had lost you forever."

This hulking brute of a woman speaks in a voice so soft it sounds like she might cry.

"Who are you?" I demand. "Are you a Dusker?"

"No." Her response is quick, sharp.

I take a step backward, but her voice is gentle when she speaks again.

"I was one for a short time, but it was for my own reasons. I was part of a movement to overthrow the Duskers and set up new laws."

She motions to the ink design on her hand.

"The rebels? They're real?" The disbelief in my voice is plain.

"We call ourselves the Solguards, or guardians of the sun. But I assure you we are very real." Jadem draws her finger along a scar that runs from her missing eye to the bottom of her pointed chin.

"And this is where you live?"

She gestures to the cave we're standing in. "This fortress was built to offer a safe haven for the Solguards, where we could plan the overthrow of the Duskers."

I have no fewer than a thousand questions. "So Dayne is one of you, too?"

Jadem sighs. "Yes, and no." Her distorted features pinch together in sadness. "Dayne and I worked together to infiltrate Malarusk and learn the Duskers' secrets. But the plan was uncovered, and the Duskers imprisoned us for many years. By the time we got out, we were both changed."

She looks like she has more to say, but then changes her mind. She clears her throat. "It was after my return that I heard about my sister, and how she and my niece had been murdered by a Halve."

Sister? Niece?

My mouth opens and closes without producing a sound.

"I heard you were dead," she continues, almost pleading. "I never met you, but I heard about you and knew who you were the moment I saw you."

Pain deepens the creases on her face. She swipes a hand across her glistening blue eye.

"Hemera," she murmurs. Another tear tracks down her ruined cheek. "My beautiful niece."

CHAPTER 19

This woman is…my aunt? Impossible. And yet….

Even though her face is scarred and distorted, there's unguarded emotion written all over her features. In spite of all logic, more than a small part of me wants to believe her.

If what this woman says is true, if she's really my mother's sister….

My mind whirls with possibilities. There's so much she could tell me. She must have hundreds of stories about my mother from before I was alive. She must know what my mother was like as a child, what kind of person she was when she was my age. She can tell me what my mother's interests and passions were before she became Lady Harkibel.

But no…everyone in my family is dead. When I look at the woman's distorted face, there is none of my mother's beauty. The blue eye, perhaps?

I banish the questions I really want to ask, forcing my lips around something more practical. "If you're my aunt, then why did my mother never mention you?"

Jadem cocks her head as she studies me, like she's trying to decide how much to tell me.

"If you wish for an answer to that question, I'm afraid I must make some rather unfortunate remarks about your father."

"My father?" It was the last thing I expected her to say.

She raises her eyebrow as though asking for my permission.

I wait, too curious to try and stop her.

Jadem sighs. "As Captain of the Subterrane, your father belonged to the Duskers."

"But he wasn't a Dusker—"

She holds her hand up.

"No, he wasn't. But if Zeidan wanted to keep his position, he needed to show the Duskers he wouldn't suffer a traitor back into his Subterrane, even if she was family. He made it clear what would happen if I ever tried to contact my sister or return to the Subterrane."

"That doesn't make sense," I say. "Even if what you say about my father is true, my mother wouldn't have gone along with it."

"She had no choice," Jadem says. This time, her voice is hoarse with sorrow and regret. "The Duskers knew I had been building a secret fortress for the rebels for more than a decade, but they couldn't find it. They suspected my sister had been helping me, and intended to arrest her along with me as soon as they found me. Your father bargained with them for her life. The agreement was that she could live, in the custody of Captain Harkibel, only so long as she never spoke of me again."

I shake my head, my brain rejecting Jadem's words.

"You said you were sent to Malarusk, yet here you stand." The challenge in my voice is plain. Everyone knows that no one sentenced to the dungeons in Malarusk ever returns.

"That's not my story to tell." Jadem doesn't blink when her one eye meets my black ones. "But I swear by the sun what I say is true."

There is something about the way she says it that makes me believe her.

"By the way," she clears her throat. "I'm not sure I ever properly introduced myself. My name is Jadem. Aunt Jadem, if you wish." Her voice is husky, and a deep blush darkens her scarred cheeks.

I glare at her. "Why should I believe anything you say? You have no proof you are who you say you are."

Dusker law or not, I can't imagine a world where my parents didn't at least mention I had an aunt.

Jadem's lopsided smile fades. "Oh, Mer."

Her use of my mother's nickname for me makes my breath hitch. I can feel my careful mask begin to disintegrate.

"We have so much catching up to do." She reaches up a hand to touch my cheek, the black rays of the sun inked onto her hand dancing as though they're alive. I flinch away.

Jadem lowers her hand. "If you wish for proof of who I am, Dayne can vouch for my trustworthiness."

"And how do you know Dayne?" I press.

A shadow crosses Jadem's face, but then she laughs. "So many questions, so like your mother. Let's end this interview for now." She searches my face with her eye. "If my knowledge of weary travelers serves me correctly, your company will be wanting a good meal and sleep."

"Wait."

I look Jadem up and down for some resemblance to my mother. Even without the scars, her broadness is nothing like my mother's delicate features. They couldn't have been related.

But she used my mother's nickname for me. Only my mother ever used that name.

"Where did my mother grow up?" I ask, testing her.

Jadem quirks her eyebrow at me.

"Subterrane Harkibel, just like you. Although it was called by a different name then."

We both look up as a kynthia bird flies into the cave and lands on Jadem's broad shoulder. Jadem reaches into a pocket and pulls out a few seeds, which the bird plucks from her calloused palm.

"They were her favorite." Jadem looks at the bird. "They remind me of her." In those words, I hear all the sadness of a woman who has lost her sister.

I gape at her. "You're telling the truth," I whisper.

Jadem nods.

Aunt Jadem. I test out the unfamiliar words in my head.

A desperate need, fiery hot, lurches up inside me. Jadem really did know my mother—grew up with her. There is so much she could tell me, so much I long to know.

"Tell me a story about her."

Jadem gives me a lopsided smile.

"A good one," I clarify.

She plucks a white flower growing against a leafy vine and brings it to her nose. "Your mother loved stories," Jadem says. "She loved to hear about the wild creatures that lived beyond the mountains. She would badger every traveler who came through the Subterrane to hear about the places they'd been. She used any excuse she could find to leave the Subterrane and explore new territories."

I absorb her every word about my mother, willing them to fill the gaping hole that has been inside me for as long as I can remember.

"There was one time," Jadem laughs, remembering, "your mother was furious because our parents wouldn't let her compete in the Dark God festival. So naturally, she decided we would make our own." My aunt laughs again, and the sound fills the tunnel. "She convinced all the children in the Subterrane to set up obstacles, and even commissioned the Cloaker to make us banners and the goldsmith to fashion trophies."

She shakes her head, remembering.

"What happened?" I breathe, afraid to interrupt.

Jadem's lopsided mouth quirks. "She won it all." She shakes her head again. "Sent one little boy to the healing cave with a broken rib after her version of the wrestling."

I can see it all. My mother. Brave, strong, smart….

"I can already tell you are very much like her," Jadem says.

Her words open a chasm in my heart, making me swell with emotion until I could almost burst. I'm like a Dweller who's starving and just happened on a feast, only to be told she can only eat a single bite.

"Tell me—"

"Later, Mer." My aunt's voice is gentle. "There will be time enough for reminiscing."

Jadem takes my arm and steers me back through the waterfall to Dayne and Wokee. Dayne's eyes flick over first Jadem and then me.

Jadem's voice is light, as though revealing herself as the aunt I never knew existed is normal. "I believe it's dinner time. Shall we make our way to the dining cave?"

Wokee lets out a whoop, undisturbed by Jadem's appearance now that there's the promise of food. He skips after Jadem as she leads the way. Vlaz trots along behind, twitching his wings as he swats at a corner of Wokee's cloak. Dayne and I follow.

My mind hums with everything Jadem has told me.

We walk along a wide, stone-walled path lined with bunches of white flowers. The ceilings here are so high that the golden sunlight streaming in from above stops before it could touch even the tallest of these people, but is still bright enough to bathe the tunnel in a warm glow. The mist from the waterfalls gives off an earthy, clean smell.

"What is this place?" I hear Wokee ask ahead of us.

"This is Solis." Jadem raises her hands up to the high ceiling.

"What?" Wokee wrinkles his nose.

"The Solguard fortress," Jadem says. "We are known as the rebels to some." She stops to water a bed of flowers from a copper watering can on the path's edge.

"So, you fight the Duskers, then." Wokee takes out his small dagger like there might be a Dusker around the next corner.

A strange look passes across Jadem's face. "Some do, but others simply wish for a safe haven where we can live under our own rule rather than the Duskers'."

"Are we in the Banished Lands?" Wokee asks.

Jadem nods. "The Duskers assumed the Banished would die off, either by Halves or the sun, but the people dug new caves and survived."

"I lived in the Banished Lands," Wokee says, his face screwed up in confusion, "but none of my people were like yours."

"Most of the Banished people only wished to be left alone when they were exiled," Jadem explains. "But there are some of us," she glances down at the sun tattoo on her hand, "who wish for something better than mere survival, something more."

"But," Wokee raises a small, bony finger, "If you're a threat to the Duskers, how come they haven't killed you yet?"

To my surprise, Jadem laughs.

"Because," she gives Wokee a conspiratorial wink, "they don't know how to find us."

"I want to be a Solguard," Wokee announces.

Dayne's face goes stormy, but Jadem laughs again. "Well in that case, you must learn how to use the glide."

"What's the *glide*?" Wokee licks his lips. "Is it food?"

Jadem motions toward a dark hole in the side of the tunnel.

"The cave fortress is quite large," Jadem explains, "so we built the glide."

Jadem steps into the darkness and then sits down on the ground with her long legs stretched out in front of her. She moves gracefully for her size and girth. Her hand rests on a thick iron bar that sticks out from the rock.

"This," she motions to the blackness before her and the iron lever, "is how we save ourselves a bit of time. Pull the lever as many notches as you need, and you'll find yourself deposited in the right tunnel."

"Huh?" Wokee tilts his head.

"If I want to go to the dining cave, which is on the second level, I pull the lever two notches," Jadem explains. You'll learn your way around soon enough."

Jadem pulls the lever to the second notch, scoots herself forward, and disappears.

"Where'd she go?" Wokee squats in front of the hole, squinting into the darkness.

"Come on," Dayne rolls his eyes.

He lifts Wokee onto the lip of the darkness, pushes him into a sitting position, and pulls the lever.

"Keep your feet out in front," Dayne instructs as he gives Wokee a push.

"Wheeeeee!"

Wokee's squeals of delight echo back up to us from wherever he's gone.

"You next, Hemera."

"You must be joking," I look from Dayne to the blackness. The familiar suffocating feeling that followed me through the Subterrane like a shadow returns. I step back from the hole.

"There's an awful lot of steps between here and the dining cave. Off you go." Dayne nudges me forward.

I sit at the edge of the hole, feeling metal beneath me.

"Dayne, I can't—"

With a push, I'm falling. A scream rips from me as the whoosh of air fills my ears. Faster and faster I go as my body hurtles along the smooth metal.

I'm swept around a sharp corner. Panic sets in as the faint outline of ten or more tunnels appears in front of me. I have no ability to control my direction. As I fly toward the place where the tunnel branches, my body is slung against a metal wall and into the second tunnel.

Without warning, I shoot out of the darkness. I'm airborne for a stomach-flipping moment before I land hard on my side, rolling twice.

Winded and hoarse from screaming, I scramble to my feet.

I've barely regained my balance before Dayne comes shooting out and over me, landing on his feet.

"That was so cool!" Wokee is dancing around us. "Can we go again? Please?"

My heart is knocking against my ribs. But the raw terror is gone. It was how I always imagined it felt for the kynthia birds when their wings caught a rare breeze. Wokee is right; I want to do it again and again.

"How do we get back up?" I ask when I've regained my breath.

Jadem quirks her lip. "You climb the stairs, of course."

CHAPTER 20

J adem points us toward the dining cave.

"Is that…" Wokee sniffs the air, "Meat? And bread?"

Jadem laughs. "You'll find that our resources here are less sparse, since we don't pay the Duskers' tithe.

I stare at Jadem—my aunt—but I'm not seeing her. I'm thinking about Subterrane Harkibel. I knew most of the jewels we mined went to Malarusk, but it never occurred to me that my father sent them our crops, too. A knot of anger forms in the pit of my stomach as I think about the Sustum bricks we were forced to choke down when fresh food was scarce.

Jadem ushers us along before putting a scarred hand on Dayne's good shoulder and steering him in the opposite direction. Before I can ask where they are going, they're gone.

With a glance between us, Wokee and I step into the wide, open chamber. Flecks of gold and silver shimmer in the rock walls and the thick pillars around the cave.

Sweet music accompanies the chatter and clink of bowls being passed down the long tables. Four women play wooden instruments to a rhythm that makes my feet tap of their own accord. A strange sound echoes through the cave. It takes me a moment to recognize it as singing. In Subterrane Harkibel, music was only heard during the Dark God festival.

Men and women dance, together. Their arms wind around each other as they step to the beat of the music. Such closeness would never be allowed publicly in the Subterrane, even between married couples.

The way they look at each other makes my heart ache for Brice.

Blinking quickly, I stare around the room. Narrow waterfalls trickle down from the ceiling and collect in small pools at the sides of the room. White, yellow, and pale pink blossoms growing from the rock crevices waft a scent almost as intoxicating as the food. My mouth waters at the sight of heaping platters of meat, bread, and fruit that are making their way across the long tables.

Wokee has already seated himself at one of the tables next to a young girl. They are chattering as Wokee helps himself to a laden basket of bread.

On my way over to the nearest table, I trip over a crack between the stones and just manage to right myself before I bring down a platter of sliced meat. I hunch my shoulders, praying no one has noticed.

I seat myself on the edge of one of the long benches, nerves still jittery from my near-fall. I pull on my hood to keep my eyes covered in shadow. Should I reach for a platter or wait for someone to pass one to me? I should have sat with Wokee….

"You're the one who came in with Dayne Clarion, right? I'm Wade. Who are you?"

Drawing my face deeper into the hood of my cloak to keep my eyes hidden, I look at the man who was the first to recognize Dayne. The sunlight reflects in his golden eyes. It's almost difficult to look into their brightness. Except that unlike my eyes, the effect of his unusual color is dazzling rather than terrifying.

Even though I couldn't think about anyone that way except for Brice, I can tell just from looking at him that this boy gets more than his share of attention from girls.

"I'm Hemera." *Jadem's niece*, I almost say, but it feels too strange to say aloud.

I pull on the collar of my cloak, which has started to strangle me.

"Nice to meet you." Wade smiles. "So, do you know what Dayne Clarion is doing here?"

Wade makes rapid gestures with his hands as he talks. He has the Solguard sun inked onto the back of his right hand, too. He isn't wearing his cloak, and the outlines of his taut muscles show through his white shirt.

"Er," I stutter. "We were traveling together and then some…Solguards…snuck up on us. But I guess Dayne had it in his head to come here anyway."

Not that he bothered to mention it to me.

Wade shakes his head in disbelief. "Those guys must feel like idiots." A devilish smile crosses his lips. "I'm never going to let Ry hear the end of this."

I have no idea who Ry is, but I have more important questions, and Wade seems to be the only person willing to answer them.

"How does everyone know Dayne, and why are you all so excited to see him?"

"You mean you don't know?" Wade stares at me like I just sprouted a second head. "I thought you said you were travelling together!"

"We were…I mean we are…but he never mentioned he was famous." My cheeks redden again. I give my hood another tug to make sure my face is hidden in shadow.

"Wow, I thought everyone knew about Dayne Clarion." Wade tears off a chunk of bread with his teeth. He chews as he passes a tureen of soup to me.

The smell makes my mouth water as I ladle the rich broth into my stone bowl.

Wade narrows his eyes at me. "You know that he and Jadem were in Malarusk together, right?"

"Yes," I lie. The smell of the broth is dizzying.

I dip my spoon into the bowl and sip. I choke from the heat and drop my spoon with a clatter.

"I thought the Duskers never release anyone from Malarusk," I say when I stop coughing.

"Yeah, that's the point," Wade waves his hand impatiently. "No one had ever escaped from Malarusk until Dayne Clarion was sent there. He figured out how to do it, and he and Jadem got out. I think they killed a bunch of Duskers, too, but Jadem would never tell us how they did it. Anyway, that's why Dayne is famous."

I chew a bite of meat. This soup tastes nothing like the thin liquid we were rationed in the Subterrane. *Because there's no Dusker tithe here.*

"You mean to tell me you were traveling with Dayne Clarion, and he never told you about his escape?" Wade's shoulders hunch in disappointment.

I shake my head.

"Do you think you could introduce me later?" His face brightens.

"Sure, I guess," I say, thinking about the scowl Dayne wore every time one of the Solguards shook his hand.

"Excellent." Wade grins.

I bite into a round, orange fruit, all the while feeling Wade's gaze on me.

"You don't have to keep your hood up, you know," he says. "The Burn won't reach you down here."

"I know." I sink deeper into the shadow of my hood. And then, searching for a way to distract him from wondering what I'm trying to hide, I say, "You sure talk a lot."

Wade makes a helpless gesture with his hands. "I've been like this my whole life." He grins. "It gets me in trouble. Sal says I should have learned better by now, but, you know," he grins, "I haven't."

I don't know who Sal is, but right now, I have more important questions.

Tread carefully, Hemera, I warn myself. I still don't know much about these people. I don't want to arouse suspicions or give them any reason to lock me up.

"Have you always lived here?" I ask.

A good, safe question.

"No way!" Wade straightens up. "Jadem built this place before she was sent to Malarusk, but the rest of us have trickled in as our settlements were destroyed or the Duskers tried to recruit us."

I look around at the smiling people in this hall filled with flowers and sunlight. The Duskers always made it seem like civilization was impossible beyond the Subterrane territory.

"It's different here from what I would have expected from rebels," I say carefully.

Wade raises his eyebrows. "We stand for everything the Duskers hate—choice, freedom, the simple joy of living…." He puts his right hand on the table, clenching his fist so the rays of the sun dance across his skin.

"Because the Duskers pray for darkness?" I guess, staring at the tattoo.

Wade nods. "We are soldiers of the sun," he says. "It's a promise that one day, people will be able to live without fear of the Duskers or Halves." Wade's mood darkens. "All the Duskers bring is death."

"They don't kill, they protect," I recite. But the words of the Dark God prayer I've repeated countless times are beginning to sound hollow.

Wade frowns. "You see that girl over there?" He points at the child talking to Wokee. "The Duskers raided her settlement and took all their weapons—to protect them—they said." His words are filled with bitterness. "Hours later, the Halves attacked."

Wade bangs his fist on the table. Soup sloshes over the side of his bowl, but he takes no notice.

"The Duskers could have killed the Halves. But they let them come. The Duskers *let* the Halves slaughter her settlement."

Wade continues, saving me from having to come up with a response. "The few of them who were left after the attack would have died in the settlement's ruins if Jadem's scouts hadn't found them."

There is a sick feeling in the pit of my stomach. I push away from the table and the scent of food. I'm not hungry anymore.

I think of my father, and the black armband of the Captains he wore whenever the Duskers came. Did he know the Duskers were deceiving all of us?

I search for something to say, but words stick in my throat. My eyes land on Wade's tattoo.

"So, I take it you don't have any Dusker God statues around here."

I meant it as a joke, but there is a fierceness in Wade's gaze that wasn't there before.

"The Duskers' promise of the darkness is nothing more than a desire to control that which should be left alone."

I shake my head. "But the darkness gives people hope. Shouldn't Dwellers—er, people—be able to want something better?"

"Everyone seems to forget the sun also brings life." Wade crosses his arms over his chest. "Are you satisfied to just hide away and pretend the darkness is coming?"

I shake my head slowly.

"We'd rather live, here and now, with all the sun provides."

The red-haired archer who brought us here passes by the table. Without her hood up, fiery curls spill in every direction and bounce with her every step.

"You're not giving up all the Solguards' secrets to the first pretty girl you see, are you?"

Pretty? I feel myself blush, but Wade doesn't look the least bit shamed.

"Of course I am," he winks at me.

If I could crawl all the way into my cloak to hide, I would.

The archer gives him a light smack on the side of his head. "Don't pay any attention to him," she tells me. "Wade could be happy talking to a rock. And he's a helpless flirt."

"I am not!" Wade gives her an affronted look. And then, after a thoughtful pause, he says, "I might be willing to concede that part about the rock, though." His smile comes so easily I can't help but feel lighter in his presence, too.

"Whatever you say, flirt." She turns to go, but as she does, she leans over and whispers in Wade's ear.

She says, "lowest day," but I miss the rest.

She gives me a curious look, and then walks away.

"That's Ry," Wade says, as though no more explanation is needed. "Rylin, actually," he amends, "but no one calls her that."

I give him a pointed stare. "What's happening at lowest day?"

"Hm? Oh, nothing." Wade is concentrating on arranging the crumbs on his plate.

"If you're worried about me telling Jadem about whatever it is, don't be. I'll be gone by the next low day, anyway."

"You mean you're not staying?" Wade stops fiddling with his spoon to look at me.

I shake my head. "I'm going to Tanguro. The Halves took—someone—from my Subterrane, and I'm going to free him."

Wade stares hard at me, probably trying to decide whether or not I'm crazy. Finally, he asks, "You're going to Tanguro? With Dayne Clarion?"

I nod.

To my surprise, Wade smiles. "Well in that case…." He leans across the table. His voice is so low I can barely hear him over the clink of cutlery and merry chatter.

"Jadem would have us locked up if she found out, but some of us have organized a company to attack Tanguro."

Wade tightens his fists and looks down at the sun tattoo as though it gives him strength.

"Sal, our leader, thinks a Dusker figured out how to control the Halves and is building up an army of them at Tanguro."

"A Dusker?"

Panic curls in my stomach. If there's a Dusker in charge, that means there are Dusker armies guarding the prisoners, too. I hadn't accounted for that.

Wade crosses his arms. "Didn't you wonder why the Halves are capturing humans? They're not smart enough to organize the guarding of prisoners, and they would have no need for it, besides. The only possibility is that a Dusker has found a way to make the Halves capture the prisoners for him."

I suck in a breath. "But why? Why wouldn't the Duskers just take their prisoners to Malarusk?"

"Like I said, they're building up their army." Wade shrugs.

The possibility sends a shiver of dread down my spine.

"Our scouts have reported there are hundreds, maybe thousands of Halves gathered in Tanguro," Wade continues. "And more than a hundred prisoners."

Thousands of Halves? Even with Dayne's help, I could never defeat thousands and rescue Brice and the others.

Wade leans so close to me I can see a muscle flex in the sharp curve of his jaw. His voice is a whisper.

"Our company is well-trained, but there aren't many of us. Sal figures once we kill all the Halves and free the prisoners at Tanguro, we'll have ourselves an army. We'll be able to attack the Duskers."

My mind races. A Solguard army would have a real chance against the Halves. If I could join them….

Wade continues, "Once we've overthrown the Duskers, the Banished can come back to the Subterrane territory. People won't need to live in fear anymore."

Wade takes a breath.

The musicians have put down their instruments to drink from silver goblets. The men and women on the dance floor go back to their tables, arm-in-arm.

"Why all the secrecy?" I ask. "This is Solis, isn't it?"

Wade huffs. "Jadem has forbidden all attacks on the Duskers since she and Dayne got out of Malarusk. She thinks we can just hide here and keep this fortress safe forever." His eyes flash with anger, but in a moment, he's smiling again. "With Dayne in our company, though, it wouldn't matter if we're outnumbered."

That's why he's telling me all of this.

"You want me to convince Dayne to go with you."

"Having Dayne Clarion would just about secure our victory. You could come too, if you bring Dayne along," he grins.

I swallow my annoyance. "What about Wokee?"

"You mean the kid who looks like a stiff wind would knock him over?" Wade shakes his head.

I glare across the table.

"Look," Wade holds up his hands, "the journey will be difficult, and at its end there will be a battle where we're outnumbered. You wouldn't be able to keep him safe."

A part of me knows Wade is right.

I sigh. "I'll talk to them."

He flashes me a smile.

"When will your company be leaving for Tanguro?"

"Two weeks. We're almost ready."

"Two weeks?" I demand. "The prisoners could all be dead by then." *Brice could be….*

I can't even think the word.

Instead, I tell Wade about Taniel's warning. *TNGR. Help.*

Wade's golden eyes flash. "Then we'll have to be ready sooner."

A dizzying mix of relief and anticipation flows through me.

Wade lowers his voice again. "Come to our meeting at lowest day. We'll tell them what you told me and that Dayne Clarion is coming. That'll warm the rest of the company up to you...no offense."

"They won't want me?"

"It's nothing personal," he shrugs. "Like I said, Jadem would lock us all up if she ever found out what we were doing."

I sink deeper into the hood of my cloak. *If these people don't trust me now, what will they do if they find out what I am?*

CHAPTER 21

Wade comes to get me from the snug cave Jadem assigned to me and my companions. Dayne still isn't back from wherever he disappeared to, and Wokee said something about going to see a flesh-eating plant. I haven't been able to tell either of them about the Solguard company.

I follow Wade up the winding stone stairs, losing count after seven-hundred.

"Why wouldn't you build a glide that goes both ways?" I ask.

Wade laughs as I wipe the sweat off my brow and try to muffle my panting. If the Solguards think I seem weak before we've even set out, they'll never let me come.

Trust the Halves to give me their strength without endurance, I grumble inwardly.

Wade pulls on his cloak as the air inside the tunnel grows hotter. The buzz of insects surrounds us when we step out into the blazing sunlight. Tools clink on stone as people work in the gardens. They laugh and sing as they work.

Wade greets everyone we pass, exchanging jokes with some of them and giving vague excuses about where we're going. I keep my gaze lowered so no one gets the idea to try and look me in the eye.

"Can anyone live here?" I ask.

"Sure," Wade says. "As long as you're not a Halve, and you don't mind the Duskers reserving a special kind of hatred for you."

I think about that. Perhaps once I've rescued Brice, we could live here together. I allow myself a moment to consider what it would be like if we didn't always have to sneak around. If we could dance together, hold each other, in front of everyone….

A smile parts my lips.

It would be different if people here knew what I am, I remind myself.

"Jadem is quite the gardener," Wade says over his shoulder, snapping me out of my fantasy. "She tends the plants herself." He points to the red and yellow flowers that are blooming in spite of the merciless heat.

Aunt Jadem. Those two words together are as strange as they were the first time she introduced herself to me.

We follow a narrow trail for more than an hour before low voices cut through the buzz of insects. The path curves, and the meeting place appears.

My breathing sharpens. *This is a mistake. They'll find out what I am. I should never have come here.*

"Don't worry," Wade flashes a smile at me. "Sal is more like a father to me than my real one ever was." His expression darkens. "Anyway," he clears his throat, "you'll love him. And the rest, well—" Wade shrugs. "They listen to Sal."

"Great," I say, stealing a nervous glance at the clearing. "That makes me feel so much better."

There are at least fifty men and women gathered here. The well in the center is rusted, overgrown, and looking every bit unused. The Dark God statues, which guard every water source in the Subterrane territory, are nowhere in sight. A balding man with a sword slung across his hips leans against the well's crumbling foundation.

The man steps forward when he sees us enter the clearing. His face is creased with age and speckled with dark spots from the sun. His beard is nothing more than a few white strands that hang down to his sunken chest. But even with his slight stoop, the man carries himself with all of the pride of the Solguards. He must be Sal, the company's leader.

"Ah Wade, my boy." The man smiles in a way that makes his entire face light up.

"Hiya, Sal." Wade and Sal exchange a look that makes me long for my mother.

"Isn't it a bit late to invite new ones to the company?" a short, beefy man with squinty eyes growls as soon as he catches sight of me. "She doesn't even look like a soldier. All looks and no brains, I'll wager."

The way he sweeps his eyes over me makes the hair on the back of my neck prickle. I pull my hood up farther and look at the ground.

The red-haired woman—Ry, Wade called her—steps toward me. "You any good with a sword?"

"She's killed Halves. Lots of them," Wade tells her. "And she came here with Dayne Clarion."

The others exchange eager looks at the mention of Dayne.

Sal raises a hand and the clearing falls silent. He fixes his gaze on me. My face feels hot. I try to yank on my hood without anyone noticing so my eyes stay hidden.

"You must forgive us for being suspicious." His voice is kind as he addresses me. "But if Wade has brought you here, then we have every reason to trust you." The creases around Sal's eyes pucker as he smiles at me. I like him immediately.

Sal puts an arm around Wade's shoulder. The two exchange a knowing look, one full of love and respect. It sends an unexpected ache through me, reminding me of the way my mother used to look at me.

I glance at Wade, who nods for me to join Sal at the front.

Don't trip. Everyone's watching. Don't trip.

I'm almost by Sal's side when my foot catches on a hidden tree root. With a muffled *oof* I am milliseconds away from sprawling head-first into the abandoned well. But Sal puts out a hand, steadying me. He gives me a smile as I regain my balance. But unlike the Dwellers, his smile is kind rather than mocking. I give him a grateful look before I turn to face the others.

Taking a deep breath, I say, "I was traveling to Tanguro on my own before I learned the Solguards existed." My voice sounds small and frightened, like a child's. I clear my throat. "The Halves killed my family, and I want the ones at Tanguro destroyed."

I keep my black eyes focused on the ground.

"And what is your name, my dear?" Sal asks.

"Hemera."

"It's a pleasure to make your acquaintance, Hemera." He takes my hand and gives it a firm shake.

He continues, "I don't want to make a habit of inviting new soldiers to our company, but I know there isn't one among us who wouldn't welcome the protection of Dayne Clarion."

There's a murmur of agreement. At everyone's expectant looks, I am gripped by a cold fear. *What if Dayne won't come?*

"I heard a rumor," drawls the squinty-eyed man, "that you're Jadem's long-lost niece."

The corner of his fat lower lip sags in what could either be a smile or a grimace. The others turn accusing stares on me.

Ry stuffs an unruly red curl back into her hood before rounding on the man. "Why don't you keep your rumors to yourself, Gorgoran?"

"Easy, Ry." Sal steps between them.

Muttering to herself, Ry steps back.

I smile at her. No one has ever defended me like that before. I open my mouth to say something to her, but then shut it before any words escape.

If she knew what I really am, she'd hate me.

"It's not a rumor. I heard it from Jadem's own mouth," someone else says.

"You're her niece? Then—" Wade's face is a combination of surprise and betrayal, but he goes silent at a small shake of Sal's head.

I should have told him. *Why didn't I tell him?*

"It's true." I dig my nails into my palms to keep my voice from wavering. "But if I betrayed you, I would do more harm to myself than to anyone else. The one I love is a prisoner in Tanguro."

The voices die down.

Sal's stare is sharp and intelligent. "I believe you will be true to your word," he says. "We must now put it to a vote. All for the joining of Hemera and Dayne Clarion to this company?"

After a pause during which I hold my breath, most of the soldiers in the clearing raise their hands.

"Then that settles it." Sal puts his hand on Wade's shoulder. "Boy, I'll expect you to have her trained and ready to go. Hemera, you can bring Dayne to the next meeting. He, of course, won't need any training."

I bite my lip, wanting to speak but not knowing if I should.

"What is it, Hemera?" Wade asks, reading my indecision.

After another hesitant pause, I tell them about the message Taniel carved on his skin.

A lot of shouting and arguments ensue until Sal quiets everyone down. The rest of the meeting is taken up by a discussion of Taniel's warning and what to do about it. After much debate, it's decided we will set out in six low days. It feels like an eternity.

Wade chatters on our way back to the cave fortress, but I don't hear a word he says. *What if we're too late for the prisoners? What if something happens to Brice before I can reach him?*

"Take the glide to level four," Wade interrupts my worrying when we reach the top of the black hole. "We'll start your training next low day."

I settle myself on the metal sheet and pull the lever. All of my worries vanish.

The rush of air and weightlessness of my body are even more exhilarating now that I know I'll still be alive at the end. When I reach the part of the tunnel that branches off, I'm gripped with the fear I'm moving too fast. I'll be flung into the wrong tunnel or smash up against one of the metal partitions.

At the last moment, the metal wall thrusts me into the right tunnel. I come shooting out the bottom, waving my feet to try to keep myself airborne for another second or two. I manage to land on my feet before I fall forward and roll. My heart thuds against my ribcage as I pick myself up, rubbing my elbow where it struck the stone floor.

By the time I get back to the cave my travel companions and I share, Wokee and Vlaz are asleep. They're curled up together on top of a feathered mattress, the thin quilt a heap on the floor. How long has it been since I last lay in a bed? My leaden eyes barely stay open as I stumble past them.

A single candle flickers in the dark room. Dayne sits on his bed. He's holding his lute but isn't playing.

"Where have you been?" His voice is curt.

I throw one longing glance at my empty bed, and then go to sit beside Dayne. I stifle an enormous yawn before launching into a description of everything that has happened since I met Wade.

"They want us—well you, really—but they said I could come, too. I'm not sure about Wokee yet, but I'm sure you could convince them."

I'm breathless.

"Hemera—"

"But it'll be perfect!" My stomach twists at the look on Dayne's face. "We were going there anyway, and now we'll have a whole army behind us."

"Hemera," his voice is soft, and he puts a hand over mine. Perhaps it's sleeplessness, but the creases in Dayne's face have deepened. "I can't travel with this company of yours."

My heart sinks. "Why not?" A thought occurs to me. "Is it because Jadem wouldn't like it?"

Dayne's face darkens for a moment. "I don't follow her orders anymore." He rests his lute on the wooden table beside his bed. "I have gotten information I must pursue."

"Now?"

Dayne nods. "I'm afraid it's urgent."

I can tell it would be pointless to try to argue with him. A lump in my throat makes it difficult to swallow.

Even though we've only been together for a short time, I assumed Dayne and Wokee would be with me when I reached Tanguro. They're the first friends I've had since I lost Destinel.

Even thinking about her makes sadness crash over me like a wave. *What if the same thing happens to Dayne or Wokee?*

I swallow. "Is it dangerous where you're going?"

"A bit, but not to worry, I'll get through." Dayne pats my hand.

"I'm afraid I'll never see you again." My voice is a whisper.

"I promise when my errand is complete, I'll come find you." He meets my black eyes with a steady gaze.

There is something about that look I've seen before. It's like waking up from a dream and almost—but not quite—remembering what it was about.

"And one more thing." Dayne's voice startles me out of my thoughts. He motions toward the outline of Wokee's body curled around Vlaz. "We both know Wokee wouldn't survive the journey. That boy adores you and will do as you ask. You must tell him to stay here. If I could make you stay, too, I would."

I watch the peaceful rise and fall of Wokee's chest. Dayne is right. "I'll talk to him tomorrow."

Dayne rests his hand on my shoulder. "Keep yourself safe until I return. And don't let anyone find out about you." He looks into my eyes. "Many fear what they don't understand. Keep your hood drawn up, and with any luck, no one ever needs to know."

I nod.

"Good. Now get some rest."

I climb into my bed, thinking of nothing except the delicious coolness of the sheets. Dayne's face is illuminated by the single candle as he sits on the edge of his bed, deep in thought. I close my eyes.

CHAPTER 22

T ime to get started, Hemera," Wade chirps.

I lift my head from the pillow. At some point during the high day, Vlaz left Wokee's bed and is now sprawled out across my feet, his tiny wings rising and falling with each breath. Dayne and Wokee are asleep.

I groan as I rouse myself from bed. Remembering Dayne's warning, I pull on my cloak and draw up the hood. I throw an envious look at my sleeping companions before following Wade up the thousand steps I've come to loathe. We go through the waterfalls and stone tunnels, and finally reach the dense trees outside the fortress. Wade keeps up a mostly one-sided discussion about Sal and the other Solguards the entire way.

I'm not really listening; my conversation with Dayne rests heavy on my shoulders. I need to tell Wade that Dayne isn't coming, but not yet. Maybe when he sees I can fight, he'll convince the others to let me join the company anyway. I need the help of Sal's army if I'm going to rescue Brice.

Ever since Wade mentioned the rumors of a Dusker at Tanguro, an unsettled feeling has been growing inside me. If the Duskers have found a way to control the Halves, is it possible they sent the beasts to look for me? Is it because they know what I am? Could that be the reason one of them was carrying Brice's drawing of me…because it was searching for me?

After more than an hour of steady walking, we duck under a wall of overgrown tree branches into a large clearing. Wade scoops away the dirt piled up at the base of a tree to produce swords, knives, and a bow and arrows from a hole in the ground.

He shakes off the dirt before handing me a set of padded armor, gesturing to me to put them on. "We don't want any injuries," Wade explains.

I notice he doesn't take any of the padding for himself.

Wade picks up one of the swords and nods for me to take the other. I grasp the hilt and anchor my stance. Between the padding and my cloak, I feel about as mobile as a tree trunk.

With a flick of his arm, Wade moves to knock the sword from my hand. I twist my body to the side to block him.

Being the Captain's daughter was not without its perks. Even though I was never gifted with any weapon except for the sling—my feet were too clumsy to truly master hand-to-hand combat, and I could never make my arrows fly true—my father made sure I was at least competent with all of the weapons in the smithy.

The blades clank against each other as I block another strike. Wade moves back, circling me. Inwardly, I groan. As long as my feet stay planted on the ground, I'm as good a fighter as any. But as soon as my stupid feet need to move….

I hop to the side, but Wade knocks me off balance. My legs get in their own way. I feel myself beginning to fall.

"Widen your stance," Wade says.

I do what he says and manage to keep from tumbling into a heap of useless limbs.

"Better." He jabs at my padded chest. "Now, anticipate my next move."

I narrow my focus and sense the moment his weight shifts. I flick the edge of my sword, which sends his weapon flying from his hands.

"You didn't tell me how fast you were," Wade gasps.

"Beginner's luck?" I shrug, turning away so he won't try to look me in the eye.

Wade shakes his head. "I've never seen anyone move so fast, and I've trained with the best Solguards in the fortress."

I laugh. "Don't be ridiculous."

"Did Dayne train you how to fight like that?"

"Yes," I lie, relieved to have an excuse.

A branch snaps somewhere in the brush. We both stand still.

When the squinty man steps underneath the branches into the clearing, Wade's posture relaxes.

"I heard you a mile back," the man growls.

"Sorry, Gorgoran," Wade shrugs. "Gotta train."

Gorgoran glares at me. There is an uneasy feeling in the pit of my stomach as I draw the hood of my cloak tighter around my face.

"So, you're going to make a soldier out of this one."

Before either Wade or I can reply, Gorgoran produces a long, curved dagger from a sheath on his back. He runs his pink tongue over his fleshy lips.

"Let's see what you've learned today." He gestures at me with his blade.

"Gorgoran—" Wade starts.

But before he can say anything more, Gorgoran lunges at me. I roll to the ground to avoid his blade. Wade shouts something, but all of my attention is focused on my attacker. When he comes at me again, I grab one of the swords on the ground to knock his dagger from his hand.

Gorgoran snarls. He throws his entire body at me, fingers grasping for my throat like claws.

I don't have time to move out of the way before he's on me. Dropping the sword, I shove him away from me.

Gorgoran sails backward through the clearing at least ten paces until he slams into a tree's midsection. His body crumples to the ground.

Wade gapes at me.

"How did you—"

"I didn't mean to push him so hard." My head throbs as I hurry forward.

I didn't kill him, did I?

Wade shakes his head. "You didn't push him. You *flew* him." Wade waves his hands through the air to demonstrate.

We both approach the body.

Wade kneels in front of Gorgoran. "Just knocked out," he reports.

I sag with relief. The man's body is twisted in a way that will cause him pain when he wakes, but Wade does nothing to untangle him.

"I had no idea he was going to try to hurt you. Are you alright? I mean, of course you're alright. Look at what you did to him!"

"What should we do with him?" My voice hitches.

"Leave him. He'll wake up eventually. But Hemera, how did you do that? He's twice your size."

I occupy myself with collecting the weapons so I don't have to respond.

"You know something? I bet even Dayne Clarion couldn't have done that."

I snort in reply, but Wade's face is serious. "I mean it. You're...more than you seem." He cocks his head, giving me a quizzical look.

I keep my face angled downward so he can't see my eyes.

"Come on." I go back to piling the weapons back in the hole. "Don't we need to be heading back?"

CHAPTER 23

I s that the best you've got?" Wade pants. "I thought yesterday you might stand a chance against me."

Wade keeps up a constant stream of chatter as we fight, telling me where to put my feet and how to move without landing in a heap. With the memory of what I did to Gorgoran fresh in my mind, I let Wade pin me to the ground with his sword pointed at my chest.

He whoops. "And that, my dear Hemera, is how it's done."

Maybe I don't need to be too *easy on him.*

I twist around and grab his ankle. Yanking him to the ground, we roll over the hard stones as we wrestle for the sword. I hold back my strength, but even so, Wade can barely keep up with me. His face shines with sweat.

"I've never lost a practice fight," Wade grunts between labored breaths, "and you're crazy if you think I'll go easy on you just because you're Jadem's niece."

I let Wade pry the sword from my grasp as he uses his body to keep me on the ground. He gives me an insufferable, victorious grin. I let him keep me pinned. I let him think he's stronger.

"Dayne says he won't come," I blurt out.

As soon as the words have left me, I'm filled with dread. I turn my face away before he notices my black eyes.

Wade sits up and studies me.

"Given the way you fight," he says, "we'd be lucky to have you, but some of them—" he shrugs his shoulders.

"Don't trust me," I finish.

Wade nods.

"I have something I could give the company in exchange for bringing me with you." Reaching inside my cloak, I take out Brice's map.

"It has all the travel caves marked." I point to the black spots dotted along the scroll. "It will save you time trying to find a cave every high day."

Wade's face brightens as he takes the map from me. I hold onto it for a second longer than I should. Sharing Brice's map feels like sharing a part of him.

Wade doesn't seem to notice my reluctance. "This is brilliant! We still hadn't worked out where we would sleep during high day. Now they'll have to let you come."

I sink to the ground as though a tremendous weight has been lifted from me.

"You really want to be part of the company, don't you?" Wade raises his eyebrows at me.

"Well I won't be able to get past thousands of Halves on my own," I reply.

"And then what?" Wade asks. "What's your plan for after you rescue what's-his-face?"

Wade's question makes me pause. Before I came to Jadem's fortress, all I wanted was to rescue Brice and get revenge for my parents' deaths. But meeting Jadem and Wade and hearing their stories…learning that so much of what the Duskers made me believe is a lie….

My eyes find the place on Wade's gloved hand where I know the sun marking to be. I think about the mission Sal is leading, to free the prisoners at Tanguro and gain an army. What would it be like if the Subterranes were freed from the Duskers?

"You know," Wade moves closer to me. I can almost feel the warmth of his skin as his hand brushes against my cloak. "You could take your hood off every once in a while."

He reaches down to pull back my hood.

"Don't!" I jump to my feet.

"I'm sorry, I didn't mean—" Wade looks away from me, but not before I see the hurt in his golden eyes.

"No, it's fine. I just…can't let anyone see."

Wade turns back to me. "There are lots of people here with Dusker scars, if that's what you're worried about. Your aunt, for one…."

"It's not that." I pull on my hood, drawing it more tightly about my face.

"Listen, we're all here because we've lost something. Some of us have lost everything…." He trails off.

"What have you lost?"

Wade pauses for so long I think he isn't going to answer at all.

Finally, he says, "I lost my entire family because I killed my father."

He must take my silence for shock, because he adds, "It was an accident."

"I'm sorry," I say, not knowing what the appropriate response is in this situation. "What happened?" And then, realizing that was probably the wrong question, add, "You don't have to tell me if you don't want to."

"It's not like it's a big secret around here." There's a scratchiness in his voice that wasn't there before. Wade clears his throat. "The Duskers found out my brother was a Solguard. They were going to take him to Malarusk and torture him for information about Solis' location, but our mother found him a place to hide."

Wade rubs his eyes. I look away until he continues.

"My father was one of the Captain's guards. When the Duskers came and no one could find my brother, my father went looking for him." Wade's carefully-schooled features melt away, leaving behind a mountain of pain and regret I understand too well.

"He found my brother and was going to tell the Duskers." Wade stares hard at the ground. "I tried to convince him not to. Begged him. But my father believed in the Duskers' lies. We fought. I didn't mean to hit him that hard." Wade pauses to clear his throat again. "When he fell, his head hit a rock. I never wanted to kill him—"

My throat is so tight I can't breathe.

When Wade speaks again, his voice is steadier.

"The Duskers found my brother and arrested him. When my mother tried to stop them, they took her, too. It all happened while I was fighting with my father." Wade swallows hard. "I didn't even know they'd been taken until it was too late."

"What happened to them?" I ask in a whisper.

Wade picks at a plant, not looking at me. "They were both executed."

He works his fingers around the roots and snaps them away from the ground. The look in Wade's eyes makes my chest ache.

"Am I talking too much?" Wade asks. "I have a tendency to do that." He gives me a weak smile.

"Not at all." I bite my lip, trying to reach a decision. After a brief pause, I say, "I know how it feels to have a terrible secret."

We're standing in the shade of an overgrown tree. Not even a sliver of sunlight peeks through the canopy of leaves. Before I can think better of it, I pull back my hood so my eyes are no longer covered in shadow.

Wade looks at me. His mouth forms into a perfect O of surprise.

"They're like the Halves," he says, leaning away from me.

What was I thinking? I yank my hood back up. *How could I do something so stupid?*

"No, I didn't mean it like that." Wade reaches up with a tentative hand to pull my hood back. The look on his face keeps me from pushing his arm away. "I mean they are like the Halves, but not really."

Wade moves closer. With a finger, he raises my chin so my black eyes meet his golden ones. Where I expect to see disgust and fear there is only curiosity.

"How'd it happen?" he asks.

I force myself to hold Wade's gaze as I tell him.

Wade doesn't say anything until I've finished. I hold my breath as I wait for his response.

"That's why you're such a good fighter," Wade says. "You have their speed and strength."

I nod.

"Except even the Halves couldn't do the things I've seen you do. It's like you're stronger, faster somehow, for being both Halve and human."

I don't know what to say.

"You shouldn't be ashamed." Wade smiles at me. "It's actually kind of awesome."

"You mean you're not terrified of me?"

Wade scoffs. "I don't scare easily."

"You can't tell anyone," I warn.

"I can keep a secret." He winks at me, and I can't help but return his smile.

"Hey," he says, like he's just realized something. "You weren't holding back when we were fighting just now, were you?"

When I don't respond right away, Wade continues, "You didn't *let* me win, did you?"

The devilish grin I give him is all the reply he needs.

CHAPTER 24

I rub my eyes, groggy with sleep. "What time is it?"

"An hour into low day."

I push myself up against the headboard. Dayne and Wokee are gone, their beds a mess of pillows and crumpled blankets. Wade is standing over me.

"What's going on?" I yawn as I stretch out my arms.

"Get up. One of the scouts reported there's a band of Halves headed this way."

"*Halves?*"

I throw myself out of bed, falling in my haste.

The entrance to the cave fortress is crowded by the time we join the other Solguards. Some I recognize from the secret meeting by the old well. Voices shout orders from every direction. There's a constant ringing as swords are drawn from scabbards. My pulse quickens.

A guard hands me a sword from a pile at the top of the stairs. The sword is lighter than the one I've been practicing with and fits snugly in my palm.

I draw the hood of my cloak farther over my face and follow the others toward the stone archway separating the fortress from the Outside. As I take my sling from my belt and place a stone in the leather pouch, a hand closes around my arm.

My aunt stands behind me. Her eye is narrowed on the sword in my hand.

"Come with me, Hemera." She turns around, her boots clipping against the stone floor.

I follow her, glancing back at the activity in the tunnel, until she veers off onto an empty path. She turns to look at me. Her balled fists rest on her wide hips.

"Hemera, I appreciate that you want to help defend the fortress, but I can't allow it. You're too precious to me."

My eyes dart to where soldiers are filing out to meet the Halves.

"They killed her." I'm shaking with rage. "The Halves killed my mother, your sister! I have as much right as any to kill them."

"Let me tell you something, Hemera." Jadem rubs a hand over her one good eye, her exhaustion plain. "It was around the time your parents married that I turned all of my attention on the Solguard cause. I believed in it. I was willing to give up the possibility of love, a family, life as a Dweller…." She trails off, lost in her own thoughts. When she sees me staring at her, she continues, "I underestimated the Duskers' power, and in doing so, paid too great a price." The sorrow of whatever happened in Malarusk lurks behind the scars across her face. "I learned then that we lack the strength and numbers to take on the Duskers and the Halves. The most we can hope for is to stay hidden."

"That's not enough." My words come out strong, almost fierce.

"I can't lose you now that I've found you," my aunt pleads.

"I didn't even know you existed! You abandoned us, and now my mother is dead. I don't owe you anything!"

I know my words are unfair, but right now, I don't care.

"Mer," Jadem's voice cracks. "Please."

I don't look at my aunt's face as I turn back toward the tunnel. Jadem calls after me but doesn't follow.

The heat of my anger pulses through me as I step out into the sea of soldiers. The air hums with shouting voices. The entrance to the fortress is ringed with archers. Ry, a bow in her hand, is barking out orders.

I step between two men I've never seen before, both of whom grip a sword in one hand and a dagger in the other. When I stoop to pick up a stone for my sling, a movement in the trees to the west catches my eye.

"Halves, in the trees!"

It takes the others milliseconds to notice what I've seen. There's a roar of voices as others rush to meet the enemy. I wind my sling as I run. A hideous cry erupts from the Halve as my stone lands its mark. I take down three more with my sling before they're upon me.

I duck out of the way moments before a club smashes into the ground beside me.

Too close, Hemera.

Someone jumps in front of me. With a single, clean stroke, the Halve's head separates from its body. I only have a moment to see it's my aunt before she's already moving on to cleave another Halve.

There are dozens of them. The Halves dwarf even the largest Solguards among us. As their beady, black eyes come into focus, I forget the complicated footwork Wade taught me and hack at everything in my path.

I tug my sword from a Halve's tough hide and stand mesmerized as the thick, brown blood drains from its body. A familiar voice cries out, snapping me back into focus.

I spin around at the sound of Wade's voice. He's trying to pull his sword from a dead Halve with one hand while using his other to keep the corpse from crushing him. Another Halve is running toward Wade with a sharpened tree trunk grasped in its fist.

I jump over sprawled bodies and duck underneath clubs that smash into the ground behind me. Kicking and punching, I fight my way toward Wade, who is still wrestling with the corpse as its dead weight presses against him. The other Halve is upon him.

The Halve throws its wooden spear.

"No!"

I dive toward them, catching the spear in my shoulder just before it pierces Wade's neck. Pain rips through me.

Dark spots blink at the corner of my vision. A club comes swinging at my face. Letting out a wild cry, I lift my sword and drive it into the belly of the Halve.

Thick blood spurts around the hilt of my sword.

Someone is screaming my name. There's another flash of pain through my shoulder, and then darkness.

CHAPTER 25

Make way! She's injured!"

Voices surround me, but I can't see anyone. It's dark in here. Too dark. The air smells like blood.

"Tie her down. She's lost too much blood."

Where am I?

"It needs to come out. Hold her down."

"She won't survive—"

Bright, white light.

Something is crushing me. I can't breathe. And then, mercifully, darkness.

The low murmurs are the first sign I'm still alive. *I know these voices.* My shoulder feels like it will split apart from the rest of my body.

I open my eyes against candlelight that makes my head throb.

"Have I lost my arm?"

"You still have both your arms. Lie still, my dear niece."

"Jadem?"

I try to sit up, but daggers of pain shoot through my arm.

The memory of the battle comes into focus. "Wade, where's Wade?"

"I'm here. You saved my life, Hemera." Wade sounds far away. "Dayne is here too; we're all here."

Nausea surges into my throat when I try to move my arm. I blink against the soft light that makes my head feel like it will split open.

I'm lying on a bed covered in clean linens. Dried herbs and medicine bottles line the stone shelves built into the wall. Jadem, Dayne, and Wade hover at my bedside.

Something seems out of place. Ignoring the shooting pains and the pleas to lie still, I raise my head.

"Where are the healers? Where are the others who were injured?"

Jadem and Dayne exchange a look.

"What? What aren't you telling me?"

But one look at my aunt's face, and I already know. Panic churns with the nausea in my stomach. I swallow the bile that gathers in the back of my throat.

Finally, Jadem speaks. "When you were first brought here, my healer thought you were not going to…." her voice cracks.

"She tried to bandage you." Dayne picks up the story in his steady voice. "But your blood touched her skin."

My heart is in my throat. I know what he's going to say before the words are spoken.

"She's dead, Hemera. When your blood touched her skin, it was the same as if she had been poisoned by Halve blood."

A healer is dead because of me.

I feel tears gathering in my eyes. Destinel was training to be a healer. If Destinel wasn't already dead, cut down by Halves, she could have been the one I killed.

My face is burning up. And then I'm surrounded by a sinking cold. I begin to shake.

The Dwellers were right all along. I am one of them.

"It's not your fault." Dayne's voice is stern as he reads my thoughts.

"I need to leave. Now, before anyone else gets hurt." I sit up, sucking in my breath against the pain.

"No one need fear you so long as they don't touch your blood," Jadem says as she presses me back down onto the bed.

"If I had told people, your healer would still be alive," I say.

"You didn't want to be treated like an enemy." Jadem shakes her head. "No one can blame you for that."

But it's my fault.

"There's something else you should know." Jadem and Dayne exchange a look. "You would have bled to death, but the wound closed itself almost as soon as the spear was pulled from it. I wouldn't have believed it if I hadn't seen it with my own eyes."

Just like after my lashing in the Subterrane, when the cuts on my back disappeared before the end of the high day....

It's that part of me—that non-human part—that is the reason for my healing.

"I'm a freak."

I give in to the pain in my shoulder and sink back onto the pillow.

"You're not a freak, Mer. You're a *gift*," Jadem bends over me.

I swallow. "I'm not human or Halve. I don't belong anywhere."

"If you were wholly either, you would be dead," Jadem says. "You are more than the sum of your parts."

I look at Dayne and Wade, who are both nodding in agreement.

"I'd guess that if you are protected from the poison of the Halves' blood, then you might also be immune to the sun's rays." Jadem searches my face. "Am I right?"

I glance at Dayne, but there is no hint of surprise on his face. He must have guessed as much already.

"This is unbelievable," Wade says, no longer able to stay quiet. "Think of what an advantage that could be—" He falls silent again at a look from Jadem.

My aunt turns back to me. "You have taken the best from both Halves and humans, making you better than either could ever be. You are indeed more than the sum of your parts."

Dayne pulls the blanket up around me and then steps back. "Sleep now, Hemera."

✳ ✳ ✳

I cradle my arm as I position myself at the top of the glide. It's been one day since the battle, but my shoulder is almost healed. Jadem's words still echo in my ears as I pull the lever and push off.

You are more than the sum of your parts.

The air whistles in my ear as I fly down the glide. The hood of my cloak whips back as my hair fans out behind me. I fall faster and faster.

When I soar out the bottom, I land without stumbling for the first time. A smile tugs at the corner of my lips.

As I near the dining cave, the lightness I felt from the glide is replaced by a crushing weight. No matter what Dayne and Jadem say, it's my fault the healer is dead.

The gentle notes of two voices singing in harmony reach around the corner of the tunnel and keep me from turning back toward the stairs. The song is mournful and makes my heart ache. I stand transfixed until the song's ending is met with subdued applause.

I duck around the waterfall and step into the dining cave. The air is warm and smells like food and flowers. I take a step toward my usual table, and then stop.

The hall has gone silent. A few people nudge each other and point at me. Everyone is staring through eyes filled with fear and hatred and distrust.

Gorgoran, leaning against the wall with arms folded across his chest, chuckles. "Little monster girl."

My cheeks are on fire. I lower my black eyes to the ground, tugging my hood up, willing myself to disappear into the depths of my cloak. A longing for Brice, so intense it steals my breath away, crushes me under its weight.

I turn to flee, but as I should have expected, my own body betrays me. I trip over my own miserable boot laces.

Some part of me registers the humiliating squeal of my body sliding across the stone floor before it comes to rest. I don't even feel any pain, even though my bare elbows hit the ground first.

I can't move. I beg the ground to swallow me up.

"Hemera, there you are!"

Wokee is running toward me, heedless of the dark stares that follow him. A flutter of black feathers extends beside him as Vlaz trots in his wake.

The sight of them is enough to make my eyes fill with tears.

"I've been looking all over for you," Wokee announces when he gets to my side. His voice is too loud in the silent hall.

He hauls me to my feet.

"Dayne said we could have dinner in our sleeping cave. It's meat stew tonight." Wokee links his arm through mine and steers me away from the glares pressing into our backs.

CHAPTER 26

Dayne is waiting for us in our sleeping cave. He gives me a sympathetic look as we come through the narrow opening. The room is lit with soft candlelight. There is a wooden table set in the middle of the room laden with bread, fruit, and a tureen of stew.

"You okay?" Dayne asks as we settle ourselves around the table.

I nod, swelling with emotion.

"It's not your fault," he says, putting a hand on my shoulder.

I don't trust my voice enough to reply.

"Jadem gave me a tour of her orchards," Wokee announces, oblivious to the somber mood. "Did you know she figured out how to grow plants underground, in the caves?"

When neither Dayne nor I say anything, Wokee keeps talking. "Not just any plants either, but trees." He pauses long enough to splash stew into his bowl. "I didn't even know that was possible, but she told me all about how she does it." Pride is written all over his face. "She said I have a quick mind."

"That so," Dayne says without much enthusiasm.

I watch Wokee as he wipes a puddle of broth from the table with his shirt sleeve. In the last several days, his bony shoulders and knobby knees have filled out. His hair, no less unruly than when we first found him, has taken on a golden shine. His cheeks glow with energy.

Vlaz splits his time between rubbing his soft wings against my hand and waiting beside Wokee for crumbs to fall his way.

As soon as Wokee pauses in his explanation of Jadem's orchards, Dayne gives me a nod. I clear my throat.

"Wokee, I'm leaving for Tanguro with Wade and some of the others. It's a secret, so Jadem can't find out."

Guilt tightens my stomach. I hadn't thought about how going on this mission would mean betraying my aunt. I look down into my still-full bowl of stew, no longer hungry.

"I know," Wokee says. "I knew something was happening when you kept going out to train with Wade. Dayne said you were in love and had to go rescue someone."

He wrinkles his nose at the mention of love. Dayne's lips quirk into a smile.

"I could come, you know," Wokee looks at me.

"No!" Dayne and I both answer at the same time.

Wokee's face falls, so I add, "I thought Jadem was going to teach you all about tending the orchards."

"Yeah, but—"

"Growing the fruit is the most important job in the fortress," Dayne says.

"Really?" Wokee's eyes widen.

Dayne shrugs. "I wouldn't want to see a hungry Solguard." He gives Wokee a meaningful stare. "Would you?"

Wokee thinks about it. "No, I definitely wouldn't. That'd be really scary."

I duck my head to hide a smile.

"You'll come back?" Wokee's eyes are big and pleading.

"I will," I tell him.

Wokee sniffs. "Promise?"

"Promise." *As soon as I've rescued Brice and killed those murdering, monstrous—*

"Oh! I almost forgot." Wokee jumps up from his chair, sending a glob of stew flying out of his bowl. Vlaz is ready and catches it in mid-air.

Wokee rummages underneath his bed and pulls out a wrapped brown parcel.

"For you," he gives the package to me.

Wokee watches as I untie the coarse brown strings. When I pull away the wrapping, blue silk spills out like water. I run my hand over the material.

It is like nothing I've ever felt before, smoother than the petals on Jadem's white flowers and softer than the hunters' most prized furs.

"It's a new cloak for you," Wokee says. "You know, since you don't need to wear your heavy one anymore. I can't believe you really can't get the Burn."

I stare at Wokee, unable to speak.

"I found the berries that make the color," Wokee points to the silk. "Mama taught me to boil them down into dye."

"It's beautiful," I breathe.

Wokee's smile stretches across his entire face. "The silk is lighter and will keep you cool. And the threads are covered in a paste Jadem makes that will keep the whole thing from frying in the sun."

I let my fingers run over the silk. It's soft and light and unlike any clothes I've ever worn.

"Blue was Wodell's favorite color," Wokee says. "He always said if freedom had a color, it would be blue. I told Jadem we should dye everyone's cloaks this color."

I can't take my eyes off the cloak.

"Well go on," Dayne says. "The Solguards know what you are now, so there's no point in wearing a heavy cloak you don't need."

"Jadem helped me make it, but I did the most important parts," Wokee announces as I put on the delicate garment.

Unlike my other cloak, which hangs on each side of me like a tent, this one clings to the curves of my body. When I walk, the material flows in elegant ripples.

"You look good in blue," Wokee says.

I hug Wokee for a long time, fighting down the lump in my throat.

"Okay, okay, you're squeezing me too tight!" Wokee slides out from my grasp, which turns my sniffle into a laugh.

"Good boy," Dayne nods at Wokee. He honks his nose into a handkerchief.

"You'll need to take Vlaz with you." Wokee looks at the cub, who is fluttering his wings in an effort to reach a piece of meat dangling from the edge of Wokee's bowl.

Vlaz, too, has changed. He's at least twice as big as he was when we first found him. His wings are sprouting new feathers, and there is the outline of muscles around his neck and shoulders. Still, he's too small to be of any use to the company of Solguards. He'll only get hurt or worse.

I turn back to Wokee. "I need you to keep him safe with you here. Can you do that for me?"

"I will, I promise!" Wokee wraps his arms around my waist.

Dayne stands up to blow out the candles. "Alright you two, it's off to bed."

❋ ❋ ❋

"Hemera," a voice hisses. I open one eye. Wade is kneeling at the side of my bed.

"What's...."

"Plan's changed," he whispers.

"What happened?" I'm already out of bed and pulling clothes over my sleeping gown.

"Jadem knows. Someone must have talked, or she overheard something. We leave at the beginning of low day."

"*This* low day?!"

"Shh! Get your things. I have weapons and supplies already packed for you."

"But everyone knows I'm—" I swallow, unable to finish.

Unnatural. Not like them. A Bisecter.

"After what you did for me, Sal insisted you come. I gave him your map, too, so no one else will make any trouble. Even without Dayne, we need you."

I don't argue. My mind buzzes with anticipation. *We're going to Tanguro.*

I pull the sky-blue silk cloak over my head. It is weightless compared to the cloak I'm so used to wearing.

Wade tries to help me pull my injured arm through the sleeve, but I wave him away. The wound that should have killed me is now little more than a scratch.

164

"We meet at the old well an hour after low day begins. Do you remember how to get there?"

I nod.

"Good. I'll meet you there."

He's gone before I can reply.

My hands tremble as I rush around the cave to collect my sling and the pack I carried all the way from the Subterrane. *We are going to free the prisoners. Brice.*

"You didn't plan to leave without saying goodbye, did you?"

Dayne sits on the edge of his bed, his lute beside him, watching me.

I put down my armful of supplies and go over to him.

"Are you sure you won't come?" I look at Dayne.

He shakes his head. "There is something else I must do."

My throat tightens. "So, this is goodbye?"

He holds out a hand. "For now."

I throw my arms around him. When we pull away, I blink back tears.

Dayne points to a bundle in the corner. "I packed a few extra supplies for you."

"Thank you," I whisper.

I tuck my sling into my belt beneath my cloak and strap Brice's dagger to the leather cord around my thigh. I hoist both packs over my shoulder.

When I'm ready, I tiptoe over to Wokee's bed, where Vlaz is snuggled against the boy's side. I scratch the cub's large, flopped ear as he nuzzles my hand. I bend down and kiss the top of Wokee's soft hair. His snoring stops for a moment, but he doesn't wake.

Dayne looks at me. "Don't be afraid of what you are. Jadem was right, you are a gift."

He gestures with his hands as though there's more he wants to say but can't find the words.

I look back as I step through the cave's archway. "Take care of yourself, Dayne."

"And you, Hemera."

✳ ✳ ✳

When we reach the clearing, there is a small group of soldiers clustered around the old well.

I look around. *Where is everyone?*

I make my way over to Wade and Sal, who are giving instructions to the scouts. Out of habit, I try to pull up my hood, but the silk is too fluid to conceal anything. I stand off to the side hoping no one will notice my blue cloak and black eyes.

Wade notices my presence and shoulders his way to me.

"What's going on?" I ask.

"Er, nothing," Wade rakes a hand through his hair. When he doesn't say anything else, I grow even more suspicious.

"Tell me."

Wade sighs. "News of…you know…spread." His gaze flicks to my shoulder. "Some of the soldiers were afraid you might do something to them." He rolls his eyes.

"So, they're not coming? Because of me?"

My voice is shrill, and some of the others stop what they're doing to eye me suspiciously.

"Their nonsense is not your problem," Sal says, joining us. "Everyone knows Gwendil's death was an accident."

Gwendil, the healer who is dead. Because of me.

Sal puts a hand on my shoulder. "You saved Wade's life, and for that I will be forever in your debt."

There is a brief pause while Sal exchanges a look with Wade.

He continues, "And your map will save us days of wandering around in search of caves."

"How many are staying behind?" I look from Sal to Wade.

"We lost about twenty," Sal admits. "But with your abilities and the map, you're worth at least that many, so by my estimations, we have lost little." He gives me a tired smile.

"Forget it, Hemera," Wade says. "You're coming with us."

Sal steps into the center of the clearing. He clears his throat, and the murmurs die down.

"Today has come sooner than we expected, but we're ready. Never in my life have I met worthier soldiers. Our strength won't be diminished by the loss of a few."

All eyes in the clearing turn to me. My cheeks flush, but I keep my gaze fixed on Sal.

Sal peers at each member of the company. "Let us remember who our enemy is. Let us take strength from each other."

The Solguards in the clearing fist their right hand over their hearts. I imitate them. Even though they all wear gloves, I'm conscious I am probably the only one without the blazing sun tattoo.

"Go in—" I begin out of habit, expecting choruses of "Go in darkness" to surround me, but Wade elbows me hard. I duck my head at the menacing stares that turn toward me.

Sal brings everyone's attention back with a few more encouraging words. Then, orders are given and supply packs are slung over shoulders. In a matter of minutes, we're putting Solis behind us.

Energy surges through me. *I'm coming, Brice.*

The ground slopes downhill toward a valley as we walk. Everyone is silent, tense. I keep my eyes moving for any sign of Halves.

"My brother stayed behind because of you," a ruggedly handsome man I've never seen before hisses as he brushes past me. "Gwendil saved my brother's life."

And I killed her.

"She was covered in those welts from your blood," the man continues. "She died in agony."

Others marching nearby nod in agreement.

I remember the Dweller man who was poisoned by Halve blood. I remember the way his skin hissed and dissolved before my eyes.

"Shut your mouth, Jarosh," Wade says.

"Yeah, ignore him." Ry moves as silent and graceful as a stag along the outskirts of our company, bow in hand. "Jarosh has a very pretty, very empty head. I'm grateful for all you did during the battle, especially for Wade."

Jarosh glares, but falls back into the line of soldiers, like he isn't willing to challenge Ry.

She watches his retreat, and then tucks her bow under her arm to stretch out her gloved hand to me. "I'm Rylin, by the way. But most people just call me Ry."

I give her a hesitant smile, hoping it conveys the overwhelming gratitude I feel toward her.

We trudge on, each lost in our own thoughts. It's not until the hairs on the back of my neck prickle that I know someone is watching me.

I load my sling and have it winding in a second before I see the thickset figure of Gorgoran appear from behind a tree. He gives me a twisted smile as he falls into step beside me.

"Monsssster girl." He hisses it like a snake.

When I pick up my pace to put more soldiers between us, I hear his menacing laugh behind me. I wish he was one of the ones who stayed behind when he learned what I am.

CHAPTER 27

Sal keeps Brice's map in his hands and looks at it every so often, muttering to himself. A part of me hates that I gave up this piece of Brice, even though it was necessary to join the company. At least I still have Brice's drawing, but even that feels like it's no longer my own. The thought of it gripped in that dead Halve's claws is almost unbearable.

The land is becoming rockier. Somehow, the air here feels even hotter. By the time the sun falls to lowest day, my silk cloak clings to my sweaty skin. I crane my neck to catch the smallest of breezes against my cheek. Before it disappears, I strip off my cloak and let the air pass through my sodden clothes beneath.

Like Dayne said, there's no longer any point in trying to hide what I am now that everyone knows.

"Jadem was right." Wade looks at me in disbelief. "That's incredible."

I feel heat rise to my face. I glance at Wade and see his face is full of genuine awe. It makes me feel like maybe my differences aren't all bad.

And then I notice the others, who are staring at me with a combination of resentment and disgust. I keep walking, forcing myself to look straight ahead rather than meet their accusing stares.

By now, Jadem knows we're gone. What did my aunt think when she found out I went with them? I grind a stone into dust beneath my foot.

Even though I've only just met her, the thought of disappointing the leader of the Solguards is almost unbearable. She's the only family I have left, and I just abandoned her.

Just like I abandoned both of my parents when they needed me.

A shudder wracks my body in spite of the heat. I huddle in my silk cloak.

What if I never see Jadem again? What if I never get the chance to hear more about my mother?

I never got a chance to ask her about her life before Solis, or about the scars on her face, or what happened to her when she was in Malarusk. I never asked her about how she created Solis and came to know so much about growing things.

My gaze comes to rest on the line of mountains far ahead. There's no time for regrets.

We stop once at a stream to refill our waterskins. While others splash water down the neck of their cloaks, I rummage through the additions Dayne made to my pack. There are two more daggers and a spare pouch filled with stones for my sling. There's also cured meat, a loaf of bread, and a few pieces of yellow fruit.

"What's that?" Wade points to Brice's drawing of me before reaching into my pack to sneak one of the fruits.

I explain how I found it in the hands of a dead Halve.

Wade wipes yellow juice from his chin. "Why would a Halve take something like that…and then keep it?"

I shrug.

"It's like it was looking for you." Ry leans on Wade's shoulders to squint at the drawing. "But I've never heard of Halves doing that."

I shudder, shoving the drawing away. Whatever reason the Halve had for taking it, it can't be good.

As the sun climbs back toward high day, Sal takes out Brice's map. He points to our position and then taps his finger on a small dot.

"Looks here like we'll reach a travel cave big enough to hold us just before high day."

"How do we know the travel cave is abandoned?" Gorgoran growls. "Could be a Dusker trap." He gives me an accusing look.

"Yeah, you expect us to follow a map she *gave* you?" the soldier called Jarosh demands.

I cross my arms. "I've used this map to find other caves and never had trouble."

*Except for Vlaz's mother….*But I decide not to mention that.

The thought immediately reminds me of my friends, and I feel a pang for them. I know it was right to leave Vlaz behind; he'll be able to keep Wokee company after Dayne leaves the fortress. Still, I miss them.

"There's always a risk," Sal replies. "I trust that sword on your belt is more than just decoration?"

Ry laughs. Jarosh scowls.

We reach the cave with minutes to spare before high day. Mercifully, it's abandoned and large enough to hold our company.

We all throw our packs down, claiming a spot. Sal lights two candles while the scouts pull the stone door over the cave's opening.

"Well done, Hemera." Ry yawns as she stretches out.

Well done, Brice.

"Go in darkness, indeed," someone murmurs, which draws laughter.

We huddle around the candles and divide our provisions. With full stomachs and twelve hours' rest ahead of us, some of the other soldiers grow friendlier.

"Is it true your Halve blood healed you from a fatal wound?" one of the Solguards asks.

I try to duck the question, but Ry insists. So I tell them about the strange circumstances of my birth.

As the others drift off to their claimed sleeping spots, I say quietly, "I'm a Bisecter." For the first time in my life, those three words fill me with strength rather than an overwhelming desire to hide.

We set out as soon as it's low day. Gorgoran marches behind me, muttering threats every time I'm near enough to hear him. I try to shut my ears to him and think about Brice, which helps a little.

My mind keeps wandering to Dayne, Wokee, and Vlaz. I miss their company, especially now that I'm surrounded by strangers. Wokee is probably working in the orchards right now, helping Jadem and discovering new plants. And Dayne—

What was his errand, and where did it take him? I had been too preoccupied with my own plans to even bother asking. Will he be in danger?

And what about my aunt? She must be furious with me for leaving. Guilt hardens into a pit in my stomach.

A low whistle comes from somewhere to the east. *The scouts' warning.* I take my sling from my belt as others unsheathe their swords.

I see their scarred hides just as the soldiers begin to shout.

CHAPTER 28

alves!" Wade yells.

I release the stone in my sling. A moment later, the Halve drops.

The other soldiers are running with their weapons raised as I let another stone fly. The sound of dying Halves surrounds me. *Good*, I think as I run toward the next one in my path. Every one of them deserves to die.

The force of my sword in the beast's belly is already in motion when I see something impossible.

There is a glint of fear in its black eyes.

A scream draws my attention away from the Halve. Jarosh, the soldier who has not missed a chance to remind me I'm a murderer, writhes on the ground. His face is spattered with drops of brown Halve blood and covered in welts.

Without thinking, I abandon my blade in the Halve's stomach and run to Jarosh. I press my bare hands to the oozing wounds on his face in a vain effort to wipe the blood away. When my fingers touch his skin, the welts sizzle and hiss. Jarosh writhes against my touch. Without knowing what I expect to happen, I press my hand more firmly against his skin. My fingertips throb as though all my blood has rushed into them.

Jarosh stops screaming.

I remove my hand as a great wave of exhaustion washes over me. *What was I thinking? Did I kill him faster?*

"Wade, Sal, someone—" I spin around in a frantic circle.

A movement from Jarosh makes me turn back. He sits up and raises his hands to his face. We both gasp.

The welts that had already begun to spread down his neck have turned to nothing more than angry red splotches on the skin's surface. My own hands are red like Jarosh's face. Something, fear or exhilaration, or perhaps both, sends a shiver through me.

Sal and Ry, who ran over at my call, stand watching with their sword arms stalled in midair.

"My dear, how did you do that?" Sal's voice is as unsteady as if he'd just seen a ghost.

"I—" I look from my hands to Jarosh. "I just touched his face and the welts disappeared."

"It's your blood!" Ry waves her sword. "You must have absorbed the poison for him. You know," she continues at the blank look everyone gives her, "like how you told us you did for your mother before you were born."

I stare, dumbfounded at her.

"Do you realize what this means?" Wade asks.

I can save people who have been poisoned by Halve blood.

The very idea of it is insane; no one can reverse the effects of Halve blood poisoning. And yet...*I just did.*

Exhilaration courses through me. I want to laugh, shout, hug someone....But then I remember something else.

Could I have saved Gwendil?

"Don't go down that road," Wade warns, reading my thoughts as accurately as though I had spoken them aloud. "You didn't know then what your blood could do, and anyway, you were unconscious when it happened."

I'm grateful to Wade, even though I don't feel like I deserve his compassion.

"No more feeling sorry for yourself," Ry announces. "You just saved someone's life!"

We all look at Jarosh, who is sitting on the ground. He looks dazed, but very much alive. He stands up and then holds out his hand to me. I take it, returning his hesitant smile.

The battle is over almost as quickly as it began. The Halves are all dead, and the scouts report there are no others lying in wait. Sal gives orders to soldiers waiting nearby. As he does so, a few of them stare at me with something that feels like awe.

I can't help but hold my head a little higher. Whatever else I've done, Ry is right; it doesn't diminish the fact that I just saved Jarosh's life. For the first time, I feel something like pride at my abilities.

Everyone is accounted for except Gorgoran, who was out scouting before the battle and hasn't returned. *I hope the Halves got him*, I think, before feeling guilty.

Sal orders the Halves to be piled up and burned so no passing Duskers will have reason to suspect we're nearby. If the rumors about a Dusker leader at Tanguro are true, we can't leave evidence of this slaughter to alert him that we're coming.

I help drag the Halves' bodies to the smoking fire, trying to avoid their still-open, black eyes. What is it about these Halves that seems different?

As I throw another body onto the fire, it comes to me. *There are no clubs or other weapons among the dead.* These Halves carried nothing with them except for the filthy cloths that cover the lower part of their bodies.

They weren't looking to attack us. We must have crossed paths with them by chance.

I think of my mother, with her beautiful face twisted in fear even in death, and my father, surrounded by a ring of Halves.

"How does it feel being on the other side?" I kick one of the corpses onto the fire.

"Hemera, are you talking to the dead Halves?" Wade pants as he and Ry heave another body onto the pile.

Low day isn't over yet, but Sal orders us to make camp in the nearest travel cave.

"Shouldn't we keep going? Taniel's warning said—"

Sal interrupts me before I can finish. "We've had enough excitement for one day, I think."

Gorgoran reappears when the work is finished and we're descending into the cave. No one else seems to notice, though, so I don't say anything.

The odor of burning flesh lingers, or perhaps it only remains in my imagination. A noisy argument breaks out as the soldiers boast about who killed the most Halves.

I climb back out of the cave. I don't want to talk about the Halves anymore or suffer Gorgoran leering at me.

As I gather up firewood, my thoughts turn to Tanguro, to Brice and the other prisoners. I kick at a rock on the ground.

"You'll get used to it, you know, all of them arguing about who has killed the most."

I spin around, nearly knocking Wade over.

"These Halves don't matter. It's the ones at Tanguro we need to figure out how to kill."

"I know," Wade says.

There's sympathy in his voice, but I'm too frustrated to give it more than a passing thought.

"While there's low day left," I throw my hands up at the sun, "we should be moving on. Every minute we delay…."

Brice would have understood my desperation. He always understood when it came to the Halves.

"I know." Wade puts down his armful of sticks and walks over to me.

I feel jittery, like I have too much energy and nothing to do with it. I should be using my strength to reach Tanguro. Instead, I'm gathering sticks for a cookfire and wasting time. I go to kick at another rock, but I lose my balance.

I curse as my feet tangle up in each other. I close my eyes, waiting for the impact as my backside hits the ground. All I feel are warm arms encircling me.

"Careful," Wade breathes as he sets me on my feet. "How would I explain it to everyone if our most valuable weapon injured herself?"

Most valuable weapon?

I'm about to reply, but I realize Wade's arms are still around me.

"Thanks," I say. "I'm good."

"Wade!"

Sal's voice makes us both jump.

"Come on boy, I need you scouting before high day comes. And you, Hemera, let's hurry up with that firewood."

For once, Wade doesn't offer a witty remark or joke. I look at him, but he's already walking away from me. I bend down to pick up the firewood I dropped and wait for the thudding of my heart to slow.

Anger—at Wade or myself, I'm not sure—wars with confusion inside me.

What just happened?

❋ ❋ ❋

After we've eaten, we all try to carve out a space for ourselves in the cramped, stuffy cave. The soldiers' banter turns to low murmurs. As weariness overtakes me, I'm pressed back into a memory I forgot I still had.

It was my eighth birthday, and my father decided it was time for me to learn how to hunt. He took me into the woods and showed me how to track the capy pigs that left muddy hoofprints on the rocks near the river. Their meat is stringy and tough, but they're slow-moving and make for easy targets.

When we found the herd, my father gave me a dagger and told me to kill one. I chose a capy pig rooting in the ground away from the others. I snuck up on it, but at the moment before my dagger struck, the capy sensed me. It turned to look at me and let out a terrible cry.

Its eyes had the same frightened, knowing look I saw in the Halve today.

When I open my eyes, sweat pours down my face. It's not until I sit up that the glassy eyes of the dead Halve fade.

❋ ❋ ❋

We're forced to slow our pace as the landscape changes from forest to bare rock. Every time I take my eyes off the ground, my ankle turns on a jagged stone. We have abandoned our tight formation. Everyone fans out as we pick our way over the rocks in a drunken fashion to make semi-northward progress.

The sun is relentless, and there is little shade to offer relief. When I can't stand it for another minute, I take off my cloak and tuck it into my pack so I'm wearing only my thin shirt and cotton pants. Everyone else wilts under their heavy cloaks.

"Must be nice," Jarosh mutters, but there's no malice in his words. We haven't spoken much since I saved his life, but on more than one occasion, he's hushed a soldier for trying to talk about what I did to Gwendil.

"Did you always know about everything you could do because of what you are?" Ry asks as we pick our way across a stretch of flatter land. Her curls, dark with sweat, hang limp against her face.

I laugh. "You ask more questions than anyone I've ever met."

"Tell me about it," Wade mutters, but he's grinning as Ry elbows him.

"Psh, like you're one to talk," Ry laughs. "Since all you do is talk…all the time."

"I can do a lot more than talk," Wade says, giving her a wink.

"Gross." Ry screws up her face.

Their easy friendship sends an unfamiliar twinge of jealousy through me.

"I knew I was strong and fast," I say. "I didn't put it together about the healing or that I can't get the Burn until more recently, though."

And now I can add healing people who have been poisoned by Halve blood to the list.

Ry opens her mouth to ask something else, but at that moment, a black arrow whizzes past her cheek.

There's a sound like the fluttering of hundreds of wings, and then the sunlight dims as arrows fly toward us.

"What the—"

"Run!"

CHAPTER 29

We all take off, desperate to get out of the arrows' path.

"This way," Sal calls, trying to herd our company.

I put out a hand, blocking an arrow headed for my face. The point goes straight through my hand. A cry rips through me, but I don't stop. I snap the arrow in two with my other hand as I run. With another scream, I yank it free from my flesh.

"Take cover," Sal commands.

Shouts come from every direction.

"Those rocks over there," Ry gasps. She releases her arrows as she runs, her eyes tracking movement I can't see.

Beside me, Wade stops running. I grab his arm and yank him along beside me.

"Sal," he yells, trying to break free from me.

"He'll—be—fine—" with each word, Ry lets fly an arrow.

We have outrun the worst of it, but we don't stop until we've thrown ourselves behind the giant rocks that serve as a natural barrier from the attack. Wade struggles, trying to go back out to where Sal and the archers are exposed. Jarosh and I hold him back.

"Your sword can't help them!" Jarosh yells at Wade. "You'll get yourself killed."

I'm shoved to the far edge of our shelter as the rest of our company squeeze in beside us.

"Get away from me, freak." Gorgoran, the first one to make it into the shelter, jabs me hard in the ribs. I bare my teeth at him before turning my attention back to the fighting.

"Over here!" Ry is shouting just past our hiding place. She gestures between shots. Squinting, I see movement all along the mountain's base. I hadn't noticed it before because the Duskers' gray cloaks make them almost invisible against the bare rock.

It takes three tries for my fumbling fingers to take a stone from my leather pouch, but we're packed too close together for me to wind the ropes of my sling. By the time I manage to shove my way past Gorgoran and into the open, the Duskers' arrows are spent and they've disappeared from view.

"Will they be back?"

"They're out of arrows. Those cowards won't come down and fight like men."

"Or women," Ry corrects as the others make their way out from behind the safety of the rocks.

Arrows litter the ground where we had been minutes earlier. Incredibly, there are no bodies on the ground.

Jarosh, making the same observation, lets out a whoop. "Take that ya bastards!" he shouts, kicking up a spray of dirt in the general direction of the mountain.

"They knew we'd be here," Wade says, echoing my own thoughts. "How could they have known?"

"Maybe we have a Dusker spy in our midst." Gorgoran makes a point of directing his full gaze on me.

I scowl back at him.

"They'll be back." Sal calls over his shoulder, his voice hoarse. "We need to reach the western edge of the range before high day."

He takes two drunken steps forward. His legs seem to give out beneath him, and our leader crumples to the ground.

"Sal!"

Everyone surges forward, but Wade is the first to his side.

The rest of us form a protective semi-circle around them, the archers taking up positions on our outside. Wade crouches on the ground beside our leader and raises him to a sitting position. We all suck in a collective breath at the sight of two black arrows sticking out of Sal's chest. Patches of blood make a neat circle around each of the arrows.

Oh no. Bile surges up from my stomach.

Wade is holding up Sal's head, talking to him, telling him everything will be fine. My heart aches for them both.

"Never," Wade says to whatever Sal has just whispered. Both of their faces are Dusker pale.

"Are there any healers in the company?" someone demands.

"There was only Gwendil...."

My stomach turns.

"Leave me." Sal raises his voice enough for the rest of us to hear.

"Those arrows need to come out," Jarosh says, ignoring the command.

A large bottle of brown liquid appears from someone's pack and is passed forward. Wade tilts Sal's head back and lets the liquid trickle past his lips. It makes him cough and gasp. Two men move into place on either side of our leader to hold him still. Wade places one hand on Sal's chest and wraps the other around the arrow's shaft. I stifle a gasp.

I clap a hand over my mouth to keep my own screams from mingling with Sal's. Blood leaps up and speckles Wade's face.

"I'm sorry, I'm sorry, I'm sorry," Wade chants as takes hold of the second arrow.

I don't want to look, but I can't tear my eyes away from the scene in front of me. Sal goes quiet as he collapses in a faint. The rocks beside him are spattered with blood.

A roll of tightly-wrapped cloth is passed to Wade, who rolls it around and around Sal's torso. Blood seeps through each layer of cloth.

"Maybe roll it tighter?" I venture.

"It *is* tight," Wade snaps through gritted teeth.

"We need help," another man states the obvious.

"And where do you expect that help to come from?" Ry demands.

"If we can get him to Tanguro maybe...."

"Oh yeah." Wade's voice drips with bitterness. "I'm sure the Halves keep loads of medicine on hand."

"No, but the Dusker there might," I point out, ignoring his sarcasm.

"We can't just stay here and wait for Halves or Duskers to come for us," Ry says. "We have to try." She grips her bow with both hands.

"There are hyenair in the mountains, too," someone else says. "They'll smell the blood."

The mention of hyenair makes me think of my friends back in the fortress. If Dayne was here, he'd know what to do. He'd be able to save Sal.

"He can't walk," someone gestures at Sal's crumpled form.

The look on Wade's face makes me feel sick. I have to do something.

"I can carry him," I offer.

A few of the men snort in response. Wade is the only one in the company who knows how strong I am. I look at him.

"It's too far." Jarosh covers his face with his hands, but it doesn't hide the agony in his voice. "He'll never make it."

"He'll make it." Wade leaps to his feet, his eyes molten fire.

We set to work tearing off leather straps from our packs to fashion a makeshift harness. Wade doesn't leave Sal's side for a moment. He presses a wet cloth to the older man's feverish skin, muttering soothing words to him all the while. I remember the way Wade and Sal looked at each other that first time in the clearing. Wade said Sal was more like a father to him than his real one had been. If anything happens to Sal….

Fatigue and heat exhaustion hang on the company. No one needs reminding about the urgency of our task.

When everything is ready, Wade helps Sal off the ground.

"Hemera, I should be the one—" Wade begins, but I interrupt him.

"You can walk next to us and talk to him. He'll want to be able to see you when he's awake."

It takes three men to lift Sal and strap him to the harness on my back.

When I take my first step, everyone crowds around me, convinced I will collapse under Sal's weight. When I don't falter, there are a few appreciative murmurs and a few sighs of relief. I don't wait to hear what they're saying about me as I set a course north, straight for the mountains.

Ry glances at the angle of her shadow and then at Brice's map. "We should be able to reach the next travel cave by high day." She frowns. "I think."

"We'd better," Gorgoran growls. "I'm not going to be Burn vulture food."

As the sun climbs toward high day, our company scrambles up the steep, uneven rocks. Heat from the ground scorches my feet through the soles of my boots. The others are straining under the weight of their cloaks. Their huffing and grunts as they clamber up the hillside are interrupted only by the rocks we dislodge and send rolling behind us.

Between breaths, Wade encourages Sal. Our leader rarely replies with anything more than a moan. At least I can feel the quick pulse of his heart against my back. I don't have to ask Wade if the bleeding has stopped; I try not to think about the wetness pressing through the material of my own shirt.

Hold on, Sal.

As we make our way up a slow-rising cliff, the rocks become larger and smoother. I try to jostle Sal as little as possible as I pull myself up each ledge. Some of the rocks are too high for me to climb with Sal on my back. At every ledge, we unharness Sal while I scramble onto the rock, and then reach down as the others lift Sal up to me. Our progress is agonizingly slow.

There is less than an hour before high day. Blisters from the Burn are already starting to form on some of the Solguards' faces. Their hair drips with sweat. Our last sips of water were drunk hours ago.

I glance at Wade. Despite the heat, his face is ashen. He grips Sal's limp hand as he walks beside me. My chest aches for what I know he's feeling.

Sal, who has been silent for some time, begins to moan again. "Let me down," he gasps.

Wade undoes the straps binding Sal to my back and lowers him to the ground.

I stifle a groan at the sight of our leader. His body quivers, and his face is twisted in pain.

"Sal, please. You're going to be fine," Wade begs as he kneels beside him. He uses his sleeve to wipe the sweat from Sal's brow.

Sal reaches an unsteady hand toward Wade, who clutches it and cradles it against his chest.

A lump too big to swallow is lodged in my throat.

"Leave me here," Sal demands in a raspy voice.

Wade looks up at the cliff we have partly climbed. "It's just a bit farther."

"You have a mission." His chest rises and falls, the crimson patch spreading with even that tiny movement.

"We can't do this without you," Wade pleads, his voice breaking.

"You must." Sal struggles to sit up but can't muster the strength.

I feel tears sliding down my cheeks but make no attempt to wipe them away.

"I won't leave you." Wade shifts his own body to cover the top part of Sal in shade.

A few of the soldiers who fought most ferociously against the Halves, and who didn't bat an eye at the Duskers' attack, watch with red-rimmed eyes as Wade pleads with Sal. A man has turned away, his shoulders shaking with silent sobs.

Sal's lips are tinged blue. A rattling sound comes from his labored breathing.

Do something, my inner voice screams. But there's nothing to be done.

I'm not sure if we have been here for minutes or hours. I look from Sal to the cliff's peak, which is a hard climb away. If we don't make it to the next cave on Brice's map by high day, the rest of the company will die.

Sal opens his eyes. "Wade."

He mutters something for Wade's ears alone.

With a long, ragged sigh, Sal stops shivering. His free arm, the one not clutched between Wade's hands, slumps by his side. His eyes are open and glassy.

"Sal!" Wade shakes him.

"Wade—"

"Sal, get up. We have to keep going. Get up!"

Ry tries to pull Wade away from Sal.

"No, let go of me." Wade shakes Ry off. "Sal!"

Jarosh leans close to Sal, and then in a broken, exhausted voice, announces, "He's gone."

"He isn't gone!" Wade pulls away from Ry. "Sal, get up. Please get up!"

Wade collapses to the ground. He gather's Sal's body in his arms, burying his face against him. "Please. Please."

I can't bear to watch anymore. No one speaks.

"Wade, we have to go, and we can't bring him." Ry's voice breaks. She wipes her eyes with her sleeve. She kneels beside Wade, putting a gentle hand on his shoulder.

Wade doesn't move. He lowers his head in the folds of Sal's cloak as his body is wracked with quiet sobs.

Looking down at them is almost like looking through a mirror of the past. If someone had been watching me sob over my mother's body, they would have observed the same scene. Even as my heart breaks for Wade, I know there's nothing I can say or do to ease his pain.

It's maddening.

We all look at each other, our own heartbreak and anger reflected on each other's faces.

Wade wipes his sleeve across his face and then sits back on his heels. He closes Sal's eyes before bending to kiss his forehead. As he does so, Wade slips a pendant tied on a string over Sal's neck and pulls it over his head. Before the pendant disappears beneath the nape of Wade's cloak, I see it's the spiraling sun, plated in gold.

"I can't stand the thought of animals getting to him," I hear Jarosh say to another Solguard.

I remember my own fierce need to bury my mother's body after she was killed. Somehow, it had given me the smallest measure of relief. I look around at the barren landscape. The ground is too hard to dig, and we have no tools, besides. But we could at least protect his body under a shield of rocks so the Burn vultures won't be able to defile him.

Without saying anything, I start to collect rocks. Tentatively at first, I start a pile of rocks around Sal's body. The others see what I'm doing and start to help.

In less than a quarter of an hour, Wade is placing the final stone atop our makeshift grave. Ry hands him a branch with some dried leaves—the closest any of us could find to flowers in this desolate landscape—and Wade bows his head as he places the branch on top of the pile.

When he straightens, his eyes are dry.

"Wade?" Ry asks.

For some reason, he looks at me. "The Duskers are going to pay for this."

* * *

Unlike the stories and laughter that helped pass the time before, now, we're silent. Sal's loss weighs on us all. Some of us sneak glances at Wade, who is staring straight ahead without seeing.

We all know we need to keep moving. Sal's last order was for us to continue on, to complete the mission. Still, it feels wrong to move forward when our leader is gone.

"Here." Wade thrusts something into my hands as we walk. "Sal would want you to have this back now."

I look down at Brice's map. A bloody fingerprint is smeared across the edge. I want to say something comforting to Wade, but I know from experience there's nothing I can say to make what happened any less awful.

"He really loved you," I say after a long pause.

Wade gives me a short nod and then turns his gaze toward the mountains. "He was my whole family."

"No, he wasn't." Ry moves to loop her arm through Wade's. She looks at him, unabashed, as tears continue to stream down her face. "I'm your family, too," she tells him.

Ry wraps her arms around Wade as his shoulders begin to heave. It's a private moment, and I know I should look away. But the sight of them like that makes me ache for my mother. Ry holds Wade the way my mother did every time a Dweller said something cruel to me.

Even five years later, knowing I'll never see her again leaves me with an aching heart and an emptiness that steals my breath away.

After a sleepless high day, we're back to the slow, laborious climbing.

We clamber up the steep mountainside, catching each other as rocks slip beneath our feet and send us sliding backward. Someone makes a wry joke about wishing we had the glide to get us up the mountain, but no one has the heart to laugh.

I look back to where the mound of rocks covering Sal is no longer visible. There's a flash of color as something moves behind a rock. I stop walking.

But when I blink, there's nothing. I shake my head. Lack of water is making me imagine things.

At lowest day, we reach a ledge protected from the sun by an overhanging rock wall. A stream trickles through the first bit of greenery we've seen in days. There's a spacious cave nearby, built deep into the mountainside. We all agree we won't find a better place to rest before the last steep part of the climb.

We sling our packs down on the hard ground. While the others are stripping off their cloaks, I step out to the edge of our shelter. My gaze is pulled down to the rocks below. Something is moving.

A hint of a gray cloak is visible before it disappears behind a boulder.

"Duskers!" Wade and I yell at the same time.

CHAPTER 30

The Duskers are using the tall rocks and sparse trees for cover, so it's impossible to tell their number. I pace back and forth at the edge of the summit as I wait for a target.

The glimmer of a sword shines up from behind a boulder.

"Fire at will!" Ry calls to the small group of archers surrounding her.

It takes only a few moments before all of our archers' remaining arrows are spent.

There is no sign of movement below us.

"Did we get them?" Ry peers down.

The Solguards grow restless as they pace along the summit's edge, weapons in hand.

"Scouts need to go down and report back," Jarosh says.

"*You* go down there if you're so keen," one of the scouts retorts.

"I'll go." Wade ends the argument.

"No." I grab Wade's arm. "It's too dangerous."

"What do I care."

The deadened look in Wade's eyes makes my heart clench. *I know what it's like,* I want to tell him.

Before I can stop him, Wade drops beneath the ledge of the cliff. I move to follow him, but Jarosh puts a hand on my shoulder. "Your sling will be more use to him from up here," he points out.

Knowing Jarosh is right, I kneel down to peer over the ledge. It's too steep for me to see Wade, but I can hear the loose stones crumbling away from the sheer rock wall as he descends.

Minutes go by. And then more time passes.

I start to fidget. The others guess at how many Duskers there might have been and which archer killed the most. I ignore them, my eyes fixed on the spot where Wade disappeared.

What's taking him so long?

Everyone stops talking at the sound of feet scrambling on rocks.

"Wade? Is everything okay down there?" Ry calls down.

The top of Wade's head appears. I step forward to pull him up, but as soon as I bend down, a different voice snarls, "Everyone back up."

A curved blade is pressed against Wade's neck. The hand is covered in a Dusker's gray cloak. The Dusker uses Wade as a shield against an attack from our company as they make the last of the climb up to the knoll.

Wade's expression is full of a dark fury. The Dusker's face is hidden in the shadow of his gray hood. When he speaks, his voice is muffled.

"Where is the man I am looking for? Where is my spy?"

We all look at each other uncertainly. *Spy? What is he talking about?*

And then I remember…the Duskers hiding in the mountains. They knew we'd be there, and the only way they could possibly have known was if….

"Come now," the Dusker speaks into the silence. "I come from Malarusk. If you do not reveal yourself, you will die with the rest of these fools." He points at the rocks below us. "My army waits for my signal."

I start at the feeling of steel against my neck. I look down to see a droplet of blood snake its way down to the collar of my cloak.

"Gorgoran, what the hell?!" Wade strains against the blade pressed against his own throat.

Gorgoran steps around from behind me, twisting the blade so the tip is poking the back of my neck. In his other hand, Gorgoran holds up a Dark God pendant.

"I am the one you seek." His squinty eyes dart from the Dusker to me. "You are right on time." His lip curls in a twisted smile.

"But you're a Solguard," Jarosh says.

I can't turn my head to look at him, but I can hear the betrayal in Jarosh's voice.

"Fools," Gorgoran sneers. "Did you think you could defeat the Duskers? Not even Jadem can protect you now."

"What have you done?" Wade's voice is strangled.

"You made it just so *easy* for me," Gorgoran gloats, pressing the point of his dagger deeper into my flesh. "Didn't you ever wonder how the Duskers knew where you were…always seemed to be one step ahead?

"They knew because I told them," he answers his own question, cackling. "I have also kept them informed about the goings on in Jadem's little cave fortress, for which they have paid handsomely."

"Why?" Ry yells. Spit flies from her mouth.

Gorgoran's smile widens. "They have promised me something of great value."

Gorgoran steps closer to me. He draws the point of his blade along the edge of my throat and down the front of my shirt. He leans in and flicks his pink tongue over his fleshy lips. When I wince and jerk away, he laughs.

He moves to stand in front of me as he moves his dagger lower. "How'd you like—"

Before Gorgoran can finish, the Dusker throws off his cloak and hurls his knife in a single motion.

There is a deafening shriek. Gorgoran clutches at the hilt of the curved dagger that is stuck in his neck. Droplets of blood bead up along the blade's edge.

Gorgoran takes several steps backward, teetering on the cliff's edge. He waves his hands in front of him as though trying to grasp some invisible railing. His stunned eyes pass over me once before he topples backward off the cliff.

For a moment, no one moves. It's like time is standing still.

And then we all squeeze onto the ledge to watch Gorgoran's body tumble down the sheer rock wall. He utters one more piercing cry before his body hits a boulder. A plume of thick dust rises into the air.

"I have to imagine that cleared up a mystery or two."

I recognize the voice that is no longer muffled by the Dusker's uniform. "Dayne?!"

My friend and traveling partner stares back at me. He wears a heavy cloak the same blue color as mine. The gray uniform of the Duskers lies in a heap beside him.

Dayne's graying hair is dark with sweat. The wrinkle in his forehead is more pronounced, making him look older, but he is otherwise the same as when we parted.

All thoughts of Gorgoran flee from my mind. *Dayne is here.* I feel safe in a way I haven't since we left Jadem's fortress.

I want to throw my arms around him, demand to know where he's been. I want to tell him I never want him to leave again. But already, there is a chorus of voices.

"How did you know about Gorgoran? How did you find us? Is there really an army of Duskers waiting for us?"

Dayne holds up a hand to stop the flurry of questions. "I happened on a party of Duskers." His scowl deepens the crease on his forehead. "The scout I captured told me about the Solguard spy. I did the figuring and knew it would be all of you who turned up."

"There were at least a hundred of them and dozens more archers in the mountains," Ry says. "How did you get past them?"

"I impersonated the scout I captured," Dayne says. "But by now, they'll know their scout isn't returning and they'll be after us. We need to get moving."

"Will you stay with us now?" There is undisguised hope in my voice.

The rest of the company echoes my pleas for Dayne to stay and lead us now that Sal is dead.

Dayne makes no promises, nor does he answer any of the dozens of questions that fly from all sides. Instead, he says, "We need to get moving. I wasn't lying about other Duskers being close by."

For the first time since we lost Sal, everyone in the company is in agreement.

"Did you take care of your errand?" I ask Dayne as we walk.

"To a degree," he says.

"I'm glad you're here."

Dayne stops walking and turns to look at me. When he smiles, I notice the dark circles under his eyes.

"Dayne," panic creeps into my voice at a new thought. "Gorgoran said Jadem couldn't protect the Solguards anymore."

"Indeed." His face is grim.

"Do the Duskers know…." I trail off, the horrible truth of what Gorgoran has done sinking in.

Dayne gives a short nod. "He told them everything. By now, every Dusker in Malarusk knows the location of Solis."

CHAPTER 31

Aunt Jadem…Wokee….

It's only the thought of Brice, imprisoned in Tanguro and surrounded by monsters, that keeps me from sprinting all the way back to warn them. That, and the party of Duskers not far behind us, courtesy of Gorgoran. According to Dayne, there are at least a hundred of them—and they would pick us off one by one if we tried to go back down the mountain. There is no other choice but to keep moving forward.

The pain from Sal's passing is less raw now that Dayne is here, which leaves room for new worries. My mind is torn between thinking ahead to what we'll find at Tanguro, and the danger Solis is in now that its location is exposed.

During the high day, we sit in silence, each lost in our own thoughts about those we've left behind. The travel cave is large with many alcoves, and one by one, the soldiers drift away from the fire to find a spot for themselves. Dayne takes Brice's map from me and disappears, muttering about needing to plan our route without unsolicited advice. Soon, Wade, Ry, and I are the only ones still sitting by the fire.

"They'll be okay," Ry says. "Jadem knew it would happen eventually. She's been preparing for this."

She looks at us for confirmation. Neither Wade nor I speak.

I hate feeling so helpless. I can't stand the thought of Jadem and Wokee and the rest of the Solguards being in danger, and being unable to help. Wade and Ry look miserable, and I know they're having similar thoughts.

Is this what it's like to be a Solguard…to feel a responsibility not just for the people you love, but to want to make life better for everyone?

I stare at the tattoos on the back of Ry and Wade's hands. The center of the sun begins as a spiral, curling outward into elegant black rays. It's almost hypnotizing.

"It's beautiful," I say.

Ry follows my gaze to the marks on her hand.

"It represents everything the Duskers fear. It's the only thing in this world with more power than them."

"I want to join the Solguard." I put words to the thought that has been churning around in my mind ever since Sal's death. "After everything that's happened…." I can't finish the sentence. I look from Ry to Wade. "I want to help."

My whole life, I've been separate and apart from everything and everyone around me. *I want to be a part of something bigger, something more.*

"All you have to do is—" Ry begins, but Wade interrupts her.

"You don't know what you're asking," he says. "The Duskers will kill anyone with the Solguard mark on sight."

"My eyes are more recognizable than your marks," I argue. "They would kill me on sight with or without the tattoo."

"She's got a better chance of surviving all of this than the rest of us," Ry points out.

I think about Wokee and Aunt Jadem. "I have as much reason to fight them as anyone." I take a breath to calm myself. "And I want to fight them as one of you."

After a brief glance at Wade, who shrugs, Ry says, "If you're sure, you'll have to swear allegiance to the guardians of the sun and swear to fight for freedom from the Duskers."

"I'm sure."

"It's for the rest of your life," Wade tells me, his golden eyes burning with the intensity of his words. "You can never stop being a Solguard."

I nod. *I want this.*

For a long moment, no one speaks.

"And the tattoo?" I press. "How is it done?"

"It's powdered blackwood mixed with water and ash." Ry shrugs her shoulders. "If there was a blackwood tree around, I could do it now."

Before she has even finished speaking, I'm rummaging through my pack. I pull out the stub of blackwood pencil I've been carrying since I left the Subterrane and hand it to her.

"The mark won't fade," Wade tells me. "You'll never be able to go back to the Subterrane territory."

"My parents are both dead; there's nothing left for me there. But I can help the Solguards."

"It's fitting in a way," Ry says as she crushes the pencil against a stone. "Unlike the rest of us, the sun can't hurt you." She adds a few drops of water to the powder to make a kind of paste.

As she works, I think about my father, loyal servant to the Duskers. What would he think if he could see me now? Would he think me brave? Foolish? A traitor?

When the paste is ready, Ry heats the blade of a dagger in the blue part of the fire. She rolls the tip of the blade in the blackwood paste and presses my palm flat against the ground in the light of the fire.

"This will hurt," she warns.

"Just don't get any of my blood on you," I tell her.

The first cut makes me bite down hard on the inside of my cheek. Black spots dance across my vision as Ry carves the black swirls into my hand and down my fingers. Blood fills the cuts.

I don't look at Wade. I don't want him to see the tears leaking from my eyes.

"Do you want me to stop?" Ry's face swims in and out of focus.

I shake my head as I let out an unsteady breath. "Just get it done with."

A steady pressure moves to my back, making the pain a little less biting.

"You're doing great, Hemera." Wade's baritone comes close to my ear.

My vision is too hazy for me to see, but I think it's his hand on my back offering silent reassurance as Ry's blade scrapes deeper into my flesh.

What must be minutes seems to take hours. When Ry is finished, and the feeling that I'm going to be sick starts to pass, I inspect the bloody lines that cover my hand.

"Welcome to the Solguard," Ry smiles.

CHAPTER 32

I sleep badly. The pain in my hand changes from a roar to a nagging, pulsing ache that is inescapable.

When the activity of others packing their belongings wakes me, I hold up my hand to the flickering candlelight to inspect the damage.

"Wow!" Ry grabs my wrist as she peers at the marking. "It's healed."

The skin around the elegant swirls is still red and angry, but the deep cuts are gone.

"Watch out Duskers," Ry winks at me. "Here comes the Bisecter."

I almost laugh out loud. When she says it like that, being what I am starts to feel like the gift my aunt said it was. I look down when I realize I'm grinning like a fool.

We follow the narrow cliff until the ground levels out. We round a cluster of tall boulders before taking our first steps onto the other side of the mountain. I suck in my breath at the sight.

The land that sprawls between the mountains and Tanguro is nothing like the bleak, stony terrain we climbed to reach the mountaintop. The slopes leading down are a tangle of wild, unfamiliar trees of every shape and color. At least a dozen shades of red, purple, and green dot the slope leading down to the valley.

I've never seen anything like it. It's like something out of one of my mother's stories, where everything was shinier and brighter than it is in the real world. Except this place *is* real.

"It's beautiful," I breathe, not wanting to blink and lose even a single moment of staring at the vibrant colors melting together on the other side of the mountain.

"It's anything but beautiful." Dayne's tone breaks the spell, and I turn to look at him.

"How could you say that?" I ask.

"Listen here." He points a gloved finger at me. "This place is evil. Don't touch anything. Try not to even look at anything for too long."

"I think you might be getting paranoid in your old age," I try to tease.

Dayne doesn't show even the hint of a smile.

"I take it you've been here before?" Ry asks, hearing our conversation.

"A long time ago," Dayne says without elaborating.

To the rest of the company, he says, "Stop gawking. We've still got a ways to go."

Dayne doesn't look north toward Tanguro, though. His eyes are fixed on my hand. His frown deepens.

Dayne glares at me before turning back to the expectant company. "From here on out it will be more dangerous." He pauses. "Tanguro is wilder than any place you can imagine. Everything here is made to thrive in the sunlight and is more powerful for it."

We look down at the sprawling, tangled colors before us.

Dayne squints against the brightness below. "Halves are not all we have to worry about in this territory."

The slope down the mountain is less treacherous than the incline. But the moment we begin our descent, the temperature rises. Impossibly, the sun is even hotter and brighter here. I glance at the others, who labor under their heavy cloaks. Heat presses against us from all sides. The air shimmers from it.

There is so much to see my eyes don't know where to turn. Sparkling silver birds with eight wings perch in copper-colored trees. Fish that have a different color for each scale on their bodies swim in purple-tinged pools nestled into the mountainside. The fish leap five or more paces into the air to clamp their jaws over the birds on which they prey. When I shut my eyes against the brightness of it all, colored spots dance across my vision.

I see now what Dayne meant. Everything here is more intense, fiercer—from the magenta script trees to the two-headed lizards that hiss and bare their inches-long fangs as we pass.

"We no longer have any choice of avoiding the North Road." Dayne breaks into our silent awe. "It will be used by Halves, but the alternative would mean facing a forest more perilous than any you have ever encountered. Everything, from the flowers to the creatures, has a taste for flesh."

But not even Dayne's gloomy words can keep energy from surging through me. We're almost there. *I'm coming, Brice.*

The forest is more brilliantly colored than anything I could have imagined. Still, there is something sinister about this place. Bright eyes gleam at us from holes in tree trunks. Strange, unfamiliar sounds surround us. Even the branches and shrubs rustle at our passing as though resentful of the interruption caused by our presence.

I take the map out of my pack. The thick stripe of the North Road cuts through the forest in a straight path from the mountains to Tanguro. Every detail on this map, from the angles of the mountain's peak to the bend in the river, is perfect.

For the hundredth time, I wonder how Brice came by this map, and why. Even as a scout, he never travelled far enough to know these lands in detail. There must be an easy explanation for how it wound up in his possession, but still, the feeling that something about it all is not quite right continues to nag at me.

We stop just shy of the North Road to make camp for the high day. There are no caves on the map, but the tree branches overhead are lush and tangled enough that no sunlight passes through. Even so, the heat is almost unbearable.

"There will be no stopping once we step onto the road," Dayne says as he sharpens his axe blade against a stone. "It will be a hard march." He seems to be the only one with energy to spare in this heat.

I rest my hand against the trunk of a purple-leafed tree. At my touch, a vine wrapped around the trunk begins to quiver. I stare, transfixed, as brilliant yellow flowers unfurl before my eyes. They waft an inviting scent.

Dayne's warning echoes through my head, but almost against my will, I move closer. *They're just flowers, what danger could they be to me?*

I breathe deeply. A lazy sort of stillness comes over me. My feet feel leaden. Transfixed, I watch as the petals peel away to reveal a dozen or more sharp fangs, each as long as my index finger.

Flowers don't have fangs, I think.

And then the leaves leap toward me. Snapping, biting, tearing. Their fangs click together as they search out its prey. I have only an instant to realize that prey is me before the flowers' teeth sink into my shoulder.

I cry out and try to tear at the vine.

Angry hisses come from the plant, and I have just an instant to wonder whether I'm losing my mind before the vine slaps a violet hand-shaped leaf over my mouth, cutting off my shout.

But then that intoxicating scent returns, and I'm calm again. I don't want to move away from this place. Not even when more of the flowers are on my neck, clicking their fangs together. A floral tongue darts out, and I could swear I hear the flowers repeating the word *tasty.*

The next thing I know, Dayne is beside me, hacking at the vine with his axe. When the vine recoils, still snapping its teeth, we're both dripping with blood. The petals make a slurping noise as they close back up and the shredded vine settles back against the tree.

"What was that?" I gasp, squeezing my right hand over the torn flesh on my shoulder.

"It's called a Love Bite," Dayne replies.

"It's a *what?*"

"Try not to touch anything else," Dayne says, inspecting the wounds in my arm that are already beginning to heal.

I take the first watch, since I know I'll never be able to sleep. This place is too strange, and I'm too close to Brice.

"How's your mark healing?" Wade joins me as I stand surveying the land.

I look at the back of my right hand. It's been less than a day, but all the pain has disappeared. There's not even a scratch left from the dagger's blade. All that remains are the intricate swirling rays of the sun.

Just the sight of it makes me feel strong.

"You are really something," Wade says, looking straight at me.

* * *

I dream I'm back in the cave behind the waterfall with Brice.

"I love you, Hemera," he whispers. His body is molded around me, and his heart beats against my chest.

Brice's lips meet mine. A shiver runs through me as he runs a hand down my back. I breathe in the woods and mist from the waterfall. Brice's scent.

I open my eyes. Desperately, I stretch my mind to hold onto the memory of Brice's face and the feeling of his touch. Too soon, his face is swallowed up by the eerie lights of the Tanguro forest. But I haven't lost the feeling of Brice's hand in mine. It's warm and strong and fits my hand perfectly.

As I awaken, it's clear it is not the phantom of Brice's touch, but someone's actual hand I'm holding. I follow the arm linked to mine to Wade's familiar outline.

I wrench my hand back as I scramble into a sitting position. To my relief, Wade's chest continues to rise and fall in sleep. I must have reached out to him as I dreamed about Brice.

"You okay, Hemera?" Wade mumbles.

"Fine, go back to sleep," I whisper as I reposition myself farther away from Wade and wait for my heartbeat to settle.

* * *

The sunlight is different here. Its brilliant orange, red, and pink rays blaze with an intensity the likes of which I've never felt. Many of the soldiers are getting Burn blisters even beneath their cloaks. I feel the blazing heat, but even though I wear nothing over my blue silk cloak, no blisters appear.

Dayne's mouth is set in a deep frown as we walk. He hasn't said a word since we broke camp.

"What's wrong?" I ask.

"Scouts left hours ago," Dayne mutters, almost to himself. "They should have been back by now."

"We'll bump into them once we're out on the main road," I try to reassure him.

I can't be worried when we are so close to Brice and the other prisoners. Every step brings us nearer.

We hack our way through a tangled mess of trees that shift their branches to block our path. It takes hours to cut away enough leaves to pass through. When we do, we stumble onto the North Road.

We all draw our weapons, ready for an attack. But the road is empty as far as the eye can see. Everything is quiet.

We have walked for almost an hour when a solitary figure appears in the distance. I grip my sling, ready for Dayne's signal.

"Scout," Ry says, lowering her bow. "Hold your fire."

As the scout comes into full view, it's obvious something is wrong. He's moving too slowly and seems to be dragging one of his legs. Dayne runs forward and catches the man in his arms as he collapses. His cloak is covered in blood.

"Halves," the scout manages to gasp.

The man tries to speak again, but only manages a gurgling sound. Blood spurts from a wound in his neck. Dayne presses his fingers over the wound, and his hand is instantly covered with blood.

After a few moments, the gurgling sound stops. Dayne takes his fingers off the scout's neck and lays him down on the road. A cloud of dust rises from the North. The ground vibrates.

The Halves are coming.

CHAPTER 33

There must be more than a hundred of them. They move fast and are soon in full view.

"They're coming for us." Dayne grips his axe in both hands.

Without waiting for a command, I take down two with my sling as the others draw their swords. The beasts are on us in seconds.

I draw both of my daggers and slash at the Halves' legs and stomachs. These Halves are different from the others I've fought. They're taller, wider, and their hides are thicker. They carry stone clubs instead of wooden ones. They know how to fight. The beasts duck away and use their clubs to block our swords.

A scream, Ry's, makes me turn away from the Halve I'm fighting. Two Halves are closing in on her. Her sword is on the ground. I clutch the hilt of my dagger and throw it.

One of the Halves falls. I put a stone in my sling and wind the ropes to bring down the other. I take a step forward but am blocked by a Halve standing in my way.

I meet the Halve's black eyes. The coppery scent of blood fills my nostrils. The Halve wraps one of its scaly arms around me and lets out an earsplitting roar.

Blinding anger fills my insides. These *beasts* have taken everything from me.

I elbow the Halve's sunken chest. The Halve stumbles backward, falling onto the ground. I dart away from its flailing legs.

Leaping into the air, I throw my arms around a Halve that holds a club in each of its deformed hands. With an almost feral shout, I yank the beast back, away from the others.

There's no time for me to move before it collapses on top of me. I'm caught underneath the beast's swollen midsection.

I have barely managed to shove the body away before five Halves surround me. I'm dizzy with the scent of their rotting flesh as they close the gap between us. I fight off two of them, but four more take their place. There are too many of them for us to defeat.

Despair starts to close in on me, but then I remember the Solguard tattoo now emblazoned on my hand. The others aren't going to stop fighting, and neither will I. My fury at the Halves overcomes my fear. I fight for all I'm worth.

It takes seven Halves to drag me across the road as I continue to kick and claw at their thick hides.

The Halves throw me forward onto the ground. I leap to my feet, but I'm surrounded. Other Solguards are pushed into the space beside me. None of us have weapons.

I feel arms around me, but this time, they're human.

"You're alright, you're alright!" Dayne's voice is raspy from the heat.

Wade appears beside me. He grasps my arms in a vicelike grip as though to reassure himself I'm really there. Ry stumbles toward us. There are festering welts across her cheek bone.

"Halve blood!" she gasps as she reaches a hand to me.

Ry screams as I press my palms over her skin to absorb the searing poison into my own hands. A hissing sound erupts from the place where my hands meet her skin.

The red spots on Ry's cheek are the only evidence of the sores that had been there moments before. My palms are covered with deep welts that are already beginning to heal. Ry throws her arms around me.

There isn't time to marvel over what I have just done.

Two other Solguards were touched by the Halve blood, and I heal them, too. Dayne stays beside me like he's afraid I might disappear in the sea of

Halves surrounding us. When there are no others to heal, Dayne turns his attention to the anxious faces waiting for his orders.

"Not much to be done now, I'm afraid," he says. "My guess is they'll march us to Tanguro to join the other prisoners. Best not to aggravate them just yet. For now, focus on staying alive."

A question echoes in my mind that I don't dare ask out loud. *Why haven't the Halves killed us already?*

The Halves move forward without warning. One-by-one, they each grab a soldier by his wrists and drag him away. Four Halves take hold of me. There is one on each arm, one in front, and the other behind. Together, they drag me out of the circle. Despite Dayne's warning, I twist away from their repulsive touch.

"Get away from me," I snarl.

The moment they sense my resistance, the Halves throw me to the ground. The wind is knocked out of me by the force of the fall. I lie gasping for air until the Halves lift me up again.

Hatred simmers deep in my bones. *I'll kill each and every one of you*, I vow.

Once every member of our company is in the grips of his captors, we're forced to march northward.

* * *

The Halves move quickly. Whenever my pace lags, they drag me forward by my wrists. Their weight on my arms is more painful than the effort of jogging between them, so I push myself on.

Lowest day passes. The sun climbs. The weightless silk of the cloak Wokee made for me invites what little breeze there is to cool my skin, but the others don't have this luxury. Every time I try to turn to see how the others are faring, the Halves shove me forward.

I'll kill each and every one of you. The promise is my only comfort as we're pushed, dragged, and yanked forward long after our strength has dissolved.

It is not until the Halves slow our pace that I'm able to look down to see the mud that has been making my steps even heavier. Through my exhausted haze, my brain makes the connection. *Water.*

As soon as the Halves release me, I drag my aching body to the streambed. I plunge my entire face into the cool, clear water. The sounds of tramping feet and ragged breaths vanish as I submerge my head.

After we have drunk from the stream and refilled our waterskins, the Halves push us off the road and under a thick canopy of blue trees. The branches are so dense no sunlight reaches the ground. The Halves make a tight ring around us as everyone peels off their sweat-soaked cloaks.

I lie on the ground, too exhausted to move. Wade and Ry collapse beside me.

A gap between the Halves' bodies is wide enough for me to see the road ahead of us. In the distance are two white, shining structures that seem to melt into the sky. I've never seen anything like them. In Subterrane Harkibel, the only above-ground structures were small wooden sheds used to store farming tools. But these reach up as far as the eye can see.

Maybe Brice is inside one of them.

A chill—of excitement or fear, or perhaps both—passes through me. We're so close now.

If we could just escape from these Halves.

CHAPTER 34

Two Halves drag me to my knees. I must have fallen asleep as I was walking. I didn't even know that was possible. Panic grips me as I try to recall where I am and how I got here. Focusing on the white structures ahead, which are almost blinding against the bright orange sky, makes my memory return.

As we close the distance to Tanguro, more of the surrounding area comes into view. The two white structures are bordered by a stone wall. The wall is twice as high as the one surrounding Subterrane Harkibel. Both sides of the stone wall meet at tall wooden gates, which loom before us at the end of the North Road.

My sore feet resist the pace the Halves set. Every muscle in my body screams in protest. But the Halves leave me with no choice but to keep up.

The two Halves working either side of the wooden gates are churning the cranks, but the gate is slow to creak open. Our captors, too eager to get us through, are pushing and shoving the prisoners. There's a bottleneck as too many people are forced through too small a space. The Halves shout and grunt in their guttural language, but it doesn't help us move any faster. I've lost sight of my companions; unfamiliar prisoners from other lands surround me. They all look as exhausted and beaten as I feel.

A Halve shoves me, and my captors lose their grip on my shoulders. For a moment, I'm left unguarded.

My heart thrums in my chest. If I'm going to slip away unnoticed, now is the time. Even as I start to separate myself from the crowd, an image of my father comes unbidden into my mind.

You abandoned him to the Halves, a voice in my head says. *Are you going to leave your friends at their mercy, too?*

But if I can get away now, I can be of more help to them. Instinct tells me I won't have another chance to slip away.

Before I can lose my nerve, I crouch low and sneak between the Halves, bumping against their disgusting, scaly hides. They are too focused on getting everyone through the gates to notice me. Besides, they seem more concerned with keeping the prisoners from getting out to notice one slipping in. I squeeze through a narrow opening between the outer part of the gate and the stone wall.

Once inside, I find myself in a courtyard of sorts. The open space is bordered by rows of the strangest-looking trees I've ever seen. White leaves spring up from the trunk and spill all the way down to the ground. The branches sway back and forth even though there's no wind.

In front of me is the first white building. The other is farther inside the stone wall and is blocked from view by the first.

An orchard with some kind of spiked, blue fruit stands between me and the building. The ground between the trees is dotted with vines, flowers, and other unfamiliar plants. Remembering Dayne's warnings and those bloodthirsty flowers, I take care not to touch anything.

Halves are everywhere. Luckily, they're too preoccupied to notice me. They're carrying pieces of stone to fortify the wall that is already taller than the height of several men combined. The Halves are turning this place into a fortress above ground.

The rumors of a Dusker here must be true.

The Halves could never figure out how to create all of this on their own. The Dusker in charge must have found some way to control them. But for what purpose? And what use could he have for human prisoners?

A commotion draws my attention back to the gates. The Halves are panicking. A plume of dust rises as they shove each other. A black shadow passing between them is the source of their terror.

There's no mistaking the ruffled black fur, fluttering wings, and one flopped ear. Flying through the air on small, unsteady wings is Vlaz. His teeth flash in the sunlight as he snaps at the Halves that scatter out of his path. A strangled laugh escapes my lips even as the Halves gallop toward me.

How did Vlaz get here? Is Wokee here, too?

The thought of Wokee amid all these monsters makes my insides clench. I search for my friend, but the courtyard is too crowded with people and Halves for me to recognize anyone. Prisoners abandoned by their captors run in every direction.

Vlaz launches himself in the air. Claws extended, he fastens onto the back of a Halve. The Halve shrieks and twists its body.

"Vlaz!"

It seems impossible Vlaz could pick out the sound of my voice above the pandemonium in the courtyard, but the cub veers away from the Halves and flies straight to me. I catch him as he bathes my face with his wet tongue. He's grown so much he barely fits in my arms. I bury my face in his fur.

It doesn't take long for the Halves to regroup. Some stay behind to corral the prisoners. The rest race toward us, brandishing their stone clubs. Vlaz lets out a low growl and flies out of my arms to meet them.

For a brief moment, all the Halves' attention is on Vlaz. His snarling and snapping fangs are holding them off for the moment. If I'm going to escape, I need to go now. I throw a last look at Vlaz, who seems unconcerned with taking on enemies many times his size, and run.

I race through the orchard, dodging away from plants that stretch out their leaves to wrap around my legs, to the first white building. It's farther away than it looks. I pass through three orchards of yellow and pink fruit before the building looms ahead of me. When I turn back, the Halves are just a mass of pale, moving specks in the distance. Vlaz is nowhere in sight.

If they hurt him….

And what will Dayne do when he realizes I'm gone? Will he think I was captured and try to find me? Wade and Ry will be worried, too.

I file away my guilt for later. Right now, I need to focus.

I crane my neck up at the building before me. I need to figure out where the prisoners are being held. Freeing them is the only way we'll have a chance against the Halves and the Dusker controlling them.

I touch the white siding of the building, and then draw my hand back in surprise. It's not burning up, or even hot. In fact, the material is cool.

The siding looked smooth from far away, but it's actually covered with large pieces of material sewn together. I look from the building to the rows of white trees. Every part of the tree, from its smooth bark to the long, thick leaves that drape around it like a cloak, are purest white. It takes a moment to figure out that the building is covered in leaves from the white trees.

I walk once around the enormous building. There are seven entrances. Each is fitted with a stone slab at least twice my height and wide enough for three Halves to move through the opening abreast.

Deep grooves in the ground show where the stone doors slide away from the entrance. I choose the door with the smallest groove and fewest Halve footprints at its base. It's far too large for any normal human to budge, and probably takes two Halves working on either side to move it.

With one hand, I push the stone door aside.

A shiver runs through me at the change in temperature as I step into the coolness. When I pull the stone door shut behind me, not even a single ray of sunlight follows me inside. I blink as I wait for my eyes to adjust to the dim torchlight.

Inside, the building is crudely made. Through the cracks in the wooden slats overhead, I can see there are at least ten levels above me. It's so strange for a fortress to reach up into the sky rather than deep below the earth. If it weren't for the walls that are made of wood rather than dirt, I wouldn't believe I was above ground.

The grunts and thudding footsteps of dozens of Halves reach my ears before I see them. The sour stench of their sweat threatens to choke me. I try to melt into the darkness, covering my mouth.

Halves are everywhere.

I slip behind a tall pile of stone debris where I can peer around at the Halves without being noticed.

I flinch as a tremendous noise cuts through the building. A crude iron contraption with a round stone in its center has begun to whir. The Halves rotate a crank that turns the stone, which they're using to sharpen thick blades. The screech each blade makes as it touches the rotating stone makes the hairs on the back of my neck prickle. The metal shavings that fly up from the machine make the Halves choke and sputter.

A new kind of horror grips me. These aren't the clumsy wooden clubs of the Halves I've fought before.

If the Halves could destroy whole Subterranes with just their clubs, what kind of ruin will they bring about with these?

From my hiding place, I can see up through a hole in the ceiling to the next level. There, Halves sit on the ground as they whittle tree trunks into spears. If any of them looked down, they'd be able to see me. But they're too busy with their work to pay attention to anything else.

Somewhere far above, I hear the clink of what I assume are metal weapons being tossed onto piles. There must be thousands of blades, spears, and clubs in this building, and the Halves are still making more.

I didn't know the Halves even possessed enough intelligence for these simple tasks.

I watch with a combination of horror and fascination. Who taught the Halves how to make weapons? Even as the question enters my mind, I know the answer. It must be the Dusker.

Maybe now that the Duskers know where Solis is located, they're planning to use these Halves to destroy the last people who have resisted their rule.

The thought makes me want to sprint back to the Solguards to warn them. I want to get Wokee and Aunt Jadem as far away from there as I can. But there's a voice nagging at the corner of my mind that tells me there has to be something else going on here, some greater purpose to all of these preparations. I just have no idea what it could be.

Without warning, the Halves stop their work. They march in formation away from the piles of weapons and away from me. There is the sound of scraping, and then I catch a glimpse of great ladders being raised to cut-out holes in the levels above. One by one, the Halves ascend the ladder. I duck back behind the pile of stones before one of their gazes lands on me. If even a single one of these beasts spots me, I'm done for.

When the floor I'm on seems clear of Halves, I slip out from my hiding place. Maybe they're keeping the prisoners on the upper floors of this building. If I can follow the Halves, maybe they'll lead me to Brice and the others.

I take small, cautious steps in the direction where the last Halves disappeared. The ground is littered with fragments of stone and partly-whittled spears. One wrong step could send a pile of the precariously-balanced weapons crashing to the floor. The last thing I need right now is for my clumsy feet to alert every Halve in the building to my presence.

I'm so intent on my every step that it takes me several moments to register the dark shadow that has crossed my path. Confusion turns to fear as I follow the shadow's length to two misshapen, hairy feet.

My mouth opens in a silent scream.

CHAPTER 35

A Halve stands before me. This one is taller and less stooped than the ones that captured our company. One of its arms is at least a foot longer than the other, which makes its entire body seem lopsided. A few thin, greasy strands of hair hang from its otherwise bare head.

The Halve's wide, black eyes stare straight into mine. It reminds me of the expressionless face of the Halve that murdered my mother. It stood there, just like this one is now, right before it killed her. Terror and hatred pulse deep within me in equal measures.

Every muscle in my body screams for me to run.

But if I run now, I might be throwing away my one chance to find the prisoners. Beads of sweat run down the sides of my face as I stand rooted to the ground. My eyes search for something—someone—to help. But I'm alone.

You are more than the sum of your parts, Hemera. Out of nowhere, my aunt's words return to me.

I grab one of the heavy blades from the ground and hold it out in front of me.

"Come on," I hiss, flicking the blade at the Halve.

There are piles of stone clubs and blades on either side of the Halve. Instead of reaching out for a weapon, the Halve extends its deformed arms toward me.

I keep my blade raised high as I stare at the Halve in confusion.

The Halve beckons me with its shorter arm as it takes several steps backward. It gestures with its arm again.

I've never seen a Halve act like this.

Could this just be some kind of distraction to capture me? It seems unlikely the Halves could mastermind such a plan, and besides, there would be no need. The Halve could just make a noise and summon the others.

Holding the blade until my knuckles are white, I take a step forward. The Halve's hideous face reveals no expression, but it nods like I've done what it wanted.

The Halve takes two steps back toward me, gestures again, and then walks away. Almost of their own accord, my legs begin to follow.

As I walk behind the Halve, every muscle in my body prepares for an attack. I peer into the depths of the building to try and see any other Halves that might be lurking in the shadows.

Instead of walking straight back, the Halve turns to the side of the building. It stops when it reaches a section of wall that is not illuminated by the torches. My heart thuds in my chest.

It takes me a moment to see what the Halve is pointing to in the darkness. As my eyes adjust, a ladder affixed to the wall appears.

The Halve nods once to me, and then grasps the sides of the ladder with its gnarled, scarred hands. It hefts its bulk onto the ladder. The rungs sag under the beast but hold as it climbs higher and higher.

There are large square cut-outs in each floor of the building. The Halve keeps going past each level, and I have to stand at the ladder's base to watch its progress as it gets farther from the ground.

When the Halve reaches the top of the building, it pulls itself onto the wooden parapet and turns back to look down at me. The beast beckons to me with its longer arm.

None of this makes any sense. I hesitate, filled with uncertainty.

The sound of a door below creaking open makes my decision. I drop the blade and grasp both sides of the ladder.

When I reach the parapet of the next level, I take a quick glance around. There seems to be nothing there except for metal-tipped spears organized into high piles. I keep climbing, all the while wondering if this is a horrible idea.

Every other level in the building either holds weapons or supplies that would be needed to sustain an army of hundreds of Halves. When I reach the final parapet, I scramble to my feet in case the Halve plans to attack me while I'm unbalanced. It makes no move toward me, however. The Halve just shakes its head from side to side and covers its twisted mouth with its hand. I take this gesture to mean it wants me to keep quiet. *Not that I need reminding.*

The Halve stoops, fiddling with something against the wall. There is a dull click followed by the grating of stone against wood. The Halve slides a panel away from the wall.

Sunlight spills onto the path. The Halve pushes away the stone door and ducks through the opening. I follow, blinded by the bursts of orange imprinted on my eyes. It's only when I'm out in the fresh air that I realize I haven't taken a real breath since entering the building. I draw greedy breaths of air that is free of Halve sweat and rock dust.

I'm standing at the edge of a wooden bridge that connects the two white buildings. When I look down, my stomach lurches.

What am I doing?

The bridge is narrow, with nothing to hold onto on either side. A fall from this height would mean certain death, healing powers or no. The trees on the ground far below send up dazzling streaks of color that are almost blinding in the sunlight.

Still, there was no sign of the prisoners in the other building. The fastest way to find out if they're in the second building is by crossing this bridge. I take a deep breath. *Be brave,* I tell myself. *For Brice.*

I take one step forward and sway on the narrow wooden slats. Already dizzy from the height, I try to steady myself.

If the Halve weren't a mindless creature, I would demand to know what it wants from me. I would demand to know why it's here and what it plans to do with me. But I know asking the Halve would be pointless.

For the hundredth time, I ask myself why I'm still following it instead of killing it. I wonder why it hasn't killed me. And still, I follow it because it feels too late to do anything else.

The Halve is already partway across the bridge. *Get moving,* I tell myself.

I take small steps across the bridge at first but find it's easier to keep my balance if I move faster. I keep my eyes on the section of bridge straight in front of me. My hands feel cold even though the air is hot enough to give any normal person the Burn.

When I look up to where the Halve is waiting for me, my foot catches on an uneven plank. My body pitches to the side. As I get a glimpse of the ground far below, dizziness takes hold of me.

A scream is lodged in my throat.

First one foot, and then the other, slips off the bridge. I cling to the wooden slats, but I'm too unbalanced. My feet swing as they search for purchase, but there's nothing but air below.

This can't *be happening. I can't have come so far just to fall off a bridge....*

One sweating hand slips off the bridge. My other hand, gripping the wood, is all that keeps me from plummeting to my death.

Even as I feel my hand slip, a firm grip closes around my arm. The Halve pulls me until I'm standing upright on the bridge. It watches me as I take deep breaths to steady my quaking limbs.

A Halve...saved me?

I wrench my arm free from the Halve's grip as soon as I've regained my balance. The Halve's arms hang limp and uneven by its sides. It takes a step back from me.

Guilt edges into my consciousness before I push it away again. *It's a* Halve.

The Halve turns to unlatch the stone covering on the building before us, which looks identical to the one we just came from. The whole of its exterior is covered in the white leaves that somehow keep everything inside from frying. The building stretches so high its top gets lost in the sun's orange haze.

The Halve pushes aside the stone covering, sniffs the air inside the building like an animal, and then steps through the opening. The Halve looks back once and gestures for me to follow.

The inside of this building is dark and stuffy, and it's impossible to see more than a few feet in front of me. I climb down the steep ladder, feeling my way from rung to rung as my eyes adjust to the dimness. At the bottom of the ladder is a tall stone archway, closed off by roughly-fitting stone doors. A lantern, which hangs from the top of the arch by an iron peg, is the only light source.

The Halve takes hold of one of the stone doors, straining against the boulder's weight. The muscles in its shoulders bulge and flex until there's an opening wide enough for its body to squeeze through. The Halve looks back at me once, beckons with its longer arm, and then disappears.

I hesitate, peering through the dark gap between the stone doors where the Halve disappeared. The smell of dank earth makes me feel like I'm back in the narrow tunnels of the Subterrane. My breathing becomes sharper. I close my eyes.

Gulping, I follow the Halve through the narrow opening. I step into a wide tunnel lit with lanterns hanging from the stone ceiling. There's enough room for me to stand upright in the tunnel, but the Halve has to crouch to keep from knocking its head.

The silence is broken by a muffled cough. I stop moving.

Did I imagine the noise? It could have just been the sound of my heart knocking against my ribs…. But then it comes again, followed by a distinctly human groan.

The prisoners. They're here.

I glance around. On either side of the tunnel are round, stone doors fitted across enclosures that could only be the prisoners' cells.

Every nerve in my body is on fire.

"I'm going to get you out of here!" I call.

Whispers, and then shouts, echo my call.

"Hemera?"

The voice is hoarser than I remember, and muffled from the stone enclave, but it's his voice.

CHAPTER 36

The Halve watches but doesn't try to stop me as I race down the path and wrench the stone door open. I stumble into the cell and fall into Brice's arms.

I've thought about this feeling every day since he was taken, but the memory is nothing compared to the reality. Strong, comforting arms wrap around me. I'm so happy I want to weep. And I do. Brice holds me, like I'm the one who has been locked up in a cell all this time and needs to be comforted, rather than the other way around.

"Hemera!" Brice's cry is muffled against the side of my neck where his lips are pressed. "Is it really you?"

I can't tell if I'm laughing or crying, or a little of both. It doesn't matter. Brice is alive. And we're together.

I wrap my arms around him, trying not to think about how I can feel each of his ribs.

"I've missed you so much," I say, my words barely audible because my face is pressed into his shoulder.

Brice takes my face in his hands and kisses me.

The kiss awakens a longing so fierce I can't breathe. *More,* my body screams. I twine myself around him, pressing closer, until there's no longer a place where I end and Brice begins.

"I love you," I say.

The words come so easily and feel so right. A giddiness takes hold of me.

Brice is here. He's alive. And we're together.

There are tears on my face. I don't know if they're mine, or his, or both of ours. I stop thinking about it…stop thinking about anything…except for this moment.

"Forgive me," he breathes between kisses. "Hemera, please forgive me."

I pull back just enough to look up at his dirty, too-thin, perfect face. There is a desperation in his eyes I don't recognize.

"There is nothing to forgive." I cling to him, wanting—needing—this moment to last. "We're together. Nothing else matters."

Like some spell has broken, Brice is pulling away from me. "Hemera, you have to get out of here." His eyes flick to his open cell door. "If he finds you…."

"Do you think I came all this way to just abandon you?" I trace the edges of his jaw and curve of his lips with my fingers.

"Please," his voice is desperate. "You have to go. I can't protect you from him."

"I won't leave you." I wrap my arms around him, trying to make him understand.

When I reach up to touch his face, his cheeks are wet with tears.

"Brice—"

"Please, Hemera. *Go.*"

"Not without you."

He looks down at his ankles, which are bound by a thick, tangled rope. "I don't think I'm going anywhere."

I suck in my breath in hopeless dismay, until I remember the small knife tied to my leg.

I unstrap the knife with trembling fingers and begin to saw through the thick ropes. "What happened?" I ask. "Why were you brought here?"

I look up from my cutting, only to see a strange emotion pass across Brice's face. *Regret?*

He opens his mouth, closes it, and opens it again without making a sound.

"Tell me," I urge.

"The—Master—he's training an army of Halves."

That much I had gathered. "But why?"

"To be able to take control of everyone." Brice snarls. "Duskers, Dwellers…you name it." He curls his hand into a fist and punches the wall. "And the Halves just love it. They just love to torture us—"

"Don't!" I stop him from hitting the wall again and cradle his bloodied knuckles in my hands.

"Why the human prisoners, then?" I ask as soon as I'm sure Brice won't try to punch anything again. "What use does he have for you?"

Brice won't look at me.

"Brice?"

"The Master needs us for the jobs the Halves are too dumb to do, which is mostly everything. Digging new tunnels, harvesting the specere leaves…." Brice's voice is filled with a bitterness I don't recognize. "He's chosen some of the more…brutal…of his prisoners to be his personal guards. They're the ones who deliver his orders."

Brice is so angry. I've never seen him lose his temper, but his nerves are frayed and there's a wild look in his eyes.

You have no idea what he's been through, I remind myself.

It was foolish for me to think I would find him unchanged. He's fragile and uncontrolled in a way I've never seen before. I'll need to be patient with him while he finds his way back to himself.

I kiss his brow. At the touch of my lips, Brice flinches almost imperceptibly.

I swallow the tears threatening at the corners of my vision. *Give him time*, I remind myself.

I go back to cutting through the ropes, needing a distraction. "Specere leaves?"

What happened to you? What aren't you telling me? is what I want to ask.

"The white trees," he replies. "Their leaves reflect the sunlight. I don't think they exist anywhere but here."

"Has he—the Master—killed any of the prisoners?" My voice is a whisper.

Brice nods his head, his face a storm of emotions. "Once prisoners are taken down to the catacombs, they don't come back."

"Catacombs," I repeat.

"It's where he experiments on them. I think he calls it the catacombs because so many of them die." Brice still won't look at me. "He cuts them up just like Taniel…." His voice breaks. "I didn't know…I had no idea…." He covers his face with his hands and slumps against the cell wall.

I put a tentative hand on his chest. This time, he wraps his arms around me in response to my touch. His heart thuds against me.

"Hemera." He says my name on a sigh. "There's something I have to tell you."

When he turns to face me, his eyes are tortured. I've never seen him so vulnerable, so uncertain. It frightens me.

"Your father," Brice begins.

"Is dead," I finish. "Halves attacked the Subterrane after you were taken."

Brice shakes his head. "You don't understand."

There is a satisfying snap as I pull the rest of the rope apart with my hands.

"Let's go." I pull him up from the ground.

"Hemera, wait." Brice shrinks back into the corner of his cell. "He can't see you. He can't know you're here. You have to leave now." His words are pleading, desperate even. "I haven't told you—"

"Whatever it is, you can tell me when we're away from here." I give his hand another tug. "We need to get the prisoners out and figure out how to defeat this…Master…and his army of Halves."

Brice rises and lets me lead him from the cell.

Relieved not to have to drag him, I ask, "Are all of the prisoners kept here?"

He sighs in resignation. "Except for the ones in the catacombs."

I move toward the cell's opening, but Brice pulls me back.

"It's no use, Hemera. These stone doors are impossible to open." He rubs the place on his ankle where the ropes chafed his skin and then stares up at me. "How did you get my door open, anyway?"

I bite my lip. I need to tell Brice everything I kept secret in the Subterrane. Guilt gnaws at me for everything I should have said long ago but didn't because I just wanted to feel normal around him. *Later*, I promise myself. As soon as we're free from this place, I'll tell him everything.

"Come on," I tug his arm. "Get your cloak."

I step into the tunnel and go to open the next cell door.

"Wait." Brice holds my wrist. "If you're really set on doing this, we'll need weapons to kill the guards. Otherwise they'll just round us back up and tell Him."

"So, we have to leave them all tied up in here until we have weapons?"

I hate the idea of leaving anyone in here for another second.

"Yes. But the only place to get those—"

"Is the other building," I finish.

"You've been to the weapons building?" Open horror is written across Brice's face.

"Come on." I take Brice's hand and tug him onto the path between the cells. The Halve that led me here is gone.

I decide to say nothing about it to Brice.

"This way." Brice leads me in the opposite direction from which I had come.

"What's on the other levels of this building?" I ask.

"More prisoners and the Halves guarding them," Brice replies. His green eyes darken with hate.

I count forty cell doors, twenty on each side of the path, before we reach a cross-section. *So many*, I think. *What is the Dusker doing with so many prisoners?*

The passages to the left and right seem identical to the one we just walked through, with the same number of cells on each side. Brice moves past the ladder in the center of the floor, skirting the edge of the opening between the floor we're on and the one beneath. He motions for me to be silent. In the dim light, I can just make out the hunched figure of a Halve sitting beside the ladder on the level below.

"Why aren't there any guards on this floor?" I whisper.

"They'll be back," Brice says.

My gut twists at the anguished calls from inside the cells.

There's a ladder at the far end of the row. It's rickety and looks unused. This is the one Brice uses to climb all the way down to the bottom floor of the building.

Brice slaps his hands against the two stone slabs blocking what must be the way out. He lets out a string of curses as he shoves all of his weight against them. They don't budge.

"Here, let me." I press my hand against one of the stone slabs and it gives way.

Sunlight streams onto the path through the crack between the stones. Brice leaps back as he pulls his cloak on.

Brice stares at me in amazement.

"I uh…." I stammer, not knowing what to say.

My cheeks heat, and I curse myself again for having kept this secret from him. I look for fear or pride or anything else on Brice's face, but I can't tell what he's thinking.

"It's true, then?" he asks. "You really are as strong as the Halves? And the sun, it doesn't hurt you?" He eyes my new silk cloak.

I'm saved from answering. Just beyond the stone doors are dozens of Halves. They haven't noticed us yet, but there are too many to fight.

"Is there any other way out of here?" I whisper.

"The river," he says. "It'll take much longer to get back to the courtyard, but we won't have to deal with any Halves." He continues to stare at me like he's never laid eyes on me before.

"Lead the way."

"Hemera," Brice begins.

"I'll explain later," I tell him. "I promise."

Right now, we need to get back to the weapons building without fighting an entire army of Halves.

As we run back along the path, choruses of pleas echo from behind the cell doors. I look at Brice, but he just shakes his head. "We won't be any help to them without weapons," he says.

Just beyond the last pair of cells is a dark tunnel that descends underground. There are no candles to light this passageway. The air is stagnant and the walls seem to press in against me. I reach for Brice's hand.

The sound of running water grows louder with each step. As we round another corner, my face is bathed in a spray of cool mist. I catch faint glimmers of white as the water froths in the darkness.

The path ends without warning. My legs kick out and meet nothing but air.

CHAPTER 37

I plunge into frigid water. It's colder than anything I've ever felt. I can't breathe.

"Hemera!" Brice shouts my name over the sound of the swirling water.

We somehow manage to clasp hands. The river is flowing too fast to do anything besides allow ourselves to be carried along by the current. I cling to Brice with numb fingers as we're carried into the darkness.

Even when I dove deep into the river near the Subterrane, the water was still sun-warmed. But this…the way it makes my teeth chatter and my hands bone-white…is like nothing I've ever known. For the first time, it makes me wonder about the darkness we've always been taught to pray for. Without the sun, would everything be like this?

As we're swept around a bend, I forget about the cold. A gasp escapes me.

The river deposits us into a lake that glitters as though lit from above by hundreds of blue and gold candles. The lights shimmer on the water's surface and reflect off the wet rocks. When I look closer, I see they aren't candles. They look like long blue and gold tails that swing from the domed ceiling.

"Glow snakes," Brice answers my question before I ask it. "At least, that's what I call them."

"They're beautiful." I crane my neck to look up at the dazzling lights.

We paddle to the stony bank and pull ourselves out of the water. Our sodden clothes cling to us. Water drips off the ends of my hair and makes me shiver as it runs down the back of my neck.

Brice leads me away from the water toward an overhang of rock. We duck underneath the narrow space to find ourselves in a spacious chamber. A mist fills the air from the waterfall that pours out of a gap in the rock wall. It steams and froths as it spills into the lake.

"Seems we're fated to be together only where there are waterfalls," Brice says.

I know he meant it as a joke, but his words still make me sad.

We sit on the rocks at the base of the waterfall. I move closer to Brice and examine his face in the soft light of the glow snakes. Brice reaches up and cups my face with both of his hands.

"I love you, Hemera. Whatever else happens, I need you to remember that."

"I love you, too," I whisper, hardly daring to breathe for fear he'll let go of me.

There is a fierceness in his green eyes. Brice pulls me to him and crushes his mouth against mine.

I melt into his arms. He's so warm, so *alive*. Every part of me strains toward him. His touch fills all of the empty places inside me, awakening both desire and longing.

I cling to Brice as his lips move down my neck. I wind my hands around his waist, drawing him closer.

"Hemera." He says my name like a prayer. When he pulls away from me, his eyes are smoldering. "There's something I have to tell you."

"Me first." My words are dulled against the pounding of my heart.

I begin speaking before I lose my nerve. "It's not just my eyes that are different. I'm strong and fast like them, except not really." I pause. *How can I explain this?*

I try again. "I'm stronger and faster than the Halves. It's like being part of both Halves and humans has made me somehow…more. The sun doesn't hurt me. And any wound I get, no matter how deep it is, heals itself in a matter of hours." I pause to take a breath. "Oh, and I can heal people who have been poisoned by Halve blood."

Now that the words are out, all I can do is wait for Brice to react. A long time passes before he says anything.

"It was true, all this time." There's a hollowness to Brice's gaze that cuts me to my core. "And you never told me."

I feel sick at having betrayed him for so long. I never should have kept a secret like this from Brice. All along, he's been nothing but honest with me, and yet I lied about a part of myself because I wanted to feel…normal.

"I'm so sorry," I whisper.

Silence hangs between us for several moments.

"I should have told you sooner," I try to explain, "but I only knew a small part of everything when we were in the Subterrane, and I guess I was afraid…."

"It doesn't matter now." Something in Brice's voice makes it clear the conversation is over.

My shoulders slump in disappointment. I don't know what I expected from Brice—understanding? Forgiveness?

"What was it you wanted to tell me?" I ask Brice, desperate for a change in subject.

Brice stares out at the water for a long moment. When he turns back to me, there's something in his eyes that makes my heart splinter. He lets out a heavy sigh. I hold my breath, waiting for whatever he's going to tell me.

But all he says is, "You're shivering. We'd better go."

✳ ✳ ✳

We spill out of the mouth of the tunnel into blinding sunlight. A red sky stretches above us, interrupted by the apricot globe of the sun. I shut my eyes and watch the flashing orbs against the blackness of my eyelids.

Our legs churn up silt as we step out of the water and onto a sandy alcove surrounded by steep boulders. Brice wrings out his cloak, careful not to allow any sunlight past the protective material. I notice him eye my silk cloak again.

Logic tells me he needs time to adjust to everything I've told him. My heart just wants everything to be the way it was before all of this.

"Let's see where we've ended up." They are the first words Brice has spoken since we left the underground lake, and he doesn't look at me when he says them.

What did I expect? I'd probably react the same way if he'd been less than honest with me all this time.

We both go still at the sound of footsteps crunching on sand. Brice's face turns pale. I motion him over to a hidden spot between two boulders.

The footsteps are followed by the harsh, wheezing breaths of at least four Halves. One of their shadows crosses our hiding place.

I put a hand over my mouth to stifle the sound of my breathing. For the space of several seconds, nothing happens. Then, the Halve bends down to look inside the rocks where we're crouched.

Black eyes gaze directly into mine.

CHAPTER 38

It's the Halve that led me to Brice, the one that saved me on the bridge. I hold my breath as we stare at each other.

The Halve nods almost imperceptibly. It doesn't even look at Brice before it turns back to the others. Their grunts turn to other sounds I've never heard a Halve make as they slosh through the shallow part of the river. Their volume rises and falls almost conversationally.

I tilt my head to hear better. They *are* talking to each other, and they're talking about me. They're trying to find me.

I gape at Brice.

The Halve that saw us is telling the others to follow the river back the other way to look for me. Their voices recede as they move farther away from our hiding place.

I don't know whether I'm more surprised the Halves can speak, or that one of them lied to protect me.

"That was close." Brice lets out a long breath as he pulls himself out into the open. "I could have sworn that one looked straight at us."

I stare at Brice, puzzled. "It *did* look at us. Didn't you hear what it said?"

Brice looks at me like I've gone crazy. "Halves don't talk," he says.

"But didn't you hear them?"

Brice shakes his head like he can't even believe we're having this conversation. "I heard their grunts and snarls. No *words*."

"You didn't understand them."

The realization that I can understand the Halve language stops me cold. I never got close enough to one—never even thought—they could be intelligent enough to speak. *And I can understand them.*

But why couldn't Brice make sense of what they were saying?

Maybe I'm the only one who can understand them. The thought rings with a truth I can't deny.

I feel like I'm standing on an island, all alone, as a storm rages around me. I want Brice to tell me it's alright, that it makes sense I can communicate with the Halves, but he's still giving me that look that says *I don't believe you, and if I did, that would be even worse.*

"That Halve was protecting us," I say, and then, realizing I haven't told Brice about how I found him, "It's the one that led me to you."

Brice scoffs. "The Halves aren't that smart, and even if they were, they'd sooner kill us than help us escape. *Trust me* on this one."

I shake my head. If the Halves are searching for me, that means the Dusker knows I'm here. And he knows what I am. A shudder of realization courses through me.

There is now no doubt the dead Halve I found gripping Brice's drawing was sent to find me.

"Hemera?" Brice's eyebrows are knit together in concern.

I want to tell Brice…to see what he might know and to share the burden of my growing unease. But if he thought I was in any more danger, he might want me to leave now all the more.

"Nothing," I say. *No point in worrying him,* I reason.

The river brought us far to the east of the white buildings. It's a long way back.

"Careful!" Brice grabs my arm as I step past a yellow flower that drips a thick golden syrup and wafts a sweet scent. "Don't get so close."

Brice plucks a leafy branch from the ground and brushes its top against one of the yellow flowers. Almost too fast to see, the flower launches out of the ground, shooting its syrup at the branch. For a moment, nothing happens. Then, the branch quivers in Brice's hand. Its green leaves turn black. The branch shrivels into itself. There's a small *pop*, and then the blackened branch disintegrates into a cloud of dust.

"Notty nellies," Brice says, looking with disgust at the yellow flowers. "They killed a couple of the prisoners before everyone learned to avoid them. The animals are just as bad, too. You can't trust anything in this place."

"I—"

"We could run, you know." Brice's eyes gleam with a ferocity I don't recognize. He grips both of my hands in his. "We could find someplace to live on the other side of the mountain. I could keep you safe."

I look at Brice. There was a time when I would have accepted his offer without a second thought. I allow myself a moment to imagine what it would be like. Just me and Brice, living alone in a cave behind a waterfall, beholden to no one except for each other.

But that was before I knew what I know now.

"The Duskers lied to us." I search Brice's face. "The Banished Lands weren't for dangerous criminals like they said. The Duskers just wanted to keep control over the Dwellers."

I draw my right hand from underneath my silk cloak to reveal the Solguard marking.

"The resistance still exists, and there are people in the Banished Lands who want to go back to the way things were before the Duskers. They want people to be free."

Brice stares at the curling rays of the sun design on my hands.

"I met my aunt, who is the leader of the Solguards," I hurry on.

"The rebels," I clarify in response to Brice's puzzled look. "My aunt built a fortress to keep the Solguards safe, but now the Duskers know where it is."

Brice's silence makes me babble. "They're my friends, and they're going to need help. Once we free the prisoners here, we'll have an army to attack the Duskers."

"We?" Brice asks.

"My friends," I falter. Brice's face is awash with doubt. "I want to help. Not just because of what happened to my parents, but because I believe in them, in what they're trying to do."

"Hemera, these—Solguards—" he pauses, choosing his words. "How do you know you can trust them?"

I think about Dayne, helping me to fight the Halves even after learning what I was…Wokee seeing my strength for the first time and being impressed rather than afraid…Wade and Sal fighting to keep me in the company even after what happened to Gwendil….

"I'm finally part of something bigger," I say. "And they accept me. Not like the Dwellers. Some of them even admire what I can do."

"Maybe if you had told me about everything sooner—" he breaks off, shaking his head. "Maybe things would have turned out differently."

A wave of hurt crashes over me.

"I didn't know about all of it, at least not the part where I could go out in the sun without my cloak and heal people from Halve blood poisoning. I only figured it out after I left the Subterrane to find you."

Brice's face turns Dusker pale. He swallows.

"Okay, then," he says. "If that's what you want."

I want to throw my arms around him, but instead, I give his hand a squeeze. "Thank you."

Before he can reply, a dark shadow passes overhead. We both look up.

"Burn vulture!" Brice grabs me and pulls me to the ground as the shadow looms closer.

The shadow's one flopped ear comes into focus just before it reaches us. "It's not a Burn vulture; it's Vlaz." I disentangle myself from Brice and jump to my feet.

The cub's small wings pump as he flies straight into my arms.

Laughing in relief that he wasn't hurt by the Halves, I try to turn my head away as Vlaz bathes my face with slobbery hyenair kisses. He wriggles free from my arms to race around me in a circle, whimpering.

"What in the sun?" Brice is staring at Vlaz. His hand rests on his belt in the place where his knives used to hang.

"You've almost grown enough to fit into your ears." I ruffle the fur on Vlaz's head. He blinks up at me, his purple tongue lolling out of his mouth.

"Of all things, to befriend a hyenair. Honestly!" Brice rakes a hand through his hair in exasperation.

Vlaz cocks his head at Brice. It's then that I see the blue silk collar wound around the cub's neck.

When I look closer, I see the blazing sun stitched on the collar in black thread.

"Did Wokee send you to me? Is he alright?" Vlaz flutters his wings and rises off the ground to lick my cheek.

Tears prick at the corners of my eyes. The Duskers wouldn't have attacked the fortress yet, would they? If anything has happened….

It's an effort to get my panic under control.

"Care to explain?" Brice raises an eyebrow.

I recount the story of how I met Dayne and Wokee, and how we killed Vlaz's mother.

"The Halves are terrified of him," I smile, remembering the way they fled from him.

Brice still looks doubtful. He stares at me for several moments without saying anything.

"What?" I demand.

"You're different, you know that?" He turns away from Vlaz to look at me.

"Maybe I am," I admit. "I'm glad I don't have to wear my stupid cloak or try to hide my eyes every time someone looks my way. I don't want to pretend I'm less than I am anymore."

"I understand." Brice turns away, but not before I see the look on his face.

Is it confusion? Disappointment? I don't know, and I'm not sure I want to.

I keep walking so I don't have to see his expression. In the distance, the pale flash of a Halve disappears behind a thick-trunked purple tree.

Brice, who has bent down to splash river water onto his face, hasn't noticed.

I take out my sling and place a stone in the leather pouch. "I'll be right back."

I step around the clusters of notty nellies as silently as I can manage. As I near the tree, I begin to wind my sling. I walk almost all the way around the trunk before I see it.

The Halve is bent over the carcass of a dead animal. Its mouth is stained blue from the animal's blood. Insects the size of my fist circle over its head, but the Halve doesn't seem to notice. The air is heavy with the smell of rank meat.

The Halve pauses when it sees me, the dripping blue haunch raised partway to its open mouth. It's the one that brought me to Brice and saved me on the bridge.

It drops the meat. Two of the insects swoop in, grasp either end of the bloodied haunch, and fly off. The Halve wipes the oily blue blood from its mouth with the back of its hand. I recoil as the Halve stands to face me.

"Can you understand me?" I ask.

The Halve looks at me. It nods its head.

I lick my lips, which are dry and cracked from the heat.

"I'm Hemera." I point to myself. "You?"

The Halve makes a noise that sounds like something between a sneeze and a cough. It sounds like "Ekil."

"I'll call you Ekil, then?"

The Halve nods.

"Why are you different from the others?" I ask.

What I really mean is *why are you helping me instead of trying to kill me?*

"I wasn't always a slave," he says.

"Oh." I don't know what else to say to that.

"And my blood is changed."

His blood is…changed?

I decide not to ask how blood can be changed, or even why. Instead, I slip off my pack and reach my hand into its soggy contents to pull out Brice's drawing. It is stained in places from the water, but the image is still recognizable. I hold it out to Ekil, who looks from me to the drawing.

"I found this with another Halve far away from here. Is the Dusker—er, Master—looking for me?"

Ekil opens his mouth, but then turns his head. His eyes widen.

"Brice, no!"

A long, gnarled branch crashes down over Ekil's head.

CHAPTER 39

You sick…disgusting…bastard….” with each word, Brice brings the branch back down on the Halve.

"Stop, it!" I grip Brice's forearm to keep the branch from falling again. Brice struggles against me for a moment, and then releases the branch.

"Get out of the way." Brice's voice is colder than I've ever heard it.

"No. You'll kill him."

"*Him?* And yeah, that's the point!" He's shaking with rage. "My parents…your mother—" Emotion floods his eyes. He raises the branch again.

"Brice, you don't understand," I begin.

"No, you don't understand!"

Vlaz bounds toward us. He growls a warning at Brice before sitting, legs splayed, at my feet. Ekil begins to tremble at the sight of the cub. His black eyes dart from the branch in Brice's hand to Vlaz.

"I thought you understood," Brice says. The look of betrayal in his eyes as he meets my gaze is like a knife between my ribs. "I thought you felt the same."

"I did, I mean I do," I grasp for words to explain the jumble of thoughts in my head. "But this Halve isn't the one responsible for all of those things. This one showed me where you were. He protected us." I think back to the weaponless Halves our company slaughtered after leaving Solis, and the terrified look in their eyes. "I don't think they are the ones we're after."

Brice's face is red and he's breathing fast.

"I think someone else—the Master you told me about—is forcing them to attack us," I continue.

"One man couldn't control all the Halves in existence," Brice growls. "Do you have even a shred of proof?" The look in his eyes is one I've never seen before.

I remember seeing the Halves in the strange white building, with their orderly piles of weapons, and knowing the work they did was not for themselves. I shake my head. "Just a feeling."

Brice scoffs. "I've been a prisoner here." He spits on the ground at Ekil's feet. "I think I know more about these monsters than you."

I put a hand on his arm. "I want revenge for everything that has happened as much as you do—"

"It doesn't seem like it," Brice says.

"But if it hadn't been for this one," I continue as though he hadn't spoken, "I never would have found you."

"And you think it *intentionally* brought you to me?" he spits.

Vlaz growls again.

"Why don't you believe me?" My own temper rises. "We're together and we're alive. That should be proof enough for you."

We glare at each other for a minute, and then Brice drops the branch on the ground. Ekil moans.

"Where are you going?" I hurry to catch up with Brice.

"I didn't realize when you talked about your *friends* you were talking about the Halves."

The sting of his words brings me to a halt.

"I could have just stayed in the Subterrane if all I wanted was to befriend some Halves." My voice wavers, betraying my emotion.

"I know." Brice softens. "I'm sorry. But it could have killed you. You're giving the Halve credit for things that are just coincidences."

Exhaustion weighs on me. I don't want to argue anymore.

"Just promise you won't hurt this Halve. I'm not on their side, I just want to know you won't kill the one thing that brought us together. We owe it for that."

I walk back over to Ekil, who wipes blood from the back of his head with his rough, scarred hands. When Vlaz follows me, Ekil cowers on the ground.

I rip off a piece of my shirt, dip it into the stream, and go to Ekil.

"Here," I say as I hand him the cloth. "You don't need to fear us."

Vlaz sniffs the Halve but doesn't growl.

"We need to free the prisoners," I tell Ekil as he mops the back of his head with the cloth. "Can you help us get back without anyone seeing us?"

"Hemera…you're grunting," Brice says. He's looking at me like I sprouted a second head.

"I'm…what?" I turn away from Ekil to stare at Brice. I can't tell if the look on his face is wonder or fear.

"You're grunting," he says again.

"I show you." Ekil's reply keeps me from having to think about the fact that I'm somehow speaking a different language without even realizing it.

"Let's go," I say to Brice carefully, as though to make sure I don't slip into the hideous, guttural language of the Halves. "Ekil is going to show us the way."

The Halve's strides are much longer than ours, and we need to jog to keep pace. Brice keeps a considerable distance between himself and Ekil. He doesn't say a word. Vlaz flies beside me and gives my cheek encouraging licks.

The air is sweltering as the sun rises toward high day. Sweat streams down Brice's face as he labors under his heavy cloak.

"Everything in this place is unnatural," Brice grumbles, skirting one of the yellow flowers and swiping at the sweat on his brow.

I bite my lip, unable to shake the feeling that he's talking about me, too.

Ekil stops when we reach a grove of the white-leafed specere trees. "Follow the river until you reach the western door. No guards there."

Ekil starts to walk away.

"Wait!" I say. "What about the drawing?"

"He wants you," Ekil replies without turning back.

My stomach tightens. "Why? Why are you helping us?"

Ekil is already too far away to hear.

When I turn back, Brice is giving me that look again. "They're not like us, you know."

For some reason, I think about the last time I ever spoke with my father. He warned me Brice might feel differently if he knew the whole truth about me. He said he sent Brice away to protect me.

Could he have been right?

I feel guilty and disgusted with myself the instant the thought crosses my mind.

"Come on." I yank up the hood of my silk cloak and wince as the material tears. "We need to reach the buildings before high day."

True to Ekil's word, the western side of the building is empty and blocked from view of the main courtyard. We approach slowly. When Vlaz doesn't growl or bare his teeth, I pull the heavy stone door open.

We step over the piles of discarded stone and timber to the stacks of weapons. The stone clubs are too heavy for any human to wield, but the long iron blades are easy enough to carry.

Brice stands still, staring at the piles of spears and clubs. "There's something I have to tell you." His face is pained, but he doesn't look at me.

I stumble on some unseen debris on the ground, and one of the blades slips from my arm.

Not now, Hemera!

It's too late. The blade falls into a precarious pile of other weapons. For one, terrifying second, the pile teeters. And then the metal blades crash to the ground. The sound is loud enough to wake the dead.

It's followed by the Halves' guttural cries.

CHAPTER 40

Come on!"

I bend down to gather as many of the weapons as I can hold and race toward the ladder on the other side of the building. Balancing the weapons in one arm, I climb.

When we reach the top, I look down. A group of Halves are staring at the mess on the ground, gesturing and grunting in confusion. None of them look up at us.

"Fools," Brice mutters, and then he looks at me, and his lip quirks. "I'm glad to know not everything about you has changed." He gives my feet a meaningful glance.

I smile back at him, and just like that, I'm reminded of how easy it always was to be with him. No matter how clumsy I was, Brice made me feel graceful. He always seemed to know what I needed.

The tension between us melts.

Brice takes my hand. "Come on."

I unlatch the stone fitting the way Ekil had earlier and step into the sunlight.

Brice shields his eyes against the brightness. "How did you know about this?"

Knowing he won't want to hear the true answer, I just say, "I found it when I was looking for you."

Brice carries the blades across the bridge in two trips. He moves as effortlessly across the rickety planks as though he were traveling over flat ground. When I cross, Brice stays one pace behind me, keeping his hands on my waist to steady me. Vlaz flies just above us.

The cub's long ears are alert. He snaps his jaws at the giant insects that swarm around us, keeping them at bay.

"Careful," Brice warns, as I push aside the stone door on the other end. The smell of unwashed bodies hits me as soon as I step into the darkness.

My eyes have barely adjusted to the candlelight when the Halve's enormous shadow rounds the corner. I have just enough time to register it isn't Ekil before the Halve swings its stone club at me.

"Duck!"

I throw myself against the wall of the cave to avoid the blow. The club crashes into the wall just over my head. Vlaz snarls and lunges at the Halve.

The Halve shrieks as Vlaz sinks his teeth into its leg but doesn't retreat. The Halve raises its club again. This time, its weapon is aimed at Vlaz's head.

I leap forward, using one of the blades to block the club. I see the flash of Brice's blade as the Halve stumbles backward.

"Watch its blood!" Brice calls as he pushes his blade deeper into the Halve's gut.

Another Halve appears before I can correct Brice. It lunges toward me, but Vlaz meets it in the air and takes hold of the loose skin around its neck. The Halve roars as Brice moves in for the kill.

It's not long before both Halves are stretched out on the ground in pools of their own blood.

"Stay behind me." Brice grips a blade in each hand as he inches along the path. "There might be more of them."

The first row of cells seems to be empty of guards. We wait for a few moments to make sure no Halves are waiting for us.

Brice cups his hands around his mouth and calls, "All clear?"

Almost immediately, voices travel back to us.

"Brice, is that you?" A deep voice cuts through the rest. "We thought you were taken to the catacombs."

"Everything's fine. We're getting out of here."

A chorus of excited voices erupts as we reach the first cell. I drop my armful of blades to wrench open the first stone door.

Vlaz squeezes through the opening first. Brice and I follow. The single candle that burns on the cell wall illuminates a tall, muscular man with jet black hair and a pointed chin. His ankles are bound in thick ropes.

"What the hell is going on around here?" the man demands as he scrambles as far away from Vlaz as the ropes will allow.

"He won't hurt you," I tell him.

"Brice? How did you get in here? How did you escape? What's going on?"

"Calm yourself, Thutmose. This is Hemera and her pet hyenair."

Brice kneels down and begins to hack at the ropes. "Thutmose has been here the longest," he explains by way of introduction.

"I'll get the rest of the doors open for you," I say, already ducking out of the cell.

It's only a matter of time before more Halves come.

Cries follow me from cell to cell as the prisoners, still bound in their ropes, beg to be freed. Vlaz stays by my side. He gives my hand, raw from the unforgiving stone, encouraging nuzzles.

"Please, I'm next for the catacombs." A weak voice calls out to me. I pull open the stone door and step inside the cell.

A girl who looks about my age stretches her filthy hands toward me. She's shorter than I am, and too thin. Her knobby shoulders make points in the fabric of her cloak. Her nose is curved in the middle and swollen, like it was recently broken.

"No one is taking you to the catacombs," I assure her.

I take my blade and begin to saw through the ropes that bind her.

"You're the one he's been waiting for, aren't you?" The girl keeps her eyes focused on the fraying ropes around her ankles.

My shoulders tense, but I keep cutting. "The Master? What makes you think he's been waiting for me?"

"He needs you for his experiments. And I recognize your face."

I stop cutting and stare at her. Dread curdles my stomach.

I know the answer, but I have to ask. "How do you recognize me?"

"I was there when he showed the picture to the Halves meant to track you," she says. "He thought I might be good for his experiments because I look like you." She screws up her face, making it clear how she feels about being compared to the likes of me.

I take my pack off my shoulder and fumble to open it. My hands are shaking so badly the contents of my pack spill onto the floor of the cell. I reach for Brice's drawing. Smoothing out the piece of script tree bark, I hold it up to the candle.

"Is this what you saw?"

"Yes," she whispers.

CHAPTER 41

I finish cutting through the ropes and hurry to the next cell without looking back at the girl. A sinking dread has begun to close in around me.

My palms, bloody from an especially stubborn door, have already healed. I brush away the dried blood as I grasp the iron handle of the next cell.

"Don't worry, I'm here to free you," I call to the prisoner.

"Hemera, is that you?" a voice calls through the narrow opening.

I pause with my hand on the iron ring of the door.

"*Wade?*"

"You're alright!"

I open the cell door and run to him. I throw my arms around his neck as he pulls me to him. When Vlaz tries to squeeze between us, he gets tangled in the ropes and we all fall to the ground in a heap of laughter and Vlaz's slobbers.

"We lost track of you at the gates," Wade is saying, "and then we all got split up. But I knew if anyone could find a way to get us out of here it'd be you."

"What about Dayne and the rest of the company?" I ask as I disentangle myself from Wade and begin to saw through his ropes.

Wade's smile fades. I stop cutting.

"What happened?" My voice cracks.

"Those filthy guards took him," Wade says. "We couldn't find you, and then there was all that madness at the gates." He swallows. "I thought they might have taken you, too."

"We need to find him." Panic tightens my chest.

Wade nods. "Ry's a few cells down. The others are here, too."

I finish cutting through the ropes. When he's freed, I turn to the cell opening, but Wade grabs my hand. He pulls me back with so much force I slam into him.

Wade doesn't give me a chance to catch my breath. In a fluid motion, he cups my neck with one hand and twists his body to dip me back against his arm. He leans over me and presses his lips to mine.

"Get your hands off her." Brice's voice at the door startles us both. I right myself, pushing Wade away.

"Brice, this is Wade," I stammer. "He's a—friend who helped me get here."

"Pleasure," Wade says. The light of the candles flickers in his golden eyes. He looks like he's enjoying himself as Brice glares at him.

"We need to free the rest of the prisoners and find Dayne. Now." I look from one to the other.

A tense moment passes before Wade says, "Come on. I'll show you Ry's cell."

When I open her cell door, Ry is tied down with so many ropes she can't take a single step.

"She almost escaped," Wade announces.

It takes all three of us to cut away her ropes. When we manage to free her, Ry wraps me in a bone-crushing hug.

"We thought they took you, too!" Her curls bounce as she jumps up and down. "So, what's the plan for rescuing Dayne?"

"Do you know where the catacombs are?" I ask Brice.

"They run beneath this building," he replies. "There's only one entrance, and it's guarded by Halves."

"Take us there. Now." I resist the urge to wrap my arms around myself at the sudden ache I feel for Dayne. "We're not too late." *We can't be.*

"What should we do about the rest of the prisoners in here?" Ry asks. Their cries for rescue echo down the rows of cells.

"Thutmose and the others can take care of it." Brice glances at me. "They won't be as fast as you, but they'll manage."

I nod. "Let's take a few of these blades and leave the rest for the prisoners. That way they can defend themselves when the guards come back."

"We'll only need enough for you three." Ry reaches beneath her shirt to untuck a scalloped dagger. "They didn't search me well enough to find this," she says with a devilish grin.

We squeeze through the groups of freed prisoners. As an afterthought, I walk back to Thutmose who labors beside three other men to open a single door.

"Once we're out, barricade all the entrances." I look around the path crowded with freed prisoners. "If we're not back before lowest day, get everyone out and head for the mountains."

I rush after the others as they stride down the path between the cells.

Brice stops to wait for me. "Want to explain what happened back there?" His eyes flash even in the darkness.

"It's not what you think." I can hear the defensiveness in my voice. "Wade thought I'd been taken to the catacombs and was just relieved to see me alive."

Brice scoffs. "I was captured with some other guys who were on scouting missions, and we got pretty close." He pauses. "But I never started kissing them."

Fury consumes my guilt. I fly around to face him. "I came here for *you*! And you stand here, questioning my loyalty—"

"I'm sorry," Brice interrupts me. He steps back, eyeing my clenched fists. "You're right. Who am I to talk about loyalty, anyway?"

"What's that supposed to mean?"

"Just...." He seems to be waging some kind of internal battle. "I did something awful, and I'm afraid you're going to hate me."

"You both coming or what?" Ry, hands on hips, waves us forward.

I wait for Brice to say something else, but he's looking at Ry, who is tapping her foot in impatience. His shoulders sag. "I'm just sorry, okay?"

"Okay." I give his hand a quick squeeze.

"By the way, you never told me who this Dayne person is," Brice says as we hurry after the others.

Dayne.

Fresh waves of panic roll through me. I pick up my pace. "He was my guide and saved my life more than once. He's my friend." My voice breaks on the last word.

Brice slips an arm around my shoulders. "We'll find him."

I swallow around the lump in my throat.

When we reach the end of the path, everyone else pulls their cloaks on while I push open the enormous stone doors. Sunlight floods the path.

"Is it high day?" Wade calls from where the others are hidden outside of the path of direct sunlight.

I step out into the heat to measure my shadow. The sunlight comes in streams of pink and red. It's so hot I can hardly breathe. "We still have about an hour," I call back.

The others follow me outside. Burdened by their cloaks, they seem on the verge of fainting.

"What are we looking for?" I ask Brice.

"Start near the doors and work your way out," he instructs. Even the shadow from his hood can't disguise how red his face is. The beginning of a Burn blister is smoking on his chin.

He wouldn't be putting himself at risk right now if it wasn't for me. *And I just....* I glance at Wade, and then look away before he catches my eye.

"The entrance will be disguised," Brice continues as he scans the ground, "but also recognizable to the Halves."

The land outside the door is nothing more than notty nellies, a few specere trees here and there, and rocks scattered about. I give the flowers a wide berth as I lift the dangling leaves of the specere trees to see if there are any secret tunnels hidden beneath.

"Over here."

I run back to where Brice is kneeling. I swerve to the side just in time to avoid the syrup of a notty nelly that spits up at a small white bird flying just overhead. In seconds, the bird collapses on the ground in a sizzling, blackened heap.

Brice points to what looks like nothing more than a tuft of grass.

"Can you smell it?" he looks at me.

He takes a great whiff as the rest of us exchange puzzled glances.

"Cammamoss." Brice motions for me to bend down and smell it. It has a deep earthy scent, not altogether unpleasant.

"Cammamoss?" I peer at the grass.

Brice plucks a handful from the ground, which transforms to the sandy color of his cloak. Its rich scent fills the air.

"Did that stuff just change color, or is the sun making me blinder than I thought?" Ry scratches her head through her hood.

Brice holds the moss next to a notty nelly, careful to avoid touching the flowers, and the moss turns yellow.

"It camouflages to look like whatever it's near so predators can't see it to eat it. Scouts use it all the time to cover their tracks," Brice says. He scrapes away more of the moss to reveal the flat stone hidden beneath. "See?"

Vlaz squeezes between Brice and me to sniff the stone. He paws at the ground and begins to whine.

I dig my hands under the stone and give it a yank.

Beneath the stone is a black hole. As I blink into the depths, the hazy pink sunlight leaves my eyes. What I thought was darkness is a tunnel lit by candles. Steep stairs are carved into the earth and stone.

Vlaz cries louder as he paces back and forth in front of the hole, wings fluttering.

"Let me go first," Brice says, putting a protective hand on my back.

Before he can argue, I grasp the rungs of the wooden ladder and lower myself down into the tunnel. He's already put himself at too much risk for my sake. Brice, Ry, and Wade grip their blades and follow me. Vlaz howls after us but doesn't follow.

The stench of decay fills the air at the bottom of the ladder. The others choke and gag, muffling the sound of footsteps ahead. I hold out my blade.

"Ekil?" I ask.

The Halve steps around the corner, but it's too stooped to be Ekil. The Halve strides toward me with incredible swiftness and grabs my throat with one of its rough hands.

"Wait," I gasp. "I need your help."

The Halve loosens its grip on my neck and opens its mouth like it's about to speak, but it doesn't make a sound. It just stands there with its mouth hanging open. I look down.

The point of a blade protrudes from the Halve's stomach. Its thick blood has already begun to puddle on the ground.

"Did it hurt you?" Brice puts his foot on the Halve's back to dig out his blade.

I let out a groan. That Halve was about to say something. *It might have known where Dayne is being kept.* To say as much to Brice, though, would be useless. I swallow the anger that surges through me.

Another Halve appears around the corner.

"Wait—" I begin, but Ry has already thrown her knife into the folds of its neck.

It lets out a roar as it thuds to the ground.

"No!"

I run to the Halve and kneel by its side. It's still alive—barely.

"What's going on down here? Where are the prisoners?" I support the Halve's neck with one hand to keep the blood from pooling there and choking it.

The Halve looks at me with something between surprise and fear in its black eyes. It tries to say something, but its words are too filled with blood for me to understand.

The Halve's head drops heavy and lifeless against me.

"Were you trying to talk to it?" Wade asks.

"Hemera, is that its blood on you?" Brice wipes the blood off my face with the sleeve of his cloak. "You'll die!"

"I told you before. Their blood can't hurt me." I push away his hand, trying to ignore the look on his face. We stare at each other until Ry clears her throat.

"Shall we?" She raises her eyebrow and makes an exaggerated gesture for us to continue.

When we round the next corner of the tunnel, a horrific stench strikes me like a blow to the face. Choking, I try to shield my nose with my silk cloak.

"Ugh, what is that?" Ry asks in disgust, her voice muffled from the sleeve of her cloak as she presses it over her face.

"Rotting corpses," Brice answers.

"Dayne?" I run down the dark passage, not caring who might hear me.

The tunnel ends abruptly. Its farthest corner is flanked by four cells identical to those in the prison building. I wrench open each door, leaving the others to go inside and start sawing through the prisoners' ropes.

I open the last door and let myself inside. The smell is sour, a combination of blood and urine. The only light in the cell comes from the candles in the tunnel. A body covered in rags is huddled in the corner of the cell.

Please don't let this be Dayne.

When I take a step into the cell, the prisoner begins to scream.

"It's alright, I'm not going to hurt you!"

At the sound of my voice, the screaming stops. The prisoner is silent for a moment. "Hemera?"

CHAPTER 42

ayne!" I cross the cell in two steps.

"No, not you, not you!" His voice is hoarse.

Even in the darkness of the cell, I can tell his hair is matted with dirt and dried blood. His forehead shines with sweat.

"Come on, we've got to get you out of here." I keep the silk over my mouth and nose, fighting the urge to wretch.

I tug on Dayne's tattered cloak. The stickiness of fresh blood coats my hand. "Time to go," I repeat as panic and nausea roil in my stomach.

When Dayne doesn't move, I pick him up as gently as I can. I carry him through the cell door before his ranting trails off and his body goes limp.

Ry and Wade also carry a prisoner between them who is either dead or unconscious. I would guess from the matted hair dragging on the ground the prisoner is a woman, but she's too covered with blood to tell for sure.

"The others are dead," Brice says helplessly.

We carry Dayne and the other prisoner past the bodies of the two Halves. Together, we manage to pull the limp bodies out of the tunnel and into the blinding sunlight. I draw Dayne's filthy cloak more closely around his body.

"This one doesn't have a cloak," Ry's voice comes from inside the tunnel. "She'll fry."

"There's a specere tree a few paces away," Brice calls down. "Keep her under your own cloak as much as you can until we reach the tree. She'll be safe under there until we can find another cloak."

As we carry the prisoners from the tunnel to the specere trees, Brice stops to cut a red branch from a leafy bush.

I push Dayne's body through the white leaves first and then turn back to help Ry and Wade with the other prisoner. We would be closed entirely in darkness under the canopy of the specere leaves if it were not for the branch Brice carries, which bathes us all in a scarlet light.

Vlaz noses his way under the tree. He sniffs at Dayne, still whimpering. The woman opens her eyes and begins to scream. Ry tries to calm her, but it's no use. She shrieks as she struggles against Ry's grip.

"You lost your cloak," Ry tells the woman as she pulls her back from running through the specere leaves. "You'll die."

"She'll bring every Halve in the fortress here," Wade says.

Ry reaches underneath her cloak to rip off a piece of her shirt. "I'm sorry," she mutters as she stuffs the cloth into the woman's mouth.

The woman's eyes roll back into her head as she faints. Brice catches her and lowers her to the ground. Dayne is moaning, "Not her. Leave my family alone."

"Dayne, it's Hemera. It's me." I stand in front of him, but his eyes are unfocused and he seems not to see me.

"What do we do now?" Wade asks.

I use one hand to keep Dayne from falling to the ground. "First, someone needs to get a cloak for her. It won't be long before an army of Halves comes, and we—"

"Oh no," Ry moans.

She bends over the woman's body and looks up. A tear slides down Ry's cheek, which looks like blood in the light of the red branch. "She's dead."

"It's the Halve blood," Dayne whispers. "Inside us."

I inhale. It never occurred to me that the blood covering Dayne's face might not be his own. I look closer at the slash marks across his neck and shoulder. The wounds are the same as the ones Taniel had when Brice and I found his body in the woods.

With shaking hands, I press my fingertips to the cuts.

I feel the searing pain as the poison is drawn from Dayne and burns into my own skin. There's a hiss as a small amount of smoke escapes from the place where my hands are pressed to Dayne's wounds.

"Hemera, what the—?" Brice starts toward me, but Wade holds him back.

Dayne shivers as the poison leaves his body and flows into mine. My legs give out beneath me and I collapse onto the ground. Every part of me feels like it's on fire. Sweat pours down my face. My lungs scream for air, but I can't take a breath.

The pain is more savage than anything I've ever felt. Healing Jarosh was nothing compared to this. I claw at my own skin as I try to rid it of the burning poison. It's like Dayne's body held more Halve blood than his own.

Just when I think I can't take it anymore, the rawness of the pain begins to recede. Gasping, I hold up my hands to examine the place where I absorbed the poison. The bloody rawness is magnified by the branch's red light. New skin materializes even as I inspect the wound.

"Hemera!" Dayne's eyes snap back into focus. He grabs my arm with surprising strength. "I must speak with you. Now."

I pull myself up to a sitting position with an effort. "We're going to a safe place," I reply wearily.

"Nowhere is safe!" he looks around, as though he expects one of us to transform into a Halve. "Now, here, alone."

"We'll keep watch," Ry beckons to the others, "and bury this body."

"But it's nearly high day," I protest.

"There's still a few minutes, at least."

"Hemera." Brice shifts on his feet.

"Go!" Dayne commands.

Brice gives me an uncertain look.

"Please," I tell him.

With a sigh, Brice ducks out from under the tree's canopy. Ry and Wade lift the woman's body. They check their cloaks, and then duck under the leaves.

Dayne sits up and rests his back against the trunk of the tree.

"Thank you," he says when the others have gone. "But you should never have come here."

"What are you talking about?"

"It's you he wants; it's your blood he's trying to replicate. That's what he's doing, mixing Halve and human blood, to try to make others like you."

"He's trying to make others like…me?" I feel sick.

"Oh Mer, how can you forgive me?" Dayne cries. "I've kept so many secrets."

I give him a sharp look. "You've never called me that before."

Dayne sighs. "We have little time, so I'll speak plainly." He blinks, as though fighting to stay conscious. "I wanted to be there to help you and watch you grow up. When I left Subterrane Harkibel—"

"What were you doing in my Subterrane?" A nervous tingle spreads through me. I look at Dayne, and it strikes me like a blow. I stagger backward.

How did I not see it before? His eyes…that blue…that familiar crease at the edges when he smiles. He's my—

Dayne sees the recognition on my face and nods. "Brother." He pauses to take a deep, shuddering breath. "Well, half-brother. We share the same mother."

CHAPTER 43

I swallow hard. "Why…why didn't you tell me sooner?"

"Because I was ashamed. If I hadn't become a Solguard, our mother might still be alive." He stares at the ground. "Not a day goes by that I don't regret abandoning you."

I don't know what to say. In spite of the heat, a chill takes hold of me.

Dayne continues, "When I found you, when I learned you weren't dead like I thought, all I wanted was to stay with you, to protect you. I thought if you knew who I really was, you wouldn't want anything to do with me." Dayne reaches a hand toward mine where it rests in the dirt. "Can you ever forgive me?"

"But the Captain isn't your father, then?" I manage to choke out.

"No. Before she married the Captain, our mother was with another man. Clarion was his name. He was a Solguard, and died in a skirmish with Duskers a few years after I was born. Our mother married Zeidan seven years later because she saw the qualities of a leader in him." His expression darkens. "She was right, but just not the way she thought he was going to be."

Dayne swallows, and then shakes his head. "When I was fifteen years old and you were just a baby, I ran away to join Jadem and the Solguards. Our mother told me some of what my father had done, and I wanted to help finish the work he had started."

"You were with Aunt Jadem? The whole time?" My mouth feels dry. Exhaustion is beginning to edge out every other feeling.

Dayne nods. His thin, lined face is filled with grief.

His gaze darkens. "Of course, once Zeidan found out, he forced our mother to disown Jadem and I and never speak of us again. Our mother knew if she tried to come with me, Zeidan would never stop searching for you, and she feared what he would do when he found you."

I try to see the man Dayne is describing, but all I can picture is Captain Harkibel, fearlessly defending the Dwellers as the Halves closed in around him. The Captain might have been difficult to know well—all I knew about him before he was the Subterrane captain was that he was a healer—and he might have been traveling outside of the Subterrane more often than he was inside it, but he protected me from the Duskers. He made difficult decisions for the sake of the Dwellers.

"It's not possible," I whisper. "My father would never…."

But even as I say the words, I feel a seed of doubt take root.

"Believe me he would," Dayne says with a bitterness I've never heard before. He takes quick, shallow breaths. "Zeidan has many spies. When he learned that Jadem and I had infiltrated Malarusk…."

"He wouldn't—"

"He sold us out to the Duskers. And they rewarded him for it."

My father is the reason why Jadem and Dayne were imprisoned? I don't know what to say.

Dayne grimaces. "Neither Jadem nor I would give up the names of any of the other Solguards or the location of the cave fortress. We were tortured and left in the Malarusk dungeons to rot. It was eight years before we escaped."

Eight years. Dayne's lined face and gray hair make sense now.

Dayne continues, "When Jadem and I broke out, we came straight to Subterrane Harkibel to see you and Mother. We were going to take you both away from the Captain. But we were too late." He sags against the tree trunk. "On our way, we learned from one of Jadem's spies that you and our mother were killed by a Halve."

"Me and our mother? Killed by a Halve?" My brain is slow to register his words.

Dayne looks at me with desperate, pleading eyes. "We saw both of your headstones in the forest where the spy said the Halve attacked. I never dreamed your headstone was…fake."

I sit numbly as Dayne's words wash over me. I remember Aunt Jadem saying something when I first met her…something about hearing that her sister and niece were killed by a Halve.

She must have been with Dayne, then.

Betrayal, at no one in particular—at everyone—washes over me. A single question emerges from the fog swirling around my head.

"How could my mother—my own mother—not have told me? How could she stand to lie about her own sister? Her son?"

"Haven't you been listening?" Dayne growls. "She didn't tell you because she couldn't. Telling you would have put us, and you, in more danger." He pounds the ground with his fist.

I shake my head. *Is it possible my parents lied to me for my entire life? About my own family?*

"I never knew." I turn away so Dayne can't see the angry tears spilling down my cheeks.

Dayne says, "After we heard about your deaths, Jadem returned to the cave fortress, but she stopped all her Solguard work. She said too many sacrifices had been made. But I was angry. I wanted someone to pay for what happened to you and Mother."

I remember the tension between Dayne and Jadem. Now, I understand why.

Dayne continues, "I went out on my own to do damage to the Duskers where I could. It took me five years to work up the nerve to go back to kill Zeidan."

"You were going to kill…my father?"

"Yes. But on my way to the Subterrane, I found you. I recognized your eyes, and then when you told me your name…."

I've been holding my breath, and force myself to let it out.

Dayne says, "I could have come back for you sooner if only I'd known."

Too many emotions are at war inside of me for me to think of a response.

Dayne's face twists in bitterness. "I sacrificed everything for the Solguards. I was rotting away in Malarusk when I should have been there to protect you."

Dayne nods at the tattoo on the back of my hand, which glows red in the light of the branch. "And now you will make the same sacrifice."

"Joining the Solguard was my choice," I say.

Dayne's anger disappears. "I'm so sorry." A tear slides down his cheek.

I can't make sense of any of this. First an aunt, and now a brother? My parents…both of them lying to me….

Remembering what I had wanted to know before, I ask, "What was the urgent errand you left Jadem's fortress for?"

Dayne's gaze is far away. "You told me everyone in Subterrane Harkibel was killed by the Halves, but then one of Jadem's scouts brought word the Captain survived."

I leap to my feet.

"He's alive? My father's alive?"

Dayne nods.

"And you didn't tell me?!"

Dayne looks up at me. "I couldn't explain to you why I needed to kill him without telling you who I was. There wasn't time to explain it all to you then."

Dayne was going to kill my father. It's only the destroyed look on Dayne's face that tempers my fury.

There is truth in Dayne's eyes, and there would be no reason for him to lie. But I still can't imagine Captain Harkibel…my father…making a fake grave for me and giving up his wife's family to the Duskers.

He wasn't the kind of man to be cruel for cruelty's sake…was he? I'm struck, once again, by how little I really knew my father. He was so often away, and when he was in the Subterrane, his time was taken up by the guards and scouts. Outside of the Dusker inspections and weapons training, which stopped after my mother's death, I barely saw him.

Destinel was an orphan and Brice's parents died soon after my mother, so it never felt strange to me to have so little to do with my father.

"Hemera, he's the reason why I thought you were dead…for *years*," Dayne says. "He's the reason I wasn't there to protect our mother."

There is so much anguish in Dayne's blue eyes. Now that I know, it's impossible not to notice their resemblance to our mother's.

"Did you do it?" There is no emotion in my voice. "Did you kill my father?"

Dayne shakes his head. "Right before I left to go in search of him, I discovered Gorgoran was a Dusker spy. I came to warn you."

I'm filled with relief, but the feeling is temporary. Footsteps pound the ground outside the specere tree. Vlaz, who had been lying beside Dayne, jumps up as Wade lifts one of the leaves and ducks his head in.

"Time to go," he beckons us. "Halves are coming."

"No, there's more," Dayne grabs my cloak to keep me from leaving.

"*Now*," Wade says. "There's an army after us."

I give Dayne my blade and unwind my sling. When we duck out from the specere tree, the Halves are galloping toward us on all fours. Within seconds, we're surrounded.

There's no point in trying to talk to these Halves; they would kill me before I could even get close enough. I place a stone in the leather pouch of my sling, wind it in two short rotations, and then let it fly.

I reload my sling before the first Halve has even hit the ground. Vlaz is in the air, snarling and biting. The Halves scatter out of his immediate path, but don't flee as they had before. Beside me, Dayne slides his blade through two Halves in a single motion.

An enormous Halve runs at me with its stone club poised to strike. I reach for another stone, but my leather pouch is empty. The Halve swings its club at my head. I duck under the blow, and then bring my elbow down on its curved back. *Crack.*

The Halve lets out a terrific roar as it sinks to the ground.

"Hemera!"

Brice tosses his blade to me. I catch it, and dive under a club that narrowly misses my head. I drive the blade into the Halve's gut. Thick blood oozes out of the wound as I draw the blade out.

The Halve's black eyes go wide. White froth flecked with blood erupts from its mouth as I use the blade a second time to end it.

Five Halves surround me in a tight circle. I dart between and around them as they swing their clubs. These Halves are better fighters than any I've encountered, but I'm faster.

I use my fist to break one Halve's arm. It howls as its stone club falls to the ground. I pick up the club and throw it at another that is closing in on me. The club strikes its head, and the Halve collapses.

"Look out!"

I turn, catching the side of a Halve's rough fist as it hits me in the jaw.

My eyes swim with tears. I blink to clear my vision as the sound of their heavy footsteps draws nearer. I throw wild punches, listening for the crack as my fists connect with the Halves' bones.

My vision clears enough for me to see the club just before it connects with my upturned face. Everything goes black.

CHAPTER 44

I open my eyes. The light shining from the lanterns makes a fiery pain erupt in my head. *Where am I?*

I'm lying on a strange bed. My arms and legs are stuck against my body as though a blanket is wrapped tightly around me. *Too tightly.*

Every breath is an effort. If I stay still, my head throbs less viciously. There is a smell in the air, familiar yet repulsive. Sweat, fear, and death.

I ignore the surge of nausea as I lift my neck to look around. Beside my bed, there's a wooden box draped with a once-white cloth, which is now speckled with dried blood. Fine-tipped knives crusted with blood rest on top of the cloth.

Beside the box are two iron cauldrons on a raised platform with clear tubes running between them. One of the tubes carries red liquid, blood, between the cauldrons. The other tube carries a liquid that is more of a rust-brown hue, like the blood of Halves. Pools of congealed blood have gathered in the divots on the uneven stone floor.

Built into the walls are carved-out spaces for crude, human-length boxes.

"I'm in the catacombs," I say out loud.

"You are, indeed," agrees a voice. The sound bounces off the stone ceiling, which gives the effect of being everywhere at once. The voice is familiar but does nothing to lessen my growing unease.

I try to sit up but find I can't move anything below my neck. Glancing down, I see it's not a blanket, but rather iron chains that have immobilized my body. My bed is nothing more than a thick wooden board resting on an iron scaffold.

"Welcome, daughter."

I raise my head enough to see my father, flanked by at least ten enormous Halves. Behind the Halves are two filthy men with long, tangled hair. Each man carries a leather whip in one hand and a dagger in the other.

"It can't be." I must have hit my head harder than I thought.

I shake my head, trying to clear it. This man standing before me can't be my father. "I saw you surrounded by Halves. You couldn't have survived."

Even with everything Dayne told me, I still can't shake the image of Captain Harkibel, surrounded by an ever-tightening ring of Halves. Whatever else he might have been, my father cared about his people. He would have done anything to protect the Dwellers; he was willing to give his own life for them. He wouldn't have imprisoned them. He wouldn't have tortured them.

My father steps closer to where I can see him without raising my head. He looks the same, except his salt-and-pepper beard has grown long and tangled. He has traded his sand-colored cloak from Subterrane Harkibel for a gray cloak of the Duskers. The crease of his brow and tight-lipped smile, once so familiar, now seem to have an edge of malice.

A feeling of dread creeps down my spine.

I twist my body to loosen the chains. At a command from my father, the Halves leave his side and surround me before I can break loose. Each one grips me with a scaly hand.

"I need you to be calm, daughter," my father says. "You and I need to talk."

"It's you." My voice sounds like it's coming from somewhere farther away than from inside my own throat. "You're the Dusker…the Master everyone is talking about."

"Indeed, I am," he agrees.

I'm too surprised, too overwhelmed, to feel anything else.

As the pain begins to ebb, my thoughts grow clearer. "How…how did you survive the attack on the Subterrane?"

My father shakes his head. "*Think* Hemera." He says it the way he did when I was trying to puzzle out the riddles he told me as a child. He stands waiting for the look of recognition to light up my face.

When I don't say anything, he sighs. "The Halves are under my command. Their attacks on the Subterrane territory weren't random. I *ordered* each and every one of them."

"But…why?" My voice sounds strangled.

"Because the Duskers were beginning to grow suspicious of my extended absences, and I knew it was only a matter of time before they tracked my activities to Tanguro. I needed more time. Fabricating my own death was the solution." He cocks his head. "Although I do regret any pain that mistaken notion might have caused you." He *does* look sorry for a moment, and then his face smooths back into an unreadable mask.

"Destinel." My breathing has gone short and ragged. "She was my best friend. You couldn't have. You wouldn't."

"I know she was your friend," he says, "but the only way for you to move forward was to have a clean break from the past."

The tears gathering in my throat are choking me, making me cough and splutter.

"It was your job to protect her—to protect all of them!"

"It is my job, first and foremost, to protect you." With a careless wave of his hand, my father dismisses the lives of hundreds.

I don't believe you, I want to say. *You're joking.* But my father never jokes.

"Taniel," I say as the missing pieces begin to fit together. "He escaped to warn us about—you?"

A strange smile plays on my father's lips. "Taniel's escape was made possible because I ordered it."

At the look of sheer bewilderment on my face, my father says, "Think of Taniel as the unwitting breadcrumbs that led you here. If it hadn't been for him, you wouldn't have known your destination."

"You tortured him," I persist, ignoring all else his words imply.

"Torture implies punishment. No," he shakes his head, "this was about progress. This was about you."

My father cocks his head at me, like he's waiting for understanding to dawn on my face.

"About me?"

Tears are still leaking out of my eyes. I want to wipe them away, but the Halves are keeping my arms pinned at my sides. I can't stand being so vulnerable, especially when my father just revealed he's the reason why Destinel, Sirrel, and so many others are dead.

"I'm not cruel, Hemera." His voice is disapproving, like he's trying to explain an important truth to a sullen child. "Destroying the Subterranes, all of them, is a necessary part of all of this." He turns to look at his two guards, who nod back at him.

My father stares at me, like he's expecting approval to dawn on my face. If it wasn't for the pain in my head, I would think I was dreaming all of this.

When I don't say anything, he comes closer, bending over me so I can see straight into his eyes. "I'm doing what is necessary for *you*."

I shake my head until my vision begins to blur. "I never asked for any of this."

"Once my work is completed, we'll possess all the power, and the Duskers won't be able to challenge us. You'll never have to hide again. You'll be free."

Free?

My father taps the swirls on my hand with one of his fingers. "You've learned the truth about the Duskers. They are oppressors, murderers. They would keep you weak so they can stay strong."

I try to snatch my hand away, but the Halves hold me still.

"Why do you wear the cloak of the Duskers if you hate them?"

My father looks down at the gray cloak. "I wear the cloak because I couldn't risk having my true identity exposed before everything was in place."

"You have your army." I jerk my head in the direction of the Halves. "If all you wanted was to overthrow the Duskers, what are you waiting for?"

"I was waiting for you, daughter."

I stare, uncomprehending, at him. My throat has gone too dry for me to swallow.

"You are a Bisecter, both human and Halve, yet stronger than both. The most powerful force in the world." He taps a finger above each of my black eyes. "I have put all of my resources, everything I learned when I was a healer, into trying to replicate you here. But the final, necessary piece was to bring you here in the flesh. Only you have the necessary strength to help carry out my plan. With your abilities, and my leadership, we'll rule men and Halves together."

"None of this makes any sense," I say, working around the pain that throbs in my temples and slows my thinking. "You didn't bring me here. I came on my own. There was no way you could have known…."

My father gives me a knowing look before turning to his guards. "Bring him in."

CHAPTER 45

The two guards disappear through a tunnel. In seconds, they have returned with a prisoner struggling between them. They throw him down at my father's feet.

The gasp has left my mouth before the prisoner has raised his head. *Brice.*

My father looks down at Brice with evident distaste. "Would you like to tell this part of the story, or shall I?"

"Hemera, please. I didn't know—"

"Oh, you knew," my father interrupts. "You *chose* not to believe."

"What's going on?" I glare daggers at my father. "What have you done?"

My father raises an eyebrow. "I only offered what your lover most desired."

"What are you talking about?" I demand. And then, more softly, "Brice?"

Tears track paths down Brice's cheeks. "He promised if I helped get you here," his voice breaks, "he'd make me Captain of the Subterrane."

"What?" I stare dumbfounded at Brice, his words jumbling together into nonsense.

My father looks at me like he pities my ignorance. "Did you think I didn't know my best scout went missing during his shifts, and that, coincidentally, you were reported missing from your work assignment at the same time? Did you think my spies didn't inform me about what was between you?"

"Then why didn't you say anything?" I can feel my face turning hot.

"I thought I could use your indiscretion to my advantage." My father shrugs. "And, as it turns out, I could."

Brice tries to stand, but the guards keep him pinned to his knees. "Hemera, I'm so sorry."

"No. No, this doesn't make any sense. The Halves captured you. They brought you here as a prisoner."

"Hemera—"

"I don't believe you!" I struggle against the Halves surrounding me, but they hold fast. "This is all just…some sick joke."

Please just let this be a misunderstanding. Please let this be a dream.

Brice doesn't speak. He doesn't need to. The truth is written across his tormented face.

Images flash through my mind like the rush of a waterfall. Brice's lips on mine. The way he looked at me when he told me he loved me. His hands moving across my bare skin in the darkness of our secret cave….

The Dwellers' whispers, which had begun to feel like a distant memory, return in full force. *What could he possibly see in* her…?

"It was all a lie," I say. The walls of the catacombs begin to close in around me. My lungs squeeze.

"It wasn't, I swear." Brice holds out his hands, pleading. "I loved you—I do love you. I fell for you long before your father made me…his offer."

My eyes sting like they're being pricked by a thousand tiny daggers, but something stronger keeps my tears in check.

A dozen things that hadn't made sense…how my father knew about our cave behind the waterfall, the way Brice sometimes seemed far away even when we were inches apart, the look on Brice's face when he deciphered the message on Taniel's arm….

"You knew about Taniel," I say. "You knew what my father did to him, and you still helped lure me here?"

It can't be. It can't—

"Please." Brice tries to wrestle his way to me, but the men hold him back.

Anger clears my vision. "How could you?"

"I should have told you. I wanted to tell you. But it was real. Hemera, I swear it was real."

"I trusted you." Like a fool, I believed every word. Because I wanted to believe…had been so desperate to belong *somewhere.*

Brice holds his hands out to me. "Hemera, please. Being Captain would have given us the power to do what we always planned…hunt the Halves ourselves. It was the only way to give us both the revenge we always wanted."

The revenge we always wanted. *Is that what I wanted?*

"I wanted you," I choke on the words.

"You have me." Brice's voice breaks. "You always will."

I round on my father, snarling. "And you told him exactly what to say to make me believe—" *make me believe he needed me as much as I needed him.* The unspoken words hang in the air.

My father knew, at least on some level, the guilt I carried for my mother's death. He must have known exactly how I'd react if Brice was threatened with a similar fate—must have known I wouldn't sit idly by a second time while the person I cared for most was at the Halves' mercy.

"I never wished to hurt you, daughter," he says.

A bizarre cackle comes out of my mouth.

"I did warn you Brice might not want you if he knew all of what you are," my father says. "Coming here was the only way you would see both him and yourself for what you really are."

My father's words from what feels like a lifetime ago return to me now. *If the scout knew what you can do…if he knew your differences were more than just your eyes….* A choked sound escapes my throat. I turn my head away from them both.

"Hemera, of all people, you have to understand why I did what I did," Brice pleads.

"How dare you." My heart beats a furious rhythm against my ribs.

"You have to believe me." Brice's voice is even more desperate now. "I never knew how far he meant to go—"

"Stop it." I try to clap my hands over my ears, wanting nothing more than to block out the lies and betrayal and sound of my heart shattering. But the Halves keep my arms pinned by my sides. "Stop it, stop it, stop it!"

"Get him out of here." My father waves a hand.

The two filthy men wrench Brice to his feet. One of them shoves Brice while the other gives him a swift kick in the gut. Brice doubles over.

"Don't be too hard on him," my father says in the silence that follows. "Ambition is a powerful drug." He frowns. "For what it's worth, I believe he did love you." He cocks his head to the side, thinking. "At least, he loved the person you were when you were trying to be like the rest of them." His mouth twists in disgust.

A muffled cry comes from Brice as the guards drag him away.

"He was never your prisoner." My voice breaks. "He was working for you the whole time."

"He was working for me until he saw the full extent of my work here," he corrects. "When his weakness overcame his ambition, Brice was no longer any use to me. He didn't have the stomach to oversee my experiments, and so I confined him with my other slaves."

"How could you do this…to me?" I choke out. "I'm your child."

Betrayal. The word thrums in my chest.

"*To* you?" My father shakes his head. "I did all of this *for* you."

My father begins to pace back and forth in front of me. "I knew after you found out he had been taken you would go back to your cave behind the waterfall."

A wave of sickness passes through me at the reminder. My father knew about our special place. He knew everything about us. *Because Brice traded it all.…*

"I left the map so you wouldn't waste time wandering aimlessly," my father explains.

"*You* left the map?"

For a moment, I imagine lunging at my father and wrapping my hands around his throat.

"Can you imagine another who knows these lands so well?" he counters.

"And it was you who gave Brice's drawing to the Halves, wasn't it?" I say through gritted teeth.

My father nods. "In spite of your strength, you were yet untrained. I sent some of my more obedient Halves to make sure you arrived unharmed."

"Why not just save yourself the trouble and make the Halves bring me here by force?" I ask bitterly.

My father shakes his head. "If I had brought you by force, you never would have learned your true strengths. Making the journey on your own was the only way to prepare you."

I raise my head, ignoring the wave of dizziness. "Let me go," I snarl at the Halves.

The Halves' eyes flick from me to each other. Even through the haze of my fury, I see an intelligent gleam in their black eyes I hadn't noticed before. It's familiar in a way I can't quite place.

A few of them begin to loosen their hold, but at a nod from my father, the two guards stride forward. They lash out at the Halves with their daggers and whips. The Halves cower.

"You cannot stop the wheel of change, Hemera," my father says. "You can either climb aboard or be crushed beneath its weight."

I'm choking on fury and betrayal. I can't speak.

He narrows his eyes at me. "Would you like to hear my plan?"

He doesn't wait for me to say anything. My father clasps his hands behind his back in the same way he always did in the Subterrane when he was giving a speech.

"The Duskers would have annihilated the Halves. But I saw their potential. For years, I have been experimenting with blood sharing between Halves and humans."

"Blood sharing?!"

"To recreate what happened to you in the womb." He says it like it's obvious. "Think about it…an army of Bisecters." He stares down at the puddles of blood on the floor. "I have managed to enhance the potency of some of the Halves' blood," he waves a hand at the ones holding me.

Now I know what it is about these Halves that's familiar. They have a look about them—both more intelligent and more alert—that reminds me of Ekil. I remember when I asked Ekil why he was different from the other Halves, he mentioned something about his blood being changed. I hadn't understood it at the time, but now it's starting to make sense. My father has been experimenting on them…enhancing their blood….

"But Halve blood alone is not enough," my father continues. "My human subjects are too weak."

If I wasn't seeing it all for myself, I never would have believed this man standing before me is the same one who defended his Subterrane from the Halves. I would never believe it was my father killing people and enslaving Halves. I'm too angry to feel hurt or betrayed or a thousand other emotions I know I should be feeling.

My father is a murderer.

I think about Destinel, my best friend in Subterrane Harkibel. I remember how she was there for me after my mother died. I remember how, after that, she was always the first one to defend me when the others called me a freak. I remember her face, streaked with blood.

A sick feeling grips my insides.

"How many people have died in your insane experiments?" I ask. "When does it all end?"

He walks over to one of the cauldrons. I follow the direction of his gaze and suck in a breath. The tube dripping brown blood into the cauldron is connected to my forearm.

It's *my* blood being drawn into the cauldron. I stare up at my father, wild-eyed.

My father motions to one of his filthy guards. "We have what we need." A yelp escapes me as he pulls the tube out of my arm. "Preserve the blood, and guard it with your life."

The guard scuttles out of the main chamber, hugging a small vial to his chest like it's a baby.

"I still don't understand—"

"Your blood is the answer to everything!" My father sweeps his hand up in an arc. "We can make more of you. You will no longer be the only one of your kind."

"More…Bisecters?" The full weight of what he's doing finally hits me.

"Think about it." He resumes pacing. "We will have the strength to overthrow the Duskers…unlike those pathetic Solguards." He spares a glance at the tattoo on my right hand. "We will usher in a new era, one in which your abilities will be celebrated rather than feared. You will no longer have to deny what you really are." His face flushes with passion.

I open my mouth, but no sound comes out. *I would no longer have to deny what I really am. I wouldn't be the only one of my kind.*

My father is watching me with narrowed eyes. "You see the brilliance of it, don't you?" His voice is quiet now.

You're insane, I should tell him. But instead, I find myself considering his words. What would it be like to live in a world where there were others like me? No one would ever have to die from the Burn or Halve blood poison again.

What would it be like to walk through a crowd and not hear whispers and feel their fear as if it was some living thing? Maybe then Brice would have been free to love me as I was, and not because of what my father promised him….

"What makes you think any of them—any of us—would follow you? Anyone with my strength wouldn't follow an ordinary human like you."

Something dark passes across my father's features before his face becomes impassive again. "That is why I need you, daughter. With everything I've discovered, and with your natural abilities, we will rule them all."

A ruckus draws my attention to the opening of the cave. Three of the guards drag Dayne, bound in ropes, across the blood-stained floor.

CHAPTER 46

L eave him alone," I shriek.

No one pays any attention to me. The Halves grip me.

"We found him snooping around outside," one of the guards reports.

"Dayne Clarion." My father says the name like it tastes foul in his mouth. "You are a fool for coming here."

"Let her go." Dayne's voice breaks. "You have no right—"

My father steps closer to Dayne, shoving him onto his knees in a single, fluid motion.

"*You* have no right. You are nothing." His voice is quiet. "As inconsequential as a gnat to a Burn vulture." He lifts a hand to strike Dayne.

"How dare you." I'm shaking with rage. "All this time….and you never thought to tell me I have a brother?!"

"The Duskers would have seized your mother for any association with her traitor sister and son," he hissed. "Putting them both firmly in her past was the only way to keep her, and you, from the same fate."

"You could have told me—"

"She lied to me!" my father roars. "She betrayed me!"

It takes me a second to realize he's talking about my mother.

He swipes a hand over his brow. When he looks back at me, his face is twisted in pain. But then, just as quickly, the raw emotion is gone. When he speaks again, his voice is calm.

"She would still be alive if she hadn't sought to betray me."

"You're a liar," I snarl.

"She was going to the Solguards. On your twelfth birthday, the day she died." He gives me a look as if to say *you remember that day, don't you?*

"We were picking rupyberries—"

"She underestimated my spies," he says as though I hadn't spoken. "She entrusted Taniel with a letter meant for the Solguards. He, of course, brought the letter straight to me. It explained all about her plans to leave the Subterrane with you so she could join them."

"You? You sent the Halve…to kill her?!" I don't even care that I'm hysterical.

"The Halve was supposed to capture, not kill." His voice is so quiet I almost don't hear over the throbbing in my head.

"But it did, and it's your fault. You killed her!"

"She killed herself with that final act of deception," he snaps.

My father takes a deep, shuddering breath. "It was soon after that Jadem and Dayne escaped from Malarusk. When I heard they planned to return to the Subterrane, I did the only thing I could to keep them away. I made them believe you had died alongside your mother."

"I wish those Halves killed you back at the Subterrane like I thought," I say.

A darkness flits across his eyes before it's gone again. "It is that spirit that proves I was right all along." He smiles out of the corner of his mouth like he's letting me in on a secret. "We will make an insurmountable team, you and I."

"I'll never help you. You're the reason my mother is dead. You're worse than the Duskers."

I miss whatever my father says next because at that moment, a shadow slips out of the tunnel behind him. When it takes another step forward, the shadow's arms stretch unevenly across the lighted floor. *Ekil.*

Adrenaline courses through me. All of the pain in my head disappears.

Forcing myself to wait until Ekil has taken a few more steps, I use all of my strength to break free from the Halves' grip. The iron chains snap away from me like I was bound by nothing more than dried twigs.

The force of my movement sends the ten Halves surrounding me stumbling back. I leap off the table before they can recover.

"Don't harm her!" my father yells.

Out of the corner of my eye, I see Dayne on his feet, cracking his elbow into one of the guard's faces.

I catch the other guard's whip around my hand and yank it from him. A fresh wave of pain sends me reeling as something strikes the corner of my head. The guard, who either didn't hear the Captain's command or chose not to, plunges his dagger into my side.

Ekil is beside me, but his words to the other Halves sound far away. I watch as Ekil swings his stone club at the Captain's guards.

"Kill it, kill it!" my father screams.

Ekil cradles me in his arms as he races for the tunnel. The dagger jostles in my side with each step. Barely aware of my own actions, I clutch the handle and draw the blade from me.

Warm blood slides down my side and soaks my hand when I press it to the wound. It's strange how I don't feel any pain.

"Why...helping me?" My words slur together.

Sunlight pours through the opening of the tunnel, but my vision is growing darker.

"The Master has made us slaves," Ekil's voice comes from somewhere far away. "His men take our blood. He forces us to kill. You can help us."

"Just run away." I try to blink away the spots darkening my vision. "He couldn't stop you."

I'm so tired.

"The Master will send his Zeroes after us."

I see the opening of the cave through a veil of darkness.

CHAPTER 47

Hemera, Hemera," a voice groans.

I open my eyes. I'm underneath a specere tree lit by a golden branch.

"Hemera?" Brice cries in disbelief as I blink up at him.

I try to sit up, but two pairs of hands push me back down.

"What happened?" I murmur.

"You were dead!" Dayne croaks. "You lost so much blood, and then your heart stopped."

Dayne and Brice are kneeling over me. Vlaz is trying to squeeze between them. Eventually, he contents himself to curl up and rest his head on my legs.

Brice lifts the fabric of my cloak to inspect the wound. He sucks in a breath. "It's almost healed!"

I touch my side. Sure enough, the hole left by the blade has sealed itself off.

"Your blood is stronger than I guessed," Dayne marvels. "I would not have thought it possible." His face darkens. "No wonder he wants you."

Brice looks at my side like he can't make up his mind whether to be relieved or terrified.

With that single glance, everything that happened before I was stabbed rushes back to me. My storm of emotions is mirrored in the fleeting glance Brice gives me before he clasps my hands in both of his and bows his head.

"I never meant to hurt you," Brice's voice is rough. "If I could take it all back, I would. A thousand times…a million…I would."

Even though the anguish is plain in Brice's green eyes, it does nothing to ease the gaping hole in my heart.

"Leave her alone," my brother growls.

Brice looks at me. Whatever expression is on my face makes his shoulders slump in defeat. I turn away so I won't have to interpret the swirl of emotions I feel just from looking at him.

"He killed her." I say to Dayne, my voice raspy. "My father sent that Halve after her. He killed our mother."

Dayne gives me a short nod, telling me he suspected as much already.

"Where's Ekil?" I ask, trying to will the furious tears back into my eyes. "Where's the Halve?"

"It went back before we left the tunnel," Dayne replies. "You've been unconscious, or verging on dead," his voice breaks on the word, "for the entire high day."

Thinking about Ekil reminds me of what he said before I lost consciousness, "Do you know what a Zero is?"

Dayne shakes his head.

"Never heard of it," Brice says. His attention is back on my healed side.

"Can you walk?" Dayne asks, concern etched into every line of his face. "It won't be long before Zeidan's servants find us."

I stand without taking the hand Brice offers. "We need to get back to the others."

* * *

When I pull open the stone doors, we're assaulted by a group of prisoners gripping Halve blades. There would be little to fear even if we had been the enemy; most of them look like they can barely lift the blades, let alone wield them.

"Stand down!" I hear Wade's command. "Damn you, stand down. Give them some space."

"What happened?" he demands when he sees the bloodstains on my cloak.

"Nothing, I'm fine."

Brice glares at Wade as he puts an arm around my waist. When I twist out of his grasp, Wade smirks.

"I have something for you," Dayne says, interrupting the tension. He pulls a sling and a cloth bag filled with colored stones from beneath his cloak.

"I made it during the high day, while you were—" His voice breaks.

"Thank you." I touch the braided ropes. The sling isn't as well-made as the one from my father, but at least this one won't remind me of him.

My father. The reason my mother is dead.

Rage swells in me. *Not now*, I tell myself.

As though reading my thoughts, Dayne leans closer to me so only I can hear his words.

"We're going to kill him, Hemera." There is unrestrained fury in his voice. "We're going to kill him."

Instead of answering, I turn to the weapon in my hands. I put one of the stones in the sling's pouch and flick it into motion. When I release the stone, it sails through the air and blasts through the building's high ceiling. People leap out of the way as a beam of sunlight filters in through the hole.

The hum of activity in the building has stopped. Every pair of eyes is on me.

I clear my throat, uncomfortable to have everyone's attention.

"So, what's the plan?" I ask Dayne.

Dayne scratches his chin. "Seems to me you're the one in charge."

"*Me?*"

"You got us all out, didn't you?" The hint of a smile curves his lips.

"But I don't know the first thing about battle strategy," I protest.

"You're better at staying alive than anyone I've ever met." Wade steps forward and places his right fist, the one emblazoned with the rebel sun, over his heart. "I can't think of a more fitting leader." His voice catches on the last word, and I know he's thinking of Sal.

I look around at the others. Most nod or offer a faint smile. A few look dubious.

"Well just a minute now," the huge man—Thutmose, Brice had called him—says as he steps forward. "Seeing as I've been here the longest, I think I might make for a better leader."

He looks around at the other prisoners for support.

"Look at her eyes," he continues. "She opened those cell doors like they were nothing. How can we trust her?"

Before I can speak, someone crosses the circle to stand before Thutmose. It's Jarosh.

"Thutmose, you and I grew up in the settlement together. You know my word's better than most." He crosses his arms and waits for Thutmose's nod of agreement. "So, when I tell you Hemera is a fitter leader than any among us, you'd better hear me."

Jarosh walks over to me and says loudly enough for everyone else to hear, "You saved my life. I'll follow you into battle or anywhere else you care to lead me. You have my trust."

Ry whoops in agreement. To Jarosh, she says, "I knew there was a brain lurking somewhere in that big head of yours."

Expectant faces turn to me.

"Well," I falter, but Dayne gives me a nod of encouragement. "If we can divide their army, it will be easier than trying to fight all the Halves at once."

"Speak up!" someone calls. "We can't hear you from back here."

I'm conscious of everyone's attention on me as I take a few steps closer. My feet tangle on themselves, and I lurch forward. I catch my balance just before I fall, but not before Wade has seen.

Wade grins, but there's no malice in it. Instead of trying to hide under the hood of my cloak like I usually would, I shrug and grin back.

"We need more weapons," I say to the others with more confidence. "Sharp stones, branches, anything we can use. If we attack soon, we might be able to catch them unprepared."

There is a deafening noise as the men and women surrounding me stamp the ground in anticipation. They are no longer the bedraggled prisoners who cowered in their cells, but soldiers heading into the fight they've been waiting for since they were first brought to Tanguro.

I clear my throat. "There's something you need to know about the enemy."

My cheeks flush, but my voice is steady.

"I know you've all been imprisoned by the Halves, but they are slaves just as you were."

I pause to let my words sink in.

"It's not an easy request to make," I glance at Brice, "but I ask that you only kill the Halves when your own survival is threatened. It's the Captain's—my father's—guards who must be killed."

There are some shouts of surprise mixed in with angry mutterings.

"If any of you don't agree to this request," I raise my voice in an effort to sound bolder than I feel, "you can leave now and flee to the mountains while there's still time."

I wait for several moments. No one moves.

"Alright, then." I take a deep breath. "Here's what I think we should do."

After I outline my plan, the circle disperses as everyone goes to carry out my orders.

"Will you be alright here?" Brice asks as he readies a team of scouts.

An almost irresistible urge to touch him fills me. I long to press myself against him and feel his arms wind around me.

And then I remember he lied to me. He used me. An almost overwhelming loneliness sweeps over me, and for the first time since escaping the catacombs, my father's offer returns to me. *More like me…never have to hide again….*

But then I remember the blood streaked across the floor of the catacombs. The people he murdered. My mother. I remind myself of the price he's paid, and is still willing to pay, for the sake of power and strength.

I take a step back from Brice. There is no more than a pace between us, but it could just as easily be a mile. The hurt and longing and regret in Brice's eyes mirrors my own feelings.

"Take Vlaz with you," I say. "He'll scare off any Halves you meet."

For now, the prison building is ours. I wish there was a way to get some of the spears and blades from the weapons building, but that's where all of the Halves are now; there would be no way to get in there without being seen.

We're doing what we can with what we have here. Every available space has been turned into a work area where materials and anything that could be used as a weapon is gathered. Some men sharpening branches into spears put down their work as I come near.

"We're indebted to you, Captain Hemera," one of them says with a nod of his head. "We've been here for a year and had all but given up hope. It's our honor to fight alongside you."

My face flushes. "Just call me Hemera," I stammer.

I turn away to hide my embarrassment, but then a thought occurs to me. "Since you've been here for so long, you must know the plants around Tanguro."

One of them raises his eyebrows. "'Course. What do you have in mind?"

"We need weapons. Any plants that could help us…."

"Say no more," the man holds up his hand.

"One last thing," I say as they put down their work. "Have you heard of Zeroes?"

Neither of them has.

"Is there anything else we can bring you?" the first one asks.

I run through a list in my head.

"Cammamoss," I say. "As much of it as you can find."

CHAPTER 48

Thutmose, Jarosh, and ten others return carrying armfuls of the most colorful plants I've ever seen. Most of them hold their arms away from their bodies, as though afraid the plants will erupt in a fiery explosion at any moment.

Three of the soldiers appear empty-handed but hold their arms at an unnatural angle like they're carrying an unseen load. The cammamoss's powerful scent trails in their wake. When the soldiers put it on the ground, there is a flicker as the cammamoss changes to the color of the packed-dirt ground.

The soldiers arrange the plants into neat piles against the wall of the building. Each pile gives off its own glow of color so bright it looks like we're outside, rather than beneath the sun-proof specere leaves.

"What's that one?" I point to a tangled silver root.

Thutmose nudges the plant with his toe.

"We call this one 'cursed stammeroot.' It's a deadly poison when it's crushed and boiled. It'll just take a drop or two to turn a Halve into a puddle of acid." He smiles.

I give Thutmose a sharp look.

"Er, I mean…." he trails off.

"It will be useful against the guards at any rate," I say. "What are those?" I point to a pile of round, richly purple pods the size of my fist.

"Touch-me-nots, but not like any you've seen before." Thutmose looks relieved for a change in subject.

He lifts one of the pods on the edge of a blade and hurls it at the far end of the building. It pings off one of the cell doors and lands on the ground.

There's the sound of popping as the pod swells and then separates into a dozen new versions of itself.

Each of the new pods explodes, shooting fiery-red spikes in every direction.

Instead of the regular needles of the touch-me-nots, these needles erupt into sparks. I jump to the side as one of the needles passes near to where I'm standing. Each spike burns a hole in the ground where it lands.

A commotion at the door draws my attention away from helping to stamp out the small fires. Vlaz soars into the tunnel, followed by Brice and his team of scouts.

"The Halves are assembling between the two buildings and have blocked the exit," Brice reports. "They're all armed." His voice is brusque, like he's delivering a report to a Captain rather than to me.

"How many?" I ask trying to ignore the ache in my chest.

Brice exchanges a look with one of the other scouts. "Must be more than a thousand, and they're still coming."

A thousand of them, and….

I scan the length of the building.

Two-, maybe three-hundred of us.

"Any sign of the Captain and his guards?"

"No."

"Alright," I wrack my brain for an idea that won't end with all of us getting killed. "We'll attack in waves. If the battle starts to go badly, a few of us can distract the Halves long enough for everyone else to escape to the mountains."

✳ ✳ ✳

The soldiers in the first wave cover themselves and their weapons in cammamoss until they're all but invisible. Even though I'll be leading them, I don't take any cammamoss for myself.

I wrap one of the purple touch-me-nots in a cloth so it won't explode and place it in the pouch on my belt. Thutmose passes around animal hide containers filled with the cursed stammeroot brew. With any luck, it will be enough to scatter the Halves and distract the Captain's guards.

I still have the small knife I keep strapped to my thigh, which I unhook and put into my belt. Dayne, Ry, and Wade, who are leading the second, third, and fourth waves, are shouting orders. There isn't enough cammamoss for them, but hopefully the cursed stammeroot, touch-me-nots, and notty nellies will be enough to protect them. But against thousands of Halves, our preparations seem like child's play.

After a few hasty instructions, we're ready. I wonder whether I'm supposed to give some kind of speech to this haggard band of prisoners-turned-soldiers. They don't need my words of encouragement, though. Men and women stomp their feet and thud their weapons against the ground. As Dayne and I ready the first wave, the tunnel erupts into a chorus of battle cries.

The fight they have longed for has come.

"Forward!" I call.

The rest of the prisoners roar with approval and clink their weapons against mine as I lead the first wave, invisible under the cammamoss, through the stone doors and into the blinding sunlight.

A cloud of dust swirls around the Halves marching toward us. I glance back at the army of freed prisoners behind me. All that is visible are the faint glimmers of a blade or corner of a cloak as the cammamoss shifts under their movement. Even their footprints are masked by the swirling dust.

I feel a surge of hope. For the first time, I think we might have a chance.

I keep my gaze focused on the Halves in front of me rather than staring at the troops stretched out on all sides as far as the eye can see.

"Now!" I shout as soon as the Halves are within range.

As we race forward, the Halves look from side to side and spin around in confusion. They seem to sense the soldiers' presence, but not well enough to land a blow. They swing their weapons, more often striking each other than any of the humans. Dozens of the Captain's guards are among the Halves, using their whips to try to reorganize the befuddled Halves.

Even though I'm the only one who doesn't wear any cammamoss, the Halves don't attack me. I'm not sure whether it's because of my father's orders or something else.

I aim the stones in my sling at the Halves' legs to make them stumble. Wounds appear on the Halves' legs and arms from the invisible weapons. The soldiers seem to be following my orders, using small amounts of the cursed stammeroot liquid and touch-me-not pods to scatter the Halves rather than kill them. Not knowing where is safe, some of the Halves begin to flee.

Triumphant shouts erupt all around me. *My plan is working.*

My stomach flips as a Halve's shriek cuts through the other sounds of the battle. The ear-splitting scream is taken up by others. Around us, panic-stricken Halves are dropping their weapons and shoving each other to escape. Not even the guards' whips can keep them in line as the air fills with the sound of their screams. A Halve stumbles and falls to the ground beside me.

"What's happening?" I shout as its terror-stricken black eyes meet mine.

"Reptors," it wheezes before it scrambles to its feet and gallops off.

Human screams are added to those of the Halves.

I weave through the stampeding Halves and jump onto a boulder to see what's happening. A monstrous creature is cutting a wide path through the Halves. A terrible coldness fills every crevice of my being.

From slimy snout to barbed tail, the reptor is longer than three men laying foot-to-head. It looks like some kind of a giant lizard…that can swallow men whole. Its thick hide is the color of mud and is covered in spikes. The reptor moves on six legs that are so short it almost seems to slither across the ground like a swollen serpent. Still, it moves fast enough to outpace the Halves.

The creature lets out a tremendous roar that shakes the ground. The sound raises the hair on my arms and sends a chill down my spine.

The reptor's open mouth displays teeth as long and sharp as daggers. When it closes its jaw, a man who had been in its path disappears.

There is another roar, and then another. A line of reptors appears from a large hole in the ground at the far end of the courtyard. Their ugly bodies squeeze through the open tunnel one after the other. Their slitted, yellow eyes shine with an unnatural brightness.

The creatures cut a path toward the main part of the battle. Humans and Halves disappear into their gaping maws.

I jump down from the boulder, yelling out orders to anyone who will listen. Some of the Halves spare me the briefest of glances as they continue their stampede off the battlefield. Their attention gives me an idea.

CHAPTER 49

H elp us!" I yell to the retreating Halves. I gesture at the human soldiers scrambling to reform their lines.

Some of them seem to understand me. They clutch their clubs and blades as they fall into line alongside the invisible army. I can guess at the expressions on the soldiers' faces beneath their cammamoss as the Halves join our ranks.

The wretched stench of the reptors fills the air.

I unwrap the touch-me-not, place it in the pouch of my sling, and release my weapon. The small, purple pod hits a reptor's horned back and bounces off. For a moment, nothing happens. And then there's a fiery explosion.

The reptors snarl, opening their mouths wide to display their hideous fangs. They lash their spiked tails as the embers burrow into their thick hides. While the reptors thrash about, I lead the humans and Halves forward.

A group of Halves swarms around one of the reptors. The Halves are faster than their bulk would suggest, and they take turns darting between the reptor's claws to strike blows.

I only have a moment to feel gratitude before I'm surrounded by the reptors.

I strike out at them with my sling and my fist. The first punch leaves my hand bloody and raw. Screams fill the air. A reptor rears up on its back legs and slices the front of my cloak with a dagger-sharp claw. I double over as blood spills from the slice across my stomach.

When the reptor opens its mouth to swallow me, I clench my fist and punch its snout with all of my strength. The creature lets out a roar as it flips over from the force of my blow. The wound in my stomach tears wider.

A fall now would put me right in the reptors' waiting jaws. I fight to stay conscious.

Before it can attack again, Dayne, Wade, and Ry are beside me. They throw themselves at the reptor.

I press a hand over my stomach and try not to think about the warm wetness coating my fingers.

The reptor roars, and I almost retch from the reek of its hot breath. The creature thrashes its horned tail.

"Watch out!"

Dayne pushes Ry out of the way, catching the force of the blow himself. He flies through the air like a ragdoll and lands a few paces away. Dayne stumbles to his feet, looking dazed but alive.

Regaining my focus, I leap toward the reptor.

"Get out of the way," I yell to the others.

"Hemera, what are you—"

Blinking away the darkness, I grab one of the reptor's legs and pull.

The leg, as thick as a script tree's trunk, detaches from the reptor's body. Foul-smelling blood sprays over me, leaving a fierce stinging where it touches my bare skin. The reptor rears up on its other five legs, roaring. I duck under its snapping jaws and drive my blade into its throat.

Blood sprays from its neck as the reptor hurtles backward on its remaining legs. It moves almost as fast as it had with all six.

I run a hand over my stomach as I watch the reptor's retreat. There's no new blood flowing through my shredded cloak. The gaping wound seems to have sealed itself off.

I try not to think about how much it took to bring down one of these creatures. I try not to think about how many more of them are wreaking havoc all over the battlefield. The screams of the prisoners…my soldiers…are impossible to ignore.

Dead soldiers litter the ground. Some are partially covered in cammamoss, others not at all. Some of their faces are covered in blisters from the Burn. Others suffered gruesome wounds from the reptors; their mouths are still twisted in the agony of their death.

Burn vultures circle overhead as the sun creeps back up toward high day. And still, the reptors keep coming.

Focus, Hemera.

"Come on!" I shout, my voice hoarse, as I try to rally the flagging soldiers.

A shadow passes overhead. My heart leaps as Vlaz, dark against the blazing sun, descends from the sky. He dives straight for a reptor and sinks his claws into the creature's eyes. The reptor roars in agony.

Vlaz flies up and down, weaving between their snapping jaws and thrashing tails. He flies down to bite and scratch at their faces before rising again. The reptors scream in fury as their jaws snap shut around empty air. Cheers erupt from the soldiers.

Blinded by their own blood streaming into their eyes, the reptors stumble around, biting and tearing at each other.

The humans and Halves attack the reptors with renewed vigor. They work together, with the Halves reaching up to rain blows on the reptors' snouts while the humans use any weapon they can find to slash at the creatures' legs. I wrestle one to the ground and squeeze the life out of it with my bare hands.

The harsh blowing of a horn cuts through our frenzied slaughter. It's coming from the direction of the fortress's entrance.

"Duskers!" someone shouts.

No, it can't be. It isn't possible....

But the gray, hooded cloaks of the Duskers are unmistakable. They're approaching the wooden gates.

Panic ripples through us all. *What are they doing here?*

"Gorgoran," Wade yells in response to my unasked question. "They knew where we were going."

"They'll kill us all!" Ry's eyes are wild.

My ears are full of the sound of the soldiers' screams.

"There are too many!" Dayne yells. "We need to retreat."

"The only way out is through the gates," Brice argues.

The Duskers' swords flash in the sunlight as they hack at the gates' hinges. Their crossbows fire black-feathered arrows one after another, felling Halves and humans alike through the gaps in the wooden bars. There isn't a full army of them, just the ones that attacked when Sal was killed. Still, the Duskers block our escape from the courtyard, and the reptors are still advancing. We're outnumbered and overpowered.

The cammamoss has fallen off the soldiers who had it, and all of our makeshift weapons are spent. We have nothing to use against the Duskers. Many of the prisoners here wear the Solguard marking; the Duskers will torture us for information and then kill us one by one. Panic squeezes my chest.

Soldiers are fleeing in every direction. I try to call everyone back, but it's no use. The Halves are still with me, but they've sustained heavy casualties, too. We don't have the numbers or the strength to split our forces for yet another enemy.

Giving up on breaking through the gate, a group of Duskers fans out to the stone part of the wall nearest to where our army is huddled. Using sledgehammers, they begin to chip away at the stone.

There is a loud crack as a Dusker manages to swing his sledgehammer through a weak spot at the wall's base. A large break shivers up one of the foundation stones. As the rock shatters, the ones above it begin to waver. It takes a moment before the wall crumbles on itself.

It reminds me of the cracked pillar in Subterrane Harkibel that caused the cave-in that nearly killed me. Instead of the helpless dread I normally feel at the memory, watching the Duskers fight their way through the wreckage of the wall gives me an idea.

Turning to the others, I say, "Get everyone far away from the gates and buildings. As fast and far as you can."

"Where are you going?" Brice demands.

But I'm already running.

CHAPTER 50

The Halves use their bodies to shield me from the Duskers as I race past.

"Get your armies away from here if you want to live," I yell to them.

As I near the edge of the courtyard, I have no choice but to step over the swollen bodies of the dead to stay on my path. I look straight ahead to keep from staring into their lifeless eyes, trying not to guess whether they are Halve, or human.

Anger wells inside me…at the Duskers…at my father. My anger burns like a life force inside me, pushing me forward, giving me strength.

It takes longer than I expected to find what I'm searching for because of the rubble littering the ground. Entire trees have been uprooted and lay on their sides. Their brightly hued corpses somehow make the slaughter more terrible.

I find the tunnel from which the reptors came by following the reek wafting up from the gaping hole. Between the dead Halves and reptor corpses draped over the tunnel, there is a space just large enough for me to lower myself down. My head reels from the stench of whatever dead animals the reptors last fed from.

The tunnel is pitch black. I keep my hand on the wall to steady myself as I follow the snaking path underground. It's easy to follow; the tunnel is wide, smoothed and hollowed out from the reptors' bulk pressing against the dirt.

The feeling of suffocation, my constant companion in Subterrane Harkibel, closes in around me and threatens my resolve. I take quick, short breaths of the stinking air.

What if I'm wrong about these tunnels, and the only place they lead is to a pit filled with reptors? What if these caves aren't connected the same way they were in the Subterrane? What if—

The path levels off at the same time that the ceiling opens up high above me. I sag in relief. These tunnels are built like the ones in the Subterrane, supported by thick stone columns every ten paces. I hold my breath, hardly daring to hope my desperate plan might work.

If I can disrupt a few of the support pillars in this tunnel, it might set off a reaction that will collapse all of the interconnecting tunnels—just like it did in Subterrane Harkibel. The Duskers on the ground overhead would be pulled down into the cave-in, destroying both them and my father's catacombs.

I have no idea if I'm strong enough to bring down one of the pillars. Each one is many times my height and girth and made of solid rock. But we're out of weapons and options. I have to try.

Four stone pillars support the ceiling in this part of the tunnel. I walk between them, looking each one up and down, trying to find one that might already be weaker than the rest. As I might have suspected from tunnels built under my father's supervision, though, none of the pillars display a single crack.

So, I choose one at random.

I take a step back and kick the column as hard as I can. Nothing happens. Taking a shallow breath of putrid air, I kick again.

Nothing. Not even a hint of movement. The pillar is too thick.

Sweat mixes with the furious tears that roll down my cheeks. *Stupid.* How could I be foolish enough to think *I* could bring down this fortress?

I glare up at the ceiling, cursing the pillars and my own weakness. The Duskers are probably standing right above me. They'll kill anyone with a Solguard mark and enslave the rest. They'll murder Ekil and the rest of the Halves.

I wipe away the sweat and tears streaming down my face. Bringing down these tunnels is our only chance of defeating the Dusker army. It's the only way to save my friends. *I have to do this.*

Pushing up the sleeves of my cloak, I make a fist. I punch the column as hard as I can. My scream reverberates through the tunnel as the bones in my knuckles rattle. The smallest hint of a shock wave ripples up the column.

Forcing my bloody, trembling hand into a fist, I punch the column again. And again. When that hand can no longer make a fist, I use my other. I don't think about the agony shooting up my arms. I think about Dayne locked in the catacombs, about Brice and the other prisoners in their cells. I think about my mother.

Taking one last, deep breath, I pull back and kick the column with all of my strength.

Crack.

Lines fly up the column. A chip of stone breaks away, leaving a tiny hollow in the pillar. A hoarse cry of surprise rises from my throat. All my fury and desperation flood through me, fueling me. I *have* to do this.

I back up to give myself more space. Then, I run at the pillar. When I'm close, I propel myself into the air and kick the crack as hard as I can.

The force of the kick sends me flying backward into the wall. I land on the ground with a thud that takes my breath away.

Pieces of rock shatter away from the widening crack and litter the ground at its base. The column sways in its foundation.

I don't wait for the column to fall before I'm at the next one down the tunnel, punching and kicking and shouting. The pillar loosens in its foundation, wobbles, and then breaks off from the ceiling. There's a rush of dirt and stone into the cave before the pillar even hits the ground.

The effect of the two broken pillars shudders down the tunnel. The beams creak and groan under the weight of the shifting ceiling. Dirt rains down from above.

There's no time to feel any sense of triumph as I race down the tunnel ahead of the crumbling walls and ceiling. The ground shifts and groans overhead.

With a final crack that reverberates through the tunnel, dirt pours down around me. I throw myself against the crumbling wall, avoiding a boulder that breaks off from the ceiling and shatters on the floor of the tunnel. Muffled screams cut through the crash of stone as the Duskers are pulled down into the maze of collapsing tunnels.

Dirt fills my mouth, choking me. I try to push my way through the rubble, but it's falling too fast now. Everything above is rushing to fill the empty spaces. Dust makes it impossible to see. I press forward through the tunnel that is fast-disappearing behind me as it fills with debris.

I can't go any further. A narrow space protected by an overhanging sheet of rock is all that keeps me from being crushed by a mountain of dirt and stones. I crouch down to the ground and cover my head with my hands, gasping for air.

It's several minutes before the rocks stop falling. My lungs scream as I take small, shallow breaths. It's completely dark.

I'm trapped. In the blink of an eye, I'm a child again, buried alive in the Subterrane. Panic squeezes my throat like fingers. I can almost hear the Dwellers on the level above, just out of sight, debating my fate. Their words ring as clearly as if they were wedged into this precarious shelter with me.

She's a Bisecter. A freak. Let nature take its course.

How many times have their words invaded my dreams? And now, when death is so near, they are my only companions in this dark place.

No.

I raise my head. I won't wait for the rocks to begin falling again, or for my air to run out. There was so much the Dwellers didn't understand, but there is one thing they got right.

I am a Bisecter.

I stand up as much as the cramped space allows. I'll only have a few seconds once the rocks are disturbed before everything collapses on me.

My heart throbs as I try to steady myself. This time, instead of the Dwellers' words, Aunt Jadem's voice echoes in my head. *You are more than the sum of your parts.*

"I am a Bisecter."

I push my arms up, raising the boulder sheltering me and everything that rests above it. There is a moment when I feel nothing but the weight of all that lies between me and the surface. And then, with another hard thrust, the boulder shoots up through the layers of dirt and stone above. For the briefest of moments, there's a narrow opening in the boulder's wake.

I jump, scaling the rocks that churn and tumble beneath my feet. The moving earth drags me down, but I climb. Faster and faster.

CHAPTER 51

It's high day, and I'm alone.

Where there used to be an army of Duskers between the wooden gates and the weapons building, there is now a gaping crater. I skirt around the edge, careful not to be drawn down with the ground that is still sliding into the depths below. Patches of gray cloaks and sword hilts peek out from the mess of stone and dirt.

My pulse races every time I look down into one of the pits for signs of my army being dragged down with the Duskers.

They made it far enough away, I tell myself. *Dayne led them all to safety.*

Still, as I survey the full extent of the destruction, panic begins to creep into my thoughts. The two buildings still stand, one of them tilted at a precarious angle. Everything between them and the wooden gates is gone.

Everything is quiet. There's something strangely peaceful about being out here instead of hidden away in the caves. Once I discovered the sun couldn't hurt me, I figured I might be able to go outside during the high day, but I never tried it until now. Before, I was too worried about being attacked by Halves or revealing what I was to my companions. I never would have been able to feel…*this.*

I toss my head back, letting the hood of my cloak fall away so my face is bathed with the light of the red-hued sun. No one is staring at me. There are no voices to tell me I'm terrible or special. There aren't even any animals on the Outside. I feel the blazing sun on my bare skin without pain. I feel free.

✳ ✳ ✳

It takes my eyes several moments to adjust to the dim torchlight when I wrench open the stone door to the prison building. It fared worse in the collapse than the weapons building. The wooden floor is splintered and there are holes everywhere from the cave-in. Most of the upper floors are too warped and tilted to be useable. Part of the ground level is still intact, though.

Please let my army be in here.

"Hemera! Where have you been?" Ry demands.

"You're here!" I step back, my eyes scanning the others milling around. "Is everyone alright? Dayne and—"

"Hemera's back!"

There's a chorus of shouts and whoops as I'm surrounded. Questions and praise surround me on all sides. There is a large group of Halves clustered on the far side of the building, although I notice Ekil isn't among them. They're eyeing the humans warily, but both sides seem to be leaving each other alone.

Even after everything we've been through together in the past day, it's still seems impossible to see Halves in the same room as humans. Yet, here they are. I can't forget all the suffering and death the Halves have brought on my people, but if it hadn't been for these ones fighting by our side, we'd probably all be dead by now. If I could find the right words, I would tell them how grateful I am for their help. But a new fear keeps the words locked in my throat.

"Where is everyone else?" I ask.

Where the tunnel had been crowded before the battle, there's now only a scattering of people.

No one speaks.

"They can't all be…."

The soldiers' haggard expressions are answer enough.

Ry shakes her head. "There were two more reptors after you left." She looks around the circle and brightens. "But look how many you saved.

Everyone from our company, and a good number of the prisoners. We were so outnumbered...."

"A lot of the Duskers took refuge in the weapons building," Wade says. "I didn't see how many—"

"We should assume a number of Zeidan's guards survived, too," Dayne says.

"And the rest of the Halves?" I ask.

Wade shakes his head. "I think a lot of them got away, but I'm not sure."

Please let Ekil be one of the ones who escaped. I can't even begin to imagine where I would be—where we all would be—if it weren't for him.

"Hemera!"

Brice.

He pushes his way through the circle until he's standing before me. His shirt is torn, exposing the smooth, muscled skin of his shoulder. I remember what it felt like to touch that place. My lips tingle at the remembrance of what it was like to kiss the hollow between his neck and shoulder.

The noise of the others surrounding us fades. Can he hear the way my heart is slamming against my ribcage?

There's uncertainty and grief reflected in Brice's eyes. Even with everything that's happened, seeing his pain cuts me like a blade.

I shake my head in confusion, not knowing what to say, or even what to think.

I want to scream at him. I want to make him hurt the way he hurt me. More than anything, though, I want to go to him. I want to feel his arms wrap around me as I nestle into the crook of his arm. I want to pull him against me until not even air separates us.

"Where were you?" Dayne's voice breaks the spell. He knocks Brice aside as he pushes his way to me.

"I'm fine," I try to tell him, but it doesn't stop him from scanning me up and down for injuries.

It's strange to see the protective look in Dayne's eye. Now that I know he's my brother, I notice other similarities besides the blue of his eyes: his slender features that mask the strength that lies beneath, the gentle surety in his every movement, the way his forehead creases in concern over my well-being. When I look at him, I can almost imagine it's my mother smiling back at me.

"That was quite a stunt you pulled out there," Jarosh says. There's a deep gash across his cheek, but he still manages a grin.

"What do we do now?" Thutmose demands.

"We don't have much time." I raise my voice above the questions and excited chatter. "Some of the Duskers survived."

When I'd poked my head into the weapons building, I'd heard muffled voices and seen gray cloaks.

"Then they'll have us surrounded as soon as it's low day." Dayne's mouth is set in a grim line.

"And all we've got is a handful of wooden spears," Ry adds, cradling her empty quiver like a lost child.

"I can go out and get more of the poisonous plants," I say. "I just need to know what I'm looking for."

There's a quiet hush as everyone takes this in. *The Bisecter can go outside during high day*, I can almost hear them thinking. But no one says anything.

Thutmose clears his throat, and with a nod from Jarosh, ticks off a long list of all the plants we need and where I can find them.

I make trips back and forth, bringing cloth bags filled with the deadly plants. It takes longer than last time because I have to run past the boundaries of the fortress to land that was not swallowed up by the cave-in. By low day, color radiates from the arranged piles, giving the building and everyone in it an iridescent glow.

No one says what we're all thinking…that all the deadly plants in the world won't be enough to save our shrunken army from the Duskers.

Just before low day, we assemble at the building's entryway. Without Ekil, the Halves seem less certain about trusting me. They're willing to fight with us, but they don't say much, and they're few in number.

Jarosh and Thutmose divide up the poisonous plants. Our shrunken army looks pathetic, with soldiers gripping yellow flowers instead of swords.

"I'm leading them from their cells to their death."

I didn't realize I had spoken the words aloud until Dayne replies, "You gave them their freedom. You gave us all a chance to fight our enemies, rather than die in chains at their feet."

I try to swallow around the lump in my throat.

Dayne steps in front of me, waiting until I meet his gaze. "I'm honored to fight by your side, little sister."

Before I can begin to find the words to reply, Dayne pulls me into a hug. For a moment, I'm too overcome to react, but then, I hug him back. Tears run down my cheeks and absorb into Dayne's cloak. I don't bother to wipe them away.

I shouldn't feel safe in a place like Tanguro. I shouldn't feel like I belong. And yet, with my brother's arms around me, I feel both these things. I know that whatever we're going to face in the coming hours or days, I'm not going to have to face it alone.

When Dayne lets go of me, I give him a wobbly smile. There's no way I can ever put into words how much I appreciate him being here with me, so I don't even try. I take a shuddering breath and face my army.

It's minutes into low day when the harsh sound of the Duskers' horn carries across the courtyard. I exchange a look with Dayne, and he gives me an encouraging nod.

We're as ready as we're going to be.

With a single word from me, we're marching out to meet the enemy.

CHAPTER 52

The Duskers meet us partway between the two buildings. They strike without mercy. The thunk of their crossbows is followed by screams. A dozen of our soldiers fall before we can retaliate. We throw the touch-me-nots as soon as we get close enough, and I kill five with my sling by the time the two armies are upon each other.

"Attack!"

My soldiers let loose a volley of notty nellies and touch-me-nots. The Duskers shriek and run from the poisoned syrup and flaming spikes. We cheer their retreat, even though they're already regrouping.

"This battle is no place for a little girl," a Dusker taunts me, his voice muffled through the gray mask he wears.

"This little girl is the last person you'll ever see," I retort, stepping toward him with my fists raised.

"Ugh! Those eyes!" The Dusker stumbles back, tripping over his own feet. "What are you?"

I wrench the sword out of the Dusker's resisting hands, and lean closer.

"I'm a Bisecter," I say, just before I slice the blade across his neck.

Three Duskers throw themselves at me. I jump to the side, just missing a blow aimed at my neck, but I trip over a reptor's body and fall to the ground. My blade flies out of my hands. Two of the Duskers race around behind me, cutting off my escape. The other stalks forward, raising his sword. I'm caught between a pile of stones and a reptor's corpse.

I try to scramble back, but there's nowhere for me to go. The blade flashes in the sunlight as it descends. And then it stops...just before it pierces my chest.

The Dusker is motionless, as though time has somehow stopped. But then the Dusker falls backward. He collapses onto his side, revealing a thick blade wedged between his shoulders. Ekil bends down and yanks his blade free.

"You saved me," I gasp as Ekil stoops to help me up.

My relief at seeing Ekil here and alive is so strong it almost overwhelms my near-death. *Almost.*

"You—" My words are cut off as Ekil lets out a terrible scream. His hand grips mine as his eyes widen in pain and terror.

Thick blood runs down his side.

"No!"

I search the ground for something, anything, to defend Ekil. My eyes land on the blade that lies beside the Dusker's body. I grasp the handle and force myself to my feet. At the same time, Brice draws his sword, stained with brown blood, to strike again.

The blade slips out of my hand. "What are you doing?" I gasp.

Brice doesn't answer. There's murder in his eyes.

I hold out my hands to Brice, pleading for him to stop. "They're not the enemy!"

Brice points his sword at Ekil's heart.

"Brice, please," I beg. "Don't."

Brice and I stare at each other. I see the moment when Brice gives in. He gives a slow, reluctant nod.

"For you," he says. "I'd do anything for you."

Before I can reply, a Dusker comes out of nowhere. Brice pushes me to the side, out of the Dusker's path. We both fall to the ground. Brice is on top of me, shielding my body with his.

"Kill the Halve," the Dusker screams.

I watch in horror as three of them converge on Ekil. Ekil runs, but he's weaponless and wounded from Brice's attack. The three Duskers are herding him right toward the place where their soldiers are most numerous.

"I have to help him," I gasp, pushing Brice off me.

"There are too many Duskers," he shouts. "It's too dangerous."

"He saved my life." I get to my feet and pick up Ekil's fallen blade. "I'm going after him."

"It's just a Halve! You'll get yourself killed."

I don't wait long enough to respond to Brice. Instead, I chase them down.

The battlefield is crowded, and I keep having to change my path to get out of the way of others who are fighting. By the time I close the distance between us, Ekil is being driven straight into a group of at least ten Duskers.

I don't hesitate. I run forward, right into their midst.

The first Dusker I reach strikes my blade with such speed I don't have a chance to anchor my stance. I'm already off balance, and when another Dusker rushes me, I hit the ground with so much force I'm stunned.

The Dusker lands on top of me. He's bleeding, but it doesn't stop him from slicing his dagger across my ribcage. I scream in pain as I wrestle for the weapon. I manage to grasp the soldier's arm and twist it so the dagger points at him instead of me.

The Dusker cracks his forehead against mine, and for a moment, all I see is blackness. Something hits the Dusker from behind, and his body goes limp on top of me. I can't move. I can't even breathe.

All I can do is watch the scene before me as I struggle to shove the dead weight off me and draw air into my lungs.

Ekil is fighting two of the Duskers, but without a weapon, he won't hold out for long. A spray of brown blood arcs over him. The Duskers duck and scatter to avoid it, but they don't stay away for long.

Move! I want to scream to the Halve, but I can't find enough air to make the sound.

It's as though everything is moving in slow motion. I see the Duskers moving in, their blades poised for the killing blow. I see Ekil, his black eyes unfocused, blood still leaking from his many wounds.

I thrust the dead body off me and draw in a gasping breath.

And then time catches up. I get to my feet just in time to see a Dusker running straight at Ekil with his sword aimed at the Halve's heart.

"No!" I yell.

The only thought in my mind is reaching Ekil before the Dusker. I throw the blade in my hands. It strikes true, and the Dusker collapses.

Another Halve fighting nearby notices Ekil. This one isn't injured, and he uses his size to plow through the Duskers. I go weak with relief as I watch the Halve swing his stone club at any who come near, blasting a path for Ekil to escape the worst of the fray. I'm so busy watching their retreat to another part of the battle I barely notice what's going on around me.

Out of the corner of my eye, I see a Dusker raise his crossbow. I'm still so focused on Ekil's near miss that I don't even register the weapon is aimed at me.

"Hemera!" a familiar voice cries.

I turn my head just in time to see a black arrow hurtling across the sky, straight for me. I stare at the arrow dazed, almost uncomprehending. I can see the arrow's tip gleaming in the sunlight right before it pierces my neck.

Except it never reaches its intended target.

Something else comes flying through the air. This time, it's a person. Before I can react, before I can even think about stopping him, Brice throws me out of the arrow's path.

He hits the ground on both feet and takes a stumbling step. His beautiful green eyes meet mine for only an instant before he looks down at the arrow sticking out of his chest.

"Brice!" I scream.

Brice's red blood blooms across the front of his cloak as he collapses.

CHAPTER 53

Aside from his twitching sword arm, Brice has gone motionless.

"No!"

I fall onto the ground beside Brice, cradling his head in my lap.

"Hemera," he chokes out, his words thick with blood. "I'm so sorry." His breaths come fast and shallow. "I'm sorry I failed you."

"You didn't fail me," I gasp, searching for someone—anyone—to help.

"Thought if I was Captain, I could avenge my parents." He coughs. Blood spatters the collar of his cloak. "Didn't mean to betray you."

"None of that matters," I tell him.

Brice tries to sit up, but he only manages to raise himself onto his elbows. "I never lied about loving you," he says.

"I know." I blink tears out of my eyes. "I know."

"Hemera—"

"Shh, save your strength." I blot at his blood with the sleeve of my cloak.

Brice has survived brawls with the guards, attacks from bandits, and Tanguro. *He'll be fine.*

Brice gives me a tired smile. "'S no use," he slurs.

"I'm going to save you," I cry. I lean over him, as though by my will alone I can keep him from slipping away. "Look at me!"

A trickle of blood slips between Brice's parted lips.

The sounds of the battle fade around us. Everything becomes still, quiet.

The steady rhythm of Brice's heart, the warmth as he held me in the darkness of our cave behind the waterfall, all of our promises…it all fades as the light in Brice's endless green eyes begins to dim.

"Someone get a healer!" I yell, scanning the battlefield. There must be someone who can help. He'll be fine. All he needs is a healer....

My thoughts come in fragments. Hardly aware of what I'm doing, I disentangle myself from Brice. My brother. Dayne can save him.

"I'll be right back," I promise.

Brice doesn't reply.

I try to run, but someone blocks my path.

"No, let go of me!" I shriek and twist, but my vision has gone blurry. I have to get help—have to save Brice.

"He's dead, Hemera, leave him." Wade's arms tighten around me, pulling me away.

I wrench myself free. "He just needs a healer. Let go of me! Someone, help!"

"You can't help him." Wade shoves me out of the way of a sword that comes flying through the air. It thuds into the ground where I had been kneeling moments before. I don't care.

Brice is dead, and it's my fault. It's all my fault.

I slump beside Brice's body, no longer caring about the battle. I barely notice as Wade and Vlaz keep a Dusker from killing me. I lay my head down on Brice's chest.

"I'm sorry, I'm sorry, I'm sorry."

Any moment now, Brice will blink, and the cloudy, vacant expression in his eyes will clear. He'll open his arms to fold me into his embrace. His lips will tickle my ear as he whispers "I love you." Any moment now....

I stare at the arrow still protruding from his chest...the arrow that should have been in my heart, instead. Brice begged me not to go after Ekil. I didn't listen. And now, because of me, Brice is dead.

Tears stream down my cheeks, mixing with the blood that is already congealing on the front of Brice's cloak.

A cyclone of dust rises on the other side of the ruined stone wall. When the dust settles, it's replaced by a blue wave slicing through the Duskers and swarming across the corpse-littered ground. *Good.* Maybe it will wash all of this blood and death away. I lay my head back down on Brice's chest.

"Jadem's come!" voices all around me shout.

Jadem. The word is familiar, somehow, but I can't think of why it matters. With a tremendous effort, I lift my head back up.

As they slay through the Duskers, I see it's not water, but rather an army in blue. Their cloaks are the same shade of blue as mine, or at least the way mine was before all of the dirt and blood.

Aunt Jadem. The Solguards. *They're here.*

I should be cheering like everyone else, but instead, there is only a yawning emptiness inside me.

A Dusker, retreating from the blue army, spies me.

I grit my teeth and raise myself to my knees as he points his crossbow at me. There are no weapons within reach. My fists are cracked with blood. I'm so tired....

There's a flash of blue as someone leaps in front of the Dusker. The crossbow ricochets backward as the Dusker fires, narrowly missing his target. Unflinching, the soldier drives their sword into the Dusker's chest.

When the Dusker has collapsed, the soldier turns to face me. I let out a small gasp.

"Hemera!" Aunt Jadem stands before me. Her scarred face is twisted in worry. "Are you injured?"

"What are you doing here?" I manage to croak as Aunt Jadem draws her sword back out of the Dusker's flesh.

"Come on!" she pulls me to my feet.

I want to resist, to stay with Brice, but my body feels too heavy for me to wrench it free from my aunt's grip. Jadem pulls me away from Brice and the fighting, using her sword to slash at the Duskers who cross our path.

A wounded Dusker stumbles toward us. Jadem draws her sword, but a small soldier in a blue cloak gets to him first. He throws a well-aimed knife into the Dusker's chest.

"I got your back, Hemera!" the boy yells.

"Wokee?" The sound of his voice clears the fog in my head just a little.

"I figured you'd be needing me." He pauses long enough to throw another dagger. "I gotta go help the others, but I'll be back."

He runs off again, and I lose him in the sea of blue cloaks that is swallowing up the last of the Duskers.

"You let Wokee come here?" I demand, using the last of my energy to give my aunt an accusing look.

Aunt Jadem shrugs her shoulders. "A thousand Duskers couldn't have kept that boy behind." A grin twitches at the corner of her scarred lip. "He said he didn't trust the rest of us to help you."

In what could be either minutes or hours, there is not a single Dusker left standing. But I feel no sense of victory. A heavy numbness weighs me down and slows my thoughts. *Brice is dead.*

The words revolve in my mind in an unending loop. The numbness keeps the pain lurking just beneath the surface from drowning me.

My ears ring with cries of victory. Thutmose and Jarosh lift me onto their shoulders, ignoring my weak protests. Jubilant shouts rise from the former prisoners as the men carry me through the crowd. Solguards, all dressed in blue, hold their fists over their hearts and chant my name.

There's laughing, hugging, and tears of joy as friends find each other. Reunions long hoped for but never expected surround me on all sides.

I force the ghost of a smile onto my face in response to the gratitude and vows of friendship that follow in my wake. I don't see their faces. All I can see is Brice's still body, pierced with the arrow that was meant for me.

A glimmer of emotion flickers in me at the sight of Wokee, on the shoulders of a man I don't recognize, reaching down to slap hands with the other soldiers in blue.

Dayne, who looks dirty and exhausted, but otherwise unharmed, calls out to me. Hearing my name, Wokee looks over. He lets out a yelp of excitement as he leaps from the men's shoulders. He makes a show of tumbling into a somersault and then jumping to his feet. He bows to the cheering crowd before running to Dayne. My brother catches him mid-leap and lifts him into the air.

Vlaz capers around Wokee, whining in excitement and lifting off the ground to bathe Wokee's face with his enormous tongue. Wokee throws his arms around the cub, and Vlaz nuzzles Wokee with so much force the two of them fall to the ground. Wokee is overcome by a fit of giggles.

A tap on my shoulder draws me away from their happy reunion.

"Miss me?" Wade's mouth is quirked up in a sideways grin. The look in his golden eyes is serious, though. There's no pity in them, only understanding. I'm grateful.

"Thank you for—" I make a vague gesture. *Believing I was capable of leading this army even when I didn't. Saving me when I didn't want to be saved.*

"You'll be alright, you know," he says. "You're strong. The strongest person I've ever met." He touches my cheek with his thumb.

Before I can think of anything to say in response, a dozen other people are separating us, congratulating me on our victory. When I turn back to Wade, he's gone.

CHAPTER 54

It takes all of us to gather the dead and pile them onto flaming biers. I never stray far from the place where Brice's body lies.

Unable to stand the thought of his body being tossed with the reptors and Duskers, I go to where he is stretched out on the ground. I carry him to a tree with golden flowers, out of sight of the bonfires.

Stupidly, I arrange his blood-stained cloak to make sure his skin is protected from the sun. I snap off the arrow's shaft and throw it as far as I can. Then, I kneel beside him. My fingers brush over his cheek like they used to when he slept next to me. His skin is hot from the sun, but stiff. His eyes are unseeing. There is no hint of the fearless energy that filled them in life. Brice's soft hair is matted with dried sweat and blood. I run my fingers through the tangles, the way I used to after we swam together beneath the waterfall.

Using a piece of a broken shield, I scoop away enough dirt for a shallow grave. I lower Brice's body into the pit. When I sit back up, some part of me is gone, broken away to nestle itself against Brice in the dirt.

I look down into the grave.

"I'm sorry." I wrap my arms around myself as if to stop the chill that has taken hold of me. "I'm so sorry."

"I'm going after the Captain."

It's the first time Jadem, Dayne, Wokee, and I have found a moment alone.

I expect them to argue, but instead, Dayne says, "I'm coming with you."

"Me too!" Wokee brandishes his knife.

"No!" all three of us say at once.

"Wokee, you're needed here," Aunt Jadem tells him. "Many of the soldiers tore their cloaks during the fighting, and you're so good at cloak-making. Could you help them?"

At this, he brightens. "Did you notice all of our cloaks are the same color as yours?" he asks me, puffing out his chest. "I didn't have time to make new ones, so Jadem helped me dye the old ones. But she only helped a little." He looks down at his own cloak. "I stitched the sun on every one of them, though."

I look more closely at Wokee's cloak and see the black outline of the spiraling sun above his right shoulder.

Wokee looks at my stained and filthy cloak and sighs.

"I'll put the Solguard sun on yours when I make you a new one."

He grins. "I even made something for Vlaz," he nods at the cub's blue collar. "See? There's a sun on it, too." He twists the collar around to show me, and then looks up, as though he's just realized something. "Hemera, did you ever notice that you're the only one who can't be hurt by the sun? It's like the Solguard mark was made for you."

"Smart boy." Dayne gives Wokee a pat on his curly-haired head.

Wokee beams. He tightens his right hand into a fist, watching the way the new black markings ripple across his skin.

Ry and Thutmose, just returned from scouting for signs of my father and his guards, cut a path through the crowd.

"All the tunnels are blocked from the cave-in," Ry reports. Her red hair is plastered to her face, which glistens with sweat. "There's no sign of the Captain in either of the buildings. Either he's gone, or there are other tunnels we didn't find."

"And Ekil?" I ask.

"We found some Halves that escaped," Thutmose says, "but they all look the same to me. Some of our people are holding them until you decide what should be done with them."

"Let them go." My voice is sharper than I intended. "They're not our prisoners."

An awkward silence follows.

Dayne clears his throat. "Shall we go, Hemera?"

"Just a minute," I tell him.

I motion to Aunt Jadem, and together, we walk away from the others until we're far enough that we won't be overheard.

"I know how hard it must have been for you when I left without telling you where I was going or why," I say, "and I'm sorry." The words I've wanted to say since I left the fortress pour out of me. "I don't want you to hate me or—"

"Oh, Mer." Aunt Jadem pulls me to her. For as big as she is, her embrace is gentle. "I could never hate you. Not ever."

My chest swells with emotion.

"Thank you," I say into her cloak. "Thank you for coming."

My aunt pulls away from me and looks at me with her single eye. "When your mother was killed, I lost the most important person in my world. No matter what I did, no matter how many Solguards I saved, I couldn't bring her back." She swallows, her eye gleaming with unshed tears. "But the day you stepped into my fortress, I got a piece of her back. You are precious to me, darling niece, and there's nothing I wouldn't do for you."

"I feel the same about you," I whisper.

✳ ✳ ✳

Dayne and I set a path toward the far end of the prison building, away from the battlefield, where the cave-in didn't reach. Vlaz trots beside us. Wokee suggested we bring the cub with us *to sniff out the bad guys*. I don't know whether he'll be able to help find my father, but Vlaz's presence is a comfort.

"I saw what happened with Brice and that Halve," Dayne says once we're alone.

I keep walking without looking at Dayne. My throat burns.

"You did what you had to do."

I shake my head. "I'm the reason Brice is dead."

"You're a leader," Dayne says. "You made a choice, a choice to defend what's right."

Swallowing, I blink back the tears that swim across my vision.

Vlaz, who has been flying ahead, lands abruptly. He puts his nose to the ground and lets out a low growl.

Dayne and I look at each other, and then hurry over to where Vlaz is clawing at the ground. The smell of cammamoss wafts stronger as we come near. Dayne crouches and sweeps his hand across the cammamoss covering the ground to reveal a heavy stone. When I roll it aside, a narrow earthen staircase appears.

Without waiting for us, Vlaz bounds down the stairs into the darkness below. Dayne and I follow behind, holding our weapons out in front of us.

At the bottom of the stairs is a wide path strewn with broken rocks. Before, the darkness of the tunnel would have stolen my breath away. I would have felt like I was suffocating. I would have cowered against the wall, ready for the ceiling to come crashing down on me at any moment.

Now, that feeling is gone. I survived a collapse, and I pulled myself from the wreckage. The only feeling this tunnel awakens in me is a burning need for vengeance.

Harsh voices and tramping boots echo through the tunnel. Dayne and I exchange a look. Shadows grow against the candlelight, and then turn into dozens of the Captain's guards. Instead of pulling back into the shadows, I step into the lantern light. One of them gives a shout.

The men rush at us with swords and leather whips. Vlaz bares his teeth and growls in response.

"Go," Dayne shouts as he cleaves a man with his sword. "I'll hold them off."

"There are too many," I argue. I send another one flying into the side of the cave with my elbow.

"Find the Captain." Dayne kills another guard. "For our mother."

Dayne throws himself at the guards, his blade flashing in the light of the candles. Vlaz lets out a growl that makes the walls tremble. As the guards cower, a path emerges through their ranks. I take a few steps, and then look back, gripped by indecision.

"Go!" Dayne roars.

I hurry down the path, punching and kicking my way through the guards. There are dozens of them. *Dayne will never be able to kill them all.* Even as I'm about to turn back, a Halve emerges in the tunnel. His head towers over the guards, who shout bloodthirsty cries as they turn their weapons on him.

Ekil. He's wielding a blade in one hand and a stone club in the other as he cuts a path through the guards.

"This way," Ekil calls in his gravelly voice.

With a last glance back at Dayne and Vlaz, I follow Ekil as he disappears down a dark passage cut into the side of the main tunnel. The sound of fighting fades as we go deeper underground. At the end of the path, Ekil turns back to face me.

"I stop here," he says. "I cannot fight Zeroes."

There is the sound of shouting and cursing in our wake. The light from the guards' torches bounces along the wall behind us.

"What are Zeroes?"

Five of the guards have caught up to us.

"Go." Ekil points to a ladder built against the cave as he blocks the guards from me.

I hoist myself onto the rungs and climb. The ladder leads straight up into the main part of the weapons building. The place is eerily silent as I pull myself from the cave and into the building.

Beside me, another ladder is fixed to the wall. I climb for what seems like forever. By the time I reach the top, my legs feel like rubber. The ladder has brought me up to a stone covering in the building's ceiling. When I push away the stone and crawl up through the hole, I'm standing on the bridge that connects the two buildings.

My father stands at the other end of the bridge.

CHAPTER 55

My father waits for me, surrounded by more of his guards.

I run across the narrow wooden planks, heedless of the way the wood creaks and moans beneath my feet.

"It's not too late," he calls as I come within hearing range. "You can still join me."

"I'm going to kill you for my mother. For what you did to Brice and your other prisoners." My voice is sharp with emotion.

I raise the blade to cut down the first guard who separates me from the Captain. When I glance at the man standing before me, my hand stops midstrike. I gasp. Stumbling back, I teeter on the edge of the bridge.

"What have you done to them?" A terrible coldness shudders through me as I stare.

Four men, if they can even be called men, surround the Captain. Each of them stares at me through hollow, black eyes. Their sunken cheeks and thin lips are covered in hideous black sores. Bald heads, covered with a few wisps of white hair, shine with oily sweat.

They are so thin their every bone protrudes, making the skeletal creatures look more dead than alive. They don't wear cloaks, but instead are covered in dirty cloth rags. Their spines are twisted and they stand awkwardly. It's like they're unfamiliar with their own bodies.

Their hands, which are mangled and covered in open wounds, grip the handles of scythes. The long, curved blades gleam in the orange sunlight.

"Didn't you ever wonder how I, with only a handful of guards, could control thousands of Halves?" My father studies me as I continue to stare with horror at the creatures.

"Bisecter Zeroes, I call them, although my guards have taken to just calling them Zeroes. They're like you, or so they are meant to be." My father gives the creatures an appraising glance. "And now that I have your blood, and not just a poor substitute of my own creation, they'll be perfect." He raises the small vial filled with brown liquid before slipping it back into the pocket of his cloak. My blood.

I gape at the creatures. The sight of their ruined flesh and hollow eyes sears into my memory.

My father gives the creatures a short nod. "You are looking at the future."

He jabs the point of a knife into the back of the Zero in front. It raises its scythe and leaps toward me in a single, fluid motion.

The creature moves so fast it's a blur. And then it's upon me. It knocks me to the ground before I can raise my sling. All that keeps me from falling is the strong grip I keep on both sides of the bridge.

The Zero doesn't wait for me to stand before it raises the scythe and brings it down over me. I hurl my body to the side, making the bridge swing. The tip of the scythe slashes my shoulder.

I jump to my feet and kick the Zero with all the strength I can muster on the rickety bridge. The force would have been enough to splinter the bones of any man, but the creature doesn't even seem to feel the blow.

It brings the scythe down again. I scream as pain rips across my back. *Fast, too fast.* I've never seen anything like it.

I throw myself to the side to avoid a blow, wavering on the bridge's edge. My hands flail as they search for purchase. They grasp only air. The Zero kicks me before I can regain my balance, and I fall.

I grab the edge of the bridge at the last moment. When I glance down, I'm overcome by a wave of dizziness. The tall trees below are no more than colorful specks.

Three fingers are all that keep me from plunging to my death. My legs swing wildly. I grasp the ropes that bind the boards together with my other hand.

My eyes are level with the Zero's feet as it bears down on me.

The creature raises its scythe. Blood drips from the curved blade and speckles the boards near my fingers.

Do something, Hemera!

As the blade falls, I reach up with my left hand to grab the Zero's leg. It lets out a piercing shriek, wavers on the edge of the bridge, and then falls. I swing my body beneath the bridge to keep from being dragged down with the Zero, and then haul myself back up. The other Zeroes are upon me before I've even gotten to my feet.

I back down the bridge, too busy dodging their relentless blows to strike any of my own. Their scythes move so fast I can hear the whir as they slice through the air. When two of the Zeroes knock into each other in their haste to kill me, I sense their momentary unbalance. I throw myself at one of them and knock it off the bridge. I barely manage to keep from falling as the wooden planks tremble beneath me.

One of the other Zeroes leaps toward me with its scythe outstretched. At the last moment, I drop to the ground. Its blade cuts the other Zero standing behind me. The Zero lets out a bloodcurdling screech before turning its own scythe on the one that struck it.

Their curved blades lock together above their heads, their quarrel with me forgotten. My father's voice comes from somewhere far away, but I can't make out his words. He steps off the bridge and disappears into the prison building.

I push my way past the Zeroes that are still fighting. I'm almost at the end of the bridge when the last Zero blocks my path.

The creature raises its scythe and slashes the ropes that connect the bridge to the building.

"No!"

As though in slow motion, the disconnected end of the bridge drops away from the building. I fumble for something to hold and manage to grab onto one of the ropes between the planks. The bridge is propelled toward the weapons building where it's still attached.

Air rushes in my ears as the falling bridge picks up momentum. Even as I grasp the rope with all my strength, I feel it beginning to fray in my hands. I hear the distant screams of the two Zeroes as they plummet to their death.

I squeeze my eyes shut as the wall of the building looms closer.

The impact jolts every bone in my body as I crash through the specere leaves and wooden siding. The rope I'm holding snaps. The air is forced from my lungs as I hit the ground inside the building with a sickening thud.

I clutch my throat, fighting for breath. Still choking and gasping, I pull a wooden stake from where it's lodged in my side. Blood rushes out of the wound and puddles beneath me. My screams fill the empty building.

In moments, the blood stops as my skin begins to knit back over the wound.

I let out a groan as I roll onto my side, just out of the pool of my own blood. My father escaped. He'll flee into the mountains through tunnels he alone knows. There will be no trail to follow. I've failed.

I don't know how long I lie there—minutes or hours—before I find the strength to stand.

CHAPTER 56

Dayne is waiting for me at the tunnel's entrance.

"He escaped." My voice breaks.

"I know." Dayne's shoulders are hunched in defeat. "Jarosh and Thutmose saw him riding one of those lizard creatures toward the mountains like the Dark God himself was chasing him." Dayne scowls. "By the time the archers got him in sight, he was already gone."

"I'm going after him. I'll track him into the mountains. I'll—"

"What about all the people here?" Dayne interrupts. "Without your protection, more Duskers will come to destroy this place and everyone inside of it."

"So, should we just let him go?" The full weight of my failure bears down on me.

Dayne studies me through our mother's eyes. "That's up to you."

I look around at the rubble-strewn area inside the stone walls.

Dayne is right, of course. Where else could these people go? Certainly not back to where they came from; most of their settlements were destroyed by Halves or seized by the Duskers. And now that Gorgoran betrayed us, not even Solis is safe.

Still, the longer I wait, the more impossible it will become to track my father. I look to where the glistening white buildings stand amid the wreckage of battle.

"We need to rebuild this place," I say finally. "We should make it a fortress to protect anyone who wants refuge from the Duskers. We'll send messengers to the Banished…tell them they can find safety and freedom here if they wish. Once that's done, I'll go after the Captain."

Dayne nods. "What about the Halves?"

I turn to Ekil, who has been watching me, keeping his distance from Vlaz. "Do you want to stay here?" I ask.

"No." His answer comes without hesitation. "The Zeroes are gone. We are free."

Disappointment flickers through me. "Where will you go?"

"Somewhere the Master won't find us. Somewhere without humans."

I can't blame him, especially after everything my father has done to them.

"Well then," I take an unsteady breath, "You have my word that no one will try to stop you."

Ekil nods. He takes the hand I hold out.

"You will always be welcome here, and I will be forever grateful for all you've done." The words sound too formal coming from my lips. I give Ekil's cold hand a squeeze.

Dayne is looking at me with some combination of awe and amusement. "My little sister can communicate with the Halves." He chuckles a little. "Will you ever cease to surprise me?"

When Ekil is gone, there's an unexpected emptiness in my heart. I'm surprised to find that, like Jarosh and Thutmose, I now count Ekil as one of my friends.

Dayne and I walk back to the fortress together in comfortable silence. Vlaz trots along beside us, nudging my hand with his nose.

Even though no one has rested since the last high day, everyone is hard at work. Ry shouts instructions to men who carry armloads of provisions to growing piles. The Solguards are filling in the craters left from the cave-in. Thutmose and Jarosh are directing others who are still working to clear the bodies and debris strewn across the ground.

Their familiar faces bring an unexpected rush of comfort to me. I stay on the edge of the activity, trying to see without being seen, but some men I freed from the prison building spot me. They put down their tools and make their way to me.

One of the men holds out his hand. "You are the reason why, for the first time in my life, I'm in a place worth defending." He looks around at the ruin like it's some kind of paradise. "I would give my life to defend a place where I can live as a free man."

I don't know what to say, so instead of responding, I clasp the soldier's outstretched hand. His words ease the despair that has been trailing me like a shadow.

✳ ✳ ✳

"Can I have a word?" Wade startles me when he appears by my side. He takes my arm and leads me away from the others.

"I wanted to say goodbye." When he turns to look at me, his golden eyes are flecked with an emotion I can't decipher.

Inexplicably, I'm uncomfortable under the intensity of his gaze. I look down at the ground. "Goodbye?"

"I'm leaving."

I feel his eyes on me, but I don't look up. "Where are you going?" There is a slight waver in my voice.

"Back to Solis. It's not safe anymore, now that Gorgoran—" his voice takes on a bitter edge. "Anyway," he clears his throat, "Jadem wants me to defend the fortress until you've built up Tanguro enough to hold everyone."

The weight of his words rests heavy on my shoulders. Tanguro will be the new Solguard fortress. And I'm somehow supposed to lead it.

"But we've only just won the battle. You can't leave yet." *I don't know how to do this*, is what I want to say.

"You'll be fine," Wade says, reading my thoughts. "And your aunt will be here to help you."

"She can send someone else back," I argue. "Jarosh. Or Thutmose." *Just not you.*

Wade shakes his head. "I asked for it to be me."

"Why?" My voice cracks.

He puts a finger under my chin to tip my gaze up. Something stirs inside me.

319

"Because you need time to figure out what you want. And I need to give you the space to do it."

"I don't understand."

Wade's face is close enough to mine that I can feel the warmth of his breath on my skin. Energy courses between us.

"I'm falling in love with you." He says the words simply, without apology.

A mountain of feelings crashes down on me.

"I know," he says, reading the expression on my face even though I don't say a word. "Too much has happened. You need time to heal from…everything, and I have a lot to figure out myself now that Sal's gone."

"Wade, I…."

He takes my face in his hands. Before I can say anything else, he's kissing me.

I should pull away. I should be ashamed of wanting him, for the fire his touch awakens in me. But instead, I wrap my arms around him and kiss him back.

When he draws away, my lips tingle from the pressure of where his mouth had been. His heart beats strong and quick, echoing my own racing pulse.

We separate when the sound of someone clearing his throat tells us we're no longer alone.

"Apologies," a man in a blue cloak scratches his cheek, "but the Solguards are ready."

"I'll be out soon." Wade doesn't look away from me. He presses his lips to my forehead and then steps back.

"I want you to have this." He takes the cord from around his neck and pulls the sun pendant from beneath his cloak.

"That's Sal's," I breathe, recalling Wade slipping it from his beloved leader's neck. "I can't."

He presses it into my hand. "So you don't forget."

The pendant is heavier than I expected. The metal is smooth to the touch and warmed from Wade's skin. I hold it up and admire the etchings of the sun; its intricate swirls are cut into the metal with extraordinary precision.

"I could never forget." My voice sounds small, far away.

Wade slips the cord of Sal's pendant over my head. It rests against my neck next to my mother's silver key, warm and reassuring. Before he reaches the door, he flashes me one of his disarming smiles. Then he's gone.

CHAPTER 57

I stay in the building for what feels like a long time. When Dayne's clear voice carries back to me from outside, I force myself to rejoin the others.

They're pouring over plans for rebuilding and expanding. There are drawings of more buildings, caves, and orchards. They're all so engrossed in their discussions that none of them notice the long line of Halves filing away from the broken wall toward the mountains. Ekil's familiar, slightly bowed form is at their head.

I raise my hand in farewell. At first, I think they're too far away to see, but then Ekil stops to wave back. I watch until the Halves are no more than moving specks against the wild landscape.

I wander away from the noise before anyone notices me. All I want is to be alone. The far orchard of pink fruit was unharmed by the battle, and I make my way toward their inviting, quiet rows.

Footsteps startle me as I stand staring at a purple insect with scarlet wings. Dayne's head appears first as he ducks under a thick overhang of branches.

"Hope I'm not interrupting anything," Dayne raises an eyebrow at me as he brushes pink blossoms from his cloak. "But we need to talk."

The look on his face makes a heavy weight grow in the pit of my stomach. "What's going on?"

"I'm leaving." He says the words quietly, like it will soften their impact.

"No, not you too…." The rising pitch of my voice betrays my panic. "You can't leave. I need you here!"

Dayne lays a hand on my shoulder. "Zeidan needs to be stopped. Now that he has your blood…."

The rest of his sentence hangs in the air.

My father will use my blood to make more of the Zeroes. Except, if what he said is true, then my blood will make them even more powerful than the ones I fought. A shudder goes through me.

"I have to come with you. You can't—" My voice cracks.

"You're the leader of these people," Dayne says. "They're depending on you to keep them safe."

Making an effort to keep my voice even, I ask, "Will you be back?"

"I'll return as soon as it's done." As Dayne's blue eyes fill with emotion, he sweeps me into a hug. "Little sis," he murmurs into my ear, "I couldn't be prouder of you."

Tears burn the back of my throat. I'm only now starting to grasp how much I've come to depend on him these past weeks, and the thought of him leaving is almost unbearable.

I want to tell Dayne what it means to me that he's believed in me from the first, and that even though I haven't known him for long, I can't imagine my life without him. I want to tell him how I never would have made it this far without him…how because of him, I'm stronger…because of him, I'm better.

Instead, I manage a weak smile and say, "I'm proud of you too, big brother."

* * *

I stand alone by the broken wooden gates, as first Dayne, and then Wade and a handful of Solguards, leave the fortress. I watch long after their receding figures have melted into the wild Tanguro landscape.

Heavy-hearted, I turn back to the smoking piles of the dead and rubble. How will I ever rebuild this fortress *and* lead the rebellion?

I keep my eyes focused on the ground to keep from falling into one of the gaping holes left from the cave-in as I walk back to the ruined courtyard. When I look up, two figures race toward me. Vlaz soars into the air, outflanking Wokee.

Vlaz is nuzzling my hand and twisting his body for me to scratch behind his floppy ear by the time Wokee catches up.

"I was thinking." Wokee leans over as he catches his breath. "You'll be needing a master botanist." He screws up his face in concentration as he says the word, making it sound more like *boat-nist*. Wokee points the tip of his knife at the overturned trees. "These gardens aren't going to replant themselves."

My mouth cracks into a grin—the first since Brice….

"You're right about that," I agree, pressing the pain deep down until it is nothing more than a dull ache in my chest.

"You need me," Wokee says with confidence. "And you need Vlaz, too."

Vlaz lets out a low whine at the sound of his name and presses his body against my leg. Then, he's off, flying to greet the two figures emerging in the distance.

There is no mistaking Ry's flame-red hair and my aunt's height.

Ry gives Wokee a playful shove, which makes Vlaz growl. She takes stock of what's left of the fortress and then turns to smile at me.

"What?" I demand.

Ry's eyes sparkle with devilish delight. "The Duskers aren't going to know what's coming for them. We've got the *Bisecter* on our side." She says the word with pride.

"More than the sum of your parts." Aunt Jadem wraps an arm around my shoulders and draws me close. She brushes a finger over the sun pendant dangling around my neck. "I nearly forgot what we were fighting for," she murmurs, almost to herself. "You helped me remember."

"Don't cry," Wokee commands, seeing the emotion on my face.

His look of utter horror makes me choke out a laugh.

Surrounded by these people, somehow the thought of all we face seems less daunting. My father will have to be found and his Zeroes destroyed. The Duskers will return, and when they do, we'll need the strength of all the Solguards and Banished. But for now—

My father was right about one thing: change is coming. The Duskers' grip on us all must come to an end. When their armies descend on us, we will be ready. *I* will be ready.

"Come on," Wokee takes my free hand and starts to tug me back in the direction of the courtyard.

As we approach, the others stop their work to form a circle around us. They wait for my orders.

I look around at the people who have lost their homes, their family, and have been imprisoned in Tanguro. Their eyes shine with expectation and hope. For the first time, their lives don't belong to the Duskers or my father, but are their own.

A tiny black bird, a kynthia, lands on a tree beside me. It looks at me with its intelligent eyes, chirping out its song before it flies off again. I think of my mother, without sadness for the first time, as the kynthia disappears into the brightness.

I look down at the swirling rays on my hand, which shine almost metallic in the sunlight.

I meet the gaze of those around me without fear or hesitation. I am no longer the scared girl abandoned to die in a cave.

I am Hemera. I am a Bisecter.

THE END

* * *

Thank you for reading my book. If you enjoyed it, won't you please take a moment to leave me a review at your favorite retailer? Many thanks!

** * **

Stephanie Fazio's e-Newsletter

Sign up for Stephanie Fazio's e-Newsletter to learn about upcoming books at: https://stephaniefazio.com/subscribe/

Acknowledgements

There are many people who helped take this novel from draft to published, and for that, I am beyond grateful.

To my amazing editor Ellen Schaeffer, for helping with this novel from start to finish. Your brilliant suggestions and gentle criticisms have made all the difference.

To the incredible writers who helped me with everything from content to marketing. Special thanks to Anne Brodsky and Jacob Davis, whose suggestions and insight were invaluable throughout the editing process.

To my readers, who have taken this journey and helped spread the word. None of what I do would be possible without you.

To all the teachers and professors who helped mentor me. Special mention for Laura Iodice, Carol Cranston, Constance Harsh, and Linck Johnson.

To Rachel Fazio and Julie Gibbons: thank you for every laugh, every phone call, and every cute video that started my day off right.

To my parents, who have endlessly supported and encouraged all of my ventures. Thank you for the family nights of reading out loud that made me fall in love with books and inspired my own creativity. Thank you for teaching me how to work hard and be a good person, and everything else in between.

To Andrew, for being my biggest champion and encouraging me to take leaps I never would have been brave enough to take without a little push. Thank you for making me laugh, sharing your office, and coming to the rescue when formatting issues almost got the best of me. Your love is a constant source of strength for me. Forever and always.

About the Author:

Stephanie Fazio is a young adult and new adult fantasy author. Stephanie grew up in Syracuse, New York, and prior to writing full time, she worked in the fields of journalism, secondary education, and higher education. She has an undergraduate degree in English from Colgate University and a Master's degree in Reading, Writing, and Literacy from the University of Pennsylvania. She lives in Austin with her husband and crazy rescue dog. When she isn't writing, she's getting lost in parks, hosting taco nights, or ironically and miserably losing at word games, but having fun while she does it.

Connect with Stephanie Fazio

Visit her Website: https://www.stephaniefazio.com
Sign up for her newsletter: https://stephaniefazio.com/subscribe/

Discover other books by Stephanie Fazio

Available June 2019!

StephanieFazio.com